Dear Reader,

A few years ago I wrote a book, *The Valtieri Marriage Deal,* about a scrummy Italian doctor called Luca Valtieri. He had two brothers, equally gorgeous, who since then have clamoured for their own books. Massimo (*Valtieri's Bride*), a widower with three adorable children, was the eldest of the family, and Gio, a lawyer, was the youngest brother. They had a family friend, Anita, who planned Luca's wedding and then Massimo's, and I thought, What better than to match her up with Gio?

He's cynical, wary, commitment-phobic, and Anita has loved him her entire life. A wedding planner, she's deeply romantic and has been waiting years for him to realise that he loves her. But there's a tragedy lurking in his past—something he's never told her—and it's keeping them apart.

And then he's injured as a result of an attack, and she looks after him. They're thrown together, and there's no escape as they travel the passionate and emotional rollercoaster that ensues.

I've loved every one of these brothers, but Gio, for me, has a special place in my heart. I hope you find a place for him, too, as you travel their rollercoaster with them.

Love,

Caroline

THE VALTIERI BABY

BY
CAROLINE ANDERSON

Harlequin (UK) policy is to use papers that are natural, renewable and recyclable products and made from wood grown in sustainable forests. The logging and manufacturing processes conform to the legal environmental regulations of the country of origin.

Printed and bound in Spain
by Blackprint CPI, Barcelona

MILLS & BOON

First published in Great Britain 2012
by Mills & Boon, an imprint of Harlequin (UK) Limited,
Eton House, 18-24 Paradise Road, Richmond, Surrey TW9 1SR

© Caroline Anderson 2012

ISBN: 978 0 263 89469 1
ebook ISBN: 978 1 408 97142 0

23-1012

CHAPTER ONE

'SIGNORE Valtieri! Wait! Please, Signore, listen to me!'

Her distraught voice sliced through the evening shadows, and Gio's heart sank. Not now, he thought. Please, not now. He really, *really* didn't have the energy to deal with Camilla Ponti diplomatically, and he certainly didn't have the time.

He'd already stalled his holiday once because of her, and he wasn't doing it again.

She'd been about to take action against his client, Marco Renaldo, but Marco had insisted on talking to her before the case came to court. Gio had postponed his departure for a day so they could meet this afternoon, and she'd dropped her claim.

Not quietly.

She'd sobbed and begged and pleaded, but her former business partner had left her no choice. Drop the case, or he'd reveal her fraud and embezzlement of the company's funds. She'd given in, but she'd blamed Gio for putting him up to it, because she was convinced he'd cost her her share of the company.

It was absurd. She'd forfeited any rights to it herself. He couldn't believe she'd even thought she had a case! The meeting over, he'd sent a text to Anita arranging to pick her up at six, then, more than ready to get out of the city, he'd gone home and stripped off the exquisitely cut suit, the tasteful silk tie Anita had given him for Christmas, the blinding white shirt. He'd put away the immaculate hand-made shoes, the monogrammed cufflinks, also from Anita, and showered and pulled on his favourite jeans and sweater, the battered leather jacket and boots that had seen better days.

Then he'd pulled the refuse bag out of the kitchen waste bin, flung in the remnants of food from the fridge, tossed an empty wine bottle in on top and headed for the door.

He couldn't get out of Firenze and away from all this quick enough. His luggage was in the car, and he was looking forward to two weeks on the slopes with his family skiing, eating, and thinking about precisely nothing.

Except Anita would be there. Just thinking about it sent a tingle of anticipation through his veins. He'd missed her recently. He'd been avoiding her ever since the night of his brother's wedding when things had got a little complicated—again—but at least with his whole family present there'd be plenty of people to diffuse the tension, and he knew a huge part of the attraction of this holiday was that she'd be there.

He couldn't get there soon enough. For some reason, the cut and thrust of his job had lost its lustre recently, and after a day like today he just felt tired and jaded.

And now this.

This woman, who'd somehow found out where he lived and was lying in wait so she could carry on their earlier conversation. Frankly, he'd heard enough.

'Signora Ponti, there is really nothing more to say,' he began, groping for diplomacy, but it was wasted on her.

'You don't understand! You have to help me—please, listen to me! I need the money—'

'Signora, everyone needs money, but you can't just have it if it isn't yours, and as Signore Renaldo pointed out, you've already stolen more than enough from him—'

'It wasn't like that! I had reasons—'

'Everyone has reasons,' he said tiredly. 'Now, if you'll excuse me, I'm meeting someone and I'm already late.'

'But I *earned* that money, I really need it,' she sobbed, reaching for him with desperate hands. 'Please, you have to listen!'

He stepped back out of reach, his patience exhausted. 'No, I don't. I've heard enough,' he said flatly, and started to turn away, the bag of refuse still in his hand.

'Nooooooo!'

Out of the corner of his eye he saw her raise her arm, but it was too late to duck. His free arm was still coming up to shield his face when something large and heavy— her handbag?—crashed into his head and sent him reeling. He tripped over the edge of the kerb, twisting his ankle sharply, the pain sickening. It gave way under him, throwing him further off balance, and he felt himself falling.

He couldn't save himself.

He dropped the refuse bag, heard the tinkling sound of broken glass just too late to roll to the side, and then a sharp, searing pain in his thigh took his breath away.

On autopilot, still waiting for another blow to fall, he rolled off the bag and glared at her, but she was so distraught that he'd never be able to reason with her. It was pointless trying.

For a long moment he lay there, shocked, his eyes locked with hers, but then he became aware of something hot and wet dripping off his fingers, and he stared blankly at his hand, and then his thigh, and he realised he was in trouble.

So did she, her face crumpling as she took in what had happened.

'No! No—I'm so sorry! I didn't mean to hurt you! Please—oh, no…!'

And turning on her heel, she ran away, leaving him there alone in the dim light of the car park, the sound of her high heels rapping sharply on the stones fading as she fled.

Relief sapping the last of his strength, he slumped back against the wall behind him and closed his eyes for a moment.

Dio, he hurt.

He looked down at his foot, bent at a strange angle. No, not his foot, he realised with relief. The boot, twisted half off where he'd tripped. But his foot was inside it and the pain was just beginning to break through all the other insults, so his relief was short-lived. Maybe not so good after all.

And there was glass sticking out of his leg. He knew he probably shouldn't pull it out, but his leg was bleeding and with the glass in there he couldn't put pressure on it, so he pulled it out anyway.

Not a good move, apparently.

Wrapping his scarf roughly around his slashed hand, he closed his fingers tight over it and rammed his fist hard down on his thigh, then rummaged for his phone. He'd call Anita. There was no point in calling either of his brothers, they and their families were already at the ski chalet, as were his sisters and his parents, but Anita was expecting him. She had a meeting with a bride and he was supposed to be picking her up any time now.

She'd help him. She always helped him, she'd always

known just what to do when he'd got himself in a mess.
And she'd rescue him now. Relief coursing through him,
his whole body shaking, his left hand struggling to coop-
erate, he speed-dialled her number.

It went straight to voicemail.

He listened to the message, heard the soft lilt of her
voice and could have howled with frustration and despair.

'Why is it,' he said sarcastically when the cheery message finally ended, 'that I'm tripping over you all the time,
and yet the one time I really need you you're not there?'

He cut off and watched the blood still slowly welling
from his thigh for another few seconds before he did what
he should have done in the first place. He called an ambulance.

And then he leant back against the wall behind him,
and dialled her number again, and then again. He needed
her, and he couldn't get her, but it was somehow comforting just to listen to the sound of her voice…

Her phone was ringing.

She could feel it in her pocket, vibrating silently as she
wound up her meeting. It rang again. And again.

Damn. It would be Gio, wondering where she was. He'd
be foaming at the mouth if she didn't go soon.

'Right, I think I've got all I need for now,' she told her
client briskly. 'I'll go and put a few ideas together for you,
and then we'll get back together again when I'm back from
my holiday.'

'Oh—I was hoping we could do it all today…'

Anita's smile faltered as the phone vibrated again.

'I'm sorry, I'm already late. I'm supposed to be leaving for my holiday and I only fitted you in today because
I was delayed, I should have gone yesterday. Don't worry,

please, there'll be plenty of time to sort everything out. It's seven months to the wedding.'

She shut her file and stood up, effectively ending the meeting, and held out her hand to the bride.

The girl smiled reluctantly and got up, taking her hand. 'Sorry. I just want all the answers at once.'

'Everybody does. It's not possible, but it will happen. I'll see you in two weeks when I'm back from my holiday. I'll call you with a date.'

'OK. And—thank you for fitting me in. I'm sorry to be a pain.'

'You aren't a pain. I'll call you, I promise.'

And with one last brisk, professional smile she walked away, resisting the urge to pull her phone from her pocket before she'd left the café and was out of sight.

Six missed calls. *Six?*

And all from Gio. Damn. She really *was* late, and he'd be truly, no-holds-barred furious with her. He hated it when people were late.

Except he didn't sound furious. He sounded...

She listened to her voicemail message in puzzlement, and tried to call him.

It went straight to voicemail, again and again, but she couldn't give up, because something about his message was worrying her and she didn't know what it was.

'Why is it that I'm tripping over you all the time, and yet the one time I really need you you're not there?'

Anita frowned, and played it again. Far from angry, his voice sounded odd. Odd, and slightly desperate. As if he was in trouble—

Her heart pounding now, she tried him again, and this time the phone was answered by a stranger.

'Hello? Are you Anita?'

'Yes—Anita Della Rossa. Where's Gio? Who are you?'

'This is a nurse in the emergency department...'

She didn't hear the rest. For a second, all she could hear was roaring in her ears from the frantic beating of her heart.

'I knew there was something wrong, I've been trying to get hold of him. What's happened to him?' she asked, desperate for information. 'Did he have an accident? Is he all right?'

'Are you family?'

She nearly lied, but there was no point, they were all too well known. 'No, but I'm an old family friend. I've known him forever.' Her voice cracked, and she tried again. 'They're all away—they've gone skiing. We were about to join them. Please, tell me how he is.'

'He's had an accident and he's going to surgery. That's all I can tell you. Can you give us his full name and family contact details, please? We need to ring them urgently.'

Urgently? Her heart lurched in her chest, and for a second she thought she was going to be sick.

'Um—yes—he's Giovanni Valtieri. His brother Luca's a doctor at the hospital—a professor. Contact him. He's with the others.' She gave them Luca's number just to be certain, then raced to the hospital, her heart in her mouth. But in the hospital emergency department she met another brick wall, built, no doubt, by the same protocol.

'I spoke to a nurse,' she explained. 'I was calling Giovanni Valtieri, and the person who answered his phone said he was here. Can I see him?'

'Are you family?'

Yet again, she thought of lying, but it was pointless, so she just trowelled on the connection. 'No, but I'm an old family friend. We've been very close since we were born—almost like brother and sister.'

And ex-lovers, she nearly added, but that was nobody else's business and she wasn't going to spread something so personal all over the hospital. Not when his brother worked there.

So they wouldn't tell her any more, but that was fine. There were strings she could pull, and she fully intended to pull every single one of them. Starting with Luca...

He felt like hell.

He lay there for a moment, assessing his body. It was throbbing, and after a bit the throbbing separated out so he could catalogue it.

His right hand hurt. He tried to flex his fingers, but it didn't seem like a good idea and anyway his hand seemed to be heavily bandaged.

OK. Right thigh—well, that certainly hurt, with a deep ache close up by his groin, but thankfully not *that* close.

And his right foot. They'd cut his jeans off to get to his leg, and they'd wanted to cut the boot off—his favourite boots. It had taken ages to break them in like that. He'd refused to let them, vaguely detached from it all through loss of blood. Until they'd eased it off. He hadn't been detached then, and the last thing he remembered was the sickening pain. He must have passed out at that point.

And he had a killer headache. He frowned. She hadn't touched his head, but maybe when he'd fallen he'd cracked it on the wall behind him. Either that or she'd had a rock in that ludicrous bag.

He breathed in, caught the hint of a familiar scent and his eyes flew open, searching for her.

'Anita?'

She came into view, her warm brown eyes troubled. She was smiling, but there was a slight tremor in her lips, and she was pale. He'd never seen anything more beautiful in his life.

'*Ciao,* Gio,' she murmured, leaning over him to brush a kiss against his cheek. 'How are you feeling?'

'Fine,' he lied, but she just snorted and raised a slender, disbelieving eyebrow a fraction.

'I am. Of course I'm all right.'

'Well, you don't look it. You look like you've been partying with the vampires.'

'Very funny,' he said, turning away so he didn't have to see the worried look in her eyes.

'I called Luca,' she said, and he snapped his head back round again.

'You *what*?'

'I called Luca. They wouldn't tell me anything, wouldn't let me in to see you, so I pulled strings.'

Damn. 'What did he say?'

'He's threatening to come back.'

'That's ridiculous! It's just a scratch—'

'Gio, you don't get taken into Theatre for a scratch!'

She broke off, took a breath and then carried on in a level tone, 'Anyway, your mother snatched the phone off him before he could say much and she's pretty upset. I promised I'd get you to ring her the moment you came round.'

He let out a short, harsh sigh and closed his eyes.

He shouldn't have called her—except, of course, he would have had to because he was supposed to have been picking her up *en route.* And when he didn't turn up and she couldn't get him, she would have rung alarm bells anyway.

'You shouldn't have called him.'

'They already had. They asked me for family contact details, and they wouldn't tell me anything so I had no idea how badly you'd been hurt, but it sounded bad. They used the word "urgent",' she said drily. 'It didn't seem like the time to argue.'

No, of course not. What was he thinking? The moment he'd been admitted and they found out his identity they would have been on the phone to his brother, because he worked in the hospital and was known to all of them.

And now apparently Luca was threatening to come back and his mother was in hysterics and all because some stupid, *stupid* woman had come after him.

'So—what actually happened?' she asked, perching on the edge of the chair beside him and reaching for his hand, then thinking better of it because of the bandages.

'A client's ex-business partner hit me with her handbag,' he said, his voice disgusted, and she gave a tiny incredulous laugh.

'Excuse me? Her *what*?'

'Humiliating, isn't it,' he said drily, 'but it gets worse. I ducked out of the way, tripped over the kerb and fell over my own refuse bag. That'll teach me to do my recycling properly.'

Anita glared at him. 'Gio, how can you joke about it? They told me it was serious! What really happened?'

He gave a short, dry laugh. 'That is exactly what happened, and believe me, it feels pretty serious. I hurt like hell.'

'I can imagine.' She bit her lip, puzzled. She still hadn't got to the bottom of this, she was sure. 'So—what did she *actually* do to you? Really?'

'Apart from attempting to knock me out with her

handbag? Nothing. She didn't need to. Goodness knows what she keeps in it, the thing weighed a ton. Anyway, it knocked me off balance and I fell over the refuse bag. Then I pulled the glass out. Not a smart move.'

She rolled her eyes, then frowned, sifting through his words again and coming up with something she didn't understand. 'What glass, Gio? Pulled it out of *what*?'

'I reckon it was a wine bottle. I dropped the bag, and I heard glass breaking before I fell on it. I cut my hand when I fell, and a piece stuck in my thigh, so I pulled it out, but it wasn't a good idea because it had severed the artery. If it happens again, apparently, I have to leave it there. Don't worry, it missed the important bits,' he added drily.

She glared at him, shocked he'd been hurt so badly and furious that he was treating it so lightly when she'd been going through hell. 'This is no time for joking, Gio! A severed artery? You could have bled to death!'

He reached out his hand, then remembered and dropped it carefully back onto the covers.

'Come round this side,' he said gruffly, but there was a drip there and it was no better.

Actually, that wasn't true. It was better. She sat down beside him, threaded her shaking fingers carefully through his and closed them firmly round his hand.

Dio, it felt good to hold her. The warmth from her palm spread into him and thawed the ice that seemed to have formed inside him, and as the tension eased, he realised how tight he'd been holding himself.

For a moment they said nothing, then she frowned slightly, her brow puckering as she tried to make sense of it.

'Why did she try to attack you, Gio? Who was she? One of your thwarted lovers?'

He laughed softly. 'No. A very disappointed woman. We had a meeting with her today, the reason I had to delay leaving, and she came off worst. She feels I cheated her.'

'And did you?'

'No. I just made sure she got what she deserved from my client, which was nothing,' he said, and he watched her frown again.

'Wow. And she attacked you for that?'

'Well, to be fair I did most of it myself when I fell up the kerb and landed on the bag. Apparently my ankle isn't broken, though, which is good news. It's just bruised and sprained.'

He nearly laughed at the 'just' but he hurt too much to bother.

'And your hand?' she asked, arching a brow towards his bandaged fingers. 'I can still see all your fingers, so I guess you didn't cut them off.'

'No. They seem to be there and they all move. As I say, most of it was my own fault.'

'Mmm. That really wasn't very clever, was it?'

He snorted at the mild understatement, and her fingers tightened a little. 'Sorry. The police are here, by the way, waiting for you to feel well enough to talk to them. And you need to phone your mother.'

He nodded. 'Call her now for me—I'll talk to her first. And then I'll talk to the police. She didn't really do anything.'

'Gio, she attacked you. If she hadn't, none of this would have happened.'

'She hit me with her handbag. That's all. The police don't need to be involved.'

'And if she comes after you again?'

He shrugged. 'She won't. And if she does, I'll be ready for her this time.'

She gave up arguing. She dialled his mother, handed him the phone and then left him alone and went and found something to eat and drink.

It could have been fantastic, or cardboard. It wouldn't have made any difference, because she couldn't taste it, not with the image of him lying there like a ghost so fresh in her mind. But it was food, and she ate it mechanically while she beat herself up about not answering his first call.

What if he'd died? What if he'd rung her, and then passed out from loss of blood before he could call an ambulance? No, he must have called one first. He surely wouldn't have been stupid enough to call her so many times before he called the medical services? Maybe, if he had her on speed-dial. Maybe he'd thought it would be quicker, but then she hadn't answered, and that could have cost him his life...

She felt sick, and pushed away the last of her panini. Cardboard, she decided finally, realising she was probably being unfair, but whatever, she couldn't eat any more of it. She went back to him, and found him propped up on his pillows looking pale and drawn and very tired.

'What did the police say?'

'They're going to talk to her. Apparently she called an ambulance, so she at least has a conscience, but her phone's now switched off—'

'She called an ambulance?'

'Yes—why?'

Because it meant he wouldn't have died because of her. She shook her head, relief taking her legs out from under her, so she sat down shakily on the chair beside him. 'Nothing. I'm just surprised. So how are you feeling?'

He shrugged. 'Much the same. The doctor's been, as well, while you were gone. They're going to keep me in overnight and review me in the morning, but they think I can probably go home tomorrow. I have to have another blood transfusion. The vampires were a bit greedy.'

He smiled, but she couldn't smile back. Not when he'd come so close. She looked at her watch. Nearly midnight.

'I'll go home now, then, and I'll come back in the morning. Do you want me to bring you some clothes in when I come?'

'Please. My bags are in the car already. If you could bring the small one, it's got everything I'll need. The big one's just ski stuff. You'd better clear it with the police on the way out, or they might not let you get it. It'll be a crime scene now, apparently. I've told them they're over-reacting, but they seem to feel they need to collect the evidence. Here, my keys. It's the little Mercedes sports, by the way.'

'Where's the Ferrari?'

He smiled. 'I do too much driving in the city. It was fun, but not practical in the city streets. The Mercedes is much more sensible.'

'That doesn't sound like you.'

'Maybe I've changed.'

She just laughed at that. Giovanni Valtieri would never change. She'd given up hoping for miracles.

She took the keys from him, and bent and kissed his cheek, letting her face rest there for a moment. She could feel the slight rasp of stubble, the roughness curiously comforting and reassuring as he turned his head against hers and touched her cheek with his lips.

'I'll see you in the morning,' she murmured, and with another light brush of her lips against his jaw she straightened up and met his dark, weary eyes.

'*Ciao,* Anita,' he mumbled tiredly. 'And thank you.'

'*Prego.* You take care. No more fighting with women.'

He gave a soft chuckle and raised his good hand as she left, and she winked at him and went out into the corridor. The policeman was there, and she asked him to contact the team at his apartment building to alert them that she'd need access to his car.

Then she walked away without waiting for the OK. She was tired and emotionally exhausted, and she just wanted to get home, but first she had to get his bag. The area was cordoned off by the police, as he'd said, and she had to get them to escort her to his car and get the soft leather grip from it.

She made her way home, undressed and crawled into bed, but she couldn't sleep. She could so easily have lost him—not that he was hers anyway, but the thought of him dying—

'No! Stop it! He's going to be all right. Stop torturing yourself.'

But all she could see was his washed-out face.

'So can you go?'

'Yes, but I have no idea *where* I'm supposed to go. I can't drive like this, I can't get upstairs to my apartment, and the police have said it's not a good idea to go back to my apartment anyway until they've spoken to Camilla Ponti and assessed her state of mind, but they can't find her anywhere. She wasn't at her home address or any of the other places they've tried, and they just don't think it's a good idea for me to hang around in Firenze.'

She nodded. That made sense.

'So why not go on holiday as we'd planned? I can drive.'

'On a skiing holiday? What's the point? I won't be able

to do anything. You go and join the others, I'll just go home to the *palazzo*. Carlotta can look after me.'

She shook her head. 'They're away. They've gone to visit their grandchildren in Napoli while your family don't need them. There's no one there.'

Damn. He'd forgotten that. So what was he supposed to do?

'Well, you'd better come with me, then,' she said after a slight pause. 'I'm on holiday now, so are you—we'll go to my villa, and I can look after you.'

'No. You're supposed to be going skiing. You can't do that for me,' he objected, ludicrously tempted.

'Why on earth not? I've been rescuing you since you learned to climb trees. Why not now? You can't cook, you can't walk, you can't drive, but you can rest and recover there while you keep out of the way and wait for the police to catch her. It's the obvious solution.'

It was. So obvious he'd already thought of it and dismissed it. On the surface it sounded the perfect plan. The only 'but'—and it was a huge one—was that it meant spending the next two weeks with Anita alone, with no one to diffuse the tension.

And that was a *bad* idea.

CHAPTER TWO

It took them a while to discharge him, but finally he was wheeled to the entrance.

Anita's car was there, drawn up to the kerb, engine running. All he had to do was get out of the wheelchair and into it.

Huh. It was a nightmare, but he gritted his teeth and managed somehow. His inflexible right foot in its support bandage was the most awkward thing—that, and the fact that his wounded thigh muscles really didn't want to lift his leg, and his heavily bandaged right hand was all but useless.

It didn't help that it was tipping down with rain, either, but at last he was in, more or less dry with the help of a man with an umbrella, and the door was shut.

'OK?' she asked briskly as he was finally settled beside her, but he'd known her nearly thirty-five years, and the concern in her voice was obvious to him.

Obvious, and strangely reassuring.

'I'm fine,' he lied through gritted teeth. 'Just get us out of here.'

He turned up the collar of his rain-spattered and blood-stained leather jacket and hunched down in the seat as she pulled away. He was glad to be getting out of the city.

He didn't think Camilla Ponti posed a real threat, but the last thing he wanted was Anita in danger, however slight the risk.

She left the city streets behind, heading out of Firenze, and after a few minutes she turned her head and flashed him a smile. 'Better now?'

They were on the A1 heading south past Siena towards the Montalcino area where both his family and hers had lived for generations.

Home, he thought with a sigh of relief.

'Much better,' he said, and resting his head back on the seat, he closed his eyes and drifted off.

He was asleep.

Good. He'd lost a lot of blood, and he'd be exhausted. She didn't suppose he'd slept much last night, what with the pain and awkwardness of his injuries, and anyway, it was easier for her if he wasn't watching her while she drove, because his presence, familiar as it was, always scrambled her brains.

Even when he was fast asleep she was ludicrously conscious of him, deeply, desperately aware of every breath, every sigh, every slight shift of his solid, muscular body.

She knew every inch of it. Loved every inch of it. Always had, always would.

Fruitlessly, of course. The one time she'd felt there was any hope for them it had been snatched away abruptly and without warning, and left her heart in tatters. Anyone with any sense would walk away from him, tell him to go to hell and find his own solution, but Anita couldn't do that.

She couldn't walk away from him. Goodness knows she'd tried a hundred times, but her heart kept drawing her back because deep down she believed that he loved her, whatever he might say to the contrary.

And one day…

She gave a soft, sad huff of laughter. One day nothing. She was stupid, deluded, desperate.

'Hey.'

She turned her head and met his eyes briefly, then dragged hers back to the road.

'How are you?' she asked. 'Good sleep?'

'I'm just resting.'

'You were snoring.'

'I don't snore.'

'You do.' He did. Not loudly, not much, just a soft sound that was curiously comforting beside her. As it had been, for those few blissful weeks five years ago.

'Why did you laugh?'

'Laugh?' She hadn't—

'Yes, laugh. If you can call it that. You didn't look exactly amused.'

Ah. *That* laugh, the one that wasn't. The laugh because against all the odds she could still manage to believe he loved her.

'I was thinking about my meeting yesterday,' she lied. 'The bride thought we could wrap it all up in an hour. She was miffed when I left.'

'Is that where you were when I rang you?'

She nodded, biting her lip at the little rush of guilt, and he tilted his head and frowned.

'Anita? It wasn't your fault. I knew you were in a meeting.'

'I should have been out by then. I could have answered it—*should* have answered it.'

'I wouldn't have answered you if I'd been with a client.'

Of course not. She *knew* that, but it didn't make any difference, and if he'd died—

His hand closed over hers, squeezing gently. 'Hey, I'm all right,' he said softly. 'I was fine, and the ambulance came really quickly, because she'd already called it.'

'Well, good. I don't suppose there was a lot of time to waste, and what if she hadn't called it? What if you'd passed out?'

He dropped his hand again. 'It was fine, the bleeding was all under control,' he lied. 'And I'm all right, you can see that. Now I just have to get better. I wonder if they've found her yet.'

'Will she go to prison for it?'

He laughed a little grimly. 'What, for hitting me with her handbag? No. She didn't mean to do this, Anita.'

'You're very forgiving.'

'No, I'm not. I'm thoroughly peed off because I shouldn't even have been here, I should have been on holiday and the only reason I wasn't was because of her. I'm just a realist and anyway, it's not really me she's angry with, it's Marco. It's just profoundly irritating.'

Irritating? She nearly laughed. 'So, have you warned him? Your client? She might go after him.'

'Don't worry, he's out of the country now. He was leaving yesterday straight after our meeting, but anyway he has very good security.'

'Maybe you should move to somewhere more secure. Your apartment isn't exactly impenetrable. OK, she might be just a bit of a nutter, but what if it was someone really serious, with a real grudge?'

He shrugged, contemplating the idea not for the first time, but he loved it where he was, overlooking the rooftops. He had a fabulous view and he was loath to lose it.

Sometimes he sat out on his little roof terrace and imagined that the rolling hills there in the distance were home.

They weren't, he knew that, but sometimes he just had a yearning to be back there, and those distant hills made him feel closer. The idea of moving to some gated community or apartment complex with hefty security and nothing to look at through the windows but carefully manicured grounds brought him out in hives.

'I'll think about it,' he said, knowing full well he wouldn't, and he closed his eyes and listened to the rhythmic swish of the windscreen wipers as she drove him home.

He was asleep when she turned onto the long gravel drive that led to her villa.

It had once been the main dwelling on her family's farm, long superseded by a much larger villa, and she loved it. It was small and unpretentious, but it was hers, it had stunning views, and it was perfect for Gio's recovery because it was single storey and so he wouldn't have to struggle with stairs.

Her headlights raked the front of the villa, and she drew up outside and opened the door quietly, easing out of the car without disturbing him. She'd put the radio on quietly while he slept, and she left it on while she went in and turned up the heating.

It wasn't cold, exactly, but it was cheerless even though the rain had stopped now, and she pulled sheets out of the linen cupboard and quickly made up her spare bed for him. It was a good room, the view from the bed stretching miles into the distance, and on the top of the hill on the horizon was the Palazzo Valtieri, home to his family for hundreds of years.

The lights were off now, the *palazzo* deserted, but normally she could see it in the dark. It was quite distinctive, and at night the lights could be seen for miles. She'd lost count of the number of times she'd lain there in her bedroom next to this one and stared at them, wondering if he was there, if he was awake, if he was looking for the lights of her villa.

Probably not. Why would he? He didn't feel the same about her, he'd made that perfectly clear five years ago when he'd ended their relationship without warning. And anyway, most of the time he was in Firenze, where he lived and worked.

But still she looked, and wondered, and yearned.

'Stop it!' she muttered, and made the bed. Torturing herself with memories was pointless—as pointless as staring at the *palazzo* on the hill like a love-struck teenager night after night.

But she *felt* like a love-struck teenager, even after all this time. Nothing had changed—except now she didn't have to imagine what it felt like to lie in his arms, because she *knew*.

She tugged the quilt straight, turned it back so he could get in, and went outside, switching on the porch lights.

He was awake. She could tell that, even though his eyes were closed, and as she walked towards him, her boots crunching on the gravel, they opened and looked straight at her through the windscreen.

He didn't want to come in. She could tell that, just as she'd been able to tell he was awake. Well, that was fine. She didn't really want him to, either, because it meant keeping up an impossible charade of indifference for the next two weeks, and she really, really didn't know if she could do it.

But it seemed that neither of them had a choice.

* * *

He had to do it.

There was no point delaying it, he had to get out of the car and hobble into the house and try, somehow, not to remember the last time he'd been in there.

The night of his brother Massimo's wedding, nine months ago.

Long enough to make a baby.

That was a random thought. And if he hadn't stopped, if he hadn't walked away and got back in his car and driven back to Firenze, they might have done just that.

They'd had a great day. A quiet family wedding, with a simple ceremony in the town hall followed by a meal in a restaurant owned by a member of their housekeeper Carlotta's family.

And then Massimo had taken his bride home, and the rest of them had ended up at Luca's with all the children. Too much for him, and too much for Anita, so he'd given her a lift home, and she'd offered him coffee before he headed back to Firenze, and he'd accepted.

Except they'd never got as far as the coffee—

'Gio?'

He eased his fragile and protesting foot out of the car with his one good hand, and then swung round and stood up, propping himself on the door for a moment.

'OK?'

'Bit light-headed.'

She clicked her tongue and took his good arm, draping it round her shoulders and sliding her arm around her waist so she could help him to the door. He didn't lean much weight on her. He couldn't, she was tiny, so he wasn't sure how much of a help it was, but it gave him a legitimate excuse to be close to her for a moment.

He actually didn't need her help. So long as he took

tiny, short steps, it was OK. Not good, but OK. And if he took it slowly, he'd be fine.

Did he tell her that?

No, because he was weak and self-indulgent, and he was enjoying the feel of her arm around his waist too much, so he told himself he didn't want to hurt her feelings.

As if it would. Anita was made of sterner stuff than that. He'd ripped her head off a million times when she'd been helping him limp home after he'd fallen out of a tree or off a wall or come hurtling off his bike at some crazy break-neck speed, and she'd never once turned a hair or paid any attention to his objections.

So he kept quiet and let her help him, and enjoyed the side-effect of being close to her firm, athletic body, savouring the nudge of her hip against his, the feel of her arm around his back, her warm fingers curled around his wrist.

And the scent of her, the perfume she always wore, the perfume he'd bought her countless times for Christmas or birthdays, always apologising for being unimaginative but doing it anyway because that scent, for him, was Anita.

'All right now?'

He nodded, words failing him for a second, and she shot him a keen look.

'You really are feeling rough, aren't you? I was expecting you to tell me to let go and stop interfering and that you didn't need my help and go and do something useful like cooking—'

She broke off, meeting his eyes and then laughing as she saw the wry humour reflected there.

'Surely not? Surely you haven't finally learned to be gracious, Giovanni Valtieri, after all these years?'

'Hardly.'

He chuckled and lifted his good hand, patting her cheek

patronisingly. It always annoyed her and her eyes flared in warning.

'Don't push your luck,' she said, and dropping him there in the entrance hall like a hot brick, she stalked into the kitchen, hips swishing. 'Coffee?'

He followed her slowly, enjoying the view in a masochistic way because there was no way he would act on this crazy attraction between them. 'Only if you've got a decent coffeemaker now. I don't suppose there's any food in the house?'

'Not yet. It's in the car. I'll put the coffee on. Do you want to lie down for a while, or sit in here?'

And there it was—the sofa, an old battered leather one where he'd nearly lost his self-control last June. But it looked really inviting, and it was set opposite a pair of French doors out onto the terrace and he could see the familiar lights of the valley twinkling in the distance. His home was out there somewhere in the darkness, and if he couldn't be there, then this was the next best thing.

'Here looks good,' he said, and made his way over to it and lowered himself down cautiously. So far, so good, he thought, and stretched his leg out in front of him with a quiet groan of relief.

'Better?'

'Much better. Have you got that coffee on yet?'

'I thought you didn't like my coffee?'

'I don't, but I need caffeine, and it has to be better than the stuff in the hospital.'

She gave him a look, but got two mugs out and found some biscuits in a tin.

'Here. Eat these while you wait. We'll be having dinner in a while. I bought something ready-made so we can have it whenever you're ready.'

'Good. I'm starving.'

She laughed. 'I've never known you when you weren't starving. It's a miracle you're not fat.'

'It's my enormous brain. It takes a lot of energy.'

She snorted, but he could see a smile teasing the corners of her mouth, and he turned away so she wouldn't see him laughing in response. Then his smile faded, and he closed his eyes and sighed quietly.

If it wasn't for this intense physical tug between them which had appeared suddenly when they were fourteen and never faded, life would have been so, so much easier. They could have just been friends, just as they had all their lives until that point. They'd been inseparable, getting into all manner of scrapes together, but then their hormones had made things awkward between them and she'd started spending more time with the girls, and he with the boys.

But despite the occasional awkwardness, they'd stayed friends, and they still were, twenty years later. She was the first person he called if he had something interesting or sad or exciting to share, but since that time five years ago when they'd somehow lost their restraint and ended up in bed for a few giddy and delirious weeks, things hadn't been the same.

He hadn't called her as much, hadn't leant on her in the same way, and if she'd leant on him, he'd given only what he'd had to and no more.

He'd been easing away from her, trying to distance himself because it was just too darned hard to be so close when he could never give her what she wanted—until last June, when he'd nearly lost the plot. He'd hardly seen anything of her since then, and he'd missed her more than he would ever admit.

* * *

She heard a quiet sigh, and looked over to where he was sitting.

He looked thoughtful, sombre, and she wondered what he was thinking about. The silly woman who'd got him in this mess with her unprovoked attack?

Or the last time he'd sat on that sofa, when they'd so nearly—

'Here, your coffee,' she said, dumping it down on the table beside him. She went back for her own coffee and the biscuits, and handed them to him.

'No chocolate ones?'

'Do you know, you're like a demanding child,' she grumbled, going back to the cupboard and rummaging around until she found a packet of chocolate coated wafers. 'Here. I was saving them for a special occasion, but since you can't cope without them...'

He arched a brow, but she ignored it and tore the Cellophane and put the packet down on the cushions between them, reaching for one at the same time as him. Their fingers clashed, and she withdrew her hand.

'After you,' she said, 'since you're clearly going to die if you don't eat soon,' and his mouth curved into a slight, fleeting smile and he picked one up deliberately and bit it in half.

She looked away. He was teasing her, tormenting her, but her fingers were still tingling from the brush of his hand.

How could she feel like this still? Always, all the time, year after year without anything but hope to feed it?

Except he'd given her hope. They'd had an affair, and last year, they'd so nearly started it up again. So very, very nearly—

'Good biscuits.'

'They are. That's why I was saving them. Don't eat them all, you won't want your dinner.'

'Unlikely.'

She snorted, and put the rest away in the tin and put the lid on, and he just leant back and stretched out his long, rangy body and sighed.

He looked so good there, as if the sofa was made for him, as if it was his body that had moulded it to the saggy, comfortable shape it now was—except he'd only ever been on it once before, and she really, really didn't want to think about that time.

'How's the coffee?' she asked to distract herself, and he glanced down into the mug and shrugged.

'It's coffee. It's not great. Why don't we go and buy a coffee maker?'

'Now?'

He chuckled wearily. 'No, not now. Tomorrow? I don't know if I can cope for two weeks without proper coffee.'

'This is proper coffee. You're just a coffee snob.'

'No, I just know what I like.'

'And you couldn't possibly compromise to spare my feelings?'

He turned his head and gave her a mocking smile. 'Now, you know that's ridiculous.'

Oh, goodness, she couldn't do this! That smile cut right through her defences and left her so vulnerable to him, but there was no way he was going to know that. So she laughed and hit him lightly with a cushion, then hugged it to her chest and pulled her knees up, propping her feet on the edge of the sofa and changing the subject back to the safer one of his attacker.

'I wonder when they'll find her. She makes me nervous.'

His lips kinked in that lopsided smile that was so familiar to her and made her heart lurch once again. 'It's not a Bond movie, Anita. She's just an angry woman who's probably now very scared.'

She nodded. 'Probably. What on earth did she want from you?'

He shrugged. 'Money? They were in business, she cheated him for years, he found out and told her to go quietly and broke up the partnership, and then she decided to go after what she thought was her half. So he produced all the evidence to show she'd cheated him and she gave in, but instead of gaining money, she's ended up with a legal bill, and she blames me.'

Anita laughed in astonishment. 'Why? She didn't seriously expect to win?'

'Apparently.'

'She's deluded, then. Either that or she hasn't heard of your reputation. She should have just gone quietly.'

'Of course, but she was distraught. Much more so than I would have expected, and she was so insistent on talking to me. It wasn't normal behaviour. Maybe if I'd listened I wouldn't be in this mess now.'

He looked slightly bemused, as if he was still trying to work it out, and she reached out a hand and rested it on his shoulder. Silly of her to touch him, so risky and not really necessary, but she needed to feel his warmth, just to reassure herself that he *was* still alive, that this woman's actions hadn't actually caused his death after all.

But then he turned his head and their eyes locked. His pupils flared, darkening his already dark eyes to midnight, and it was as if all the air had been sucked out of the room. Heat scorched through her, a heat born of want and need and a deep and unbearable longing to just lean over and rest her head on his shoulder and hold him close.

For an age they said nothing, and then she pulled her hand away and got up.

'I'll get the food in from the car and cook the dinner,' she said, her voice jerky and tight, and pulling her boots back on, she went out to the car and stood for a moment sucking in the cool air and getting herself back under control.

How could she still love him, still want him, like this? Five years she'd had to get over him, and she'd thought she was doing OK, but tonight she felt as if she hadn't made any progress at all. And now they were supposed to be stuck together alone here for two weeks, and keep their hands to themselves?

They'd never do it.

He was on the phone when she went back inside with the shopping, talking to his mother.

She could tell it was her, just by the tone of his voice and the patient, slightly indulgent expression on his face.

'I'll be fine. Don't worry about me, Anita's looking after me. Of course I'll be nice to her. I know she's a nice girl.' He glanced across at her and winked, and then his mother said something else and he looked hastily away. 'Don't be silly. Of course not.'

Of course not what? Of course not, any chance of them getting back together? It would make his mother a very happy woman. Hers also. Her, too, come to that, happiest of all of them, but it was a fruitless waste of energy thinking about it any more, so she dumped the shopping down on the worktop and started to put it away.

If only she could tune out the sound of his voice, instead of catching every word as if she was eavesdropping! Not that she could help it.

She left the shopping and went into the bathroom, giving it a quick clean. Hopefully by the time she'd finished, he would have got off the phone and she wouldn't be forced to endure the warm murmur of his voice and that soft chuckle which melted her bones.

By the time the taps and mirror were gleaming and they could have eaten off the fittings, she decided the bathroom was probably clean enough. She went back into the kitchen, but he was still on the phone. To Luca, this time, she thought.

There was medical stuff—details of his treatment, a report on what hurt, what tingled, what ached—definitely Luca. And he was lying, as well. She took the phone from him.

'Luca? Hi. This is mostly lies. He hurts, he looks awful, he's dizzy—Gio, no, you can't have the phone back.' She stepped further away, listening to Luca's advice for feeding him things to replace the iron while Gio protested from the confines of the sofa.

'Will do.'

'And don't let him walk on that foot yet.'

'OK. I'll do my best.' She swatted his hand away. 'He wants you back.'

'Anita, before you go, I know this is difficult for you,' Luca said softly. 'We're really grateful to you for being there for him. You just take care, OK? Don't let yourself get hurt, and if it all gets too much, call, and one of us will come.'

She swallowed hard. 'I'm fine. Here he is.'

She handed the phone back and retreated to the kitchen, wishing she'd bought raw ingredients instead of a ready-made meal. It might have given her something to do for the next hour or so, instead of turning on the oven, putting the pan of lasagne into it and then twiddling her thumbs for half an hour.

She closed the oven door and thought about what Luca had said. Dark green vegetables and red meat, with whole grain bread and pulses.

Well, the red meat was taken care of, and she had some pâté and a mixed salad she could give him for a starter, and the ciabatta was made with stoneground flour. That would have to do for now, and tomorrow she'd go shopping.

She pulled plates out and started arranging the salad. He was watching the television now, flicking through the channels, and then he stopped. 'Oh, no, for heaven's sake, why can't they leave me alone?'

'What?'

'It's made the news. Look. The police said it might and they were going to do some damage limitation, but it doesn't sound like it.'

She put the knife down and went over, perching on the end of the sofa and watching.

'Police say Giovanni Valtieri was released from hospital at midday today following an incident yesterday in which he was assaulted. He was seen being driven away from the hospital by a woman believed to be Anita Della Rosso, a friend of the family and one-time girlfriend of the lawyer, who's been at his side since the incident.'

'What!' She plonked down onto the sofa next to him and stared at the television in astonishment. 'How did they find that out?'

He shrugged. 'They're everywhere. Listen.'

There was a reporter standing outside the hospital now, talking about how she'd been seen arriving yesterday and again this morning, and then further talk about their relationship.

'A hugely successful lawyer in his own right, Giovanni is the colourful and flamboyant youngest son of Vittorio and Elisa Valtieri, members of one of Tuscany's oldest and most respected families, and his renewed relationship with society wedding planner Anita Della Rossa is bound to be a cause for speculation. Will Anita be planning her own wedding soon?'

The screen went suddenly blank, and she looked at Gio.

His face was rigid, his lips pressed tightly together into a straight line, a muscle in his jaw jumping. He threw down the remote control and sat back, arms folded, fulminating in silence.

He was furious, she could tell, but more than that, he was worried.

He dragged in a breath and turned to her.

'I never should have dragged you into this. All this talk about our relationship—it's so public, and now they're going to point Camilla Ponti straight at you.'

She smiled a little ruefully and touched his cheek. 'Gio, it's OK. This is my private bolt-hole, a secret hideout that hardly anybody knows about. She won't look for us here, everyone thinks I live either in my apartment in Firenze or with my parents. There's nothing to link it to me, not even the address. I give my parents' villa as my postal address here. This is just like a guest villa.'

'Talking of your parents, you'd better warn them,' he said. 'If they're watching this news bulletin—'

Her phone rang, right on cue, and she spent the next five minutes telling her mother he was all right, they were at her villa and it was all just idle speculation. She was simply looking after an old friend.

'You expect me to believe that? There's no smoke without fire, Anita.'

She coloured. Her mother didn't know about their brief affair five years ago. Nobody did, not really. They certainly hadn't told anyone. Luca and Massimo had guessed, but nobody else had, as far as she knew. Well, apart from the press and now half of Tuscany—

'It's just rumour,' she said lightly. 'Ignore it. I have to go, I'm cooking supper for us.'

But her mother wasn't stupid. 'Take care, *carissima,*' she said softly, and Anita swallowed.

'I will. *Ciao,* Mamma. Love to Papà.'

She lowered her phone and met his eyes.

'Is she OK?'

'She's fussing.'

'Of course she's fussing, she's your mother. I'm surprised she's not over here right now checking the sleeping arrangements.'

'Well, she'll be disappointed, then, because I've made up the spare room for you. Do you want to eat where you are, or at the table?'

'Here? Do you mind? I can't be bothered to move.'

Subtext: it'll hurt too much, even though he'd had his painkillers with coffee earlier. She took his food over to him, with a glass of wine to wash it down.

Not that she approved, but it might help relax him and she wasn't in the mood to play his mother.

'Thanks, that looks really good. I can't tell you how hungry I am.'

She'd spread the pâté on the toasted ciabatta, so he could eat it one-handed, and he forked in the salad and mopped up the dressing with the last of the toast. 'That was good. Tasty. What can I smell?'

'Lasagne. I thought you could eat it with a fork.'

'Great idea.'

She took his plate and brought it back with the lasagne on it, and after they'd eaten it he leant back and sighed in contentment.

'Better?'

'Amazing. That was really good. I was ready for it. I haven't eaten anything proper since the day before yesterday.'

He rolled his head towards her, his eyes serious, the food forgotten. 'Anita, I hate involving you in this. You should be on holiday, not sitting here babysitting me while they gossip about us on the news.'

'Don't worry. I don't care if people talk about us.'

'Well, I do, and I'm not thrilled about them giving Camilla Ponti directions.'

'She won't come after you,' she said with more confidence than she felt. 'She's in Firenze somewhere, trying to hide from the police. Even she's going to realise she's in deep enough trouble without making it worse. And anyway, I thought you said she was mortified.'

'She was. She really didn't mean to hurt me.'

'Well, then, we'll be fine,' she said firmly. 'The outside lights come on if anyone approaches, so we can't be sneaked up on. I'll set the alarm and put the car in the garage, and nobody would know we were here, if that makes you happier.'

What would make him happier was knowing that Camilla Ponti had been found and seen by a doctor. Until then, this would have to do.

'Fine.'

'Good. Now I think it's time you went to bed.'

Their eyes clashed again, and then he levered himself to his feet.

'You'd better show me to my room, then,' he said, and

she led him down the hall and pushed open the bedroom
door. She'd unpacked his bag and laid his things out on
the top of the chest, including his painkillers.

He was pleased to see them. He'd just had some, but he
had no doubt he'd need more before the night was out. He
hobbled awkwardly past her, looked around and then met
her eyes again. 'It's a nice room. Thank you.'

'*Prego.* I'll bring you a glass of water. The bathroom's
across the hall, and I've put out clean towels and your pills
are on the chest. Will you be all right getting ready for bed,
or do you want me to help you undress?'

He gave a soft huff of laughter.

'I don't think that's a good idea.'

Their eyes locked, his dark and unfathomable. As well
as she knew him, she couldn't read them.

She could feel the heat scorching her cheeks, but she
held her ground. 'I thought you weren't feeling great.'

'I'm not, but I'd have to be dead before I let you undress
me. *Buonanotte,* Anita.'

And he closed the door softly in her face.

CHAPTER THREE

HE stood there for a moment, listening, and after a long pause he heard the sound of her banging around in the kitchen.

She sounded mad with him. Not surprising, really. It hadn't been the politest rejection, and she'd only been trying to help, but—*Dio,* just being that close to her was killing him, and he might not be feeling great today, but his body clearly didn't care about that. It was interested in Anita, and saying so.

No *way* was she taking off his clothes and finding that out!

Which meant he had to do it on his own, and frankly he wasn't sure he could one-handed. The first thing he had to do, though, was use the bathroom, because he wasn't going to wander around the house half naked. He knew his limitations, and keeping a lid on his libido was one of them. The more he was wearing when he was exposed to her, frankly, the better.

There was no sign of his washbag, so he assumed she must have put it in the bathroom already. He frowned, feeling another pang of guilt, which was silly. It was nothing he wouldn't have done for her, and he wouldn't have taken no for an answer about helping her undress, either.

Clearly his skin was tougher than hers. And she wouldn't have been so rude.

Guilt again.

He limped to the bathroom, spent a few infuriating minutes in there struggling to clean his teeth with the wrong hand, and when he opened the door she was outside.

She hadn't been able to stay away. She'd gone into the kitchen, steaming mad with him, deeply hurt—

I'd have to be dead before I let you undress me.

What was that about? He'd been keen enough for her to undress him five years ago, for goodness' sake, so what on earth had changed so much that he wouldn't even let her help him when he was injured? She'd thought they were friends still, but clearly not. They'd crossed a line when they'd had the affair, and now—now everything was different, and there was no going back.

They couldn't just undo the fact that they'd been lovers. She realised that, but this was nothing to *do* with sex! Except clearly, for him, taking off his clothes was something he did on his own, or a prelude to lovemaking. Often, for them, the only prelude, she remembered, because on occasions they'd been so desperate they'd almost torn each other's clothes off—

'Oh, stop it! This is ridiculous!'

She slammed the dishwasher shut, battened down the hatches on her memories and swiped a cloth over the worktop. The plates were in the dishwasher, the kitchen was tidy.

And still he was in the bathroom.

In difficulties?

So she'd gone to investigate, listened outside to the sounds of frustration as he struggled with something—his toothbrush?

And then the door opened, and she saw the pain etched into his face, the frustration, the tiredness, and she just wanted to hug him. He shook his head, closing his eyes briefly, and when he opened them she could see guilt written all over his face.

Goodness knows what was written on hers. It must be a mass of emotions, and it seemed he could read them all.

'I'm sorry, *cara,*' he said gruffly, reaching out one-handed to hug her, and then she was there against him, her arms around him, her face buried in his chest just breathing him in and holding on.

'I'm sorry I flounced off,' she mumbled. 'You look awful. I've been so worried about you—'

Her voice hitched, and he sighed and rubbed her back gently. 'I'm fine, Anita. Come on, don't cry. Go and make us some hot chocolate, and I'll get my clothes off. No more tears, eh?'

She eased away, sniffing slightly and scrubbing tears from her cheeks. 'Sorry. I'm such an idiot—'

'You're a lovely idiot. I'm lucky to have such a good friend.'

There. He'd said it. Friend.

Not lover.

She nodded, and walked away towards the kitchen to make the hot chocolate, and he gritted his teeth and made it the last few steps to the bedroom.

Then he looked at his foot.

The nurses had struggled to get his trousers on over it without hurting him. What hope did he have, one-handed? He couldn't do it alone.

Which meant asking Anita.

She came back with the hot chocolate while he was sitting on the side of the bed scowling.

'Problem?'

'I can't get my trousers off on my own,' he said grudgingly.

She suppressed a smile. 'No, I don't suppose you can. And you need something to keep the weight off your foot in the night.' She plonked the chocolate down on the bedside table, threw the bottom of the quilt back and put two pillows in the bed.

'OK. That should do it. So, are you sleeping in the trousers, bearing in mind that you'd have to be dead to let me help you?'

He winced at the mild tone which belied a world of hurt—hurt of his making. He deserved her sarcasm. Hell, he deserved more than that. It would serve him right if she left him to struggle on his own. So he swallowed his pride. He needed her help, like it or not, and he realised he might have to grovel to get it.

'I'm sorry. I didn't mean that quite as it came out. No, I'm not sleeping in them, but I have no idea how to get them off, I just know it's going to hurt.'

'Not if I do it—assuming you'll let me help you?' she asked more gently.

He shrugged, hating it but out of options, and unfastened his trousers, pushing them down to his knees before sitting back down on the edge of the bed. He felt naked and vulnerable. Ridiculous. He'd been fine with the nurses, so why was he worried about Anita?

Because I know what it's like to make love to her.

'Just do it, Anita,' he said, and she gave a little shrug and knelt down at his feet, which brought her eyes in line with the telltale bulge in his jersey shorts. And just south, on the inside of his muscular thigh, was the transparent dressing over his wound.

She winced. 'That was close. It could have been really catastrophic.'

'My sex life's not really your problem,' he said shortly, struggling with her proximity and wishing she'd just look somewhere else before he gave himself away, but she just rolled her eyes.

'I wasn't thinking about your sex life,' she bit back drily. 'But since you mention it, there are all those children you might never have been able to have. That would be a waste.'

'Except I'm not planning on having any children, *cara*. No way. I'm not cut out to be a father.'

She sat back on her heels and stared up at him, astonished. 'What? That's ridiculous, you'd be a marvellous father,' she said crossly. 'You're wonderful with your brothers' children. They adore you.'

He shrugged. 'So? I'm their uncle, I spoil them. It changes nothing. I'm not having children, ever. I don't want the responsibility. If I did, I would have done something about it.'

With her? Hardly. The moment their relationship had started to look cosy and semi-permanent, he'd legged it into the wide blue yonder. But one day, surely, with someone…?

'You might change your mind,' she said doggedly. 'It would be a shame to waste all the potential in those genes.'

'Potential for what?' he asked, exasperated. 'I've told you, I've got no intention of passing on my genes to anyone. There isn't a woman in the world who could talk me into it.'

Well, that was telling her, she thought, and under the resignation—because after all, she knew her relationship with him was going nowhere—was a pang of what felt like grief. She'd dreamed of it so many times, could conjure up an image of a child with his eyes and her hair, but only if she let herself, and she didn't, because she didn't want to lose what was left of her sanity. He'd had quite enough of that already.

'Well, that's a shame,' she said lightly, trying to make a joke out of it. 'I mean, I don't want to inflate your ego, but you're healthy, passably good-looking and when you aren't tripping over your own refuse bag, you're reasonably intelligent. You could have some quite nice children, so long as they didn't inherit your attitude.'

It was the sort of sassy remark he expected from her, so without thinking he came straight back at her.

'*Dio*, you can talk! What about your attitude?'

'There's no chance your children will inherit my attitude, is there? You made that quite clear five years ago.'

There was a second of shocked silence, and then he reached out a hand and touched her cheek.

'Anita?'

To his astonishment she blushed and turned her head away. 'Ignore me,' she mumbled. 'I'm just worried about you.'

He frowned. 'Well, you don't need to be.' He sighed and rammed his hand through his hair, then winced. He'd have to remember to use the other one, but right now he was so tired and sore he was ready to fall over, and her words had created a sudden, shocking image of a cheeky little girl with a sassy smile and a wit like a razor. And it took the wind right out of his sails.'I need to get to bed,' he said abruptly.

'Sorry,' she muttered, and then she hooked off his left boot and eased the trousers down, first off his left foot, then very carefully over his right. Then she peeled the sock off.

He flexed his ankle slightly and winced as she sat back on her heels and looked at it.

'It's an impressive colour,' she said, getting to her feet.

He peered at it thoughtfully. It was black and blue, the bits he could see of it around the strapping, and no doubt in time it would go all shades of the rainbow. He looked forward to it. It might hurt less by then.

He eased back onto the mattress, unable to use his bad hand to shift himself, refusing to ask her help, but she gave it anyway, hooking her arm in his armpit and hauling the bad side up the bed while he shoved the good side.

Then she plumped the pillows and covered him carefully with the quilt, hesitating to frown down at his thigh.

'Is it all right? Does the dressing need changing?'

'No. They've given me a supply of fresh dressings, but they'd told me to leave it for a day or so. It should be fine— assuming I can peel it off the hairs.'

Her laugh had a little mocking edge to it that he didn't like. 'It'll be like having a leg wax. I'm sure you'll cope, you big baby.'

He winced, and she laughed again, then her smile faded and she reached out a cool, gentle hand and laid it on his leg, just below the wound, all signs of mockery gone.

'Even if it is none of my business, I'm glad the glass hasn't done any lasting damage,' she said a little gruffly as she covered him up and gave him back some privacy.

'As you were kind enough to point out, if I hadn't been so stupid we wouldn't be sitting here having this conversation.' He patted the bedcovers beside him. 'Come here. Grab the hot chocolate and turn out the light, and come and sit with me for a bit. I'm too tired to argue with you.'

'That'll be a first,' she said drily, but she climbed up onto the bed beside him, wriggling back against the pillows and handing him his hot chocolate before turning off the bedside light so they could see the twinkling lights in the distance. For a moment he said nothing, then he gave a contented sigh.

'I love that view,' he said quietly. 'Utter blackness, with just the faintest glimmer from the villages. It's never as dark in the city, and I really miss it.'

'I do, too. The view's the main reason I wanted to renovate this villa. Sometimes I sit here at night and stare at it for hours,' she said. 'It seems odd without lights on at the *palazzo,* though. I can usually see it from all the main rooms. It's like a beacon.'

'So is that why you look out? To see if I'm there?' he teased.

Ouch. Too close to the truth for comfort, she thought, hoping she wasn't blushing. Once in an evening was enough, but at least it was too dark to see.

'In your dreams,' she said lightly. And hers, but she wasn't giving him that bit of ammunition under any circumstances!

'Have you had your painkillers and antibiotics?' she asked instead, watching him carefully in the dim light from the hall.

He nodded. 'Yes. Anita, I'm fine, really, stop fretting.'

'I can't help it. I can't believe I didn't answer your calls—'

She broke off, not wanting to broach the subject yet again, but he gave a soft huff of laughter.

'Forget it. I'm fine. It was my own stupid fault I was hurt.'

Anita shuddered. 'Not entirely. If she hadn't been there it would never have happened.'

Even in the darkness, she could see him frown, serious at last. 'I know. And I'm concerned that she's still out there. Will you do me a favour? Stay here next to me tonight?'

'What, to protect you?' she teased, but he gave a wry chuckle.

'Hardly. I was thinking more the other way round.'

'You're going to protect me?' Now it was her turn to laugh. 'Gio, you can hardly move!'

'I can stand between you,' he said quietly, and she realised he was deadly serious. His macho nonsense touched her, but the irony of it was so ridiculous she didn't know whether to laugh or cry.

'Gio, she won't come here.'

'You don't know that. If it hadn't been on the news, I wouldn't have worried, but as it has…'

His voice trailed off, and she gave in.

He wanted to protect her, and for the sake of his peace of mind, she'd let him think he was, but there was no danger from Camilla Ponti that she could see. The only danger to her in this villa was Gio himself, and she wasn't strong enough to resist him.

But she knew him well enough to know that she wouldn't win the argument, so she did the next best thing. She agreed.

'All right. If you insist. I'll get ready for bed and come back.'

'Don't forget to lock up.'

She rolled her eyes. 'Well, isn't it just as well I've got you here to remind me of something so obvious.'

It actually suited her to be beside him, because she

wanted to keep an eye on him and make sure he was all right. She just had to resist the urge to fall into his arms.

Not that there'd be much to resist. He was exhausted and injured, and if nothing else the pills would make him sleep.

And as long as he was this sick and this sore, she'd be safe.

Ish.

'Give me five minutes,' she said, and retreated.

It was OK to start with.

She was wearing pyjamas—not little bits of fluff, but real pyjamas with a long-sleeved top and trousers. She just felt safer that way—safer from herself, but she needn't have worried, because he stayed firmly on his side, and she stayed firmly on hers.

Until she woke in the night to hear him muttering and thrashing around, and she reached out her hand and rested in on his chest.

'Gio! Gio, wake up, you're dreaming!'

He grunted, and she felt the tension drain out of him with a whoosh.

'Sorry—I didn't mean to disturb you.'

'It's fine. Are you OK?'

'I am now. Come here.'

And he reached out his left arm and scooped her into his good side. She laid her head against his chest, listening to the drumming of his heart, and gradually it slowed to a steady, even beat.

She rested her hand over it and wondered what he'd been dreaming about. The attack? Probably, she thought, with another stab of guilt for not answering her phone. She tried not to think how different it might have been if the ambulance hadn't got there in time, if the woman hadn't called for help.

Very different.

She might have been visiting him in the hospital mortuary instead of lying here beside him, and the thought brought with it a wave of emotion that made her catch her breath.

Losing him because he didn't want her was one thing. Losing him because he'd been killed in a stupid accident was another altogether. She'd been without him for all of her adult life, except for a few short, blissful weeks, but she'd always known he was still walking around in the world, still out there with that razor-sharp intellect and the tongue to go with it, and just knowing that somehow made it all bearable.

To lose him to death, never to hear his voice again or see his face, never to be near him again, just didn't bear thinking about.

So she snuggled closer, resting her legs against his left one, her toes nudging his foot. Just in contact, nothing more.

Until the next time she woke, to find she'd shifted, draped her leg over his, so that his firm, hard thigh was between hers, the pressure making her ache for him in a way she'd forgotten.

No. Not forgotten. Put out of her mind, but not any more. Now, it was right back there in the forefront, and she shifted against him, trying to ease the ache.

He moved his leg, lifting it slightly towards her, and she made a tiny, needy noise.

This was crazy! He was injured, there was no way this was going anywhere, and she ought to move out of his arms and—

'Where are you going?'

'I'm lying on you. I'm afraid I'll hurt you.'

'You're not hurting me, you're fine. Stay there.' His arm tightened and pulled her closer.

She slept again, but her body was far from relaxed, and she woke again some time later from a lurid dream to the building, driving sensation of a climax on the brink.

Still half asleep and in the clutches of the dream, she bit her lip as she felt the sensation explode through her body, the shockwave stealing her breath so she could only gasp his name.

'Anita?' He turned his head, feeling the tremors running through her, the clench of her thighs against his, and need rocketed through him.

Her beautiful body was convulsing against him, his name a broken whisper on her lips. He tilted her head, his mouth finding hers and plundering it, swallowing the gasps and sighs still coming from her body as the shockwave died away. *Dio*, he wanted her. Crazily, improbably, he wanted her, wanted to bury himself deep inside her and drive into her again and again—

'Ahh!'

He dropped his right leg back to the mattress, letting the tension out of the protesting thigh muscle, feeling the nudge of the pillows against his ankle. Damn.

She lifted her head. 'Gio?'

'It's OK,' he said, ignoring the pain, running his hand over her back and soothing her. He still wanted her, despite the pain, and his mouth found hers again in the darkness, frustration killing him.

'I can't,' he groaned. 'I need you, I want you so much, but I just can't.' He swore softly, rocking against her leg, grunting with pain as his thigh tightened again.

And then she slid her hand slowly, hesitantly over his chest, down past his ribs, tightening the muscles of his abdomen as she glided over them and under the waistband of his shorts. He thought he'd die as her fingers circled him, her delicate grip torture. Then she tightened her hand, moved it slowly in firm, even strokes, and he felt the pressure mounting relentlessly.

He dropped his head back, lifted his hips and let out a long, shuddering groan as she took him over the edge and everything crashed and burned around him.

And then reality hit, like a bucket of cold water, as the pain penetrated his emerging consciousness and common sense returned.

What the *hell* was he doing? With Anita, of all people? He'd ended it five years ago, tried to stay away from her, for her sake, because he couldn't be relied on, couldn't be trusted in a relationship, could never seem to give enough to make a woman truly happy. He'd done it so she could move on with her life, find another man, settle down, have the babies she so clearly wanted. And it was working, sort of. She was dating from time to time. She'd get there, if he could only leave her alone.

But he couldn't, apparently. And now, here, when he needed her for so many other reasons, he'd gone and blown it by doing this.

He hadn't needed her by his side all night. He'd *wanted* her by his side. It was nothing to do with the Ponti woman, because he truly didn't think she'd hurt them. It was all to do with wanting Anita.

It was *always* to do with wanting Anita.

'Gio? Are you OK?'

Her voice was soft, her hand stroking his chest now,

the touch tender, as if he was a child—or maybe just an injured lover.

He wasn't her lover. He couldn't be her lover.

'Why did you do that?' he asked harshly, his voice not quite as steady as he would have liked.

There was a tiny gasp, and she pulled her hand away from his chest as if it was red hot, eased her body away from his, and he felt cold air move in to fill the space where she had been. It made his heart ache.

'I'm sorry,' she mumbled. 'I thought—'

'Forget it. I need the bathroom.'

He got out of bed and limped painfully across the hall. Hell, his foot hurt, but there was no way he was asking her to help him. Not after that.

It had been too darned personal, but it wasn't enough. He wanted to get a lot, lot more personal, starting right now.

He stood in front of the bathroom mirror for ages, staring at himself in disgust. He was still hard. He still wanted her. Even after—

He willed his body to co-operate. It took an age, and when he finally went back to bed she'd gone, her bedroom door firmly closed.

Probably just as well, he thought guiltily, easing himself back under the covers, but it was cold and lonely without her, and he cursed himself for ruining it, for kissing her, for reaching out for her. He should have just lain there and pretended to be asleep, but he'd wanted her to touch him.

Well, she had, and now it was going to be thoroughly awkward and difficult between them, and he only had himself to blame.

She didn't sleep again that night.

Instead, she lay in her bed, feeling cold and lonely and

embarrassed. How could she have been so stupid? So ridiculously uninhibited?

She gave a tiny howl of frustration and turned her face into the pillow. It was going to be so difficult now between them. It had been hard enough before. Now it would be impossible. It was going to be utterly humiliating facing him in the morning, even though it hadn't really been her fault. How could she control her body in its sleep?

But she hadn't been asleep, she reminded herself bluntly. Not for all of it. Not when she'd touched him. Not when she'd kissed him back, and slid her hand down into his shorts and wrapped the hot, silky length of him in her palm—

'No!'

She stifled the tiny scream of frustration and humiliation, and pulled the quilt up over her head. Stupid, stupid, stupid. How was she supposed to face him after that? She might not get up again.

Ever.

His phone rang at seven thirty—not too early under normal circumstances, but after the unscheduled scene in the night he'd only just dropped off to sleep again and for a second he considered not answering it.

He was glad he did.

It was the police, to tell him that Camilla Ponti had walked into the police station in Firenze in a distraught state, saying she'd nearly killed him.

'She didn't hurt me. It was an accident, but I do think she needs to see a doctor, because she wasn't rational. Do you need me to come and talk to her?' he asked, but the detective told him it was unnecessary.

'You just concentrate on getting better, and leave her to us. We'll take care of her.'

'Good. Call me if you need anything.'

He put the phone down, blew his breath out and lay back on the pillows.

They'd got her.

Which meant, of course, that there was less justification for him to stay here hiding out with Anita.

He waited for the feeling of relief, but it didn't come. Instead, he just felt a little flat. Ridiculous. He'd go back to Firenze and pick up his life where he'd left off. Maybe even go on holiday with his family after all.

Except that it was a skiing holiday and anyway, Anita was supposed to be there, too.

Oh, hell. It was all too complicated, and a more immediate concern was having a shower. How, he had no idea, but the first step was getting to the bathroom.

He threw back the covers and eased himself to the edge of the bed. He was still sitting there psyching himself up for the walk when there was a tap at the open door and she came in, wrapped in a bath robe with her hair in a towel, obviously fresh from the shower.

She smelt amazing, and he groaned inwardly as she walked over to him and leant on the end of the bed, her hands fiddling with the belt of her robe.

'Who was that on the phone?'

'The police. They've got her. She turned herself in. Apparently she's in a hell of a state.'

'Oh. Right.'

She looked down into his face, and he could see just how awkward she felt this morning. Just as awkward as him.

'About last night—'

They both broke off, and his mouth twitched into a smile and he raised a brow, gesturing with his head for her to continue.

'I'm sorry. I overstepped the mark. I didn't mean to, I was half asleep and I don't really know what happened. It won't happen again.'

He felt curiously disappointed, and nearly laughed at himself. 'Forget it. As you say, you were asleep. I kissed you, I pushed it, encouraged you—hell, I begged you, Anita, and I had no right to be so harsh with you. I'm the one who should be sorry.'

He wasn't, though, he realised. Not really. And given the choice, he'd do it all over again. So he couldn't give himself the choice.

'It won't happen again, anyway, because I'm going back to Firenze,' he announced bluntly, and she stared at him as if he was mad.

'What? Why? How? How will you manage?'

'What do you mean, how will I manage?'

She rolled her eyes and stood back, hands on hips. 'You can't manage one-handed. You can't do any one of a number of things with only one hand! You're going to have to change the dressing on your leg—what are you going to do, ring your neighbour's doorbell and ask them to do it? Don't be silly! And how will you cook?'

'The same way I always do. I'll pick up the phone.'

'And go to the door and let them in. You don't even have a lift in that building. How will you manage the stairs with that ankle?'

She was right. Maddeningly, annoyingly right.

'I'll go and join the rest of the family, then.'

'On a skiing holiday?' she said, looking pointedly at his foot. 'Sounds great.'

'Well, I haven't got a lot of options, have I, really? Carlotta and Roberto are away, so it's my apartment or the ski chalet.'

'Or you could just stay here.'

Her words hung in the air between them, fraught with the memory of last night.

He thought about it. He could stay there, sure, but would it be wise? Probably not. Safe? Unlikely. Appealing?

Oh, yes.

'On one condition,' he said, feeling himself surrender.

'Which is?'

'We go out this morning and buy a coffee maker.'

She stared at him blankly for a second, then she let out a tiny huff of astonished laughter.

'Done. I'm going to get dressed. Do you need any help?'

'No.'

Probably not true, that, but he'd manage if it killed him.

She nodded, and walked towards the door. 'OK. Yell if you need me.'

Need? He'd never stopped needing her, not for a day in the last twenty years. But he was no good for her, and the sooner she found herself a nice, decent, reliable man to make her happy and give her babies—babies without his attitude—the happier he'd be.

He frowned, put the babies firmly out of his mind and headed for the bathroom. A shower could wait. In the meantime, he could wash and dress himself, even if it was agony. He had to regain some independence from Anita if he was going to be able to manage this situation.

He could do this. He could keep his distance, accept her friendship at face value and leave at the end of the fortnight.

He just needed to toughen up.

CHAPTER FOUR

THEY skipped breakfast.

The lure of a rich, dark double espresso was calling him, and Anita knew he'd be grumpy until he had his caffeine shot. Besides, the café they were going to made the most amazing pastries, and she needed comfort food after last night.

She was still squirming with embarrassment every time she thought about it. Well, not just embarrassment, if she was honest. There was a good chunk of lust flung in there, too, and she was beginning to wonder how she'd cope for two weeks until his family came back and took him off her hands.

She must have been mad to suggest it. She should have sent him back to Firenze and let him cope. He could have hired a nurse, for heaven's sake. He had enough money.

'There's a space.'

She turned into the parking bay and cut the engine. They were as close as they could get to the café, and there was a shop almost next door that sold decent bean-to-cup coffee makers. She'd never bought one because she didn't care that much about coffee and they'd always seemed a bit unnecessary, but that was fine. He could have whatever he liked. He was buying.

'I'm ready for this,' he muttered as they arrived at the café, and he pulled out his wallet and ordered his double espresso and her cappuccino. 'What are you eating?'.

'Oh, I don't know. I can't decide…'

He ordered a selection before she could vacillate any longer, and while he was paying she found a table by the window and sat down to wait for him.

And wait.

Eventually he came over, a wry smile on his face, and eased himself into the chair with a grunt.

'Sorry. He'd seen the news—wanted to know how I was doing.'

'I'd worked it out, Gio. It's going to happen all the time. You grew up here, of course they're interested.'

'Yeah, he was interested in you, too. Were you planning our wedding yet and that sort of thing.'

Not a chance. Not now, and probably never had been, although she'd let herself believe it for a few delirious weeks. *Move on!*

'So, what do you want to do today?' she asked, completely ignoring his last remark because there didn't seem to be anything to say about it, and particularly not in public.

'Apart from buying a coffee maker?' he said drily. 'I don't know. Do you fancy going for a drive? I get cabin fever.'

'That quick?'

He laughed. 'I'm not good when I'm not busy. So, shall we do that? We could drive somewhere and stop for lunch.'

'You haven't even had breakfast yet and you're worrying about the next meal,' she teased. 'Don't worry, I won't let you starve. And sure, we can go for a drive. There's that lovely road high up on the ridge looking towards Monte

Amiata. The views are lovely and we could cut back on the other side along the Val d'Orcia and have lunch in Pienza.'

He nodded, but he didn't look enthused, and Anita began to wonder how she was going to entertain a man who lived life so hard and so fast that he had cabin fever after a day. Less than that. And she had a fortnight to get through?

'I have a better idea.'

Good, she thought, because she had none at all. Well, none that were in any way sensible or wouldn't get her into a whole load of trouble. 'What's that?'

'Let's go back to my apartment and pick up my coffee maker. I've got a spare one—I've got a built-in one now, so it's redundant. You can have it. And I need clothes. All I've got is that overnight bag and it's a bit challenged. I didn't really think it through. And trainers, so I have a shoe I can wear on this foot, and I can bring my laptop. I've got some work I could be doing on a case that's coming up.'

She nodded, relieved that he might actually find something to occupy him, apart from baiting her because they weren't doing what they both wanted to do because he'd decided five years ago that it was off the menu. 'OK.'

She looked up, smiled at the café owner who'd brought over their order and dug into the pastries. She was starving. She hadn't slept at all well last night, and when she had—

Back to that again, she thought, growling silently. Well, at least Camilla Ponti had turned up, so she wouldn't have to spend another night with him so he could 'protect' her. Fat lot of protection. She needed protecting from herself, apparently, as well as him.

'Did I say something to upset you?'

She jerked her head up and met his eyes. 'What? No. Sorry. I was miles away.'

About four miles, to be exact, lying in his bed sprawled all over him and behaving like a hussy. She could feel her cheeks getting hotter, and looked hastily away. 'Good pastries.'

So she was thinking about that, too, he thought, and gave a silent huff of laughter. Oh, well. He'd thought about it for twenty years without acting on it apart from one short and all too memorable month, so he could do it for another fortnight. And if she wanted to talk about food…

'They always are good pastries in here,' he said blandly, biting into one as she looked up.

Their eyes locked, and then her gaze tracked his mouth as he licked his lips. It wasn't deliberate, it wasn't conscious, but her pupils flared as she watched him and he just knew he was in trouble, because last night, entirely by accident, they'd broken all the rules in his little black book.

Starting with rule number one—don't mess with friends. Especially not one you've known since before you could walk. One you've already hurt because you couldn't keep a lid on your lust.

He looked down at the table, located his coffee and took a gulp. It was hot. Too hot, and he felt it burn his tongue, but at least it took his mind off Anita's body.

They arrived in Firenze shortly before lunchtime, and she pulled up next to his Mercedes sports. It was his new toy, and he'd been looking forward to driving it up into the Alps.

And then the Ponti woman—

He cut off that line of thought, got out of the car and saw a shard of broken glass lying on the ground.

He bent and picked it up, and felt a cold shiver run over him.

'Why was she so desperate to talk to me, Anita?' he asked softly, staring at the glass in his hand. 'I was only doing my job. She had no entitlement to that money, and she must have known that. So what was there to say that she so desperately needed me to hear?'

'Who knows? She's a liar and a cheat. Don't waste time thinking about her.'

She all but dragged him towards the door, and he let them in and looked at the stairs.

'Want me to carry you up?' she suggested sassily, and he glowered at her for a second, then gave a reluctant laugh.

'It's very kind of you to offer, but I think I can manage.' He could. Just about. He hopped, he hobbled, and finally they were there and he could sprawl on his sofa and look out over the rooftops to the hills in the distance while he recovered.

'Could you put this glass in the bin? You'd better wrap it. There's a pile of old newspapers in one of the cupboards in the kitchen—and while you're there, I need a coffee.'

Anita, busy taking in the changes he'd made to the kitchen area in the last five years, rolled her eyes. 'You *always* need a coffee. I don't know why I indulge you.' She dealt with the glass, then looked around. 'So, where is it anyway, this new gadget of yours?'

'Under that glass door—no, not that one, that's the steam oven. Next to it. Lift the door up and slide it back.'

She studied it. It seemed pretty straightforward, but some instructions wouldn't go amiss. 'So, how does this thing work?'

'You put beans in it from in the freezer, put a cup under it and press the button. It's not exactly rocket science.'

She ignored the sarcasm. 'Cups? Freezer?'

It would have been easier to get up, but it was more entertaining lying there watching her pottering in his kitchen, so he stayed put and gave her instructions, and every time she bent over to get something out of a cupboard, he was treated to the delectable view of her smooth, rounded bottom in jeans that hugged her lovingly.

His jeans were getting a bit more loving just watching her, and he dragged his eyes away and tried to get himself under control.

Anita threw a glance over her shoulder and saw him flicking idly through a magazine. Sarky swine, she thought. She could have smacked him, but she wouldn't give him the satisfaction. He'd been so different five years ago. He wouldn't have left her alone in the kitchen, he would have been in there, standing behind her with his arms around her, his body warm and hard and very, very close, and sometimes he'd turn her towards him and lift her so she was perched on the edge of the counter, and he'd take her then and there, his eyes hot and smoky with need, and then he'd gather her up in his arms, her legs still locked around his waist, and carry her to the bedroom to finish what he'd started.

Until he ended it, without a word of warning.

'There, was that so hard?' he asked when she set his espresso down in front of him with rather more force than was necessary.

'It's not a case of hard, it's a case of not having seen it before. I'm not an idiot—don't patronise me.'

She was cross, he realised. Cross because she was in his apartment? Cross because he was being an ass? Or cross because the last time she'd been here, he'd been telling her all the reasons why their affair should end?

'I'm sorry,' he said, meaning it. Sorry for all sorts of things. 'Thank you for making the coffee.'

'You don't have to grovel. Have you got anything here to eat?'

'No, not really. I'd run the fridge down because I was going away. There's no milk, either.'

'That's fine. I'll have it black, if it's as good as you say it is. Are you hungry? I could go out and get something.'

'Or we can order pizza.'

He pulled out his phone. It didn't surprise her that the number was on speed-dial, or that the intercom buzzed after just five minutes.

She ran down and paid and carried the steaming box back upstairs and put it on the coffee table in front of him. It was a *quattro stagioni,* with a different topping on each quarter, and she pulled off a slice and ate it hungrily.

'Oh, gorgeous. It's so fresh—where's the pizzeria?'

'Just round the corner. Literally.'

'And they know you well.'

He grinned mischievously. 'Don't tell my mother.'

She studied him, unshaven because it was too challenging to bother with, the stubble on his jaw making him look just a little wicked and slightly dangerous. She felt a shiver of excitement down her spine and crushed it ruthlessly.

'I'm sure of all the things I shouldn't be telling your mother, Giovanni Valtieri, that's the least of them.'

He winked and chuckled, sinking his teeth into the second slice of pizza. The flavour exploded on his tongue, and he sighed contentedly and demolished it, and reached for another, and another.

She left him the last slice, sitting back and wiping her fingers on the paper napkin.

'I can't remember when I last had pizza. That was amazing.'

'It is good there. They use our olives.'

'Do they? I wonder why?' she teased, and he laughed softly.

'Because they're the best?'

'My father might argue, but Massimo would be pleased to hear you say that. He works hard to uphold the family name for quality, and he's very proud of it.'

'And your father?'

She grinned. 'He thinks his olives are better. He concedes on the wine and the cheese.'

'That's because he doesn't make either of them.'

She shrugged, her eyes teasing, and he felt a pang of loss. They'd been so good together, and he'd had real hopes for them, but then reality had intruded with shocking force and reminded him of just what a lousy bet he was.

He couldn't give a relationship what it deserved. He never had, and he was afraid he never could, not even with Anita, and he'd thought it was better for her to get out of it before she got in too deep and ended up destroyed, like Kirsten. And not just Kirsten.

There was enough on his conscience already. Too much. He couldn't have Anita on it as well. Not his dearest friend.

Looking at her now, he felt nothing but regret, but that was selfish. For once, it wasn't all about him and what he wanted, and he knew he was going to have to exercise enormous self-control in the next fortnight. He couldn't let his own selfish wants and needs override his common sense and decency, however much he wanted her. Not if she was ever going to move on and find someone else.

He didn't want to think about that.

'I suppose we should get on,' he said abruptly.

'Probably.' She got to her feet and washed her hands in the sink, then looked around. 'So where's this coffee maker?'

'In that cupboard on the left—no, the next one.'

She opened the cupboard and found it, lifted it out and set it on the worktop. She eyed it dubiously. Apart from the fact that it would take up her entire kitchen, it weighed a ton and she was going to have to carry it downstairs. 'It seems a bit excessive.'

'Where coffee's concerned, nothing is too excessive,' he said emphatically. 'There are some unopened beans in the next cupboard.'

She got them out, put them with the machine and then walked towards his bedroom. She hadn't been in there since their affair, but it hadn't changed a lot.

He had a new blind, but that was it. The bed was the same, she noticed with a pang, swathed in vast acres of the finest threadcount Egyptian cotton; pure white, un-adorned, uncomplicated luxury. It was the most comfort-able bed she'd ever slept in, and she'd been happier there than she had anywhere in her life.

She'd gone out and bought herself the same bedding after they'd split up, but she hadn't been able to bring herself to use it because just the feel of it reminded her so strongly of him that it broke her heart.

'So, what do you need?' she asked, forcing herself to focus on something other than the bed.

'Underwear, socks, casual shirts, sweaters, trousers—there are some jog bottoms in the bottom drawer in the wardrobe, I think. They might be easier to get on and off over my foot. And my trainers.'

She found them, and the underwear. Soft, clingy jersey shorts that hugged his body enticingly. A heap of socks, all carefully paired. Shirts, hung by colour and style.

'You're a neat freak,' she said drily, throwing the clothes

into a heap ready for packing. He was standing in the doorway, frowning.

'Don't crease those shirts.'

'I thought they were casual? And you're going to be wearing them with jog bottoms.'

'They don't have to look as if I've slept in them.'

She propped herself against the door of the wardrobe and folded her arms.

'Do you want to do this yourself, or would you like me to help you? In which case, you need to shut up.'

He opened his mouth, then clamped it shut in a grim line. She smiled and carried on, and he retrieved a few things from the bathroom, then packed up his laptop and the documents he needed. Ten minutes later they were on their way out.

He limped slowly towards the car with his laptop bag over his shoulder while she made another trip for the coffee maker. By the time she was back with it, he was in the car with his eyes closed.

'Did you bring any painkillers with you?' she asked, and he shook his head.

'I'm fine. Let's just go.'

They went to the supermarket on the way home, to buy things for supper. She'd only done a hasty shop the day before, just enough to tide them over, so she left him in the car and worked her way a bit more systematically along the aisles for something to make that evening.

Nothing too easy, she thought. A dish that needed a bit of preparation, something to occupy her. She trawled the meat aisle, and came up with wild boar. Brilliant! She could make a wild boar casserole for supper, from a recipe she'd been given by Lydia, Massimo's new wife.

The Englishwoman had been a chef until Gio's brother had swept her off her feet, and she'd shared lots of recipes with Anita, most of which she hadn't got round to trying. But they were elaborate enough to kill time, and that was perfect for her purposes.

She gathered up vegetables, bread, milk and a few other essentials, and made her way back to the car, feeling guilty for taking so long.

She needn't have worried. He was fiddling on his laptop, and he shut it and put it back in the case as she got in.

'OK?'

'Yes, I was just catching up on some work.'

'You shouldn't really be doing that. You should be resting.'

'It's not exactly physically stressful,' he said drily, and she couldn't argue with him. It was pointless, she wouldn't win. She never did, not really, not a real argument. He was too clever with his words. They were his stock in trade, and she'd given up trying years ago.

Pity she couldn't give up loving him. It would make life a whole heck of a lot easier.

He went to bed when they got back, saying he needed a rest, and so she busied herself in the kitchen making the casserole.

Stupid, she realised later when he'd reappeared from the bedroom, because now supper was all taken care of and she had nothing, absolutely nothing, to do.

They hadn't even been there long enough to generate any washing, so she went and got a book from her bedside table that had been on her 'to be read' pile for much too long. But that didn't work, either. Somehow sitting there reading while he fiddled on his laptop seemed crazily intimate and settled—the sort of thing a couple did.

And they were *not* a couple, she reminded herself fiercely.

'You don't look as if you're enjoying that book,' he said, cutting into her train of thought.

'What?'

'The book. If you don't like it, why read it?'

She frowned down at it. She'd read the same paragraph about six times, and still didn't know what it said. With a disgusted sigh she threw it down and went over to the kitchen, opening the fridge and searching for inspiration.

'What are you doing?'

'Looking for something to cook.' Or something to do, more correctly. Something a little further away from him, that she had to concentrate on.

'What kind of something? I thought you'd already prepared our food? I can smell something really good, so I hope it's for later.'

'It is. It's wild boar casserole. Easy to eat with one hand. I thought I might make some chocolate mousse for dessert.'

'Can you do that?'

'Well, now, let me see—of course I can!' she retorted, rolling her eyes sarcastically.

She just needed to be able to concentrate, and that, with him in the room, was easier said than done, but she dug out Lydia's recipe, took eggs and dark, bitter chocolate and cream out of the fridge and worked her way systematically through the instructions. A few minutes later she spooned the soft, fluffy chocolate mixture into two white ramekins and smiled with satisfaction.

Perfect. And just enough left in the bowl to make licking it out really satisfying. She scooped the spatula round it, looked up and found him watching her hopefully.

'No. It's mine. Cook's perks,' she told him firmly, and stroked her tongue up the spatula.

Something flared deep in his eyes, and after a breathless second, he looked back down at his laptop and she turned away.

But the damage was done. He'd seen her licking the spatula, seen the smears of chocolate all around her mouth, and the urge to get up and go over there and kiss the chocolate off her lips was crippling him.

He kept his eyes firmly down, but even so he could see her, his peripheral vision just good enough that he could see every time she lifted it to her mouth, and finally he crumbled and looked up, just as she threw the spatula back in the bowl and plunged it into the sink.

'I hope you enjoyed that.'

'Mmm, *mmm*,' she said, licking her lips still. 'Did you want some? You should have asked. You'll have to wait now until after dinner.'

'You said it was cook's perks.'

'I might have given you a little taste if you'd asked nicely.'

Mischievous little witch.

'I'm sure I'll survive,' he said drily, stifling a smile. 'How about some coffee?'

'Again? No wonder you have dreams.'

'Wine, then? It's nearly dark.'

Wine? Sit with him and drink wine, to weaken her already fragile defences? She didn't think so.

'Have whatever you like. I'm going to have tea.'

'Make that two.'

'Please.'

He growled. 'Please,' he said, and she turned away so he wouldn't see her smiling. He was miffed because she'd eaten all the scrapings from the bowl and hadn't offered him any. Well, tough. She put the kettle on, took two mugs out of the cupboard and made the tea.

The wild boar casserole was wonderful, she thought, much better than any previous attempt she'd ever made, and he seemed to enjoy it, but the chocolate mousse wasn't quite set yet, so they left it for later.

They'd eaten at the table, because the casserole was a bit messy to eat sprawled out on the sofa, but as he went back to its welcoming softness, she could see he was struggling a bit.

'Are you all right?'

He sat down, propped his foot up and met her eyes. 'Do you know how many times today you've asked me that?'

She paused, plates in hand, and frowned. 'Oh, I do beg your pardon. I'm so sorry I spoke.'

He sighed heavily, and shook his head. 'Sorry. I'm being unreasonable.'

'You are. And it's difficult to know what else to say when it's quite obvious that you're not all right. I guess I just keep waiting for you to say you're feeling better, but you don't.'

'That's because I'm not—and I'm bored. I'm going to go crazy if I can't do something soon.'

'Like what?'

He shrugged, his smile crooked and mocking. 'We could go for a walk. Oh, no, that's right. I can't walk anywhere.'

'Ha-ha, very funny. Just remember it's not my fault, I'm not the one who hit you with the handbag.'

'Rub it in, why don't you.'

She suppressed a smile. 'Television?'

He shook his head. 'Nothing on. We could play chess if we had a chess set.'

'What, so you could thrash me?'

He smiled lazily. 'I thought you wanted me to feel better?'

'Not at my expense!'

'Anyway, it's academic. We should have thought about it earlier, we could have brought my chess set.'

'I've got one here,' she admitted reluctantly. 'You gave it to me years ago.'

He stared at her, his eyes unreadable. 'Have you still got it?' he asked softly, his voice faintly incredulous.

'Of course.'

He'd made it for her during a long, wet winter, turning the pieces on her father's lathe, carving the tops with a skill she hadn't known he possessed. He'd given it to her for Christmas, the year she turned sixteen, and although she hardly ever used it, it was one of her most treasured possessions.

She took it out of the cupboard, cleared the coffee table and set it up, and he reached out and picked up the knight, turning it over in his hand with a low chuckle. 'It took me so long to carve these,' he said quietly. 'I had to do about seven. I kept breaking the ears off the horses.'

'Is that why they look angry, with their ears laid back, so they don't stick up?'

He chuckled. 'It was the only way I could do it. The wood wasn't hard enough and they would have broken off anyway. Your father suggested it.' He put it back, a slight frown furrowing his brow as if he was miles away, back in the time when things were less complicated and rather happier.

She picked up two pawns, one dark wood, one pale, shuffled them behind her back and held them out in her fists. 'Left or right?'

He thrashed her.

She'd known he would, but he accused her of not trying.

'I am trying.'

'So focus.'

'I am focused,' she snapped. Just not on chess.

'Doesn't look like it. Try again.'

She tried. She really, really tried to concentrate, but he was sitting right opposite her with his bandaged foot up on the sofa, looking so enticing it was impossible to focus her mind on anything other than him.

And then he moved his knight and said, 'Checkmate.'

'What? How? How on *earth* is that checkmate?'

She stared at the board in disbelief, then threw up her hands and put the pieces back into the box.

'Quitter.'

She gave him a withering look and folded up the board with a snap. 'I'm not a quitter, but I'm not here as a prop for your ego, either.'

'So did you want me to let you win?'

'No! I wanted to be able to do it.' She shut the cupboard door on the offending game and stalked into the kitchen. Quitter, indeed.

'So, do you want this chocolate mousse?'

'Not if you're going to tip it on my head.'

She laughed then, letting out the frustration in a defeated little chuckle, and then took the desserts over to the table. She'd put a dollop of cream on top of each, and as they dug the spoons in, the cream slid down and puddled in the centre, ready for the next mouthful.

Gio felt the cool, creamy and yet intensely chocolaty dessert melt on his tongue, and he groaned. If sin tasted of anything, then this was it.

'Good?' she asked, and he flicked his eyes up to hers and smiled slowly.

'Oh, yes. Really good,' he said, taking another spoonful and savouring it slowly. And then he watched as she lifted her spoon to her mouth, her lips parting just enough to let it in, then closing around the spoon as her eyes drifted shut in ecstasy.

He nearly groaned out loud.

Dio, he wanted her. Wanted to taste the chocolate on her tongue, wanted to stand up and walk over to her and pull her to her feet and carry her to bed and make love to her until she screamed.

But he couldn't.

Not just because of his ankle and the cuts on his hand and thigh, but because Anita was out of bounds.

Rule number one—don't mess with friends.

He'd messed with her enough, both last night and five years ago. He wasn't going there again, wasn't risking her emotional wellbeing by letting her get involved with him again.

If he could have just taken her to bed and had fantastic and uncomplicated sex with her, it would have been fine. But he couldn't. No way. This was Anita, and nothing about their relationship was uncomplicated.

And she was a forever person, a believer in the happy-ever-after—for heaven's sake, she was a wedding planner! She made people's dreams come true.

He seemed to turn them all to nightmares.

He dragged his eyes off her, finished his dessert in silence and put the pot down. His mind full of Kirsten and the tragic waste of a life, he hadn't even tasted the last few mouthfuls. It could have been wallpaper paste.

'I need a shower,' he said curtly. 'Do you have a plastic bag and some tape so I can wrap up my foot?'

She blinked, a little startled by the sudden change of atmosphere, but this was Gio. He did this all the time, especially recently. She stifled an inward sigh and got up.

'Sure. What about your hand and your leg?'

'They'll be fine. The dressings are waterproof, apparently, so long as I don't soak them.'

She pulled a bag out of a drawer and held it scrunched up against her middle. 'Um—do you need a hand to get this on?'

'No. I can manage,' he said firmly.

'What about the tape?'

'I can manage. I can use these fingers now a little. I'll be fine. I'll see you in the morning.'

He walked out, limping heavily, shoulders ramrod straight, the bag and the tape in his left hand.

She watched him go, listened to the sound of him undressing. Grunts, the odd unintelligible comment that she probably hadn't needed to hear, the occasional thud.

Then she heard the bathroom door close, and a moment later the sound of running water.

He'd call her, surely, if he was in difficulties?

She was being ridiculous. He was fine. He was young and fit and the hospital had been happy with him. Of course he was all right.

She cleared up the kitchen, loaded the dishwasher and switched it on, wiped down the tops and tidied the sitting room. There. Now she'd go and sit on her bed with her book and wait for him to finish.

Not that she needed to. It didn't matter to her how long he took, because she had an en suite bathroom off her room. It was just that she wouldn't be able to rest until she knew he was all right.

The water had been turned off long ago, and she guessed he was drying himself. Slowly and awkwardly with one hand, she would think. She wondered how the waterproofing had worked.

And then she heard a yelp and leapt to her feet, running to the bathroom door.

'Gio? Are you OK?'

There was a stifled sound of frustration. 'I'm fine,' he said at last.

'Can I do anything?'

'Only tell me why women would ever contemplate having their legs waxed,' he growled, and the penny dropped.

He was changing the dressing on his thigh, peeling the plaster off the hairs. She winced and tried not to laugh. 'Ouch. Do you want me to help?'

'No, I want you to leave me alone. I can manage,' he snapped, and she retreated, muttering about ungracious men and telling herself at the same time that he wasn't really ungracious, he was just proud and hurt and trying to keep his distance.

And she wasn't making it any easier.

'I'll say goodnight, then,' she said, and walked swiftly away, leaving him to it. He didn't need her with him tonight. He'd had her last night, and look what had happened. From now on, he was on his own, the ungracious, sulky, temperamental—

'Stop! Stop thinking about him! Just go to bed!'

She went, exhausted from the strain of keeping up a neutral front, worn down by the emotional tension zinging between them.

And then, in the middle of the night, she had a dream…

CHAPTER FIVE

She was late.

They were going skiing, and she was meeting Gio at his apartment and he was giving her a lift. It was difficult, because she was dragging her skis along behind her and her bag was trundling awkwardly over the old stones, but she was trying to hurry, because he was going to be so angry with her.

She turned the last corner, hurrying towards the front door, but it was dark there, so dark, and in the shadows by the wall she could hear the sounds of a scuffle.

There was a grunt of pain, and she froze.

'Gio?' she whispered, her heart pounding. She could vaguely make out a man lying on the ground, and somewhere a long way away a woman was sobbing.

'Gio!'

'Anita—help me! I'm bleeding. You have to help me...!'

'I'm coming!' she yelled, and tried to run to him, but her feet wouldn't move. She felt as if she was running in treacle, every step a marathon, and the stones were covered in broken glass. She had to get to him, had to help him, but suddenly the place was full of people and they wouldn't let her through. They kept asking who she was, and all the time she could hear him calling her.

She began to scream, sobbing with terror. People were shaking her, shouting at her, and she tried to fight them off. She had to get to him, to help him, and they were holding her back...

'Anita! Anita, wake up! You're dreaming, *cara*! It's all right. Wake up. It's me—I'm here. I've got you.'

She heard her name, heard his familiar voice slicing through the terror and reaching out to her, and she opened her eyes and stared at him in confusion.

'I couldn't get to you,' she croaked, lifting up a hand to cradle his dear, precious, familiar face. It was warm, reassuringly so, his eyes troubled, and she felt the fight drain out of her. 'Oh, Gio, you were calling me and I couldn't get to you!' she said again, and burst into noisy, messy, uncontrollable tears.

'Oh, Anita, *carissima,* come here...'

He gathered her up against his chest, his arms wrapped firmly round her, rocking her rhythmically as he soothed her with meaningless words of comfort, and gradually the tears subsided.

He eased back, staring down at her, searching those tear-drenched, empty eyes. 'Are you OK now, *cara*?'

She sniffed and nodded, but a shudder ran through her and he knew she was lying.

'You were hurt,' she said, her voice shaking. 'You told me you were bleeding, and you asked me to help you and I tried to get to you but I couldn't run, my feet were stuck and the stones were covered in broken glass, and then everybody was blocking my way and I was so afraid you were dying—'

'Shhh,' he murmured, gathering her back up into his arms, and she slumped against his chest and let him hold her, too overwrought to care about keeping up a front. She loved him, and she could so easily have lost him. She was allowed to cry for him.

Gradually her sobs hiccupped to a halt, and her breathing slowed and eased, and he let her lie back against the pillows, her eyes staring up at him as if she still couldn't quite believe he was all right.

'I should never have let you go to my place today,' he said, his brows drawn together in a frown.

'It's not your fault. It's just my vivid imagination. It must have been seeing that piece of glass.' She shoved herself up the bed, shifting the pillows so she was sitting upright against the headboard, her hands knotted in the quilt.

She might seem all right, he realised, but she was still gripped by the dream, and the moment she fell asleep again, it would come back. He knew that. He was painfully familiar with the principle, and he was kicking himself for taking her there today.

'Hey. Why don't I make us some hot chocolate and we can sit up and drink it?'

She stared at him. 'You?'

He smiled and shrugged.

'Or I could ask you? Because you'll do it better than me.'

She gave a soft, slightly unsteady chuckle and threw back the bedclothes, slipping her legs out of bed and standing up. She was in the pyjamas again, he saw. They were meant to cover her up, but they just draped enticingly over her bottom and hugged her breasts gently, cradling them.

His hands itched to take their place, to cup her bottom and draw her closer, to feel the weight of those soft, rounded breasts in his palms once more.

'I'll just get my robe,' he said, and retreated quickly, before she could see the effect she was having on him.

Well, as quickly as he could, considering he'd almost run to her room on his damaged foot and it was giving him some significant hell at the moment.

Good, he thought as he limped hastily back to the privacy of his room. It might take his mind off Anita and her lovely, luscious body.

It didn't work.

Neither did the fact that she'd swathed herself in an ankle-length cashmere cardigan over the pyjamas. The fabric draped softly over her body, and he stifled a groan and dropped into the corner of the sofa, propping his feet on the coffee table.

'Have you got any music?'

'Mmm. My CDs are there.'

On the other side of the room.

'Just press play on the remote—it's there, on the coffee table. I can't remember what's in there.'

Jazz. Soft, smoky jazz, that filtered out of the speakers and drifted into every corner.

He leant back and closed his eyes as the lazy, haunting sound of a saxophone filled the room. It was such a sensuous instrument, he thought as the music swirled around him and through him.

Music to make love to.

He dropped his left foot to the floor and sat upright, ramming himself back into the corner and growling quietly in frustration.

'Change it if you don't like it.'

'It's fine,' he said. 'I just had cramp. I'm all right now.'

'Sure?'

'Of course I'm sure. I'm fine.'

She blinked, and then shrugged. 'Whatever. Here. Your hot chocolate.'

She set it down in front of him, and he picked it up, wrapping his left hand around the mug and propping it with the fingers of his right.

His hand was getting better, but he still wouldn't like to pick anything up with it. Two weeks, he'd been told, to allow any minor damage to the tendons to repair itself. Before then, they could tear if he over-used it, but it was too sore to want to do anything except, possibly, curl his hand gently over one of her delectable breasts and test the sweet, mobile weight of it—

He took a gulp of the hot chocolate. Too hot. He felt it scald his tongue, and he put it down again.

'Sorry, I should have put cold milk in it,' she said apologetically, settling herself in the far corner of the sofa and tucking her feet up under her bottom so she was turned to face him.

'It's fine,' he said, but his voice was a little impatient and she sighed inwardly. He really, really wasn't enjoying being cooped up with her like this—probably not any more than she was. And neither of them had needed her waking in the night from that hideous dream—

She cut off her line of thought abruptly. *Don't go there. You won't be able to sleep again if you think about it.*

'I'm sorry I woke you.'

He turned his head and met her eyes searchingly. 'I wasn't asleep.'

'Was the pain keeping you awake?'

He shook his head. 'No. I never sleep well in a strange bed for the first few nights.'

But he had, last night. Until she'd—

Stop it! Don't even slightly *think about it!*

'Well, unless I'm with you,' he added, and there it was, out in the open again, where neither of them wanted it.

'Well, I'm going to solve that for you tomorrow,' she said lightly, her voice slightly strained, 'because, after seeing your place today, I think you're probably OK to go back to Firenze. You've got the pizza place just round the corner, and you can order whatever else you need over the internet and buzz the door open. I'm sure you'll be fine.'

She glanced back at his face and his eyes locked with hers, unreadable. And then he looked away again, and nodded.

'Yes. I'm sure I will. Good idea.'

He picked up his hot chocolate, drained it even though it was still hot and stood up, yanking the belt on his robe tighter. 'I'll see you in the morning.'

And without another word, he limped out of the room and disappeared down the hall to his bedroom.

She couldn't sleep.

Every time she closed her eyes, she was back in his room with him, lying there beside him, with her hand on his chest, feeling the steady thud of his heart under her palm...

She picked up her book, but it couldn't hold her attention. She read the same paragraph she had earlier another six times, and threw it down. She was never going to get through this book as long as he was there under her roof reminding her of how much she'd missed him for the last five years.

She threw the book down in disgust and looked around.

She'd go and watch television. There probably wasn't anything decent on, and it was cold in the sitting room. February in Tuscany was not a good time to be up all night without the heating on, and she didn't want to run it unnecessarily, but it beat lying here thinking about him all night. She'd go crazy.

She got up and pulled the cardi on again, and crept out into the hall. She had to pass his room to get to the sitting room, and she hesitated at the open door.

There was a chair in his room. A comfortable, squashy armchair. She could creep in there and curl up on it and watch him. Just for a little while. He was going tomorrow, and she was going to miss him so much.

It wouldn't hurt, would it? He wouldn't even know, he'd be asleep by now, surely?

His door was wide open, the dim light from the lamp she'd left on in the hallway spilling in across the foot of the bed. She could see the lump in the bed where she'd put the cushions in it to protect his foot, and an angled lump on this side of it—his other leg, bent at the knee and turned out?

He was motionless, and she crept across the room to the chair and stopped. He'd put his clothes on it. Well, of course he had. That was one of the reasons it was in there.

So she lifted them, holding her breath so she didn't disturb him, and put them carefully down on the floor.

Something clinked against the tiles—his belt buckle? She didn't know, but she froze for a second, listening.

Nothing.

He can't have heard her, she thought, and she sat quietly down, wriggling back and tucking her feet up under her to keep them warm. And then she felt the draught from the window, and shivered and pulled the cardi higher round her neck. She wished she'd brought a throw to wrap round her shoulders, but at least the cold would keep her awake—

'Anita, what are you doing?'

His quiet, patient voice startled her, and she gasped softly. He hadn't been meant to know she was there, and she'd been so sure that he was asleep. Obviously not, or not any more.

She looked across at the bed, just as he levered himself up on one elbow and stared back at her, his features indistinguishable in the darkness. Hers, on the other hand, were clearly visible in the stream of light from the hall, and embarrassment must be written all over them.

'I'm sorry. I couldn't sleep and there was nothing on the television.' She got stiffly to her feet, the circulation cut off by her cramped position. 'I'm sorry, I'll go, I don't know what I was thinking—'

'No.' For a second he said nothing more, then he spoke again, his voice resigned. 'No. Come here, Anita. Get into bed. You must be freezing.'

She was, but still she hesitated, and then he flung back the covers on the empty side of the bed and waited.

'Well, come on. I don't bite.'

No. He didn't bite—well, not five years ago. He'd nibbled, and sucked, and trailed his tongue all over her, blowing lightly to chill the skin and then warming it again with those hot, sensuous, erotic lips—

'Is that a good idea?'

'Yes. You're cold, we're both wide awake. Just get into bed, Anita. Come on. And then maybe we'll both get some sleep.'

She closed her eyes briefly, then gave in. She knew what would happen. It was inevitable, no matter what their intentions, but somehow it didn't seem to matter any more, because the worst thing that could happen was she'd fall in love with him and she'd done that years ago.

So she peeled off the cardi and slid into bed beside him,

and he turned her away from him and hooked her back into the curve of his warm, hard body, and covered her with the goose-down quilt she'd never been able to bear to sleep under alone because of all the memories the feel of it brought back.

'Heavens, you're freezing, woman,' he said with a shudder as she wriggled her bottom closer. He wrapped his top arm firmly round her, his damaged hand resting across her ribs, his thumb just brushing the underside of a breast.

He tried not to think about it, tried not to think about the times she'd snuggled up to him like this and he'd woken her up to make love to her.

He wasn't going to make love to her. He wasn't. Whatever his body thought to the contrary. She shifted, and he stifled a groan and moved his injured foot out of reach.

'Mind my leg,' he said, and she stiffened.

'Sorry, did I hurt you?'

'No.' Not in the way she meant, but to hold her and know he couldn't have her, that he mustn't let himself do this—it was going to kill him. 'Just remember not to kick me.'

'I don't kick.'

He snorted softly, shifted his head so her hair wasn't in his face and tried to zone out a little, to go somewhere that wasn't either making love to Anita or rehashing all the reasons why this was such a lousy idea—

'Gio? What's wrong?'

'Nothing. It's OK. I just—hell, I've missed you, Nita.'

'Oh, Gio…'

Her voice was soft, and she turned in his arms, her hand settling lightly on his cheek, her fingers cradling his jaw. 'I've missed you, too. We were so good together. What went wrong?'

He didn't answer. He couldn't. Not truthfully, and he'd rather not speak than lie.

'I'm no good for you,' he said gruffly. 'You need someone sensible who knows how to have a relationship. I'm a disaster, *bella*. I didn't want to hurt you, you have to believe that. And if I did, I'm sorry.'

He was. Sorry he'd hurt her, sorry she'd come to him, sorry that in the warm, soft cocoon of the bedding, there were no barriers between them that had a hope of working.

'Anita...'

It was scarcely a whisper, but the soft huff of his breath over her face, the light touch of his hand on her cheek, the gentle and inevitable brush of his lips on hers took away the last trace of her feeble resistance.

She moaned softly, and his fingers threaded through her hair, steadying her as he increased the pressure slightly. She gave in and parted her lips, welcoming the hot, velvet sweep of his tongue as he probed the secret recesses of her mouth.

'Gio,' she breathed, and he anchored her head with his hand and deepened the kiss, turning her to fire with every searching thrust of his tongue. She arched against him, her hands on his body urging them together, closing the gap until they were in contact from lips to knees.

It nearly finished him.

The feel of her body, soft, yielding, the flesh still cool and yet somehow on fire, drove him crazy, and he shoved the pyjama top out of the way and found her breasts.

So sweet, so firm and yet so soft, so real. Her breasts were perfect. So perfect, just fitting the palm of his injured hand, soothing it. He bent his head, touching his lips to her nipple, blowing lightly on it then stroking it with his tongue, and she cried out softly, her body shuddering.

So responsive to him, just as he was responsive to her. He'd never felt so much, so intensely, with anyone else, and he feared he never would.

'Don't stop,' she begged as he paused. 'Please, don't stop...'

He laughed softly in the darkness. How could he stop? There wasn't a thing in the world that could stop him now, except Anita. He touched his hand to her face, found her mouth again with his and kissed her until she sobbed with need.

'You'll have to help me,' he said at last, lifting his head and staring down at her, brushing the hair gently back from her face with his trembling fingers. 'I can't undress you with this stupid hand.'

She reached up and kissed him, her lips brushing lightly over his, their warmth filling him. And then she sat up and peeled off her top, wriggled out of the bottoms and reached for his shorts.

'Condom,' he said gruffly, checking her as she started to move over him. 'In my wallet, on the bedside table.'

She rolled away, picked it up and took it to the doorway, and he watched her hungrily as she stood naked in the stream of light and searched through it.

She hesitated at the photograph of her, momentarily distracted that he carried one, then frowned. Where would a man keep a condom?

In another pocket, zipped in. There. Several, she saw with relief, wondering why it hadn't even occurred to her to think of it. Thank God for someone with some common sense.

She threw the wallet back on the bedside table, tore off

the foil and slipped under the covers and reached for him, her fingers shaking as the tension coiled tighter inside her.

'Easy,' he murmured raggedly, and then she was moving over his body, lowering herself slowly down onto him, and it felt as if she'd come home…

Had he known this was going to happen?

He'd been so determined it wouldn't, and yet yesterday, when they'd been at the apartment, he'd gone to the bathroom and stashed a few condoms in his wallet.

Just in case.

And now he was wishing he'd brought more. A lot more.

He turned his head and looked at her. She was sleeping like a baby, flat on her back, one hand up by her face, her head tilted slightly towards him, lips parted softly.

He could see a stubble rash around her top lip, and he rubbed a hand against his jaw and frowned. It might have been better if he'd shaved last night, but by the time he'd finished the shower he'd had enough.

He'd have to be careful how he kissed her next time.

Because there would be a next time. Now they'd done this, broken down their resistance and surrendered to it, he knew there would be no going back, not until their families came home and life intruded again.

But until then—until then, they could indulge themselves, because the damage was already done.

Her eyes flickered open, and she smiled.

'*Ciao*, gorgeous,' she said, and he chuckled.

'*Ciao*, gorgeous, yourself. Sleep well?'

'Mmm. You?'

'Not really. I've been waiting for you to wake up.'

'Oh.' Her eyes widened, and she reached out her hand and cradled his jaw. 'Mmm. Stubble. Yummy.'

'Yeah. It's given you stubble rash on your lip.'

She felt it with her fingertips, and wrinkled her nose. 'Oh. That'll look good if we go out.'

'Are we going out?'

She searched his face in the dim light of dawn, and smiled slowly.

'Possibly not,' she murmured, and reached up, drawing him down to her. 'Kiss me.'

'I'll hurt you.'

'I'll live.'

So he kissed her—but not on her mouth. He kissed her neck, her shoulders, down the warm, pale slope of her breasts. He drew her nipples into his mouth one by one, sharing his attention equally so he wasn't accused of favouritism, then he moved lower, tracing a circle around the hollow of her belly button before blowing a raspberry on the soft, smooth skin just below it.

It made her gasp, and then laugh, and she could feel him smiling against her skin, feel his shoulders shift as he chuckled, the warm, damp air of his breath huffing softly across her body as he turned his head and moved downwards.

'Gio—'

'Shh.'

She bit her lips, sobbing with need, and then he moved on again, lifting her leg up so he could stroke his tongue over the back of her knee.

She shuddered and clutched at him, and he slid his hand up her thigh and stroked her with a fingertip, his head lifted now, their eyes locked.

Black, burning coals. She'd never seen such ferocious need in his eyes, and she shifted against his hand, sobbing as he teased her with the lightest touch. Then he moved up her, the rougher texture of his body trailing fire over her skin. She was shaking all over, beyond reason, needing him, needing him so much—

'Gio, please…'

He leant over her and grabbed his wallet, and seconds later he was there, entering her with one long, slow thrust, and she wrapped her arms around him and sobbed with relief.

'Anita,' he growled, his mouth against her throat, his body taut as a bowstring as he drove into her again and again. He could feel her body tighten around him, feel the shudder of her breath, feel the deep convulsions wrap around him and take him blindly over the edge into a place he'd never been before, and as he soared and fell he knew that in that moment something, somehow, had irrevocably changed…

They didn't get up that day.

Not really. They made the odd foray to the kitchen for food, and she wrapped his foot up in a bag and they showered—or at least, that was the idea. She found a garden chair and brought it in and washed it, and they put it in the shower so he could sit on it, and then they made love on the chair under the pounding stream of hot water.

Except as they came down to earth again the water was almost cold, so they turned it off and rubbed each other dry and went back to bed to warm up again until the water was hot and they could shower properly.

And then in the evening his family rang for the daily catch-up, and when he finally put the phone down he was starving.

'Let's go out for dinner.'

'What? Really? With stubble rash?'

He laughed. 'It doesn't show. I've been very careful. And anyway, we've run out of condoms.'

'Oh. Right. I'll get dressed, then,' she said sassily, but there was a hint of shyness in her smile, and a tinge of colour in her cheeks.

He laughed softly. How could she still be shy, after everything they'd done that day? There wasn't a square inch of either of them that hadn't been kissed or stroked or touched, and apart from a few concessions for his injuries, it had been just as it had before.

Well, almost as it had. There was something deeper, some new element to their lovemaking that he didn't want to think about too much.

'So, are you going to get dressed?' she asked, standing in the doorway in her jeans and boots and jumper. Her hair was loose, curling around her shoulders, and she'd put a little makeup on to cover the ravages of their lovemaking.

And he was still sitting there on the sofa staring into space and wondering what the hell was going on and what it was that was different.

'Sure.' He got up and limped back to the bedroom, pulled on his clothes with a little help from Anita at the foot end, and they headed out of the door for what felt remarkably like a date.

It was a cold, wet night, and en route to the restaurant they called in at the supermarket. The list was short. Bread. Milk. Wicked things for breakfast. And condoms. Lots of them.

They got through the checkout straight-faced, and headed back to the car laughing like naughty children. Except they didn't feel like children, and after the first two courses in the cosy and intimate little restaurant they cut short their dinner and went home to have their very adult dessert in private.

Something was different.

She didn't know what it was, quite, but there was a change in him. He seemed—not remote, exactly, but as if he was keeping something of himself back, something she'd never been allowed to see and until now maybe hadn't even been aware of.

It was almost as if he'd just discovered he had a softer side, and he was in denial. As well he might be, because if he had such a side, she'd certainly never seen it.

And yet, maybe, she had, with his nieces and nephews. His sister Carla rarely visited her family, because she lived in Umbria with her artist husband and their children, but Luca lived in the grounds of the family estate with his wife Isabelle and their two children, and Massimo, who ran the estate, lived in the *palazzo* with his three children and his new wife, Lydia. She was just a few weeks off having their first baby together, and Anita was sure Gio would be as involved with that baby as he had been with all the others.

And he was involved, for all he might deny it. They climbed all over him, sat on him and demanded stories, made him get down on the floor on his hands and knees and give them pony rides, and he did it all without protest.

Was that a man who didn't want children? Who didn't want love?

So why was he so resistant to it?

Or maybe he wasn't resistant. Maybe he was just commitment-phobic. She'd seen this before, with some of her brides. Their fiancés would get increasingly short-tempered and unsympathetic right up to the wedding, and then they'd call it all off, or make themselves so objectionable that the women called it off. Either way, Anita ended up with tearful brides on her hands, although not usually on the day.

And most of the time it was just plain nerves. Sometimes she could talk them out of it, but sometimes the stress of a wedding highlighted the flaws in their relationship.

Well, there were no flaws in her relationship with Gio, because she didn't have one. She knew that much, and this time round she wasn't going to be foolish enough to assume that this was the real thing.

Gio didn't *do* the real thing. Just sex. Amazing, incredible sex. And now it was different from before—more intense, more focused. More loving? As if, despite himself, he was giving her more than he had ever given anyone, and perhaps was getting more in return.

And sometimes, when she glanced up, there'd be a look in his eyes that she'd never seen before. He'd mask it quickly, but not soon enough to hide it from her.

She couldn't work out what it was. Confusion? Regret? Longing for something just out of reach?

Whatever it was, he certainly wasn't talking about it, so she did the only thing she could do for now and took what he gave her at face value. He'd made himself more than clear on the subject of happy ever after, and she wasn't going to push it. Not now. Not yet.

But she wasn't happy about it. For years, she'd taken anything she could, however little, because if this was all she could have of him, if it was all he was prepared or able to offer, she'd taken it, poor deluded fool that she'd been, because as the old saying went, half a loaf was better than no bread.

And where Gio was concerned, she'd settled for crumbs.

Well, not any more. Now, she wanted more. They could be happy. This interlude had proved it. And she wanted it. She wanted him, and a family with him, and the whole bang shooting match.

All or nothing, and if she had to fight for it, and she lost, then at least she'd know she'd tried, but she wasn't letting him walk away again without any explanation.

She just had to bide her time and find an opportunity to bring it up. And that, with Gio, would be no easy task.

CHAPTER SIX

NOTHING lasts forever.

He knew that, but the end of their fortnight together was coming up faster than an express train. And when the end came, their idyll would be over.

They both knew it was coming, but they both chose to ignore it.

They went to see her parents one day, and had lunch with them, careful to keep their distance from each other so they didn't give away how it was between them, but by this time they were so used to the little touches, the exchanged glances, the wordless gestures, that it was almost impossible to keep up the front, so they didn't go again. Instead they went out for drives, dined out occasionally, but mostly they were at her house doing not a lot.

She cooked for him every night, experimenting with recipes Lydia had given her, and while she cooked, humming away quietly to herself over the stove, he sat on the leather sofa and worked on his brief.

Not for long, usually, because if there was a lull she'd come and sit by him and tuck her cold toes—always cold—under his thigh, with her arms wrapped round her knees and her chin propped on top, and they'd talk.

They made each other laugh. They always had, and he'd

forgotten how much fun it was to be with her. And they squabbled about silly things; they fought over the remote control and argued endlessly about books and music, and in the evening after they'd eaten they'd play chess. Usually he won, but sometimes she did, usually because she'd cheated by doing something distracting.

Not deliberately. She wasn't that devious, but sometimes she'd pick up a square of chocolate and slowly suck it to death while she was contemplating her next move, or sit cross legged opposite him and lean over to study the board with a little frown, her arms propped on her knees and her cleavage just *there,* and he'd lose his concentration entirely and blow it.

And then she'd tease him, and he'd slowly and deliberately put the chess board away and chase her, very slowly, back to the bedroom. He still couldn't move fast, but he didn't need to. She didn't exactly run and she always, always let him catch her.

He couldn't remember ever being this happy before. He knew it was temporary, but for now, at least, it was a win-win situation, and he couldn't think of anything that he'd lost.

Yet.

That was to come, but in the meantime, they played and they loved and they were happy, and he tried not to think about the end.

Because it would come, all too soon, and he knew that this time it would hurt far more than it had ever hurt before.

And then the phone rang one morning, and it was Luca.

'Lydia looks as if she's going into labour early, so we're coming home,' he told him, and Gio felt a crushing sense of loss.

'Is she all right to travel?'

'I think so. We've just loaded the cars—could you let Carlotta and Roberto know so they can air the house and get things ready for them? They come home today.'

'Sure. Anything else you need? Food?'

'If you could grab some milk and bread and stuff, just so we've all got something for the kids, that'd be great.'

'Sure. Will do. We'll leave it in the kitchen at the *palazzo*. You drive carefully, and give our love to Lydia. *Ciao*, Luca.'

He put the phone down and met Anita's eyes. She was watching him thoughtfully, and he tried to smile, but it was harder than he'd imagined.

'They're coming home,' he said expressionlessly. 'He says Lydia's going into labour.'

She looked away. 'And they're driving for five hours? I don't envy them, the kids will be vile by the time they get here.'

He gave a humourless laugh. 'They'll be vile long before that, but they won't be stopping. They need to get home before she has the baby.'

'Is it safe to travel when you're in labour?'

'I have no idea. It's outside my experience,' he said, feeling a sharp stab of guilt and regret twist inside him. 'But Luca's an obstetrician, and he seems to have sanctioned it, so I would imagine so. I doubt they'll hang about, though.'

'I doubt it. So, do they need us to go shopping?'

He shrugged. 'Just basics.'

She nodded. 'OK. I'll get dressed.'

'Anita—'

He broke off. He didn't really have anything to say, but maybe he didn't need to say anything after all, because she just smiled wryly and turned away, and he let out a long, slow sigh and picked up the phone and called Carlotta.

And then he went into his room and packed.

It was over.

She'd known it was coming, known this day would be here, but she'd counted on another three days, and she felt so *cheated*! She'd planned things for each one of them—a lovely drive out into the country for a picnic in the chestnut woods, then home for his favourite meal, roast chicken stuffed with lemons and rosemary, with garlic roasted potatoes and a homemade tiramisu for dessert.

A romantic, sexy DVD, with erotic little nibbles, all aphrodisiacs designed to torment the senses and wind them both to fever pitch. She was going to make the chocolate mousse again and feed it to him, spoon by spoon.

Then breakfast in bed, on their last day, with the wickedest pastries she could find and lashings of hot coffee, followed by some equally hot lovemaking.

And then talk. Before the others got back, she wanted to talk to him, to discuss their relationship, because they did have one, however much in denial he might be.

She wanted to know what it was that had kept them apart, had stopped him from loving anyone, not just her. Something had, surely, because he was so great with all his little nieces and nephews, and she knew he never forgot a birthday or a wedding anniversary, always giving thoughtful and personal gifts.

The greatest gift he gave was his time. He was never too busy to talk to them, never too busy to visit if it was an important occasion, and he was deeply involved in the family business, as well.

So it wasn't that he didn't do family. He did. Just not one of his own, and she wanted to know why.

Why he'd cut off their relationship before so abruptly was still a mystery to her. She wanted answers to that, and to why, now, he'd just taken it for granted that it would be over.

But he didn't look happy about it, so why end it?

A million questions, and as usual, no answers.

And all her plans for their last few days were wiped out in an instant. If they'd talked, if they'd hashed it all through and got to the bottom of it, and if even then he'd still wanted it to end, then they would at least have had that time, the slow winding down, a beautiful, tender farewell to their affair.

And now it would never happen.

Abruptly, without warning and before she'd had time to steel herself, it was over, the second time this had happened, and she wanted to crawl into a corner and cry.

'Are you ready?'

No crying. She was tougher than that, and this time she was going to stand and fight. She blinked, swiped away a tear that had escaped and opened her bedroom door with a smile. 'Sure. Shall we go?'

He scanned her face but said nothing, just limped out to the car with his things and put them in the boot, and he was tight-lipped and silent all the way to the supermarket. He perked up a bit for Carlotta, teasing her as she checked him over and looked at his foot and exclaimed over the bruises.

'I'm fine,' he told her, but she flapped her apron and wiped her eyes and hugged him, and then she sat him down and fed him cake. Fed both of them, because she'd looked at Anita and seen the lost look in her eyes.

'Eat! Come on, you need good food to heal.'

He looked at the slab of cake in front of him and for once he wasn't hungry. 'I've had good food. Anita's been cooking for me and she's taken very good care of me. Tell me about your grandchildren. How were they?'

'Oh, wonderful! Giovanni, you have no idea how wonderful it is to be a great-grandparent. So much easier than being a parent. You can hand them back to Mamma, and when they're clean and fed, you get them back. It's perfect!'

He laughed obediently, but Anita carried on poking the cake around her plate, unable even to smile. She was so frustrated that she'd lost a chance to talk to him, but with the family home, he'd stay here now for a while.

Maybe then she'd find a way to pin him down and find out what was stopping him, because if she couldn't change his mind about being a parent, then Gio might never know what it was to be a grandparent, because you couldn't do the one without the other.

And if he was never a parent, then she would never be, either, because after this last ten days she knew, without any doubt in her mind at all, that there would never be another man for her. She loved him so much, so deeply, that just the thought of another man touching her as he had filled her with revulsion.

'Anita, you're not eating.'

She tried to smile, but it was a poor effort. 'I'm sorry, Carlotta. I had a big breakfast, and I'm really not very hungry.'

She didn't believe her. Anita could see it in her eyes, see the sympathy, the understanding. It was no secret in the family that she loved Gio. She always had, always would, and she'd never been a good poker player. And this last week had just made it ten times worse.

* * *

Lydia had her baby three hours after they arrived back, at home, with Massimo at her side and Luca and Isabelle providing the medical backup.

They'd got back while Anita and Gio were still there, and with the baby so close it would have seemed wrong to leave at that point—rather like leaving a wedding before the bride arrived. And anyway, how was he supposed to leave? He'd need Anita's help, and she was up to her neck in children at the moment.

They were in the kitchen with his parents and the five children, Massimo's three and Luca and Isabelle's two, while Carlotta cooked up a storm to take her mind off it and the rest of them entertained the children. Francesca, Lavinia and Antonino were fizzing with excitement, but Annamaria was cranky and Maximus, Luca's youngest, was beyond tired, and so Gio battened down his feelings and picked the little boy up and rocked him off to sleep while they waited for the news.

And then shortly before five Luca came into the kitchen, a huge smile on his face, and hugged Francesca as she threw herself at him.

'Well?'

'It's a boy,' he said, beaming. 'They're both absolutely fine, and she's doing really well. Here. I took a photo. You can all go and see him in a minute.'

He showed them the picture on his phone, Francesca and Lavinia there first, then Antonino clamouring to see his little brother, and then Annamaria, Luca's daughter climbed into the fray to peer down at the picture of the smeary, streaky little baby.

'Oh, he's beautiful!' Carlotta said, looking over their shoulders and bursting into tears. *'Bellissimo!'*

He was, Gio thought, his heart clenching as he passed

his nephew back to Luca. 'Here, your son,' he said, handing over the sleeping child, and Luca eyed Gio thoughtfully but said nothing. Anita was hanging over the photo now with his mother and father, and she looked up at Gio and their eyes locked. And as he watched, the tears welled over and slid down her cheeks.

This would never be his, he realised. This happiness, this cluster of people around a hasty photograph of his brand-new baby, because there would never be a baby. The stakes were too high, the risks too great.

Pain and guilt lanced through him, and he turned away, needing to get out, done with playing happy families, and instantly Anita was at his side.

'Gio? Are you OK?'

'I need to get out of here. Can you take me back to Firenze?'

'What?' She frowned, her face puzzled. 'Aren't you going to stay here, now they're back?'

'They don't need me here.'

'They do! And you need them. You shouldn't be alone.'

'I'm fine,' he said, although he'd seldom felt less fine. He felt raw, flayed inside by all the emotion, and he just wanted to get back to his apartment and hole up for a while.

A long while.

'Well, whatever, you can't go yet. You have to see the baby, pat your brother on the back, drink a glass of something—you can't just run away!'

'Gio? What nonsense is this? You're not leaving!' his mother said, cutting him off at the pass. 'Get the Prosecco out. We need to drink to the baby.'

Luca's baby was handed to his grandmother, and Annamaria snuggled down on her grandfather's lap, and before he could protest any more he was handed a bottle of Prosecco by Luca and told to open it.

And then just as the cork popped, Massimo walked into the kitchen with the new baby in his arms, and Gio felt his heart turn over.

'They're doing girl stuff,' Massimo said with a grin. 'We've been sent out. So, *bambini*, what do you think of your little brother?'

He sat down so he was at their level, and the children clustered round him and bent over the baby, their shrill voices hushed by Francesca, ever the one to keep order between the younger ones, and Gio felt a huge lump in his throat at the sight of his brother's close-knit family.

This new baby was a huge step forward for his brother, finding happiness with Lydia after the tragic loss of his wife. It had been the year before his affair with Anita, and Gio had used the excuse that he was busy to stay away as much as he could, but in reality he'd found his pain unbearable to watch. He still felt guilty for the lack of support he'd given his brother, and now he forced himself to go over to him and do what he had to do.

'Congratulations,' he said gruffly, staring down at the tiny, precious child cradled so gently in his brother's arms. 'He's beautiful.'

The baby's eyes opened wide and he stared straight at Gio. Pain slammed through him, and he backed away. 'He's great. Gorgeous. Tell Lydia well done.'

'Tell her yourself.'

'I can't. I have to go—Anita's giving me a lift back to Firenze.'

Massimo frowned, scanning his face thoughtfully. 'Will you be all right?'

'Of course. I'm fine now. The stitches are all ready

to come out, I've just got a twisted ankle. Don't fuss. Anyway, I've got work to do.'

He nodded slowly, as if he didn't quite believe it, but the children were clamouring for attention and wanted to hold the baby, and Gio made a bid for freedom in the chaos.

'Can we go now?' he asked Anita with a touch of desperation, and she opened her mouth to protest but Luca shook his head.

'Just take him home, Anita,' he said softly, and Gio shot him a grateful look. He didn't know the facts—nobody knew, but he sensed that something was wrong, something that could never be put right, and he was cutting his brother some slack.

So Anita put his things back in the car again, and drove him back to the apartment and carried everything up for him. And then, because she knew if she didn't do it now she'd never get another chance, she tackled him.

'Gio, we need to talk.'

'No,' he said flatly. 'There's nothing to talk about, Anita. It was just a few days.'

'It was a *love affair*,' she said, her voice firm. 'I love you, Gio, and I know you love me.'

'You know nothing.'

'I don't know why you're ending it. I don't know why you ended it before. You never did explain.'

'There was nothing to explain,' he said, but he wouldn't meet her eyes. He stood staring out of the window at the distant hills, and resolutely refused to look at her.

So she left him there. He had enough food to tide him over, and as she'd told him so succinctly, anything he needed he could order in.

And then she drove all the way back to her house, walked into the bedroom she'd shared with Gio for the past ten days, curled up in the middle of the cloud-soft bedding and cried her heart out.

She thought it would get easier, but it didn't.

She resisted the urge to phone him to make sure he was all right. He had two brothers and three sisters and his parents to do that. She didn't need to get involved.

Get involved? That made her laugh. She couldn't get involved, she was already involved, right up to her neck and beyond.

She tried to bury herself in work, but curiously other people's happy-ever-after somehow didn't seem to cut it.

'You can't afford to lose business,' she told herself firmly, and rescheduled a couple of meetings for the next day, bringing them forward. She'd be ridiculously busy, but that was fine. Busy was good.

Better than sitting in the corner of the leather sofa—*his* corner—and crying.

She met with the bride she'd been with when Gio had been hurt, and of course it was all she could talk about.

'I saw you on the news, with Gio Valtieri. I didn't realise he was a friend of yours.'

'Yes. Yes, he is. I've known his family all my life.'

'They said…'

She trailed off, and went a little pink. 'Sorry. None of my business. How is he now?'

'Getting better, I understand. I'm not sure, his family's back now so they're looking after him.'

Or trying to, but she didn't imagine he'd be making it easy. He never did. He'd be grumpy and withdrawn and hostile to any offers of help or show of concern. Another reason to leave him to get on with it.

'Now, about this wedding,' she said, and dragged her mind and the bride's back into focus.

He'd gone back to the hospital at Luca's insistence for a check-up the day after he got back. They X-rayed his foot again, took the adhesive strapping off—not something he enjoyed, especially the bit above his ankle where the hair was—and then left him with a removable ankle support.

Then they took the stitches out of his hand and leg, made him move his fingers through a range of tasks, and signed him off.

He was glad about that. He'd seen enough of the hospital the first time, and the first thing he did when he got back to his apartment was have a long, hot shower. Not a good idea, because it just brought back memories of making love to Anita in the shower at her house.

Everything brought back memories, but the nights were the worst. So long, so lonely. He spent hours sitting outside on the balcony in the cold staring out at the distant hills and wondering how she was.

And then Luca came, and looked him up and down and shook his head.

'You look awful. Even worse than Anita.'

He bit his tongue so he didn't ask how she was. Not good, if Luca was to be believed.

'I'm fine. I'm just tired.'

'I can see that. You've got black bags under your eyes and you don't look as if you've eaten anything in the last two weeks.'

'One week and six days,' he correctly expressionlessly, and Luca frowned.

'Right, that's it, I'm taking you home. Go and pack your things. You're coming with me.'

'No.'

'Yes. It's not a question, Gio. Either you pack your things or I do.'

'Do what you like. I'm not coming.'

'Because Anita's there?'

He swallowed and looked away, and Luca gave a soft sigh and put his arms around him and hugged him.

'Come on,' he said, his voice softening. 'Isabelle can feed you up, and you can take over some of the office work for Massimo so he can spend more time with Lydia and the children.'

'I'm working.'

'That's not what your secretary said. She's filing her nails. She said you're supposed to be working on a case, but there's been no sign of you.'

'I'm working on it here.'

'Are you?'

He sighed and rammed a hand through his hair, the honesty that was bred in his bones not allowing him to lie. 'No. Not really.' He felt suddenly choked, and he sucked in a breath and looked up at the sky through the window.

'Let me take you home,' Luca said softly, and suddenly he couldn't fight it anymore, because he was so empty, so lost, so *lonely* without her.

He went into his bedroom, pulled out his bag and threw some clothes in it, grabbed his wash things and hesitated at the condoms.

No. He didn't need them. It was over.

He zipped the bag shut, slung the strap over his shoulder and picked up his laptop case. 'Well, come on, then, if you want to get out of here before the traffic starts.'

* * *

He was home.

Helping Massimo out, she'd heard, doing some of the company's legal work for the estate.

She found herself sitting in the dark at night and staring at the lights of the *palazzo*. Was he there? Bound to be, staying with his parents in their wing of the ancient Medici villa that was home to all of them. She wondered, now that Massimo and Lydia had taken over the larger part, which of the lights was Gio's room.

'Stop it!' she told herself when she was doing it for the fourth night in a row. 'You're being stupid. Get over him. You aren't fifteen any more.'

She moved to the chair, so her back was to the window, and there in front of her was the chess set that he'd carved for her all those years ago. She picked up one of the knights, the lovingly carved but rather angry horse so delicately detailed, and swallowed a lump in her throat. She ran her finger lightly down its Roman nose, over the flared nostrils, and remembered the times she'd won because he'd been distracted, and when she'd looked up, triumphant, there'd be that look in his eyes, the burning need, the passion simmering under the surface.

She put the little horse down, and a tear fell onto the board beside it. She wiped it away with her finger, but another fell, and then another, and she gave up and went to bed in his sheets and cried her eyes out.

And then she got up and stripped the bed at last, and threw the sheets in the washing machine and set it off before she could change her mind.

She slept in her room that night, without the memories, without the scent of him still lingering faintly on the fine cotton sheets, and when she woke in the morning she had to run to the bathroom.

Really? *Really?*

She plonked down on the travertina tiles and stared blankly across the room.

How?

They'd been so careful, so meticulous about this. There was no *way* she could have got pregnant. But she'd been feeling rough for days now, and she'd blamed it on the awful emptiness inside. But maybe she wasn't empty inside at all. Maybe...

She got slowly, cautiously to her feet, went into the kitchen and put a slice of bread in the toaster. Plain bread, a bit of dull sandwich bread which was all she'd felt like eating for the last week.

And just the smell of it toasting was enough to send her running to the bathroom again.

She waited until the nausea had subsided enough for her to eat the cold toast, and then she felt better. Slightly.

It might be a bug, she told herself, even though she knew it wasn't. She'd had bugs before, and this felt quite different. She got in the car, drove to a supermarket in the next town and bought a pregnancy test. Then she went into a café and ordered green tea, and when she couldn't stall any longer she went into the cloakroom and unwrapped the test.

Then she held her breath and waited.

One line.

Two.

Pregnant.

She laid her hand gently over her abdomen, and stared down. Gio's baby, she thought with a great welling of love, and then it dawned on her she was going to have to tell him, and she started to shake.

Well, they were going to have to talk now, she thought, and felt a shiver of apprehension.

He'd go crazy! He'd been so emphatic about it, and even though it wasn't her fault, he was going to be furious. He'd think she'd done it on purpose, to trap him. She was sure of it. He was so cynical, so wary, so untrusting of relationships, and he'd never believe it had been a genuine accident.

She could hardly believe it herself.

Her fingers trembling, she put the test back into the packet, stuffed it into her handbag and walked out through the café and back to her car. She didn't know what to do, which way to turn.

She couldn't tell her parents. They'd been unhappy enough about him staying with her, even though she'd somehow convinced them it was fine, and this would send them over the edge. They'd totally over-react, and she really wasn't up to it. Her father would go after Gio with a shotgun, and her mother would cry, and it would be a nightmare. She'd have to tell them some time, of course, but not yet.

Not now.

Now, she just needed someone who knew them both, who loved them both and could help her work out what to do.

Luca.

Relief flooded her. Luca would know what to do.

She started the engine and drove home, slowing as she passed the entrance to the Valtieri estate. Luca and Isabelle lived in the lodge just a short way up the drive, and she could see Luca's car there.

Just Luca's. Not Isabelle's. She was probably up at the *palazzo* with Lydia and the baby, and in the middle of the day there was no way Gio would be here. He'd be working in the office or out on the estate somewhere with Massimo.

She went up the drive and pulled up beside Luca's car, and he must have heard her because the front door opened and he came out.

'Anita?' he said softly, and that was enough.

His gentle voice, the kindness and concern in his eyes, pushed her over the edge and she started to cry, great gulping sobs that had him gathering her up against his side and ushering her into the house.

He led her to the kitchen, pushed her into a chair and put the kettle on, and then sat down opposite her and waited.

'I'm sorry,' she said, when she could speak again, and he just smiled and shrugged.

'Don't worry about it. You obviously needed that. Are you OK? Isabelle's out—do you want me to call her?'

She shook her head. 'No, it was you I wanted—'

She broke off, biting her lip. How could she go on? Where to start? She stared blindly at him, unable to form the words, and after a moment he sighed in realisation and gave her an understanding smile.

'Oh, Anita,' he said quietly. 'How?'

'The usual way?' she said, trying to joke about it, but it really, *really* wasn't funny. She shrugged. 'I have no idea. We were so careful—'

She bit her lip so hard it bled, but she didn't really notice.

Luca shrugged. 'These things happen sometimes. Nothing's fool-proof. I see it all the time. So—what now?'

'I don't know. I'm just so shocked. I don't know what to do—where to turn, where to go from here. That's what I wanted to ask you. What should I do, Luca?'

He tilted his head on one side, his face serious.

'What do you want to do?'

Live happily ever after with your brother?

She blinked away the welling tears. 'It's not what I *want* to do, it's what I wish I could *un*do. I shouldn't have made him to come to my house, shouldn't have insisted on looking after him. I knew it was asking for trouble, but I didn't know what else to do and I couldn't leave him alone with nobody to care for him. How could I? And now—now I'm pregnant, and he's going to hate me for it, and I just don't know how to tell him.'

'He won't hate you.'

'He will! He'll think I've done it on purpose, just to trap him, and I can't bear it. I love him so much, but he's so set against having children, so adamant that he doesn't want them, that he'll be a bad father, that he doesn't have what it takes to make a relationship work, but he's never really tried, he just walks away, every time anyone gets close…'

She tailed off, the tears welling again.

'I can't tell him I'm pregnant, Luca,' she sobbed. 'I just can't, it's the last thing he wants to hear and he's just going to go crazy…'

Luca sat back in his chair, his face grave.

'Not telling him isn't an option, Anita, I'm afraid,' he said gently. 'I'm sorry, but apart from the fact that it's shortly going to become blindingly obvious, he's standing right behind you.'

She stared at him, shock draining the blood from her head so she felt sick and dizzy.

'No!' she gasped silently. Her hands flew up to cover her face, and she just wanted to run away, to hide somewhere and wait for it all to be over, but Luca was standing up and walking past her, laying a comforting, reassuring hand on her shoulder as he went, and then Gio was sitting down where Luca had been, and his face could have been carved from stone.

'Is it true?' he asked, his voice ragged. 'You're having my child?'

She nodded, and pulled the test out of her handbag, passing it to him.

He took it, staring at it blankly as if he'd never seen one in his life before, which he might very well not have done, she thought.

'What is this?'

'It's a pregnancy test. One line is negative, two is positive.'

Two lines. Positive. Gio stared down at the test, and closed his eyes as a sea of emotions washed over him. How? How had this happened? They'd been so careful, every time. Nothing was one hundred per cent safe, he knew that from bitter experience, but…

'When is it due?' he asked, but his voice didn't sound like his and he swallowed hard, but there was a lump there he couldn't seem to shift.

'I don't know. I haven't worked it out. About seven and a half, eight months?'

He counted on his fingers, not trusting his mind with the maths. 'November? The beginning of November?'

'Probably. I can't be sure. I have no idea when it happened, but obviously in that fortnight.'

He blew his breath out slowly. He was going to be a father. Of all the crazy, ridiculous, impossible things, he was going to be a father, before the end of the year. And Anita was going to be a mother.

The mother of his child.

Shock spiralled into fear, and he swallowed again.

'We'll get married,' he said flatly. 'I'll let you fix the details. It doesn't need to be huge, just quick—'

'No.'

'No? You don't want a quick wedding?'

'I don't want a wedding,' she said, shocking him again. 'Don't be ridiculous. A few weeks ago you explained to me in minute detail that you don't do relationships, that you can't, that they always fail, that you'll be a rotten father and you'll never countenance it, and then you tell me we're getting married? I'm pregnant, Gio, not deranged. There's no way I'm marrying you because of this.'

He stared at her, another shocking possibility entering his head. 'No. You aren't planning—why did you talk to Luca?'

'Not for that!'

'Then—if you're having the baby, if you want to keep it—Anita, we *have* to get married.'

'No, Gio, we don't,' she said firmly, because the path ahead was suddenly clear and no longer so strange and terrifying. 'I won't marry a man who doesn't love me, who can't love me, who can't promise me forever—and you've made it abundantly clear that you can't. But I am going to have the child, quite definitely, and of course you can have access to it if you wish, and I hope you will, but your family will see it regularly, and so will my family, and I'll bring the baby up to be proud of his father, even if his father can't find it in his heart to love him. And I will love him, to the end of my days.'

She got to her feet, and he stood up, too, the scrape of his chair harsh in the sudden silence.

'Anita, please.'

'No. You made your feelings about being a parent crystal clear, Gio, and I won't put you in a position where you feel trapped. What kind of a marriage would that be?'

A good one, he wanted to shout, but he couldn't know that. Every relationship he'd had had failed, and the fallout, on one occasion, had been catastrophic. What made him think this one would be any different?

And so he let her go.

CHAPTER SEVEN

HE was still standing there when Luca came back in a few moments later.

He didn't ask any questions, just walked up to him, put his arms round him and held him as the tears he'd bottled up for so long fell in a torrent.

Then he dragged himself out of his brother's arms, walked over to the window and stared out at the rolling hills. He didn't see them. All he could see was a woman's face racked with grief—grief he'd inadvertently caused. Grief that had nearly killed her.

And now it was starting all over again.

'Want to talk about it?'

'Not really.'

He sat down, not knowing what else to do, and Luca put a glass of whisky down on the table in front of him and watched him thoughtfully. He looked up and met the gentle, compassionate gaze, and sighed.

'Come on, then, let's have it.'

'What?'

'The lecture on irresponsibility.'

'No lecture. Anita assured me there was no irresponsibility. I was just wondering what's happened to hurt you so deeply in the past.'

He looked away, picked up the whisky and took a gulp. 'Nothing,' he lied.

'I don't believe you.'

'Tough.'

'Gio—you're my little brother. I know you nearly as well as I know myself. And I know when you're hurting.'

He shook his head. 'Luca, don't. Just leave it, please, and if you can't leave it, then take me back to Firenze and let me deal with this my way.'

'No. You need to be here. Anita needs you.'

'Apparently not,' he said bitterly. 'I asked her to marry me, and she said no. She said—'

He couldn't even repeat what she'd said, the words hurt him so much.

'What did she say?' Luca prompted softly.

'She said she wouldn't marry a man who didn't love her.' The words seemed to flay the skin off his heart, but somehow he carried on. 'And she said she'd bring the baby up to be proud of me, even if I couldn't find it in my heart to love him—'

His throat closed, and he picked up the glass, swirling the liquid around for a moment until he felt he had a chance of swallowing it.

'It's not true, though, is it? You do love her. You've always loved her, ever since you were fifteen.'

'Well, of course, but it's not that kind of love. It's— complicated.'

'When isn't it? That's no reason to quit, though.'

'I'm not quitting.'

'It sounds like it. It sounds like you're running away.'

He looked down into the glass, then drained it and slammed it down on the table and got up.

'This is nothing to do with Anita. And anyway, you

know nothing about our relationship,' he said roughly. 'She's just a friend—that's all. That's all she's ever been.'

'Don't lie to yourself. I don't care if you lie to me, but don't lie to yourself, Gio. She's always been more than a friend. You wouldn't be having this conversation with me if she was just a friend.'

It was true. He couldn't argue with it, so he walked out, got into the borrowed farm truck and drove away. He had no idea where he was going, but the truck seemed to know, and five minutes later he pulled up outside Anita's house.

Her car was outside. Good. He'd go in, talk some sense into her and get this wedding under way, because this was one woman he *wasn't* going to let down, one baby he wasn't going to fail, and she *would* marry him.

She wouldn't change her mind.

She flatly refused to talk to him about marriage, and she wouldn't let him in, so he sat in the truck outside her house and waited.

For hours.

She had to come out eventually, he thought, but then a cold finger of fear slid down his spine. What if she'd decided she couldn't cope? What if it suddenly all felt too much, and she did something stupid? Something dreadful—

He was out of the truck and pounding on the front door again before he had time to think, but she didn't open it this time.

What if she can't?

Fear clawing at him, he ran round to the back of the house and pounded on the French doors to the kitchen, tugging at the handle.

The lever moved, and the door swung quietly open, surprising him. He stepped inside and stopped.

She was curled up in the corner of the sofa, hugging a cushion. Her face was streaked with tears, but she met his eyes defiantly.

'This is my house. I didn't invite you in. Please leave.'

He closed the door and sat down on the chair, suddenly aware of pain in his ankle. 'No. I can't. I'm sorry, we have to talk about this.'

She threw the cushion down and got up. 'There's nothing to talk about, Gio. I can't marry you, I won't marry you, and I'm having the baby. That's all there is to say.'

'No. No, it's not. I'm not letting you do this on your own. Fine, don't marry me if you don't want to, but I'm going to be here for you every step of the way. I'm not giving up, Anita. I have every intention of being part of this.'

She scanned his face, saw the implacable expression in his eyes and the set of his mouth, and knew he meant it. Gio was nothing if not stubborn, and once he'd made his mind up, that was it.

Well, she was stubborn, too, and this was her house.

'Do you want me to call the police?'

'And tell them what? The father of your baby is insisting on looking after you?'

He had a point.

'I could call my father.'

'Have you told them yet?'

She shook her head. There was no way she was going to call her father. All hell would break loose, and she needed to feel calm and centred before she opened that can of worms.

'Please, Gio. Just go.'

'I can't. I can't leave you like this.'

'Like what? Pregnant? Are you going to sit there until I give birth, is that it? Well, newsflash, Valtieri, it takes nine months! That's another seven point something to go, and if you imagine for a moment you're going to sit there and haunt my kitchen until then, you've got another think coming. You know where the door is. Use it.'

'I can't.'

'Why?'

'Because I have a duty to you and to my child.'

She rolled her eyes and sat down again.

'Giovanni Valtieri, I've listened to you talking about your feelings on this subject until I'm sick of hearing it, and now suddenly you expect me to believe you've had a change of heart? Give it a rest. You're just trying to do the decent thing, and believe me, it's not necessary. I'm fine.'

'Are you? Are you really? Because I'm not. I feel as if my whole world has been turned upside down on its axis, and I don't know what to think or feel any more. And if you feel the same, then I'm not leaving you to deal with it on your own.'

She stared at him, slightly shocked at the sudden insight into his emotions, the closest he'd come to revealing his true feelings on anything serious for—well, forever, really. And he was right. She did feel as if her world had been turned upside down, because having his child had been something she'd wished for for years, but not like this. Not in this way, with him offering to do the decent thing and not a word of love between them.

And it made her want to cry again.

'I'm not going to marry you, Gio.'

'OK. I got that bit. But you *are* having my baby, and I can't let you do it alone. It took two of us to put it there, and there's no way I'm going to let you go through your pregnancy unsupported.'

'You can buy maternity underwear,' she said lightly, but he just looked at her, his eyes raw with a pain she didn't understand.

'Anita, please,' he said quietly, that pain echoing in his voice. 'We have to make this work. I can't tell you how important it is.'

'You could try.'

He shook his head. 'Just trust me.'

That made her laugh, but the sound echoed round the kitchen, the saddest sound she'd ever heard. 'How can you ask me to trust you when you don't even trust me enough to tell me what's troubling you? Something's gone wrong for you, Gio, I know that. Tell me what it is.'

'I can't. I can't tell you. I can't talk about it, but it was nothing to do with you, nothing you'd done. It was something I did, or didn't do. Something I should have done differently—something I can't undo.'

There was a grim finality to those words that chilled her to the bone, and in his eyes was a hollow desperation that made her bleed for him.

'Tell me,' she coaxed softly, but he shook his head.

'No. Not now. Maybe one day. But—this time, I have to get it right. I have to be there for our child, and that means being with you.'

This time? 'Not necessarily. I have no intention of denying you access.'

'But you would. If we aren't living together, then, by definition, you're denying me access to a huge part of my child's day, every day. I want to be with you during your pregnancy, to feel it move, to come with you for scans, to be there at the birth and every day afterwards. It's incredibly, unbelievably important to me. I need to be with you for this.'

She could hear the conviction in his voice, but he'd hurt her so much, and she wasn't willing to give in just because this time it was him who was hurting.

'You didn't want to be with me before,' she said rawly. 'You just walked out one morning, and when you came back, it was over. No explanation, no reasons, just—finish. Do you have any idea how much that hurt me, Gio? How much it tore me apart?'

He felt gutted by her words, reamed out inside. He'd wanted to save her from pain, and in doing so, he'd caused it, far more than he'd realised. 'I'm sorry,' he said gruffly. 'I never wanted to hurt you.'

'I thought I was going to die, Gio. I had everything I'd ever wanted there with you, and you snatched it away without any warning. And now, just because there's a child involved, you want me to let you back into my life, even though you still can't say that you love me? Why?'

The pain in her voice shredded him anew. 'Because this is different,' he said roughly. 'This isn't about want. This is about rights. A child's right to have both parents. A child's right to be safe and protected.'

'It would be safe and protected.'

'It will be. I'll make sure of it.'

He had been so emphatic about not having a child, ever, and yet now there was going to be one, he was so desperately protective of it. *This time, I have to get it right.*

What did he mean, *this time*? When had it not been right? Five years ago, when he'd done something he couldn't undo?

She felt a chill run down her spine. He'd ended their

relationship so abruptly. Could that have been the reason? Something to do with a *child*?

I can't talk about it.

Because it hurt too much?

Oh, Gio, tell me. Tell me what's hurting you. Tell me what's keeping us apart.

She closed her eyes, counted to ten and gave in.

'So what do you have in mind?' she asked, and his shoulders dropped as if a weight had been taken off them.

'I move in here, and look after you. Make sure you're all right, give you whatever you need—whatever's necessary.'

'So—just as if we were married?'

'No, not if you don't want that. I'll sleep in the other room.'

'That seems a little superfluous at this stage. We seem to have moved past that.'

They had—and yet had they? Emotionally, they were still separate entities. He'd never said he loved her, never given her the slightest suggestion of a future with him— well, not until he'd told her they'd get married, which to her at least wasn't viable without the underpinnings of emotional honesty.

And he wasn't being emotionally honest yet, not completely, or he would have told her whatever it was that had put that haunted look in his eyes. But he was trying, and moving towards it, inch by inch.

But the other room? If she agreed to that, would she ever stand a chance of getting him to open up to her? Didn't she stand more chance of that by keeping him close?

He couldn't hurt her any more than she'd been hurt already. She was beginning to think she was immune to the damage he inflicted on her every time she let herself hope, but clearly she wasn't the only one who'd been hurt.

Stick to facts.

'Your sheets are in the washing machine,' she said, conveniently ignoring the fact that they could easily be dried, 'so if you're staying tonight, it'll have to be with me.'

'I'm sure I'll cope. I'll go back to Luca's and pick up my things, and I'll be back later. And don't tell your parents without me. We'll do it together.'

'My father will want to chase you down the aisle with a gun,' she warned, and he just smiled grimly.

'Sensible man. It'll be good to have him on my side. I'll see you later. I won't be long.'

He went cross country, his first stop the *palazzo,* his family home.

He walked into the big family kitchen and found all of them, Luca and Isabelle included, gathered round the table. They looked up, and all of them fell silent.

'Giovanni?' his mother said softly, her face troubled. 'What is it? You look as if you've seen a ghost.'

He swallowed hard. How true. How very, very true.

'I'm fine. I, er—I just thought I'd come and tell you something.'

Luca got to his feet hastily. 'Hey, kids, come with me, I've got something to show you.'

'But we want to see Gio!' Lavinia cried.

'Later. Come on.'

He ushered all of the children out, and the others all turned to him expectantly. 'Well?' his father said. 'What is it? Spit it out.'

He took a deep breath, then said clearly, 'Anita and I are expecting a baby—and before you ask, we aren't getting married.'

His mother stopped in her tracks, half out of her chair,

arms outstretched towards him, and her smile faltered. She sat back down again abruptly, her mouth open. 'But—I don't understand. You love her!'

He gave a soft laugh. 'No, Mamma. I don't love her—not like that. We just—we got a little carried away.'

'And you didn't have the sense to take precautions?' his father growled.

'I did. Every time. And don't you lecture me. I know how "early" Massimo was.'

His father coloured, but his mother chipped in. 'We were engaged. You, on the other hand, are not, even though you do love her, whatever you might say to the contrary, and I'm deeply disappointed in you that you haven't got the decency to ask her to marry you.'

'Well, that's where you're wrong, you see,' he said lightly, sitting down in Luca's place and picking up his wine glass. 'Because I have asked her, and she said no.'

He filled the glass, swirled the wine around and sniffed it, held it to the light, nodded and drained it like water. Then he reached for the bottle again, and Massimo's hand came out and removed it.

'No. You're not sitting there and getting drunk. What are you going to do next?'

'Pack and move in with her. She won't marry me, but she's allowing me to look after her.'

Isabelle frowned. 'That doesn't sound like Anita.'

'It isn't. I didn't give her a choice.'

Massimo snorted. 'I'll bet. I don't suppose you thought to *tell* her that you love her?'

'Will you all give up with this? I don't love her!' He got to his feet and walked to the door. 'You know where I'll be if anyone needs me for anything. I'll see you tomorrow.'

* * *

The door was unlocked when he got back there with his things, and he walked in, calling out her name.

She didn't answer. She was wandering round the kitchen with a piece of toast in her hand, looking grim.

'I feel sick,' she said. 'I thought it was morning sickness. I've been feeling sick all day.'

'Ring Isabelle. She'll have some tips. Or Lydia.'

'I thought you were going to look after me?'

'I am, but I've never been pregnant, Anita, so I can't tell you what will make it better. However...'

He sat down, got out his smart phone and started searching.

'Carbs,' he said. 'Lots of carbs. Never let yourself get hungry or dehydrated. Keep your blood sugar up. Fruit and plain toast or crackers.'

'Done that. It doesn't work.'

'Stress is bad for it.'

She gave a short, bitter laugh. 'Oh, well, that's all right then, I'll just chill out, shall I?'

He put the phone down and stood up again, walking over to her and pulling her reluctant body into his arms. 'I'm sorry. I'm so, so sorry. I really didn't want this to happen—'

'You think I don't know that?' she asked slightly hysterically, pushing away from him and heading for the biscuit tin. 'Ginger biscuits. I bought some the other day—'

'Want me to go shopping?'

'No, I want you to go, but I'm not going to get my wish.'

She found some plain biscuits, the sort that were best dunked in hot coffee because otherwise they were pretty flavourless. Perfect. She curled up on the sofa and nibbled the edge of one, and gradually the nausea subsided again.

'Better?'

'Slightly. If I could work out what I need, it would be better. I feel really hungry.'

'What have you eaten today?'

'Biscuits. Toast. Not much.'

He nodded, and walked into the kitchen and started opening cupboards.

'What are you doing?'

'Cooking for you.' He pulled his phone out of his pocket and rang Luca. 'What do I feed her?'

'Pasta or boiled rice with butter and salt. Oh, and green vegetables. Clean flavours. No meat, Isabelle says. Lydia says anything she doesn't see again in five minutes is good. Stir fry with fresh ginger in it and soy sauce. And they send their love.'

He gave a wry laugh and opened the fridge. 'OK. I can do something like that. *Ciao*.' He put the phone down and turned to her.

'They send their love. You ought to talk to them.'

She sighed. 'I ought to talk to my mother, but I feel so grim.'

'Let me feed you, then we'll talk to them.'

He pulled out vegetables—leafy greens, sprouting broccoli, peppers. He shredded them, dry-fried them in a touch of oil, put them on a bed of buttered boiled rice and added a slosh of soy sauce.

'Here—try that.'

She recoiled, but tasted it, chewed, swallowed and went back for more, and he blew out a silent breath and cleared up the kitchen. He'd made enough for two, but by the time he'd finished it he was wondering if he'd survive. He was starving, and the whole dish had lacked any kind of richness—entirely the point, of course, but it wasn't going to get him through the next few weeks.

There was some leftover pasta and sauce in the fridge, and he sniffed it. It smelt amazing.

'It's fine. I made it yesterday and couldn't eat it. I thought I might feel better today. Just—please don't heat it.'

Because it would bring out the smell. He nodded, stuck a fork in it and ate it cold, then he put the plate in the dishwasher and went over to her, perching on the edge of the sofa next to her.

'OK?'

She nodded. 'Yes. Thank you. I was just hungry, I think. I feel much better.'

'Better enough to tell your parents?'

She closed her eyes and rested her head back. 'They aren't going to understand,' she said wearily.

'They need to know. It's not fair that the others know and they don't.'

'How do the others know? Did Luca tell them?'

He shook his head. 'No. Luca would never do that. Patient confidentiality and all that. I told them. I hope you don't mind.'

She shrugged. 'It's your baby, too, Gio.'

He glanced down, and noticed she was sitting with one hand lying gently on her abdomen, cradling it. She'd be an amazing mother, he thought with a sudden rush of affection, and vowed to do everything in his power to keep her safe. It was beyond him to make her happy. Keeping her safe—them safe—would be enough of a challenge.

Her parents were delighted.

She was the last of their children to have a baby, and they'd almost given up on her, and so they were thrilled about that, if not about the situation. They were a little shocked because this had come almost out of nowhere, but the fact that they'd spent time alone together wasn't lost on them; they'd seen them together in that time, and she didn't think for a moment they'd managed to disguise the intense chemistry between them.

Not that there was any sign of it now, of course.

Gio was polite, friendly, solicitous—and driving her gently mad. He also made it abundantly clear to her parents that not getting married was her idea, not his.

Clever move, but he wasn't a lawyer for nothing, she thought wryly. Manipulating people's emotions was all part of the job, and he was highly successful at his job.

He took her home—well, she drove, but only because he was in the borrowed farm truck and it was a bit basic. But he ushered her out to the car, opened the door, closed it and went round and sat beside her and fastened her seat belt, even though it was only a few hundred yards on private roads.

'How about a nice relaxing bath?' he suggested, and she nodded.

'I'll go and run it.'

'No. You eat something. Luca said you need to eat constantly. Little and often.'

He went to run the bath and came back to find her munching salty potato sticks out of a giant packet.

He stole a few, put the kettle on and made her a cup of hot water with a slice of lemon and a sliver of fresh ginger—her mother's suggestion—and then chivvied her into the bathroom.

She was glad to be chivvied, if she was honest. She was exhausted, and it had been a deeply emotional and stressful day. And it wasn't over yet. They had the night to get through, and she'd had to put his sheets on to wash again because they'd been left in the machine overnight and she still hadn't tumble-dried them. Sort of deliberately, because she wanted him to be with her so she could catch him when his guard was down and find out what was really going on, but now she was beginning to regret that.

A little privacy might have been nice—time to lie and contemplate the enormous change that was coming in her life, not least the inextricable inclusion in it, for the foreseeable future, of Gio Valtieri—but that was never going to happen. Not for weeks, if not months.

She knew enough about him to know that when he'd made up his mind, it was made up, and he wasn't going anywhere until he was ready.

There was a tap on the door.

'How are you doing?'

'OK. I was about to get out.'

'Can I get you anything?'

Peace?

'No, I'm fine.'

She heard him walking away, his gait slightly uneven still. It had been better, and she wondered what had happened to make him limp again. She'd noticed it earlier. It was only five weeks since his attack, and he'd healed better than she'd expected, but maybe not as well as she'd thought.

She climbed out of the bath, got dried and dressed in her snuggly, full-length bath robe, then emerged from her bedroom to find logs burning cheerfully in the fireplace and Gio sitting with his feet up and his laptop on his lap.

He shut it down as she went in and got to his feet.

'OK?'

'I'm fine. Gio, please, stop fussing. I'm pregnant, not sick.'

'Sorry.' He didn't sound sorry, he sounded implacable, as in, 'I'm sorry, but that's the way it is, live with it' sorry.

'Were you working?'

'No. I was looking up the early stages of pregnancy.'

She shouldn't have been surprised. This was Gio, after all. He made it his business to be informed on any subject that was relevant to him or his work, and this, the slow and systematic creation of a living being from next to nothing, would be tackled no differently.

'How many weeks are you?'

'I don't know. Between seven and five, I guess. You go from the first day of the last period.'

She felt herself colouring—absurdly, since it was a perfectly normal thing and he had to know all about it, but that was fact and this was *her*, her body, her system, her cycle. And that made it somehow weird, despite the fact that he knew every single inch of her body because he'd spent almost two weeks very recently mapping it in minute detail.

'And that was?'

'I don't know. Sometime before we were due to go away. I can't remember exactly. It's not really relevant, I just get on with it. I know I should have been all right for the holiday.'

He nodded, and she could see his brain working.

'I just wish I knew how it had happened,' he said quietly. 'What went wrong, what we did or didn't do.'

'It doesn't matter now, though, does it?' she answered. 'The result's the only thing that really matters. Are there any of those potato chips left?'

They went to bed early.

She was exhausted, and she fell asleep on the sofa and woke up with her head on his shoulder. Strange, because he hadn't been sitting there, he'd been in the chair, and yet now he was next to her, his arm around her back, her head cradled comfortably in the hollow of his shoulder as he rested back beside her.

She stretched and sat up straight, rolling her head on her neck, and he retrieved his arm and stood up.

'Bedtime?' he murmured, and she nodded sleepily.

She needed the loo again, and she was hardly able to stay awake. How could anyone miss the signs, she thought, because her body was screaming out to her that something had changed, something was different, and she couldn't possibly have missed it.

She fell into bed, and a few moments later he joined her, settling himself down on the far side of the mattress, giving her space. It felt curiously lonely, and she knew she was being perverse but she wished he'd hold her, because she could have done with a hug.

'Did you put the fire guard up?'

'Yes, and I checked the doors were locked. Relax, *cara*. Go to sleep.'

He lay there listening to the sound of her breathing. It was slightly uneven, interspersed with the occasional sigh, and he knew she was still awake. Worrying about the future, or about them? The two were now linked, of course, and the thought made him go cold inside.

What if he let them down? What if he failed Anita, or worse still, failed the tiny and incredibly vulnerable child cradled in her body?

He couldn't fail again...

'Gio?'

He turned his head, and saw her looking at him in the dim light from the hall. 'Yes?'

'Hold me?'

Her voice was soft, a little tentative, as if she thought he might reject her, and with a soft exhalation he gathered her close and held her gently in his arms. He wouldn't fail her. It simply wasn't an option.

'It's OK, Anita,' he said, his voice slightly unsteady. 'It's going to be all right. I'll look after you.'

He would. She knew he would. She just wondered if he'd ever let her look after him, because someone needed to. The look on his face just now had been harrowing to see.

Grief?

She sensed a deep well of sadness in him. She had no idea what had happened, but something bad enough that he still couldn't talk about it, and she was horribly afraid that it involved a child.

He'd never mentioned it until today, but some time after their affair had ended Luca had told her that he didn't know what was wrong with Gio but that something big must have happened. Something tragic and heartbreaking?

And now, he was holding her as if she was the most fragile and precious thing in the world, and it made her ache inside. If only he could trust her—trust anyone. But he held himself aloof, and always had.

Everybody's friend, and yet nobody, not even his brothers, really knew him.

She laid her hand on his heart, snuggled her head down closer into the hollow of his shoulder, and let exhaustion claim her.

And as she slept, Gio kept watch over her, and knew that somehow, somewhere, he'd find the strength to do this, because he had no choice. Because it was Anita? Would he have felt like this about any other woman, or would he simply have made some tidy financial settlement, settled custody and access arrangements and left it at that?

Maybe, but Anita was different. Anita had always been different, and he'd never been able to keep a sense of perspective about her. And now there were three of them to pay the price because he hadn't been able to keep a sensible emotional distance between them, but had succumbed, not once, but twice, to the lure of the fairy tale that seemed to dangle in the air just out of reach whenever he was with her.

Well, it was in reach now. All he had to do was make damn sure that Prince Charming didn't turn back into a frog.

CHAPTER EIGHT

She had to give him credit where it was due.

For a man who knew nothing about pregnancy, who claimed that he was useless at relationships and didn't have any sticking power, he did a very passable impersonation of the ideal partner.

She woke up that first morning still in his arms, and lay there for a few minutes luxuriating in the warmth and intimacy of a totally platonic embrace. It might not have stayed that way, but for those few moments, while he was still asleep and she was feeling OK, it was wonderful.

And then the nausea hit, and she leapt from the bed and ran.

She thought she was going to die, kneeling on the cold stone floor wondering how on earth she had got herself in this mess, and then suddenly, unexpectedly, a warm, strong hand appeared and held her hair out of the way, the other hand lying gently on her shoulder offering silent support.

She sagged against his legs, and he stood there, soothing her with a rhythmic sweep of his thumb against her shoulder, waiting until everything settled down, and then he handed her a hot, damp flannel to wipe her face, and disappeared.

She got up and rinsed her mouth and followed him

into the kitchen, just in time to be handed a slice of toast smeared with yeast extract.

How did he know that? How?

She ate it ravenously, demanded more, and then snatched it from him the moment it was spread.

'Good, eh?'

'Amazing,' she said with her mouth full. 'Thank you.'

'Don't thank me, that was Lydia. Tea?'

'Mmm,' she said warily. 'Maybe. Decaff? Not strong, very little milk?'

It was perfect. Under normal circumstances she would have thrown it down the sink, but on that day—that day it was just right.

And so it went on.

She tried to work, but it was difficult. She made some phone calls to brides, pulled together a few ideas, but she just felt so *tired* all the time, and when she wasn't stuffing carbs, she spent a large part of every day napping.

And every time she woke he was there, tapping away on his laptop, writing up a brief or emailing a colleague.

'I'm going to trash your career,' she said, but he just smiled.

'I don't think so. I was due some time off. This is just routine stuff.'

She nodded, and got up to put the kettle on. He was at her side instantly.

'Hungry?'

'I could eat something. I could always eat something. Pasta? No dairy. Something clean flavoured.'

'Arrabiata?'

'I haven't got any sauce.'

'Well, isn't it a good job I got some?'

She propped herself up against the worktop and watched

him slice the vegetables. 'You know, for someone who's so rubbish at relationships, you're pretty good at this domestic stuff,' she said softly, and he glanced up and met her eyes.

'Just doing my bit,' he said lightly, but there it was again, that lingering shadow, the ghost of some remembered sadness in the back of his eyes.

'Gio, what's wrong?' she asked, catching him by surprise, and he cut himself.

He swore softly, grabbed a piece of kitchen paper and squashed it firmly on his finger. 'Nothing. What makes you think anything's wrong? Apart from the fact that I've cut myself. Do you have any plasters?'

'Sure.' She let it drop and went and found him one, wrapping it firmly round the end of his left index finger. 'Do you want me to finish cutting that up?'

'No, I'm done,' he said, scraping it into a pan and setting it on the hob, and he couldn't have told her any more firmly that the subject was off limits.

He had to go back to Firenze the following day.

Because she'd pushed him too hard? She didn't know, but she missed him. He got a lift in with Luca, and was driving himself back when he was finished, but then he called her.

'I'm going to be late home,' he said. 'Camilla Ponti wants to see me.'

'What!' She was stunned. More stunned that he seemed to be considering it. 'Are you going to see her?'

She could almost see him shrug. 'She can't do me any harm. Apparently she wants to apologise.'

'Or convince you not to prosecute her for assault,' she said sceptically. There was a long pause.

'Perhaps. I don't know. Anyway, I won't be back till much later. I'm sorry. Will you be all right?'

'Of course I will, Gio. I might spend the evening with Massimo and Lydia—get in a bit of baby cuddling for practice. It might remind me what it's all about when I feel queasy. Light at the end of the tunnel and all that.'

'Sounds like a good idea. I'll call you when I'm on the way home. You take care, *bella*. I'll see you later.'

He hung up, and she rang Lydia, arranged to go round there and spent the evening cuddling little Leo.

He was delicious, the most gorgeous baby she'd ever seen, and Lydia was more than happy to talk babies and share her top tips for morning sickness and all the other joys that were to follow.

Isabelle came up, too, and they spent a wonderful girly evening together while Massimo went down to Luca and babysat his two and left the girls to it.

But always, in the back of her mind, was Gio.

He'd said he'd ring when he was leaving, but it was almost ten by the time she went home, and there had still been no word from him, so in the end she rang him.

It went straight to voicemail, but she didn't leave a message. What was she supposed to say? 'Where are you?' She wasn't his wife, she didn't *want* to be his wife—not under the terms he was offering—and she wasn't going to behave like one.

So she went to bed, and she lay there and worried about him anyway.

'Signore Valtieri—thank you so much for agreeing to see me. I realise I had no right to ask.'

He shook her hand and pulled out a chair for her.

'Signora Ponti. Please, have a seat. I gather you want to apologise?'

'Yes. But I need your help, and I don't know where else to turn.'

His help? He stared in shock at the broken, dishevelled woman across the desk from him who sat wringing her hands. He'd expected contrition of some sort, but this was beyond anything he'd imagined, and it just underlined his feelings at the time of the attack. She'd been so desperate, so distraught. And she was now.

'I'm not sure how I can be of help to you.'

'I want you to ask Marco to help me. He won't see me.'

'I'm not surprised. I thought we'd said all there was to say at our meeting. Why you felt you had the right to come after me and assault me, I have no idea. I know you didn't mean to hurt me that badly, but I could have died because of what you did—why should I listen to what you have to say? And why on earth should I help you?'

She closed her eyes, and a tear squeezed out from under one lid. An act? Maybe—and maybe not.

She opened her eyes and looked at him, and he could see the pain in her eyes all the way down to her soul. It shocked him. This wasn't acting, this was a woman on the edge of a precipice.

'I can never apologise enough for what I did to you,' she said softly, her voice shaking. 'I'm not even sure what I did do. I don't remember hitting you. It was like a red mist came down over me, and I just wanted to lash out at you for what you'd done to me.'

'I did nothing to you. You had no case, I demolished it. It was obvious what was going to happen.'

'No. There was nothing obvious about it, not to me. The

only obvious thing was that I had to try. Signore Valtieri, do you have a child?'

He went still, motionless, but beneath his ribs his heart was pounding. 'No,' he said, knowing it was only part of the truth yet not willing to share his private pain with this woman.

'Then you won't understand what it's like to love your child so much that you'd do anything for him, even lie and cheat and steal, just to keep him safe.'

She opened her hand, and flattened out the photograph that was clutched in it. She laid it on his desk and pushed it towards him.

'This is my son.'

She slept fitfully, unable to relax completely until he was home, and then finally, at nearly one in the morning, he let himself in.

He didn't come to her room. She lay there for a while, listening and waiting, and then finally, unable to rest without knowing if he was all right, she got out of bed, pulled on her robe and went to find him.

He was sitting on the sofa in the dark, staring out over the distant valley. Most of the lights had gone now, the headlights of a vehicle moving slowly along the winding roads the only sign of life.

He heard her come in, and he turned his head and held out a hand to her. '*Bella*. I thought you'd be asleep. Come and sit with me.'

He patted the sofa cushion next to him, and she came and curled up beside him, tucking her feet under her bottom and snuggling into his shoulder.

'You're late.'

He was. His meeting with Camilla Ponti hadn't been at

all what he'd expected, and he'd spent most of the evening trying to work out what to do from now.

'Yes. I didn't mean to wake you. I'm sorry.'

'You didn't. I wasn't asleep. I tried to ring you.'

'I know. I'm sorry I didn't answer. I was thinking.'

'That hard?'

She could see his mouth twitch, just slightly, into what might almost be a smile, but it was a smile that tore at her heart. She reached up and laid a hand on his cheek.

'So how was she?'

'She wanted to apologise,' he said gruffly. 'She's fallen apart, Anita. She looked horrendous. Initially when we had our meeting all those weeks ago she was pretty self-contained at first, and you could imagine her as a successful business woman. She was elegant, smartly dressed, composed—well, until she realised she would lose. Today—what can I say? She was untidy, she looks as if she's aged twenty years and she couldn't stop crying.'

'Sounds like a good act.'

'No,' he said quietly, 'it was no act. She was genuinely distraught. She told me she needed the money because her child's in a care home. He suffered injuries in a car accident before he was born, and she can't look after him, he needs specialist care. That's what she needed the money for, why she stole from Marco for years, and why she needs her half of the business. To support her son.'

'And you fell for this?' she asked, incredulous, but he just smiled sadly.

'She showed me a photograph of him. He's a teenager now, but he can't speak and he can hardly move and it's an absolute tragedy. And before you say it, I know it's true, because after she left I checked up on it.'

Anita sighed, racked with guilt for doubting the poor

woman. 'Gosh, Gio, I'm sorry. It just sounded so implausible—how dreadful for her. For him—for both of them. Doesn't she have a husband to help support her?'

'No. He died in the car accident. It turned out he wasn't insured, so there's no compensation and the cost of his care falls entirely to her. That's why she cheated Marco all those years, and then tried to get her half of the business, to cover her spiralling debts. And when it was obviously not going to happen, it pushed her over the brink.'

'I should think it did. Oh, how awful. So how will she pay his care home bills?'

'She can't, and she's got a lawyer's bill she can't pay. And he's putting pressure on her.'

'Who represented her?'

'Bruno Andretti.'

'Did he know what it was for?'

'I don't know. It doesn't matter, she had no way of winning and he should have told her that. I wonder if he knew about the fraud? If she didn't tell him, it's not his fault. I'll go and see him, see if I can sort it out. And I'll talk to Marco. He doesn't know about the child. If she didn't tell her business partner, I doubt if she told her lawyer.'

'Is he a friend of yours?'

'No, but I know him. He's OK.'

He shifted so he was facing her, and laid a hand gently on her cheek, his eyes tender. 'You look tired, *cara.* Come on, back to bed.'

She fell asleep almost instantly, cradled in his arms, and he lay there holding her and thought of their child, of how he'd feel if anything happened to it. The surge of raw emotion shook him, and he wondered how it would feel to be Camilla Ponti, to have no way to help your child and no money to pay the bills, with your life falling apart around you.

He couldn't let it happen to her, to them. He'd talk to Bruno, and he'd talk to Marco, and see if he couldn't sort something out for her.

He went off again the next day.

'I don't know when I'll be back, but it shouldn't be too late,' he said as he left her at the door.

At the last second he leant in and kissed her, just a gentle brush of his lips on her startled mouth, and then he drove to Firenze and went to see Bruno.

'I'm afraid he's busy,' his secretary said.

'Tell him it's Giovanni Valtieri.'

She disappeared through a door, and came back a moment later looking surprised. 'He'll see you now.'

'Thank you.'

He walked through the door she'd gone through and closed it softly.

'Andretti.'

'Valtieri, *ciao*—come on in. Coffee?'

'Thank you.' He took the cup and set it down. 'I want to talk to you about your client, Camilla Ponti.'

Bruno sat back in his chair, propping one foot on the other knee and rocking slightly on the spring, a smile lurking in his eyes. 'Ah, yes. Are you better now? I heard you fell over a refuse bag. Careless, that. I take it you want to sue? Because you won't win.'

'No, thank you for your concern. I want to talk to you about your bill.'

He frowned. 'My bill? What about my bill?'

'I'm surprised you didn't tell her she had no case. Did

you know anything about her? Did you find out why she needed the money? Why she had debts?'

He dropped his foot to the floor and leant forwards. 'I didn't know she had debts. She told me nothing—only that Marco Renaldo had refused to give her her share of his company.'

'Because she'd embezzled funds from him, because she needed the money. She has a son with severe disabilities. He's in a care home. It's very expensive, but he needs specialist care.'

'She didn't tell me any of this. Am I supposed to be a mind-reader?'

'No, but you could have checked her credit rating,' he said drily. 'However, it's not too late to help her.' He picked up his coffee cup from the edge of Bruno's expensive plate glass desk and took a sip. 'I want you to waive your fee.'

'What? Don't be ridiculous—'

'I'm not being ridiculous. I'm waiving mine, and I'm going to ask Marco to help her. I know you don't have to, but it would be a gesture you can well afford.'

He stroked the surface of the desk with an idle finger, and Bruno gave a short huff of laughter.

'You owe me lunch.'

'Any time. Just not today, I have a lot to do.'

He drained his cup, shook Bruno's hand and drove straight to see Camilla Ponti.

'Your lawyer's agreed to waive his bill,' he told her gently, 'and I've paid your son's overdue fees and the next quarter to give you breathing space.'

Her eyes flooded with tears. 'But I attacked you,' she said, confused and unable to believe him. 'I could have killed you. Why would you do that for me?'

He smiled sadly. 'I didn't tell you the whole truth. I

don't have a child yet, but I will, in a few months, if all goes well. So, yes, Signora Ponti. I don't agree with what you did, but I *do* understand. And I want to help you, so that you can be there to support him.'

It still wasn't the whole truth. There was more, but it was too private, too painful and not for her ears, and so he left her then, promising to be in touch, and drove home to Anita.

It was time to explain, to tell her what had happened, and to ask her to try and understand why it was that he couldn't dare to let her love him.

She was asleep, curled up on the sofa, her hand under her cheek. She looked so young, so innocent, and he felt a wave of guilt that he'd hurt her all those years ago.

But wasn't that what he was doing now? He was no good at love. He always failed, always bailed out when it got messy or complicated. By staying with her, wasn't he putting her at risk of falling in love with a man who couldn't ever seem to deliver?

Dio, he wanted to, so much, but he wasn't sure he could. Every time he'd tried, he'd failed. He couldn't let himself fail Anita. Better not to let her ever rely on him emotionally. Physically, for practical and financial support, yes, of course. But for love?

He didn't think he had what it took, however much he might want it, but maybe he owed her that explanation. It was just finding the way to tell her that seemed so hard.

She stirred, and he crouched down beside her, brushing the hair out of her eyes.

'*Ciao, bella,*' he said softly, and her eyes flickered open.

'Gio—you're home.'

Home. The word sliced through him, and he sucked in

a quick, light breath. So welcoming. So dangerous an illusion…

'*Si.* I was done early. Can I get you anything?'

'Tea? I'm so thirsty. I keep trying to drink water but it just makes me feel rough.'

'Do you need to eat?' he asked as he put the kettle on.

She nodded. 'Probably. Not toast, though. I'm off toast.'

He found a packet of plain sea-salted crackers and put them down in front of her. 'How about these?'

She took one and nibbled the edge of it, and nodded. 'Lovely. Thanks.'

He was in a suit, she realised. Sharp suit, crisp white shirt, a silk tie she thought she recognised. Power-dressing. Why? Business meetings, of course. He must have been back to his apartment and picked up some more things.

'Successful day?'

He propped himself up against the kitchen cupboards and smiled slowly. 'Yes. I persuaded Bruno Andretti to waive his fees for representing Camilla.'

'You must have been quite convincing.'

'I was.'

Of course he was. She ran her eyes over him. The suit was immaculately cut, skimming his taut, muscular frame and subtly emphasising his masculinity. Power dressing, indeed. He looked amazing in it, and just looking at him made her mouth water.

'Go and change, and then come back. We need to go shopping. I meant to go earlier, but I fell asleep, so there's nothing to eat tonight. Go. Shoo.' She picked up her tea, grabbed another cracker and settled back on the sofa to wait for him.

They went to the supermarket and picked up a few things, and then while she curled up on the sofa in front of the television he fried chicken and cherry tomatoes, piled them in a dish and baked it in the oven while they watched the news, and then he served it with a bowl of penne pasta tossed in light olive oil and basil.

He'd stirred some mascarpone through his, because the bland and inoffensive chicken cacciatore was missing the soft and creamy cheese, but he hadn't wanted to risk cooking it which might bring out the smell. He'd learned quite early on that smell was one of the main things that set her off, and he'd taken to visiting Massimo in his office for coffee in the mornings for that reason.

'Yummy,' she said, cutting off another piece of chicken. 'This is really good. I had no idea you could cook so well.'

'Of course I can cook. You really think Carlotta let us grow up without knowing something as essential as how to feed ourselves? We can all cook.'

'Did you leave the mascarpone out?'

'Only from yours. I didn't want to upset you. Did you want it?'

'No. It's great. Just right. I was a bit worried when you said what you were cooking, but I might have known you'd get round it somehow. I'm sorry, you must be so bored with my dull diet.'

'It's not that dull, and I'm sure I'll survive, *cara*,' he said softly, and he wanted to scoop her up in his arms and kiss the guilty little smile off her face. Just in time to tell her—

Oh, this was so hard.

He cleared the table, made them a drink and sat down beside her.

'No. Go the other side. Let's play chess. I could do with a mental challenge, it might wake me up.'

He lost. He lost two games running, and then put the set away, his heart pounding.

'Why are you doing that?'

'Because I can't concentrate. I need to talk to you, Anita. There's something I should have told you years ago, something you need to know.'

Finally.

She sat back against the sofa and searched his face. His expression was serious, his eyes troubled. She patted the sofa beside her.

'Come here,' she said softly. 'Whatever it is, we can deal with it.'

He hoped so. Oh, how he hoped so, but he was very much afraid she was wrong, because there was a flaw in him that he didn't think even Anita could fix.

And he didn't dare risk giving her that chance, because in trying to fix him, she could end up broken, and who would fix her? Not him. He had no skills in that department. His only skill seemed to be in doing the opposite, and he'd passed that one with flying colours.

CHAPTER NINE

HE sat down beside Anita, put his arm around her and drew her in to his side.

He was tense, his whole body taut, and she snuggled closer and slipped her arms around him. 'Hey, relax, this is only me,' she said quietly. 'Whatever it is, it won't change what I feel about you. Just tell me, and then we'll talk about it.'

She made it sound so easy—but maybe it was. Maybe he just needed to say it.

'It was just before our affair,' he began, and she felt her heart start to pound harder. She'd known it was something to do with that time. Maybe now, finally, she was going to find out why they'd split up. He'd gone to work one morning with a tender kiss and a promise for later, and when he came home that evening, he told her it was all over. No warning, nothing. Finished. And she'd been devastated.

'It was September, and the weather was glorious,' he went on. 'I had a brief affair, with a girl called Kirsten. She was Australian and over here studying art history. She was based in the Uffizi at the time, and she was bright, savvy and we had a fling. Only she didn't think it was a fling, she'd thought it was much more serious than that. I'd kept it light, she never came to my apartment and I never spent the night with her, but somehow she fell in love with me anyway.'

Somehow? Anita nearly laughed, except she knew just how poor Kirsten felt. Falling in love with Gio was painfully easy.

'I don't know how she managed to convince herself it was more,' he said, sounding genuinely perplexed. 'I was very careful to keep it simple, as uncomplicated and casual as possible. I really, really didn't lead her on, because I didn't want her to think I was offering more than I was. It was a pleasant enough interlude, she was a lovely girl, we had fun, but that was all it was, Anita, all it was ever meant to be. So I ended it, as gently as I could, and she got upset. There was nothing else I could do, I didn't love her, I wasn't going to marry her, and I felt I'd made that quite clear all along, but she didn't want to hear it.

'She stalked me for a while until I told her firmly to leave me alone, and then she gave up and I assumed she'd got over me and moved on. And then I went to your brother's wedding, and you were there, of course, and we had rather too much to drink and danced all night. And the next day we went back to Firenze, and I took you out for dinner, and then afterwards I took you back to my apartment and made love to you for the first time.'

He touched her cheek, his eyes sad. 'It was amazing. I'd wanted to do it for so long, and it was better than I could ever have imagined. And we had fun, didn't we? Lots of fun. We did all sorts of silly things, and we spent every spare minute together, and it was great. And then one day I had a letter, at work, from Kirsten's parents. She was in hospital in Adelaide. She'd seen us together, apparently, and she'd flown home, got some pills and taken an overdose.'

'Oh, Gio, no!' She'd known something shocking was coming, but not this. She reached up, tracing her fingers over his face, seeing the lines of grief etched in his skin. 'Oh, I'm so sorry. Did she survive? Was she all right?'

'Yes. Yes, she survived, and she was expected to make a full recovery, but she told her parents she'd wanted to die because she couldn't get over me, and then after she'd been admitted to hospital the doctors realised that she was pregnant.'

Pregnant? Anita's fingers stilled against his face, and her hand dropped to her lap. She'd wondered, but...

'You've got a child?' she asked numbly.

'No. That's the worst thing.' He sucked in a ragged breath. 'She lost the baby, Anita,' he said, his voice hollow. 'She lost the baby because I couldn't love her the way she wanted me to. She really shouldn't have got pregnant. I was careful—so careful—but maybe she sabotaged that in an attempt to keep me. Or maybe it wasn't even mine. I don't know. She said she didn't realise she was pregnant when she took the pills, and I have no way of knowing if that's the truth, but it makes no difference. She tried to kill herself because I let her down, and so a baby died because of me, and I will never forgive myself for that.'

'No.' She couldn't let him believe that. She couldn't believe he did, it was so far off the mark. 'A baby died because its mother let herself believe in something that wasn't true. You hadn't egged her on, made her false promises, told her you loved her. You didn't tell her you loved her?'

'No! No, of course I didn't. It wouldn't have been true.'

'So you hadn't led her on, but nevertheless she'd painted a happy-ever-after for the two of you that was never going to happen. Trust me, it's easy to do. I know that. It's what I did in those few short weeks when we seemed so happy.

But then you came home one day, with no hint, no clue, no warning whatsoever, and told me it was over. Was that the day you got the letter?'

He nodded slowly, his eyes filled with regret. 'Yes, that was the day I got the letter. I didn't know what else to do. I was stunned, on auto-pilot, and the only thing I could think was that I had to end it before you had a chance to convince yourself you were in love with me, and certainly before you became pregnant. But you've already told me how much I'd hurt you, and you were painting happy-ever-afters, so I was already too late,' he added, his voice strained.

'Oh, Gio,' she said with a tender smile. 'It was always going to be too late. I'd been doing the same thing every time you noticed me since I was fourteen and my hormones kicked in. Only this wasn't just noticing me, it was much, much more than that, and because we seemed so happy, I let myself fall even deeper in love with you.' She shook her head. 'Gio, why didn't you just tell me about her when you got the letter? You tell me everything, but you didn't tell me that. Why not?'

He shook his head. 'I don't know. I just wanted to protect you, in the only way I knew how, which was to get you away from me as quickly as possible before I could hurt you, too.'

'Why did you think you would hurt me?'

'Because I always hurt everybody. I've had a rule, for years, not to get involved with nice girls. Only sleep with women who know the rules. And rule number one, don't sleep with your friends. And you were my best friend, Anita, and I'd broken my rule. And I thought if you fell in love with me, at some point it would get messy and I'd want out, because I always did, and I was afraid you might do the same thing as Kirsten, only you might have been more successful. I couldn't have lived with that, with the knowledge that you'd died because I'd let you believe that I was in it for the long haul. So I had to make it clear there was no long haul and never would be, because I don't seem to be able to do it.'

'Maybe you've never let yourself try.'

'I have. Of course I have. I gave up trying, years before Kirsten. She just caught me unawares, and she just proved what I'd known all along. I'm a lousy bet, Anita. I hurt every woman I touch.'

'Will you tell me something? Honestly? How many times have you told a woman you love her?'

He stared at her blankly, then looked away. 'Never.'

'Because you've never loved anyone, or because you've never committed to it?'

'I've never loved anyone. I don't seem to be able to. I like them, I'm fond of them, I enjoy their company, but none of them make me feel—'

Like you.

He nearly said it out loud, but he was glad he hadn't, because it took his breath away.

Was that it? Was the reason he'd never loved anyone before because none of them had been Anita?

'Maybe you've never let yourself love, Gio. Maybe it's never mattered enough to try and make a relationship work, and so you've never let your guard down before. Perhaps there's never been enough at stake before, and maybe now you should, because there is. There's a lot at stake here, Gio. Maybe it's time to try.'

He met her eyes, aching to believe her, but the thought of hurting her was anathema to him. 'What if I fail, Anita?' he said, his voice strained. 'What if this all loses its gloss and we end up hating each other? I'll break your heart, and I couldn't bear to do that.'

'No, you won't. No more than you have in the past. And anyway, we won't hate each other. No more than we already do. And if you're worried you'll get bored, I'll have to find ways to make it entertaining,' she said with a gentle, slightly mischievous smile.

She reached up and touched his cheek with the backs of her fingers, her caress tender. 'Gio, you can't hurt me, not unless you're deliberately unkind. I've loved you forever, and nothing's going to change that. And if we can make this work, for ourselves and for our child, isn't that better than never having the courage to try?'

He swallowed. 'I don't know,' he said after a long hesitation. 'I seem to have this fatal flaw, and I don't know if I've got what it takes. And I'm so afraid I'll hurt an innocent child. You're an adult. I worry enough about hurting you, Anita, but our baby—I couldn't hurt our baby. I've already got one child on my conscience. I can't have another.'

His words echoed in her head, going round and round.

I've already got one child on my conscience. I can't have another. Can't have another. Already got one. Can't have—

She sat back, realisation dawning. 'Is that why you're here?' she asked, shocked. 'Why you've insisted on looking after me? Because you're afraid I'll do something foolish and harm the baby? Gio, *never!* I will never, *ever* harm our child, or myself. I feel desperately sorry for your Kirsten, but I've spent my whole life knowing that you'll never love me the way I love you, and I'm not going to suddenly do something foolish because I've found out I'm pregnant, any more than you are.'

'Me?'

'Well, yes. Why not? I won't marry you under these

circumstances, and I've told you that, but I never for a moment thought you'd go off and try and kill yourself because of that. I know you better, I know your strengths, and you really ought to know mine.

'I'm tough, Gio. I can do this alone, and I will if necessary, but I'd much rather do it with you by my side, and if you find you can love me, if you find that our relationship is different to all your others and you want to stay, then maybe we *could* get married. In the meantime, I'll carry on, and you'll have to decide for yourself what kind of a relationship you want with me, long or short term, and I'll do my best to go along with it, because come hell or high water, we're going to be together in some form over this. We've got a child to bring up, and it's down to you whether we do it separately or together. And the only way to find out if we can do it is to try.'

He stared at her, and let his breath out in a whoosh. 'Really? You'd do that—take that big a risk, for me?'

It was the biggest gamble of her life, but she had no choice. If she was ever to win Gio, to convince him that he could love her, then she knew instinctively that this was her only chance.

'Why not?' she said gently. 'What have I got to lose? I *love* you. And if you give yourself a chance, who knows, maybe you can love me, too. But you have to try, or you'll never know.'

Could he trust himself enough to try? Trust her? He wasn't sure. What if she suddenly realised she wasn't as strong as she thought? What if it all fell apart and she found she couldn't take it and wanted out? If he let himself love her…

But if he didn't try, if he didn't let her try, then they'd lose it all anyway. Life had no guarantees.

'OK,' he said, feeling the ground fall away from under his feet. 'We'll try—but I'm not promising anything, Anita. I've never stuck at this in my life, and I'm thirty five. That's a long time to spend moving on.'

'I know. And we'll take it step by step, and I won't put any pressure on you, I promise. Let's just see what happens.'

Her eyes were gentle, her face so close he only had to move his head a little way for their lips to touch.

She met him halfway, her breath easing over his face in a soft sigh as their lips met. With a ragged groan he gathered her into his arms and kissed her as if she was the most precious thing he'd ever held, and deep inside her, she felt a glimmer of hope spring to life.

She knew he loved her. All she had to do was wait for him to realise it, too.

Sliding her arms around his neck, she kissed him back, kicking it up a gear, and with a groan he shifted her in his arms and stood up, carrying her to the bed and laying her down in the cloud-soft bedding.

He took her clothes off slowly, item by item. Her sweater. Her jeans, already too tight so that the stud had to be undone. Her bra, also on the small side now. The tiny scrap of matching lace that barely covered those soft, moist curls.

She was exquisite, and he wanted her so badly he thought he'd die. He stripped off his clothes, shucking off his jeans and shorts and socks in one movement, and then rolled back to her, gathering her into his arms again and covering them to keep out the chill.

He kissed her all over, paying homage to every inch of her body. He hesitated for a moment, his lips pressed low down against her abdomen, close to their child, and he vowed to do his best to make this work, for all their sakes.

She touched him gently, her fingers threading through his hair in a tender caress. 'Gio?'

He shifted back up the bed, cradling her head in his hands and kissing her deeply. He had to have her, had to make love to her before he went crazy, and he was about to reach for his wallet when he stopped himself. Not necessary. She was already pregnant with his child, and that brought a whole new dimension to their lovemaking.

It was the first time in his life he'd made love to a woman without a barrier between them, and the physical sensation was incredible, but the emotional connection was even stronger. And as he lay with her afterwards, cradling her gently against his heart as their breathing returned to normal and their heart rates slowed, he knew that nothing he'd ever experienced before in his life could touch this.

Was it love? He didn't know. Whatever it was, it was the most beautiful, most terrifying thing he'd ever experienced, and it left him deeply shaken and humbled and more determined than ever that this was going to work.

It had to. The alternative was unthinkable.

The next few weeks were the most amazing and nerve-racking of his life.

When he wasn't working on the estate or in Firenze, he looked after her, cooking for her to make sure she ate sensibly, going out for short walks to make sure she got some fresh air. And when he was working, he sent her texts, and flowers, and left notes for her inside the fridge.

He spent more and more time working in the family business alongside Massimo, taking over some of the admin and marketing work. This freed his brother up to do what he really wanted to do, which was experiment with new varieties of grapes and olives, to improve and expand their range of products, but it also meant he could go home to Anita for lunch, and sometimes lunch stretched into the afternoon…

March turned into April, and the weather was glorious. They got the cushions out of storage and put them on the benches around her loggia, and in the afternoons they lay there bathed in the slanting sun and read books and dozed.

And at night, they made love.

But still, he held something back, because he wanted to be sure, didn't want to say 'I love you' until he could be certain he meant it. Not when the stakes were so high.

And Anita waited, but the words just didn't come.

No matter. He did love her, she was more sure than ever, and she could wait. She'd waited decades. Another few weeks weren't going to kill her.

She went to see Luca, one day when Gio was in Firenze. She rang him, and he was at home, so she went to speak to him about managing her care during her pregnancy.

'How's it going?'

She smiled. 'OK. Gio's being amazing.'

'Yeah, he's around a lot. How is that?'

She felt herself colour. 'Good. Well, some of it. Luca, I've tried to convince him to give himself a chance to make this really work, but he can't believe that he can really love anyone. I don't know if he ever will.'

'That's ridiculous. Of course he loves you.'

'I know, but it's not that simple.' She hesitated, then she said, 'There was a woman, an Australian. Something happened, something I can't tell you, but it's made him so wary. It's as if it's broken something inside him.'

'Well, if anyone can mend it, Anita, it's you. I knew

there was something. I'm glad he's told you. I have no idea what it is, but he needed to talk about it, and I'm glad he's trusted you with it. It's a good sign.'

'I hope so. Luca, about the baby. Isabelle and Lydia tell me I need to sort out my maternity care and I'll need a scan, they said. Can you sort it for me, or at least point me in the right direction?'

He smiled. 'I knew you were going to ask me that. I'd rather not look after you myself, it's a bit personal and you might not want to look at me over the dinner table afterwards, but I'll get someone on my team to supervise your care, and if you're OK with it, I'll make sure I'm up to date with your notes so you can ask me anything you aren't sure about.'

She nodded, and he went on, 'You'll need a scan at about twelve weeks. I take it you're still a bit vague on your dates?'

She gave a wry chuckle. 'Well, I can tell you the only dates I could have conceived, if that helps pin it down. There's a ten day window, right smack in the middle of your holiday. Stick a pin in it.'

His mouth twitched. 'That'll be fine. I'll get the paperwork done and book you an appointment at the right sort of time. We'll be able to give you a pretty exact gestational age from the scan measurements. Anything else?'

'No. I'll leave you to get on. I know you're up to your eyes in paperwork, because Isabelle said you were. I'm sorry if I've held you up.'

He hugged her warmly. 'You haven't held me up at all. It's a pleasure to talk to you, Anita. It always is. And for what it's worth, I'm delighted you're having my brother's baby. It's about time something normal and adult happened to him. He's spent far too long chasing a lifestyle he doesn't even like.'

It was an interesting remark, and she wondered which bit of his lifestyle Luca was referring to. The work, as a lawyer? Or his love life—actually, scratch that. Not *love* life. Social life? Private life? Better. More accurate.

She tried not to think about all the women who'd been in his life. She hadn't been a nun, exactly, but there had been very few men in her life, and none of them had had a prayer of living up to Gio. And since their affair five years ago, there had been no one. If she couldn't have Gio, she didn't want anyone, and she'd officially resigned herself to being an old maid.

She went back to her house and checked her phone for messages. Oops. Some of her brides were getting antsy, and she made a few phone calls, set up some meetings and decided she really, really ought to tell the ones who were booked for later in the year that she wouldn't be available to run their wedding days, even if she was able to set everything up for them at this point.

She mentioned it to Gio when he got home, and he pulled off his tie, dropped into the corner of the sofa next to her and put his feet up on the coffee table.

'Cancel them. Tell them you aren't going to be available if you don't want to do it. *Do* you really want to do it?'

Did she? 'I'm not sure,' she said slowly. 'Some of them are just spoiled brats who want every last thing going, and I hate arranging celebrity-style weddings for empty-headed little girls who don't seem to think at all about the real meaning of marriage, but some of them—some of them are just lovely, and when it's really important to them and I can give them the day of their dreams, it's just fabulous.'

'So cherry-pick,' he said, as if it were that simple, which

maybe it was. 'You won't need the money, I've got more than enough for both of us, and you'll have plenty to do when the baby comes. Do as much or as little as you want.'

'You don't mind if I work?'

He laughed softly. 'Do I have any say in it? I'm not your husband, Anita, and I'm certainly not your guardian. It's entirely up to you what you do with your life. But no. Of course I don't mind. But before we go much further down the line, we ought to talk about where we're going to live.'

'We?' she said tentatively, but he just shrugged.

'You, then, at any rate. You and the baby. Will you stay here, or do you want to live in Firenze?'

So not we, then, she thought and felt her spirits nose-dive. 'Why not here? It's got everything I need and my family are close by.'

'It's a little small. We could do with another bedroom or two, and I was thinking the area beyond the loggia would be perfect for a swimming pool. I can just see it now—an infinity pool, with nothing beyond but the valley. Gorgeous. Fantastic.'

She laughed softly. 'Gio, I don't have that sort of money to spend.'

'But I do,' he said, his voice quiet and sincere. 'The pool is just a bit of nonsense, but the bedrooms—well, it would be nice to have it all done before you have the baby. You don't want the dirt and disruption afterwards.'

He was talking about investing his money in her house. Buying into the relationship? It sounded very much like it. Very much like commitment, but still there was no sign of those little words she was waiting for, and he couldn't seem to settle on 'we' or 'you'.

'By the way, Camilla Ponti's going to be OK,' he told

her, catching her by surprise. 'I've spoken to Marco, her ex business partner, and he's going to take her back.'

That surprised her. 'Just like that?'

He laughed. 'Well, not quite. He had no idea she had a child with disabilities. She'd never said anything about her private life, and so he had no idea what she was dealing with in terms of her finances or the personal stresses she was under. So he's taking her back, in a different role, for a small fixed salary which will be just enough to live on, and he's going to pay her son's fees for as long as she behaves. And if it goes well, she gets a pay rise.'

'Wow. That's impressive. How did you talk him into that?'

He gave a wry smile. 'I took him to the care home when she was there, and she introduced him to her son. He came away in tears.'

'Have you met the boy?'

He nodded, his smile fading. 'Yes. And I have to say, the staff there are amazing, and it's worth every cent of what she pays. He's very limited in what he can do, but they can tell when he's responding and they communicate with him far more than I would have thought they could. And so he's contented, which is more than I would have expected considering the level of frustration he must feel.'

'That's so sad.'

'It is. It's incredibly sad.' He held his arm up, making space for her next to him. 'Come here.'

She scooted over, snuggling in next to him, and he laid his hand over the little bump that was now beginning to show.

'*Ciao*, baby,' he said softly, giving her bump a gentle stroke with his fingers. 'You doing all right in there?'

'Seems to be. I went and saw Luca today, and he's going

to book me in for a scan for around about the twelve week mark.'

'May I come?'

She took her gaze from that gentle, caring hand and looked up at him. There was a curiously diffident expression in his eyes, as if he wasn't at all sure of her answer, and she hugged him.

'Oh, Gio, of course you can. It's your baby, too.'

His mouth flickered into a smile. *'Grazie,'* he murmured, and kissed her.

She laid her hand over his. 'I hope the baby's all right,' she said softly, her fears for it coming to the surface now after their conversation about Camilla's son.

'So do I, Anita, but if it isn't, if there's anything wrong with it, it won't make any difference. I'll still love it. You were wrong about that, you know. It's not that I can't find it in my heart to love our child, rather that I don't trust myself not to let it down, but until you were pregnant I don't think I really understood what it meant to be a parent. Not in a personal way. I understood the physical responsibility, and the need for emotional security, but I didn't understand what it would feel like to know that your child is slowly growing and developing, turning into a real person that's part of you. I do now, and I know that whatever happens to us, I could never walk away from this.'

'Oh, Gio.'

She tilted her head and stretched up, pressing a kiss to the rough plane of his jaw, and he turned his head and found her mouth and kissed her lingeringly.

'Are you hungry?' he asked. 'Do you need to eat soon?'

She smiled against his mouth. 'No. I've been eating biscuits all afternoon.'

'Good. Because I have something else in mind for you

right now,' he said with a cheeky grin that reminded her of the boy she'd first fallen in love with. He pulled her to her feet, took her out into the hall and turned right instead of left.

'What? Where are you taking me?'

'It's a surprise,' he said, and ushered her out of the front door.

He took her for a picnic to the chestnut woods on the Valtieri estate.

They parked the car and he got a wicker picnic hamper out of the back and threw a blanket over his shoulder and they followed the path down to an opening in the trees. The valley stretched out in front of them for miles, and they could see the *palazzo,* and Luca and Isabelle's house, and nestling in the trees was her house, with her parents' much larger villa just beyond.

'I love it here,' she said, settling down onto the picnic blanket with a contented sigh and wrapping her arms around her knees so she could see the view.

He dropped down beside her, lying out full length and folding his arms behind his head. 'You always did. If ever I couldn't find you and there'd been a ruckus of some sort, I'd know where you'd be.'

'I still come here sometimes, when I feel crowded or I need to think about stuff.'

'So do I. We spent so much time in these woods when we were kids. Do you remember?'

She lay down beside him, and he put his arm out so she could use it as a pillow. 'Of course I remember. I remember you falling out of that tree over there and breaking your leg, and I had to ride your bike down to the *palazzo* and try and find someone to help get you down, and you were so cross because you said you could have sat on the bike and freewheeled down.'

'I could have,' he said with a smile.

'And if you'd fallen off? You would have made it far worse and your mother would have killed me.'

He chuckled. 'Very likely. Do you remember when I crashed the bike into a tree?'

'Yes. You were so badly winded I thought you'd never breathe again.'

'*You* thought that?' he said, laughing. 'I thought I'd lie there and slowly suffocate, waiting for my lungs to re-inflate. It was a nightmare. I never did tell my parents about that.'

She smiled and laid her hand over the baby. 'I wonder if it's going to be a boy like you,' she said, and pulled a face. 'It'll be a nightmare to bring up.'

'I'm sure we'll cope,' he said, and there it was again, the 'we' word, hanging in the ether.

He pulled her closer, and she lay there in the crook of his arm and rested her cheek on his chest and wondered what the future held for them.

CHAPTER TEN

'I'VE got my scan appointment through.'

He hung up his jacket on the back of a chair and took the letter out of her hand. 'I'll see if I'm free. If not, I'll have to shuffle things.'

He sat down next to her, kissed her absently and pulled out his smart phone. 'OK. Here's my calendar. Yes, I can do that, I think. I'll have to move a client, but that's fine. Is this the clinic's address?'

'I think so.'

He nodded, tapping it into his phone. 'OK. You ought to have this calendar on your phone, so you know where I am at any time.'

She blinked. 'Why would I need to know that?'

He shrugged, and she smiled and leant over and kissed him, reading his mind. 'Nothing's going to happen, Gio,' she said. 'I'm fine.'

'Nevertheless, you might need to know where I am, and I'd like to know where you are. Do you have a virtual calendar?'

'Of course I do. I use it to keep track of all my weddings and meetings. I'd be lost without it.'

He hesitated for a second, then said, 'Want to swap passwords?'

She stared at him. This was a big thing for him. It didn't sound like much, but to give her access to his every movement, and to ask for hers—that was a real investment for him. 'Sure,' she said slowly. 'I'll get my phone.'

It made sense. She could see that. She was just amazed that *he* could, that he'd feel it was necessary to share all his movements with her—unless he wanted to be able to keep tabs on her because he was still worried she'd do something foolish. Either that or he wanted to know how much she was doing so he could interfere and tell her to cut back.

Or maybe, she thought, it was just as he said, that it made sense to know what both of them were doing.

They swapped passwords, so she had his diary as well as her own on her phone, and she could update it daily. And then he made her put his number in her phone as the emergency contact number.

'Just in case. You never know. I've put you in as my contact now.'

Not his parents? Not one of his brothers?

Wow. She put her phone away, and went into the kitchen and started to prepare supper, still thinking about that.

'Hey, are you feeling up to cooking, or do you want me to do it?'

'No, I'm fine with it. I'm feeling better. Not brilliant, and I won't be brewing coffee or cooking cheese any time soon, but I might let you have meat again.'

He laughed, his eyes crinkling as he looked up at her from the sofa, and she went over to him and bent and kissed him, just because she could. She couldn't believe he'd put her in his phone as the emergency contact—

'You need some more clothes,' he said, staring appreciatively down her cleavage as she straightened up. 'You're beginning to blossom.'

'Is blossom a euphemism for getting bigger breasts?' she asked drily, and he chuckled.

'It might be. And your tummy's starting to show when you stand up.'

'I don't think it's anything to do with the baby. I think it's all the relentless carbs I've been eating.'

He got up and followed her back to the kitchen, sliding his hands round under her arms and cupping her breasts gently. 'Mmm. Whatever, it suits you.' His hands slid down, linking together over her tiny bump and easing her back against him, and he bent his head and nibbled her neck.

'Will supper keep?' he asked, his voice muffled, and she turned in his arms and smiled at him.

'I'm sure it will. What did you have in mind?'

'Oh, a little this and that.'

But his eyes were smouldering, and as he lowered his mouth to hers, she reached behind her and turned off the oven. Some things didn't need to be hurried…

He shifted his client, and got home in plenty of time to take her for her scan. She was drinking water all the way there in the car, following her instructions.

'I hope they don't keep me waiting too long,' she said wryly, but they didn't keep them waiting at all. Luca was there, and he greeted them both with a hug.

'Do you want me to go, or may I stay?'

'Stay,' Gio said, not even giving Anita a choice in the matter, because he was suddenly afraid for the baby and if there was anything wrong, he wanted Luca there to talk them through it.

Funny, he'd never thought of it before, but Camilla Ponti's son had brought home to him with vivid clarity just how badly things could go wrong, and it had only been then, meeting the boy and realising the depth of her commitment, that he'd realised what they'd inadvertently signed up to with this pregnancy.

What any couple expecting a baby signed up to.

'Anita?'

Luca, checking with her. She was nodding, and then she was lying down on a couch, undoing her too-tight jeans and sliding them down just far enough. She reached out her hand, and Gio gripped it, staring at the screen as the person wielding the ultrasound wand began to scan her.

'There we are. That's the head, the spine—and see that? Fluttering? That's the heart beating.'

He felt Anita let out a breath, and he squeezed her hand. The scan moved on, checking other things—the position of the placenta, verifying that there was only one baby, taking measurements for the dates.

Early. Early in their ten-day window—that second night, when they'd made love so hastily, so urgently? She'd torn open the foil with shaking hands. Had she damaged it? Maybe. He'd been too shot away with need and longing to notice, but it seemed irrelevant now, looking at the grainy and yet somehow extraordinarily clear image of his child.

'That all looks really good,' Luca said from behind him, and he rested a hand on his shoulder and squeezed it hard. 'There. You can both relax now.'

'Want a photo?'

'Yes, please,' they both said at once, and Gio asked for two. One each, so he could have one in his wallet and carry it everywhere with him.

She got off the couch and disappeared to the cloak-room to get rid of the litres of water she'd drunk, and Luca slung an arm round his shoulders and led him out to the waiting area.

'So. How does it feel?'

'Amazing,' he said, staring down at the photo in his hand. It blurred suddenly, and he had to blink hard to clear it. 'Absolutely amazing. I can't believe it's happening.'

'Oh, it's happening. You wait. It'll feel like ten minutes and you'll be woken up first thing on a Sunday morning by a child arriving on the bed with a great big smile and a story book.'

'Are you trying to put me off?'

Luca smiled and hugged him briefly. 'I wouldn't dream of it. You enjoy it. It's fantastic. Right, I have to go, I've got a clinic, but it's good to see you and I'm glad everything looks OK.'

'Thanks, Luca. For everything.'

He smiled and nodded, and left him there staring at the image of his baby. Was it conceived that night? It had been the night he'd made love to her for the first time in five years, and in that moment, right afterwards, he'd somehow known that everything had changed.

Was that how Kirsten had felt, the night their baby had been conceived?

Oh, Kirsten, I'm sorry. I didn't mean to hurt you. I never meant our child to die.

'Gio? Are you OK?'

He pulled himself together and smiled at Anita, suddenly realising just how OK he was. The past was past. It hadn't been his fault, he hadn't taken the drugs, he hadn't known she was pregnant, he had nothing to blame himself for. And now, he had the future to look forward to.

'Yes, I'm fine,' he said, blinking away the sudden tears. 'You?'

She smiled back, her face serene. 'Never better. Shall we go for lunch?'

'Good idea. Here, your photo.'

She tucked the envelope in her handbag and took the one he was looking at out of his hand.

'I wonder what it is?'

'Does it matter?'

'No. No, not at all. I just think a girl might be slightly less worrying to bring up.'

'Only until puberty,' he said drily, and ushered her out of the clinic.

He stood at the window of his apartment in Firenze, staring out over the distant hills and contemplating his future.

His life was changing drastically, and everything about it was good. The baby was doing well, and they seemed to be getting on fine.

More than fine. Brilliantly well. He was happier than he'd ever been in his life, and she was blooming. He couldn't imagine it getting any better, and he knew, without a shadow of a doubt, that he would never tire of her. How could he when he loved her so much?

He loved her? Well, of course he did! He'd been gradually accepting it for weeks, and yet he'd never voiced it in his thoughts, never formalised it.

But yes. He loved Anita Della Rossa, with all his heart and soul, and he always had. No wonder his relationships had always foundered. They'd all been with the wrong woman.

It hit him like a thunderbolt, and he sat down abruptly. He loved her. He really, really loved her. Not just as a friend, but—how did it go? Truly, madly, deeply? He smiled, and then he laughed, and then he got up, left the apartment and drove home.

She wasn't there.

Odd. He'd checked her calendar, and she wasn't supposed to be doing anything this afternoon, unless something had come up since he'd synchronised it last night.

Maybe she'd decided to go shopping, or have lunch with the girls, he thought, disappointed that she wasn't at home when he had to tell her this vital and amazing thing, and he tried to ring her, but it rang and rang, and then went to voicemail.

OK. Maybe she was busy. He'd try her later.

Still nothing. He left a message.

'I'm back home. Call me. I've got something to tell you.'

He went to see Massimo, and found him in the kitchen surrounded by his family.

'Can we have a quick word?'

'Of course.' He stood up, kissed Lydia in passing and ushered Gio into his office. 'What's up?'

'I've been thinking,' he said, getting straight to the point. 'You've got more than enough to do here, and hardly any time for your family. I already do all the company's legal work, and there's plenty more I could usefully do, like the stuff I've been doing. How about taking me on permanently?'

Massimo frowned at him, then blew out a long breath. 'Really? You'd dump your law practice?'

He shrugged. 'Maybe not entirely. But I'm sick of it. I've had enough of juggling people's lies, and it's time to look out for my own family. I'm going to be a father soon, and if Anita'll have me, I'm planning on being a husband. I don't want to be stuck in Firenze while they're here, and I've really enjoyed working with you. I think we could build the business, play to our strengths, find other areas to expand into. What do you say? Do you think it's viable?'

His brother stared at him for a long, long moment, then let out a huff of laughter. 'Oh, yes. I definitely think it's viable. Papà and I were talking about it only yesterday, wondering how we could persuade you away from the sinful city.'

He smiled. 'I need no persuading. I just have to convince Anita that she'll have me. Do you know where she is, by the way? I thought she'd be at home, but she's not, and I can't get her. I wondered if she was with Lydia or Isabelle, but her car isn't at their house and it's not here, either.'

'Shopping? I know she had a meeting this morning, because Lydia rang her, and she said something about going on to do a bit of clothes shopping while she was in town. Try her again. She was probably just somewhere noisy. And, yes, by the way. It would be great to have you on the team.'

'Good. Let's hope you're still saying that in a year's time.' He grinned, slapped Massimo on the back and left him, pulling out his phone as he ran down the steps to his car.

He called her again, left another message, and went home. She still wasn't there, and he began to get worried.

Her meeting had been just outside Chianciano, and there were good shops there, but surely by now she'd be on her way home? He rang her, and got her voicemail again.

'Anita, where are you? I'm starting to get worried. Call me.'

He'd give her half an hour. And in that time, he'd do the intelligent thing and go into her calendar and update it, just in case.

Nothing. No changes.

So where was she?

He couldn't drive there and look for her along the road, that was crazy. There were two routes, one via Pienza and Montepulciano, the other the quiet back road that ran through the forest and nature reserve. That was her most likely route, he thought, and the one where if she'd run out of petrol or broken down, she was less likely to be helped by a passing motorist. She couldn't change a puncture now, not while she was pregnant, so she'd be sure of having her phone on her. So why wasn't she answering it?

His mouth dry, he rang her again. 'Anita, please, call me! I don't know where you are, and I think something must have happened. Please, call me, *cara*. I love you.'

He hung up, beside himself. He'd have to try and find her. He picked up his phone, set off in the car towards Chianciano and then hesitated.

Was he just being a drama queen? Maybe she was just taking time out, doing what she always did?

The chestnut woods. Of course.

He'd check on the way. It wouldn't take him far off his route, and it would be stupid to go so far if that was all she was doing.

He skidded down the track and found her car immediately, parked by the side of the track near where they'd had their picnic the other week. It wasn't locked, and her bag was in it, her phone inside, with all its missed calls and voicemail messages from him. Still worried half to death, ready to kill her, he forced himself to walk towards the clearing.

And there she was, sitting on the ground under the tree he'd fallen out of as a child, and she turned her head and smiled at him and he thought he was going to be sick with relief.

'*Ciao,* Gio. I knew you'd find me. I've hurt my ankle.'

Thank God. He'd been so afraid—

'It probably wouldn't have killed you to have your phone on you,' he said gruffly, dropping it in her lap before sitting down beside her and pulling her into his arms.

'I left it in the car. Have you been trying to get me? I could hear it ringing, but I couldn't get there. I'm sorry.'

'Don't be. What have you done to your ankle?'

She shrugged. 'Just twisted it. I must have stood on a root or something, and it just turned under me, but I can't put any weight on it.' She rested her head against his shoulder. 'I'm sorry I worried you. I knew you'd know where to find me.'

'Only because I drove past the end of the track. I was going to Chianciano to look for you.'

'Ah. I walked out of the meeting. The bride was being unrealistic and stroppy, and I didn't need to have that sort of hassle, so I did what you suggested and cherry-picked her out of my life. Then I came here to think, and I've had rather more time to do it than I anticipated. Still, it's been useful. I've got lots to tell you.'

'I've got lots to tell you, too. Can I go first?'

'Sure. Just let me get these messages. They can't all be from you.'

'They might well be,' he said drily, and she bit her lip guiltily.

She started to listen to them, and one after the other, they grew more desperate, until by the last one she could tell he was coming unravelled.

Anita, please call me! I don't know where you are, and I think something must have happened. Please, call me, cara. I love you.

She stared at the phone. Did he mean it?

'Did you mean it?'

'What?'

'You said you love me.'

He smiled ruefully and brushed his knuckles over her cheek. 'Yes, *cara*, I meant it. *Te amo*, Anita. I love you. That's what I was coming home to tell you.'

'Oh, Gio!'

She burst into tears and flung her arms around him, sobbing. 'You have no idea how long I've waited to hear you say that,' she mumbled into his shirt, and he gathered her up against his chest and held her while she cried.

'I'm sorry,' she said, pulling herself together with an effort and tilting her head so she could see his face.

His eyes were tender, bright with tears, and he brushed the hair back from her face and kissed her slowly.

'I love you,' he said quietly. 'I think I've probably always loved you. That's why I've never been able to love anyone else, because none of them were you. I should have talked to you years ago, told you how I felt, but I didn't really understand it until now, when I couldn't find you. I knew I loved you—I'd realised that this morning while I was packing up some things in my apartment, but it was only when I couldn't get hold of you and I started to think of all the dreadful things that could have happened—'

'Shh,' she murmured, pulling his face down and kissing him gently. 'I'm sorry. I'm so, so sorry.'

'It's all right. It doesn't matter now.'

He let her go, to her regret, and got up—only he didn't, not really. He went up onto his knees, then bent one leg up so the foot was on the ground, and then he took her hand. On one knee?

'Gio?' she said softly, and he smiled.

'Marry me, Anita,' he said quietly. 'I know I've been an

idiot. I should have talked to you long ago, worked it out, because it's so blindingly obvious to me now, but I just didn't realise how much you meant to me, and I had no idea what happiness truly was until now. In fact it's such a recent revelation I haven't even got you a ring, but you're a difficult woman to please and I'm sure you'll have your own ideas,' he added with a smile.

'So, will you? Please? Marry me, and let me love you and look after you and our baby, and make a life for us, here in the country surrounded by our families?'

'Oh, Gio! Of course I will. I'd love to marry you,' she said, tears welling in her eyes, and he pulled her into his arms and kissed her as if she was the most precious thing in the universe.

Then he eased away, looking down into her face and wiping away a tear with his thumb. 'Come on, let's get you home and sort this ankle out.'

He scooped her up and put her in his car, and she sent him back to fetch her shopping and her bag, and then he drove her home, carried her inside and looked at her ankle.

'Do you think it needs hospital?' he asked, and she shook her head.

'No. We could ask Luca to look at it, but later. Stick some ice on it and come and sit down and let me tell you what I've been thinking.'

'Let me guess,' he said, sealing crushed ice in a bag and wrapping it in a towel before placing it gently on her foot. 'You want to ditch your business.'

'No, but I do want to scale it back, at least until the baby's older. How did you know?'

He smiled. 'Because I've spent the last few days planning how to scale back mine.'

Her eyes widened. 'You're closing your law practice?'

'Not entirely. I'm going into the family business, but I might keep a small amount of work going, maybe more locally. I'm sick of it, Nita. I've done nothing else for too long, and now it's time to come home, to the things that really matter. You, the baby, my family.'

He hadn't called her Nita for years, not since they'd been children, and it made her want to cry with happiness.

He looked down at her hand, stroking her ring finger. 'Just one thing,' he said, 'before you go off on maternity leave. I've got a job for you. How quickly can you arrange a wedding?'

She laughed. 'Oh, Gio, you'd be amazed.'

'Good. Because I've discovered that the idea of having you as my wife is getting more and more appealing, and I've realised I don't want to wait any longer than I absolutely have to.'

'Can you give me four weeks?'

'If I must. Can you organise the sort of wedding you want in that time?'

She laughed, the musical sound filling him with joy. 'Oh, Gio, of course I can. I've been planning it in my head since I was fourteen years old. I know *exactly* what I want.'

'Well, we'd better make sure you have it, then.'

They were married in the chapel in the *palazzo* five weeks later.

It took a little longer than she'd thought because they had to stop planning every few minutes to hug and kiss and talk some more. Highly distracting, but she wouldn't have changed it for the world.

She'd spent years now creating dream weddings for other people, and she knew exactly how to achieve what she wanted. It wasn't complicated.

No hoopla, no nonsense, no fireworks or star-studded ceilings in a marquee, no entertainment or extravagance.

Just the people they loved. Their family and friends, gathered round to celebrate their union, and she had her wish.

It was a glorious day. She wore a simple lace dress that fitted her beautifully and proudly showed off her baby bump, and an ancient lace veil that had belonged to her great-grandmother, and Lydia and Carlotta cooked the most amazing wedding breakfast. They set up tables in the colonnaded courtyard in the *palazzo,* and after they'd eaten they cleared them away and had dancing.

And then, when she began to flag, Gio scooped her up in his arms and carried her down the steps of the *palazzo* to the waiting car, and they were driven away.

Not home, not that first night, because the builders were in, but to the bridal suite of a nearby hotel.

She was still in her wedding dress, and they shed confetti all the way up stairs to their room, but nobody minded. They were well known in the area, and well loved, and it was a wedding they'd all been looking forward to for years.

Gio closed the door behind them, and drew her into his arms. She was still smiling. She'd been smiling that morning when she got up in her parents' home for the last time as a single woman, and she'd smiled all day.

'Happy?' he murmured.

'Very happy. You?'

He nodded, his eyes caressing her. 'Of course. How could I be anything else? I've got the most wonderful wife in the world, we're having a baby—life's perfect.' He bent his head and kissed her.

'*Te amo,* Anita. *Te amo...*'

* * *

Four and a half months later, at the end of October and right in the middle of harvest, Anita gave birth to his son.

He was born in the morning, and by evening he was at home with them, the crib all ready beside their bed, and after she'd fed him Gio changed his nappy, a little nervously despite all the practice on his nieces and nephews, and then settled down beside her, the baby cradled in his arms.

She rested her head on his shoulder, and he smiled down at her. 'OK?'

'Definitely. I'm glad he wasn't too early. I can still smell the paint.'

Gio laughed softly. 'The poor builders. They've been here all day clearing up the last of their mess, but at least he's got a nursery when he needs it, even if he hasn't got a name.'

'We'll choose one.'

'He might have to have two. How about Luigi?'

'No. How about Mario?'

'What, as in Super Mario?'

She laughed and snuggled closer. 'How about we put all the names in a pot and pull one out and call him that?'

He stared down at his baby, a tiny frown between his eyebrows as he stroked his fingers tenderly over his son's soft, downy cheek. 'Or we could call him Georgio, after Camilla's son. After all, in a distorted sort of way we owe him for all this. Without him, she wouldn't have been in that situation, and without us being thrown together we might never have come to our senses.'

'We?' She tilted her head round so she could see his face, and laughed at him, but not unkindly. 'I never lost my senses. I've been in love with you since I was tiny, and I've always known it. You're the one who came to his senses, and you certainly took your time.'

He hugged her with his free arm, snuggling her closer, holding the people he loved most in the world against his heart. How could he ever have doubted that he loved this wonderful, brave, generous woman who'd been his life-long companion and friend? He'd fought it for years, failed Kirsten not because she wasn't loveable but because his heart was already taken. He just hadn't admitted it, but there was no denying it now, and he bent his head and pressed a tender kiss to her lips.

'Well, at least you know it wasn't a hasty decision. So—Georgio?'

She nodded slowly. 'Yes. I like it, and I like the idea of calling our baby after him.' She gazed down at their baby, perfect in every way, and felt a wave of love so strong she had to blink away the tears.

'He's beautiful,' Gio said softly, and rested his cheek against her forehead. 'Just like his mother. Did I ever mention that I love you, Anita Valtieri?'

'I'm not sure. Say it again, just in case?'

She felt his smile, then the soft graze of stubble as he turned his head and kissed her tenderly.

Te amo, carissima. Te amo...'

* * * * *

THE LARKVILLE LEGACY

A secret letter…two families changed for ever

Welcome to the small town of Larkville, Texas, where the Calhoun family has been ranching for generations.

Meanwhile, in New York, the Patterson family rules America's highest echelons of society.

Both families are totally unprepared for the news that they are linked by a shocking secret.

For hidden on the Calhoun ranch is a letter that's been lying unopened and unread—until now!

Meet the two families in all eight books of this brand-new series:

My Dear Fabulous Reader,

This story challenged my ideas of what makes family, and made me look closely at my own life. It's a hard thing not quite belonging. Being the half- or step-sibling. You're one foot in and one foot out all the time. Never quite *fitting*. And whether or not you acknowledge it, and whether or not those around you mean it, there are always subtle ways that's reinforced.

So imagine what it would do to you if it was your primary family you felt you didn't belong in. And never understood quite why. For thirty years.

Meet Ellie Patterson. Days before this story begins, dancer Ellie discovers that the man she thought was her father is not, and that she has a whole second family in small-town Texas. Despite the fact she's never left New York, she jumps in a rental car and heads south to find the family she never knew she had. She's more than ready to leave money and privilege behind in exchange for people who she might fit with.

Except then she meets Jed…a man who's learned to live with his own demons. And for the first time family isn't the biggest thing on her mind.

This was a hard story to write, but the more I got to know Ellie and Jed (and Deputy!) the more I grew to love and understand them. When 'the end' came it was quite hard to let them go.

I hope you enjoy meeting them as much as I did.

Enjoy!

Nikki

SLOW DANCE WITH THE SHERIFF

BY
NIKKI LOGAN

Nikki Logan lives next to a string of protected wetlands in Western Australia, with her long-suffering partner and a menagerie of furred, feathered and scaly mates. She studied film and theatre at university, and worked for years in advertising and film distribution before finally settling down in the wildlife industry. Her romance with nature goes way back, and she considers her life charmed, given she works with wildlife by day and writes fiction by night—the perfect way to combine her two loves. Nikki believes that the passion and risk of falling in love are perfectly mirrored in the danger and beauty of wild places. Every romance she writes contains an element of nature, and if readers catch a waft of rich earth or the spray of wild ocean between the pages she knows her job is done.

For Lesley—because mothers are always
mothers, birth or otherwise.
And for Cil—because so are sisters.

CHAPTER ONE

SHERIFF JED JACKSON eased down on the brake and slid one arm across to stop his deputy sliding off the front seat.

'Well,' he muttered to the grizzly bear of a dog who cocked an ear in response, 'there's something you don't see every day.'

A sea of loose steer spilled across the long, empty road out to the Double Bar C, their number swollen fence-to-fence to seal off the single lane accessway, all standing staring at one another, waiting for someone else to take the lead. That wasn't the unusual part; loose cattle were common in these parts.

He squinted out his windscreen. 'What do you reckon she's doing?'

Adrift right in the middle of the massing herd, standing out white in a sea of brown hide, was a luxury sedan, and on its roof—standing out blue in a sea of white lacquer—was a lone female.

Jed's mouth twitched. Ten-fifty-fours weren't usually this entertaining, or this sizeable. This road didn't see much traffic, especially not with the Calhouns away, but a herd of cattle really couldn't spend the night here. His eyes lifted again to the damsel in distress, still standing high and dry with her back to him, waving her hands shouting uselessly at the cattle.

And clearly she couldn't.

He radioed dispatch and asked them to advise the Calhoun ranch of a fence breach, then he eased his foot off the brake and edged closer to the comical scene. The steer that weren't staring at one another looked up at the woman expectantly.

He pulled on the handbrake. 'Stay.'

Deputy looked disappointed but slouched back into the passenger seat, his enormous tongue lolling. Jed slid his hat on and slipped out the SUV's door, leaving it gaping. The steer didn't even blink at his arrival they were so fixated on the woman perched high above them.

Not entirely without reason.

That was a mighty fine pair of legs tucked into tight denim and spread into a sturdy A-shape. Not baggy denim, not the loose, hanging-low-enough-to-trip-on, did-someone-outlaw-belts, de-feminising denim.

Fitted, faded, snug. As God intended jeans to be.

Down at ground level, the length of her legs and the peach of a rear topping them wouldn't have been all that gratuitous but, from his steer-eye view, her short blouse didn't do much to offset, either.

The moaning of the cattle had done a good job disguising his arrival but it was time to come clean. He pushed his hat back with a finger to the rim and raised his voice.

'Ma'am, you realise it's a state offence to hold a public assembly without a permit?'

She spun so fast she almost went over, but she steadied herself on bare feet, and then lifted her chin with grace.

Whoa. She was…

His synapses forgot how they worked as he stared and he had to will them to resume sending the signals his body needed to keep breathing. He'd never been so grateful for his county-issue sunglasses in his life; without them she'd see his eyes as round and glazed as the hypnotised steer.

'I hope there's a siege happening somewhere!' she called, sliding her hands up onto her middle. Her righteousness didn't make her any less attractive. Those little clenched fists only accentuated the oblique angle where her waist became her hips. Her continuing complaint drew his eyes back up to the perfectly even teeth she flashed as she growled at him with her non-Texan vowels.

'Because I've been on this rooftop for two hours. The cows have nearly trebled since I called for help.'

Cows. Definitely a tourist.

Guess an hour was a long time when you were stuck on a roof. Jed kept it light to give his thumping pulse time to settle and to give her temper nowhere to go. 'You're about the most interest these steer have had all day,' he said, keeping his voice easy, moving cautiously between the first two lumbering animals.

He leaned back against the cattle as hard as they leaned into him, slapping the occasional rump and cracking a whistle through his curled tongue. They made way enough for him to get through, but only just. 'What are you doing up there?'

Her perfectly manicured eyebrows shot up. 'I assume that's a rhetorical question?'

A tiny part of him died somewhere. Beautiful and sharp. Damn.

He chose his words carefully and worked hard not to smile. 'How did you come to be up there?'

'I stopped for…' Her unlined brow creased just slightly. 'There were about a dozen of them, coming out in front of me.'

He nudged the nearest steer with his hip and then shoved into it harder until it shuffled to its right. Then he stepped into the breach and was that much closer to the stranded tourist.

She followed his progress from on high. It kind of suited her.

'I got out to shoo them away.'

'Why not just nudge through them with your vehicle?'

'Because it's a rental. And because I didn't want to hurt them, just move them.'

Beautiful, sharp, but kind-hearted. His smile threatened again. 'So how did you end up on the roof?' He barely needed to even raise his voice now; he was that close to her car. Even the mob had stopped its keening to listen to the conversation.

'They closed in behind me. I couldn't get back round to my door. And then more came and I…just…'

Clambered up onto the hood and then the roof? Something

caught his eye as he reached the front corner of the vehicle. He bent quickly and retrieved them. 'These yours?'

The dainty heels hung from one of his crooked fingers.

'Are they ruined? I kicked them off when I climbed up.'

'Hard to know, ma'am.'

'Oh.'

Her disappointment seemed genuine. 'Expensive?'

She waved away that concern. 'They were my lucky Louboutins.'

Get lucky more like it. He did his best not to imagine them on the end of those forever legs. 'Not so lucky for them.'

He edged along the side of the car to pass the shoes up to her and she folded herself down easily to retrieve them.

She stayed squatted. 'So…now what?'

'I suggest you get comfortable, ma'am. I'll start moving the steer back towards the fence.'

She glanced around them and frowned. 'They don't look so fierce from up here. I swear they were more aggressive before.'

'Maybe they smelled your fear?'

She studied him, curiosity at the front of her big blue-green eyes, trying to decide whether he was serious. 'Are you going to move them yourself?'

'I'll have Deputy help me until the men from the Double Bar C arrive.'

That got her attention. 'These are Calhoun cows?'

'Cattle.'

She pressed her lips together at his correction. 'That's where I was coming from. Calling on Jessica Calhoun. But she was out.'

He paused in his attempts at shoving through the steer and frowned. 'Jess expecting you?'

'What are you, their butler?'

Again with the sass. It wasn't her best feature, but it did excite his blood just a hint. Weird how your body could hate something and want it all at the same time. Maybe that was a carryover from his years in the city. 'I just figured I'd save you some time. Jess is more than out, she's on her honeymoon.'

That took the wind from her sails. She sagged, visibly.

'Sorry.' He shrugged and then couldn't help himself. He muttered before starting up on the steer-shoving again, 'Would you like to leave your card?'

She sighed. 'Okay, I'm sorry for the butler crack. You're a police officer—I guess it's your job to know everyone's business, technically speaking.'

A pat with one hand and a slap on the way back through. With no small amount of pleasure in enlightening her, he pointed at his shoulder. 'See these stars? That makes me county sheriff. Technically speaking.'

She blew at the loose strand of blond hair curling down in front of her left eye and carefully tucked it back into the tight braid hiding the rest of it from him. Working out whether to risk more sarcasm, perhaps?

She settled on disdain.

Good call. Women in cattle-infested waters…

'Well, Sheriff, if your deputy could rouse himself to the task at hand maybe we can all get on with our day.'

That probably qualified as a peace offering where she came from.

He lifted his head and called loudly, 'Deputy!'

One hundred and twenty pounds of pure hair and loyalty bounded out of his service vehicle and lumbered towards them. The cattle paid immediate attention and, as a body, began to stir.

'Settle,' he murmured. Deputy slowed and sat.

She spun back to look at him. 'That's your deputy?'

'Yup.'

'A dog?'

'Dawg, actually.'

She stared. 'Because this is Texas?'

'Because it's his name. Deputy Dawg. It would be disrespectful to call him anything else.'

'And he's trained to herd cows?'

He hid his laugh in the grunt of pushing past yet another stubborn steer. 'Not really, but from where I'm standing beggars can't be choosers—' he made himself add some courtesy '—ma'am.'

She squatted onto her bottom and slid her feet down the back windscreen of the car. They easily made the trunk.

'You have a point,' she grudgingly agreed, then gestured to a particular spot in the fence hidden to him by the wall of steer. 'The hole's over there.'

But her concession wasn't an apology and it wasn't particularly gracious.

Just like that, he was thinking of New York again. And that sucked the humour plain out of him.

'Thank you,' he said, then turned and whistled for Deputy.

Every single cell in Ellie Patterson's body shrivelled with mortification. Awful enough to be found like this, so absurdly helpless, but she'd been nothing but rude since the officer—sheriff—stopped to help her. As though it was somehow his fault that her day had gone so badly wrong.

Her whole week.

She shuddered in a deep breath and shoved the regret down hard where she kept all her other distracting feelings. Between the two of them, the sheriff and his...Deputy...were making fairly good work of the cows. They'd got the one closest to the hole in the fence turned around and encouraged it back through, but the rest weren't exactly hurrying to follow. It wasn't like picking up one lost duckling in Central Park and having the whole flock come scrambling after it.

The massive tricolour dog weaved easily between the forest of legs, keeping the cows' attention firmly on it and away from her—a small blessing—but the sheriff was slapping the odd rump, whistling and cursing lightly at the animals in a way that was very...well...Texan.

He couldn't have been more cowboy if he tried.

But there was a certain unconcerned confidence in his actions that was very appealing. This was not a man that would be caught dead cowering on the roof of his car.

Another animal lumbered through to the paddock it had come

from and casually wandered off to eat some grass. Thirty others still surrounded her.

This was going to take some time.

Ellie relaxed on her unconventional perch and channelled her inner Alex—her easygoing baby sister—scratching around for the positives in the moment. Actually, the Texan sun was pleasant once the drama of the past couple of hours had passed and once someone else was taking responsibility for the cows. And there were worse ways to pass the time than watching a good-looking man build up a sweat.

'Sure you don't want to come down here and help now that you've seen how docile they are?' the man in question called.

Docile? They'd nearly trampled her earlier. Sort of. Getting friendly with the wildlife was not the reason she drove all this way to Texas.

Not that she'd really thought through any part of this visit.

Two days ago she'd burst out of the building her family owned, fresh from the devil of all showdowns with her mother in which she'd hurled words like hypocrite and liar at the woman who'd given her life. In about as much emotional pain as she could ever remember being.

Two hours and a lot of hastily dropped gratuities later, she was on the I-78 in a little white rental heading south.

Destination: Texas.

'Very sure, thank you, Sheriff. You were clearly born for this.'

He seemed to stiffen but it was only momentary. If she got lucky, country cowboys—even ones in uniform—had dulled sarcasm receptors.

'So…Jess just got married?' she called to fill the suddenly awkward silence. Back home there was seldom any silence long enough to become awkward.

'Yep.' He slapped another rump and sent a cow forward. 'You said you know the Calhouns?'

I think I am one. Wouldn't that put a tilt in his hat and a heap more lines in his good ol' Texan brow.

'I… Yes. Sort of.'

He did as good a job of the head tilt as his giant dog. 'Didn't realise knowing someone or not was a matter of degrees.'

It really was poor on her part that two straight days on the road and she hadn't really thought about how she was going to answer these kinds of questions. But she hadn't worked the top parties of New York only to fall apart the moment a stranger asked a few pointed questions.

She pulled herself together. 'I'm expected, but I'm…early.' Cough. A couple of months early. 'I wasn't aware of Jessica's plans.'

They fell to silence again. Then he busied himself with more cows. They were starting to move more easily now that their volume had reduced on this side of the wire, inversely proportional to the effort the sheriff was putting in. His movements were slowing and his breath came faster. But every move spoke of strength and resilience.

'Your timing is off,' he puffed between heaving cows. 'Holt's away, too, right now and Meg's away at college. Nate's still on tour.'

Her chest squeezed. Two brothers and two sisters? Just like that, her family doubled. But she struggled to hide the impact his simple words had. 'Tour? Rock star or military?'

He slowly turned and stared right at her as if she'd insulted him. 'Military.'

Clipped and deep. Maybe she had offended him? His accent was there but nowhere near as pronounced as the young cowboy she'd met out at the Calhoun ranch who told her in his thick drawl that Jess wasn't home. Least that's what she'd thought he'd said. She wasn't fluent in deep Texan.

The animals seemed to realise there were now many more of them inside the field than outside it and they began to drift back through the fence to the safety of their numbers. It wasn't quick, but it was movement. And it was in the right direction.

The sheriff whistled and his dog immediately came back to his side. They both stood, panting, by her rental's tailpipe and watched the dawdling migration.

'He's well trained,' Ellie commented from her position above the sheriff's shoulder, searching for something to say.

'It was part of our deal,' he answered cryptically. Then he turned and thrust his hand up towards her. 'County Sheriff Jerry Jackson.'

Ellie made herself ignore how many cow rumps that hand had been slapping only moments before. They weren't vermin, just... living suede. His fingers were warm as they pressed into hers, his shake firm but not crippling. She tried hard not to stiffen.

'Jed,' he modified.

'Sheriff.' She smiled and nodded as though she was in a top-class restaurant and not perched on the back of a car surrounded by rogue livestock.

'And you are...?'

Trying not to tell you, she realised, not entirely sure why. For the first time it dawned on her that she'd be a nobody here. Not a socialite. Not a performer. Not a Patterson.

No responsibilities. No expectations.

Opportunity rolled out before her bright and shiny and warmed her from the inside. But then she remembered she'd never be able to escape who she was—even if she wasn't in fact who she'd thought she was for the past thirty years.

'Ellie.' She almost said Eleanor, the name she was known by in Manhattan, but at the last moment she used the name Alex called her. 'Ellie Patterson.'

'Where are you staying, Ellie?'

His body language was relaxed and he had the ultimate vouch pinned high on his chest—a big silver star. There was no reason in the world that she should be bristling at his courteous questions and yet...she was.

'Are you just making conversation or is that professional interest?'

His polite smile died before it formed fully. He turned up to face her front-on. 'The Calhouns are friends of mine and you're a friend of theirs...' Though the speculation in his voice told her he really wasn't convinced of that yet. 'It would be wrong of me to send you on your way without extending you some country courtesy in their place.'

It was credible. This was Texas, after all. But trusting had never come easy to her. And neither had admitting she wasn't fully on top of everything. In New York, that was just assumed.

She was Eleanor.

And she'd assumed she'd be welcomed with open arms at the Calhoun ranch. 'I'm sure I'll find a place in town…'

'Ordinarily I'd agree with you,' he said. 'But the Tri-County Chamber of Commerce is having their annual convention in town this week so our motel and bed and breakfasts are pretty maxed out. You might have a bit of trouble.'

Embarrassed heat flooded up her back. Accommodation was a pretty basic thing to overlook. She called on her fundraising persona—the one that had served her so well in the ballrooms of New York—and brushed his warning off. 'I'm sure I'll find something.'

'You could try Nan's Bunk'n'Grill back on I-38, but it's a fair haul from here.' He paused, maybe regretting his hospitality in the face of her bland expression. 'Or the Alamo, right here in town, can accommodate a single. It's vacant right now but that could change any time.'

Having someone organise her didn't sit well, particularly since she'd failed abysmally to organise herself. If she had to, she'd drive all the way to Austin to avoid having to accept the condescension of strangers.

'Thanks for the concern, Sheriff, but I'll be fine.' Her words practically crunched with stiffness.

He studied her from behind reflective sunglasses, until a throat gurgle from Deputy got his attention. He turned and looked back up the dirt road where a dust stream had appeared.

'That's Calhoun men,' he said simply. 'They'll deal with the rest of the steer and repair the fence.'

Instant panic hit her. If they were Calhoun employees, then they were her employees. She absolutely didn't want their first impression of her to be like this, cowering and ridiculous on the rooftop of her car. What if they remembered it when they found out who she was? She started to slide off.

Without asking, he stretched up over the trunk and caught her around the waist to help her dismount. Her bare feet touched softly down onto the cow-compacted earth and she stumbled against him harder than was polite.

Or bearable.

She used the moment of steadying herself as an excuse to push some urgent distance between them but he stayed close, towering over her and keeping the last curious cows back. A moment later, a truck pulled up and a handful of cowboys leapt off the tray and launched into immediate action. That gave her the time she needed to slip her heels back on and slide back into the rental.

She was Eleanor Patterson. Unflappable. Capable. Confident.

Once inside, she lowered her window and smiled her best New York dazzler out at him. 'Thank you, Sheriff—'

'Jed.'

'—for everything. I'll know better than to get out in the middle of a stampede next time.'

And just as she was feeling supremely on top of things again, he reached through her open window and brushed his fingers against her braided hair and retrieved a single piece of straw.

Her chest sucked in just as all the air in her body puffed out and she couldn't help the flinch from his large, tanned fingers.

No one touched her hair.

No one.

She faked fumbling for her keys and it effectively brushed his hand away. But it didn't do a thing to diminish the temporary warmth his brief touch had caused. Its lingering compounded her confusion.

But he didn't miss her knee-jerk reaction. His lips tightened and Ellie wished he'd take the sunglasses off so she could see his eyes. For just a moment. She swallowed past the lump in her throat and pushed away her hormones' sudden interest in Sheriff Jerry Jackson.

'Welcome to Larkville, Ms. Patterson,' he rumbled, deep and low.

Larkville. Really, shouldn't a town with a name like that have better news to offer? A town full of levity and pratfalls, not secrets and heartbreak.

But she had to find out.

Either Cedric Patterson was her father...or he wasn't.

And if he wasn't—her stomach curled in on itself—what the hell was she going to do?

She cleared her throat. 'Thank you again, Sheriff.'

'Remember...the Alamo.'

The timing was too good. Despite all her exhaustion and uncertainty, despite everything that had torn her world wide open this past week, laughter suddenly wanted to tumble out into the midday air.

She resisted it, holding the unfamiliar sensation to herself instead.

She started her rental.

She put it in gear.

Funny how she had to force herself to drive off.

CHAPTER TWO

LARKVILLE was lovely. Larkville was kind. Larkville was extremely interested in who she was and why she'd come and clearly disappointed by her not sharing. But no one in the small, old Texas town had been able to find a bed for her. Despite their honest best efforts.

Remember the Alamo…

Sheriff Jackson's voice had wafted uninvited through her head a few times in the afternoon since her sojourn with the cows but—for reasons she was still trying to figure out—she didn't want to take his advice. The Alamo might be a charming B & B run by the most delightful old Texan grandmother with handmade quilts, but she'd developed an almost pathological resistance to the idea of driving across town to check it out.

Although three others had suggested she try there.

Instead she'd steadfastly ignored the pressing nature of her lack of accommodation and she'd lost herself in Larkville's loveliest antique and craft shops as the sun crawled across the sky. She'd had half a nut-bread sandwich for a late lunch in the town's pretty monument square. She'd grabbed a few pictures on her phone.

None of which would help her when the sun set and she had nowhere to go but back to New York.

No. Not going to happen.

She'd sleep in her car before doing that. She had a credit card full of funds, a heart full of regrets back in New York and a possible sister to meet in Texas. She turned her head to the west and stared off in the direction of the Alamo and tuned in to the confusion roiling in her usually uncluttered mind.

She didn't want to discover that Texan grandmother had room for one more. She didn't want Sheriff Jed Jackson to be right.

Because his being right about that might cast a different light on other decisions she'd made about coming here. About keeping Jessica Calhoun's extraordinary letter secret from everyone but her mother. From her siblings. From her twin—the other Patterson so immediately affected. Maybe more so than her because Matt was their father's heir.

She drew in a soft breath.

Or maybe he wasn't, now.

Dread washed through her. Poor Matt. How lost was he going to be when he found out? The two of them might have lost the closeness they'd enjoyed as children but he was still her twin. They'd spent nine months entwined and embracing in their mother's womb. Now they'd be lucky to speak to each other once in that time.

She didn't always like Matt but she absolutely loved him.

She owed it to him, if not herself, to find out the truth. To protect him from it, if it was lies, and to break it to him gently if it wasn't.

A sigh shuddered through her.

It wasn't. Deep down Ellie knew that. Her mother's carefully schooled candor slammed the door on the last bit of hope she'd had that Jessica Calhoun had mixed her up with someone else.

Of their own accord, her feet started taking her back towards her car, back towards the one last hope she had of staying in Larkville. Back towards her vision of kindly grandmothers, open stoves and steaming pots full of home-cooked soup.

Back to the Alamo.

There were worse places to wait out a few days.

'Well, well...'

Ellie's shock was as much for the fact that the big, solid door opened to a big, solid man as it was for the fact that County Sheriff Jed Jackson had no reason to wear his sunglasses disguise indoors.

For a man so large, she wasn't expecting eyes like this. As pale as his faded tan T-shirt, framed by low, dark eyebrows and fringed with long lashes. His brown hair was dishevelled when not covered by a hat, flecked with grey and his five-o'clock shadow was right on time.

Coherent thoughts scattered on the evening breeze and all she could do was stare into those amazing eyes.

He slid one long arm up the doorframe and leaned casually into it. It only made him seem larger. 'I thought you'd have gone with Nan's Bunk'n'Grill out of sheer stubbornness,' he murmured.

Ellie tried to see past him, looking for signs of the hand-hewn craft and that pot of soup she'd convinced herself would be waiting. 'You're staying here?'

No wonder the tourists of Larkville couldn't find a place to sleep if the locals took up all the rooms.

His dark brows dipped. 'I live here.'

She heard his words but her brain just wouldn't compute. It was still completely zazzled by those eyes and by the butterfly beating its way out of her heart. 'In a B & B?'

'This is my house.'

Oh.

She stepped back to look at the number above the door. Seriously, how had she made it to thirty in one piece?

'You have the right place, Ellie.' Ellie. It sounded so much better in his voice. More like a breath than a word. 'This is the Alamo.'

'I can't stay with you!' And just like that her social skills fluttered off after her sense on the stiff breeze.

But Texans had thick hides, apparently, because he only smiled. 'I rent out the room at the back.' And then, when her feet didn't move, he added, 'It's fully self-contained.' And when she still didn't move... 'Ellie, I'm the sheriff. You'll be fine.'

Desperation warred with disappointment and more than a little unease. There was no lovely Texan nana preparing soup for her, but he was offering a private—warm, as her skin prickled up again at the wind's caress—place to spend the night, and she'd be his customer so she'd set the boundaries for their dealings with each other.

Though if her galloping heart was any indication that wasn't necessarily advisable.

'Can I see it?'

His smile twisted and took her insides with it. 'I'd wager you wouldn't be here if you'd found so much as an empty washroom. Just take it. It's clean and comfortable.'

And just meters from you...

She tossed her hair back and met his gaze. 'I'd like to see it, please.'

He inclined his head and stepped out onto the porch, crowding her back against a soft-looking Texan outdoor setting. She dropped her eyes. The house's comforting warmth disappeared as he pulled the door closed behind him and she rubbed her hands along her bare, slim arms. This cotton blouse was one of her girliest, and prettiest, and she'd been pathetically keen to make a good impression on Jessica Calhoun.

She hadn't really imagined still being outdoors in it as the sun set behind the Texan hills.

She followed him off the porch, around the side of the house and down a long pathway between his stone house and the neighbors'.

It was hard not to be distracted by the view.

Her fingers trailed along the stonework walls as they reached the end of the path. Jed reached up and snaffled a key from the doorframe.

'Pretty poor security for a county sheriff.' Or was it actually true what they said about small-town America? She couldn't imagine living anywhere you didn't have double deadlocks and movement sensors.

As he pushed the timber door open, he grunted. 'I figure

anyone breaking in is probably only in need of somewhere safe to spend the night.'

'What if they trash the place?'

He turned and stared at her. 'Where are you from?'

The unease returned and, until then, she hadn't noticed it had dissipated. She stiffened her spine against it. 'New York.'

He nodded as if congratulating himself on his instincts. He looked like he wanted to say something else but finally settled on, 'Larkville is nothing like the city.'

'Clearly.' She couldn't help the mutter. Manhattan didn't produce men like this one.

She shut that thought down hard and followed him into the darkened room and stared around her as he switched on the lights. It was smaller than her own bathroom back home, but somehow he'd squeezed everything anyone would need for a comfortable night into it. A thick, masculine sofa draped in patchwork throws, a small two-person timber table that looked like it might once have been part of a forge, a rustic kitchenette. And upstairs, in what must once have been a hayloft…

She moved quickly up the stairs.

Bright, woven rugs crisscrossed a ridiculously comfortable-looking bed. The exhaustion of the past week suddenly made its presence felt.

'They're handcrafted by the people native to this area,' he said. 'Amazingly warm.'

'They look it. They suit the room.'

'This was the original barn on the back of the building back in 1885.'

'It's…' So perfect. So amazing. 'It looks very comfortable.'

He looked down on her in the warm timber surrounds of the loft bedroom. The low roof line only served to make him seem more of a giant crowded into the tiny space.

She regretted coming up here instantly.

'It is. I lived here for months when my place was being renovated.'

She was distracted by the thought that she'd be sleeping in

Sheriff Jed Jackson's bed tonight, but she stumbled out the first response that came to her. 'But it's so small….'

His lips tightened immediately. 'Size isn't everything, Ms. Patterson.'

What happened to 'Ellie'? He turned and negotiated his descent quickly and she hurried after him, hating the fact that she was hurrying. She forced her feet to slow. 'This will be very nice, Sheriff, thank you.'

He turned and stared directly at her. 'Jed. I'm not the sheriff when I'm out of uniform.'

Great. And now she was imagining him out of uniform.

Unfamiliar panic set in as her mind warmed to the topic. It was an instant flashback to her childhood when she'd struggled so hard to be mature and collected in the company of her parents' sophisticated friends, and feared she'd failed miserably. Back then she had other methods of controlling her body; now, she just folded her manicured nails into her palm and concentrated on how they felt digging into her flesh.

Hard enough to distract, soft enough not to scar.

It did vaguely occur to her that maybe she'd just swapped one self-harm for another.

'You haven't asked the price,' he said.

'Price isn't an issue.' She cringed at how superior it sounded here—standing in a barn, out of context of the Patterson billions.

His stare went on a tiny bit too long to be polite. 'No,' he said. 'I can see that.'

Silence fell.

Limped on.

And then they both chose the exact same moment to break it.

'I'll get a fire started—'

'I'll just get my bags—'

She opened the door to the pathway and the icy air from outside streamed in and stopped her dead.

A hard body stepped past her. 'I'll get your bags, you stay in the warm.'

His tone said he'd rather she froze to death, but his country courtesy wouldn't let that happen.

'But I—'

He didn't even bother turning around. 'You can get the fire going if you want to be useful.'

And then he closed the door in her face.

Useful. The magic word. If there was one thing Eleanor Patterson was, it was useful. Capable. A doer. Nothing she couldn't master.

She took a deep breath, turned from the timber door just inches from her face and stared at the small, freestanding wood fire and the basket of timber next to it, releasing her breath slowly.

Nothing she couldn't master…

The night air was as good as a cold shower. Jed's body had begun humming the moment he opened his door to Ellie Patterson, and tailing those jeans up the steep steps to the loft hadn't reduced it. He had to work hard not to imagine himself throwing the Comanche blankets aside and plumping up the quilt so she could stretch her supermodel limbs out on it and sleep.

Sleep. Yeah, that's what he was throwing the blankets aside for.

Pervert.

She was now his tenant and she was a visitor to one of the towns under his authority, a guest of the Calhouns. Ellie Patterson and feather quilts had no place in his imagination. Together or apart.

She just needed a place to stay and he had one sitting there going to waste. He'd dressed it up real nice on arrival in Larkville and had left the whole place pretty much intact—a few extra girlie touches for his gram when she came to visit, but otherwise the same as when he'd used it.

It might not be to New York standards—especially for a woman who didn't need to ask the price of a room—but she'd have no complaints. No reasonable ones anyway. It was insulated, sealed and furnished, and it smelled good.

Not as good as Ellie Patterson did, but good enough.

He opened her unlocked car to pop the trunk.

He'd watched her rental trundle off down the long, straight road from the Calhoun ranch until it disappeared against the sky, and he'd wondered if he would see her again. Logic said yes; it was a small town. His heart said no, not a good idea.

The last person on this planet he needed to get mixed up with was a woman from New York City. That was just way too close to things he'd walked away from.

And yet, he'd found himself volunteering the Alamo in her moment of need, the manners his gram raised him with defying his better judgement. He'd been almost relieved when she so curtly declined his help.

As he swung her cases—plural—out of the rental's trunk, he heard the unmistakable sound of Deputy protesting. A ten-second detour put him at his front door.

'Sorry, boy, got distracted. Come on out.'

Deputy looked about as ticked off as a dog used to the sole attention of his owner possibly could, but he was a fast forgiver and barrelled down the porch steps and pathway ahead of Ellie's cases.

In the half second it took to push the door to the old barn open, he and Deputy both saw the same thing. Ellie, legs spread either side of the little stove, hands and face smudged with soot, a burning twig in her hand. He only wanted to dash to her side and wipe clean that porcelain skin. Deputy actually did it. With his tongue.

Ellie gasped.

Jed barked a stiff, 'Heel!'

Deputy slunk back to his master's right boot and dropped his head, sorry but not sorry. Ellie scrabbled to her feet, sputtering. There was nothing for him to do apart from apologise for his dog's manners and place her suitcases through the door.

As if he hadn't come off as enough of a hick already.

Then his eyes fell on the work of modern art poking out of the fireplace. He stepped closer.

'I've never made a fire.'

He struggled not to soften at the self-conscious note in her voice. It was good to know she could drop the self-possession for a moment, but he wasn't buying for one moment that it was permanent. Ms. Ellie Patterson might be pretty in pastels but he'd wager his future she was tough as nails beneath it.

He didn't take his eyes off the amazing feat of overengineering. An entire log was jammed in there with twigs and twisted newspaper and no less than four fire-starters. And she'd been about to set the whole lot ablaze.

He relieved her of the burning twig and extinguished it. 'That would have burned down the barn.'

She looked horrified. 'Oh. Really?'

Deputy dropped to his side on the rug closest to the fire, as though it was already blazing.

Dopey dog.

'Less is more with fires....' Without thinking he took her hand and walked her to the sofa, then pressed her into it. He did his best not to care that she locked up like an antique firearm at his uninvited touch. 'Watch and learn.'

It took him a good five minutes to undo the nest of twigs and kindling squashed inside the wrought-iron fireplace. But then it was a quick job to build a proper fire and get it crackling. She watched him intently.

He stood. 'Got it?'

Her colour surged and it wasn't from the growing flames. 'I'm sorry. You must think me so incredibly inept. First the cows and now the fire.'

He looked down on her, embarrassed and poised on his sofa. 'Well, I figure you don't have a lot of either in Manhattan.'

'We have a fireplace,' she started without thinking, and then her words tapered off. 'But we light it with a button.'

Well, that was one step better than 'but we have staff to do it for us.' Maybe she knew what she was talking about when she teased him about being the Calhouns' butler.

'I'm sure there's a hundred things you can do that I can't. One day you can teach me one of those and we'll be even.'

Her blue eyes glittered much greener against the glow of the growing fire. 'Not sure you'd have much use for the intricacies of delivering a sauté in arabesque.'

'You're a chef?'

His confusion at least brought a glint of humour back to her beautiful face. 'Sauté onstage, not on the stove. I'm a dancer. Ballet. Or…I was.'

'That explains so much.' Her poise. The way she held herself. Those amazing legs. Her long, toned frame. Skinny, but not everywhere.

The lightness in her expression completely evaporated and he could have kicked himself for letting his eyes follow his thoughts. 'What I mean is it doesn't surprise me. You move like a professional.' Her eyebrows shot up. 'Dancer, I mean.'

Deputy shot him a look full of scorn: way to keep digging, buddy!

But as he watched, the awkwardness leached from Ellie's fine features and her lips turned up. The eyes that met his were amused. And more than a little bit sexy. 'Thank you, Jed. I'm feeling much less self-conscious now.'

So was he—stupidly—now that she'd used his name.

He cleared his throat. 'Well, then… I'll just leave you to unpack.' He glanced at the fire. 'As soon as those branches are well alight you can drop that log on top. Just one,' he cautioned, remembering her overpacked first effort. 'As long as you keep the vent tight it should last awhile. Put a big one on just before you go to bed and it should see you through the night.'

'I'll do that now, then, because as soon as you're gone I'm crawling into bed.'

'At 7:00 p.m.?' Why was she so exhausted? It couldn't just be the steer, even for a city slicker.

She pushed to her feet to show him the door. 'I think my

week is finally catching up to me. But I'm going to be very comfortable here, thank you for the hospitality. You've done your hometown proud.'

It was on the tip of his tongue to tell her Larkville wasn't his hometown, but she didn't say it to start a conversation, she said it to end one.

He moved to the door, surprised at how his own feet dragged, and whistled for Deputy. 'Sleep well, Ellie.'

His buddy hauled himself to his feet and paused in front of Ellie for the obligatory farewell scratch. She just stared at him, no clue what he was expecting, but then his patient upward stare seemed to encourage her and she slid her elegant fingers into his coat and gave him a tentative rub. She released him, and Deputy padded to Jed's side and preceded him out the door.

Jed stared after the dog, an irrational envy blazing away as she closed the door behind him. He pulled the collar of his shirt up against the air's bite and hurried back to his house. It was ridiculous to hold it against a dog just because he'd been free to walk up and demand she touch him. Her sliding down his body earlier today was a heck of a lot more gratuitous than what just happened in the barn.

Yet... The way her fingers had curled in his dog's thick black coat... Her eyes barely staying open. It was somehow more... intimate.

Deputy reached the street first, then paused and looked back at him, a particularly smug expression on his hairy black, tan and white face.

'Jerk,' Jed muttered.

Who or what Ellie Patterson touched was no concern of his. She was the last kind of woman he needed to be staking a claim on, and the last kind to tolerate it.

But as he put foot after foot up that long pathway towards his dog, he'd never, in his life, felt more like rushing back in there and branding his name on someone—preferably with his lips—so everyone in Larkville knew where Ellie Patterson was coming home to at night.

Stupid, because the woman was as prickly as the cactus out on the borderlands. Stupid because she lived in New York and he lived in small-town Texas. Stupid because he wasn't interested in a relationship. Now or ever.

He turned and stared at her door.

But it wouldn't be the first stupid thing he'd done in his life.

Deputy looked at him with disgust and then turned back to the front door of the cottage and waited for someone with opposable thumbs to make it open.

Not half the look Ellie would give him if she got even the slightest inkling of his caveman thoughts. This was just his testosterone speaking, pure and simple.

Men like him didn't belong with women like her. Women like Ellie Patterson belonged with driven, successful investment bankers who made and lost millions on Wall Street. Men like him belonged with nice, country girls who were happy to love him warts and all. There was no shortage of nice women in Hayes County and a handful had made their interest—and their willingness—clearly known since he arrived in Larkville. And right after that he'd made it his rule not to date where he worked.

Don't poop where you eat, Jeddie, his gram used to say, though she generally referenced it when she was trying to encourage him to clean his room. But it was good advice.

His gut curled.

He'd ignored it once and he'd screwed everything up royally. Sticking faithfully to this rule had seen him avoid any messy entanglements that threatened his job or his peace of mind ever since he'd arrived in Larkville three years ago.

But abstinence had a way of creeping up on you. Every week he went without someone in his life was a week he grew more determined to only break it for something special. Someone special. That bar just kept on rising. To the point that he wondered how special a woman would have to be to meet it.

Deputy lifted his big head and threw him a look as forlorn as he felt. It was exactly what he needed to snap him out of the sorry place he'd wound up. He flung himself down onto the sofa, reached for the TV remote and found himself a sports channel.

In the absence of any other kind of stimulation, verbally sparring with an uptight city girl might just be as close to flirting as he needed to get.

If she didn't deck him for trying.

CHAPTER THREE

GIVEN how many five-star hotels Ellie had stayed in, it was ridiculous to think that she'd just had one of the best sleeps of her life in a converted hayloft.

She burrowed down deeper into the soft quilt and took herself through the pros and cons of just sleeping all day.

Pro: she wasn't expected anywhere.

Pro: she wouldn't be missed by anyone. No one would know but her; and possibly the sheriff, although he'd almost certainly be out doing sheriffly duties.

When was the last time she just lay in? While all her classmates were keeping teenage hours, she'd spent every waking moment perfecting her steps, or doing strength training or studying the masters. Even when she was sick she used to force herself up, find something constructive to do. Anything that meant she wasn't indulging her body.

Now look at her. Twelve hours' rest behind her and quite prepared to go back for another three.

What had she become?

Her deep, powerful desire to pull the blankets over her head and never come out was only beaten by the strength of her determination not to. She hurled back the toasty warm covers and let the bracing Texan morning in with her, and her near-naked flesh protested with a thousand tiny bumps. Even the biggest log she'd found in the woodpile couldn't last this long and so the little room was as cold as…well, an old barn. Bad enough that she'd broken a cardinal rule and gone to bed without eating anything, she'd stripped out of her clothes and just crawled into bed in panties only, too tired to even forage amongst her belongings for her pajamas.

More sloth!

She pulled one of the blankets up around her shoulders and tiptoed over to her suitcases, the timber floor of the raised loft creaking under her slight weight. The sound reminded her of the flex and give in the dance floor of the rehearsal studio and brought a long-distance kind of comfort. They may have been hard years but they were also her childhood. She rummaged to the bottom of one case for socks and a T-shirt and dragged them on, then slid into her jeans from yesterday, her loose hair caressing her face.

No doubt, the people of Larkville had been up before dawn—doing whatever it was that country folk did until the sun came up. There was no good reason she shouldn't be up, too. She looped a scrunchie over her wrist, pulled the bedspread into tidy order, surrendered her toasty blanket and laid it neatly back where it belonged, then turned for the steps.

Downstairs didn't have the benefit of rising heat and it had the decided non-benefit of original old-brick flooring so it was even chillier than the loft. It wasn't worth going to all the trouble of lighting the fire for the few short hours until it got Texas warm. Right behind that she realised she had no idea what the day's weather would bring. Back home, she'd step out onto her balcony and look out over the skyline to guess what kind of conditions Manhattan was in for, but here she'd have to sprint out onto the pavement where she could look up into the sky and take a stab at what the day had in store.

She pulled on the runners she'd left by the sofa, started to shape her hair into a ponytail, hauled open the big timber door… and just about tripped over the uniformed man crouched there leaving a box on her doorstep.

'Oh—!'

Two pale eyes looked as startled as she felt and the sheriff caught her before momentum flipped her clean over him. All at once she became aware of two things: first, she wasn't fully dressed and, worse, her hair was still flying loose.

Having actual breasts after so many years of not having them at all was still hard to get used to and slipping them into lace was never the first thing she did in the morning. Not that what she had now would be of much interest to any but the most pubescent of boys but she still didn't want them pointing at Sheriff Jed Jackson in the frosty morning air.

But even more urgent… Her hair was down.

Ellie steadied herself on Jed's shoulders as he straightened and she stepped back into the barn, tucking herself more modestly behind its door. She abandoned her discomfort about her lack of proper clothing in favour of hauling her hair into a quick bunch and twisting the scrunchie around it three brutal times. That unfortunately served to thrust her chest more obviously in the sheriff's direction but if it was a choice between her unashamedly frost-tightened nipples and her still-recovering hair, she'd opt for the eyeful any day.

Of the many abuses her undernourished body had endured in the past, losing fistfuls of brittle hair was the most lingering and shameful.

She never wore it loose in public. Not then. Not even now, years after her recovery.

Jed's eyes finally decided it was safe to find hers, though he seemed as speechless as she was.

'Good morning, Sheriff.' She forced air through her lips, but it didn't come out half as poised as she might have hoped. The wobble gave her away.

'I didn't want to wake you,' he muttered. Four tiny lines splayed out between his dark eyebrows and he glanced down to the box at his feet. 'I brought supplies.'

She dropped her gaze and finally absorbed the box's contents. Milk, fruit, bread, eggs, half a ham leg. Her whole body shrivelled—the habit of years. It was more than just supplies, it was a Thanksgiving feast. To a Texan that was probably a starter pack, but what he'd brought would last her weeks.

'Thank you.' She dug deep into her chatting-with-strangers repertoire for some lightness to cover the moment. 'Cattle mustering, fire lighting and now deliveries. County sheriffs sure have a broad job description.'

His lips tightened. 'Sure do. In between the road deaths and burglaries and domestic violence.'

She winced internally. Why did every word out of her mouth end up belittling him?

But he moved the conversation smoothly on. 'You were heading out?'

'No, I just wanted to see the sky.' That put a complex little question mark in his expression. 'To check the weather,' she added.

'You know we get the Weather Channel in Texas, right?'

Of course she knew that. But she'd been trusting her own instincts regarding the weather for years. On the whole she was right more often than the experts. 'Right, but I'd rather see it for myself.'

Wow, did she sound as much of a control freak as she feared?

His stare intensified. 'As it happens, meteorology is also on my job description. Today will be fine and eighty-two degrees.'

Ellie couldn't stop her eyes from drifting upwards to the streak of cloud front visible between the overhanging eaves of the two buildings.

He didn't look surprised. If anything, he looked disappointed. 'You really don't trust anyone but yourself, huh?'

She lifted her chin and met his criticism. 'It smells like rain.'

He snorted. 'I don't think so, Manhattan. We've been in drought for months.'

He might as well have patted her on the head. He bent and retrieved the box, then looked expectantly towards her little kitchenette. No way on earth she was letting him back in here until she was fully and properly dressed and every hair was in its rightful place. She took a deep breath, stepped out from behind the door and extended her arms for the box.

'It's heavy…' he warned.

'Try me,' she countered.

Another man might have argued. The sheriff just plonked the box unceremoniously into her arms. It was hard to know if that reflected his confidence in her ability or some twisted desire to see her fail.

She fixed her expression, shifted her feet just slightly and let her spine take the full brunt of the heavy supplies. It didn't fail her. You don't dance for twelve years without building up a pretty decent core strength. Just for good measure she didn't rush the box straight over to the counter and, since it was doing a pretty good job of preserving her modesty, she had no real urgency. 'Okay, well… Thanks again.'

B'bye now.

He didn't look fooled. Or chagrined. If anything, he looked amused. Like he knew exactly what she was doing. The corners of that gorgeous mouth kicked up just slightly. He flicked his index finger at the brim of his sheriff's hat in farewell and turned to walk away.

She could have closed the door and heaved the box over to the kitchen. She probably should have done that. But instead she made herself take its weight a little longer, and she watched him saunter up the pathway towards his SUV, law-enforcement accoutrements hanging off both sides of his hips, lending a sexy kind of emphasis to the loping motion of his strong legs.

Then, just as he hit the sidewalk—just as she convinced herself he wasn't going to—he turned and glanced back down the lane and smiled like he knew all along that she was still watching. Though it nearly killed her arms to do it, she even managed to return his brief salute by lifting three fingers off her death grip on the heavy box in a *faux*-casual farewell flick.

Then she kicked the door shut between them and hurried to the counter before she had fruit and ham and eggs splattered all over her chilly barn floor.

* * *

Jed slid in beside Deputy and waited until the tinted window of his driver's door was one hundred per cent closed before he let himself release his breath on a long, slow hiss.

Okay…

So…

His little self-pep talk last night amounted to exactly nothing this morning. One look at Little Miss Rumpled Independence and he was right back to wanting to muscle his way into that barn and never leave. No matter how contrary she was. In fact, maybe because she was so contrary.

And, boy, was she ever. She would have hefted all one hundred and twenty pounds of Deputy and held him in her slender arms if he suggested she couldn't.

But she had done it. Thank goodness, too, because a man could only stare at the wall so long to avoid staring somewhere infinitely less appropriate. It wasn't her fault he'd had a flash of conscience while jogging at 6:00 a.m. about how empty the refrigerator in his barn conversion was. Her mortification at being caught unprepared for company was totally genuine.

So she might be snappish and belligerent, but she wasn't some kind of exhibitionist.

Which meant she was only two parts like Maggie, he thought as he pulled the SUV out into the quiet street. Maggie and her sexual confidence had him twisted up in so many knots he could barely see straight by the time she'd worn him down. It was never his plan to date someone in his own department but it was certainly her plan and Maggie was nothing if not determined.

But he was practically a different man back then. A boy. He'd taken that legacy scholarship straight out of school and gone to the Big Smoke to reinvent himself and he'd done a bang-up job.

He just wished he could have become a man that he liked a little bit more.

Still…done was done. He walked away from the NYPD after fifteen years with a bunch of salvaged scruples, a firm set of rules about relationships and a front seat full of canine squad flunky.

Not a bad starting point for his third try at life.

One block ahead he saw Danny McGovern's battered pickup shoot a red intersection and he reached automatically for the switch for his roof lights. Pulling traffic was just a tiny bit too close to Ellie Patterson's jibe about the kinds of low-end tasks she'd seen him run as sheriff but, if he didn't do it, then that damned kid was going to run every light between Larkville and Austin and, eventually, get himself killed.

And since one of those fine scruples he'd blown his other life to pieces over involved protection of hotshot dumb-asses like McGovern, he figured he owed it to himself to at least try. He'd been negligent enough with the lives of others for one lifetime.

His finger connected with the activation switch and a sequenced flash of red and blue lit the waking streets.

Time to get to work.

CHAPTER FOUR

ELLIE pulled her knees up closer to her chest, cupped her chamomile tea and listened to the sounds of the storm raging over Larkville. The awesome power of nature always soothed her, when the noise from the heavens outgunned the busy, conflicting noise inside her head—the clamoring expectations, her secret fears, the voice telling her how much better she should be doing.

The sky's thundering downpour was closer to mental silence than anything she could ever create.

Her eyes drifted open.

The crackle of the roasting fire was muted beneath the rain hammering on the barn's tin roof but its orange glow flickered out across the darkened room, dancing. The flames writhed and twisted in the inferno of the stove, elegant and pure, the way the best of the performers in her company had been able to do.

The way she never had. Despite everything she'd done to be good enough, despite sacrificing her entire childhood to the God of Dance. Her entire body.

One particularly spectacular flame twisted in a helix and reached high above the burning timber before folding and darting back into itself.

Still her body yearned to move like those flames. It craved the freedom and raw expression. She hadn't really danced in the nine years since walking away from the corps and the truth was she hadn't really danced in the twelve years before it. The regimented structure of ballet suited her linear mind. Steps, sequences, choreographed verse. She'd excelled technically but, ultimately, lacked heart.

And then she'd discovered that one of her father's corporations was a silent patron for the company, and what heart she had for dance withered completely.

The place she thought she'd earned with brutal hard work and commitment to her craft… The place she knew two dozen desperate artists would crawl over her rotting corpse to have…

Her father had bought that place with cold, hard cash.

Two air pockets crashed together right overhead and the little barn rattled at the percussion. Ellie didn't even flinch. She shifted against the sofa cushions to dislodge the old pain of memory. She'd run from that chapter in her life with a soul as gaunt as her body, searching for something more meaningful to take its place. But she didn't find it in the thousands of hours of charity work she put in over the past decade raising funds for Alzheimer's research. And she didn't find it in the company of some man. No matter how many she'd dated to appease her mother.

And—finally—she opened her eyes one morning and realised that her inability to find something meaningful in her life said a whole lot more about her than it did about the city she lived in.

The rolling thunder morphed into the rhythmic pounding of a fist on her door, though it took a few moments for Ellie to realise. She tossed back the blanket and hurried the few steps to the front door, taking a moment to make sure her hair was neatly back.

'Are you okay?'

The sheriff stood there, water streaming off his wide-brimmed hat and three-quarter slicker, soaked through from the knee down. A bedraggled Deputy shadowed him.

Surprise had her stumbling backwards and man and dog took that as an invitation to enter. They stepped just inside her door, out of the steady rain, though Jed took off his hat and left it hanging on the external doorknob. He produced a small, yellow box.

'Matches?' she said, her tranquil haze making her slow to connect the dots.

'There's candles in the bottom kitchen drawer.'

'What for?'

He looked at her like she was infirm. 'Light.' Then he flicked her light switch up and down a few times. 'Power's out.'

'Oh. I didn't notice. I had the lights out anyway.'

Maybe people didn't do that in Texas because the look he threw her was baffled. 'You were sitting here in the dark?'

Was that truly so strange? She rather liked the dark. 'I was sitting here staring into the fire and enjoying the storm.'

'Enjoying it?' The idea seemed to appall him. He did look like he'd been through the wringer, though not thoroughly enough to stop water dripping from his trousers onto the brick floor of the old barn.

'I'm curled up safe and sound on your sofa, not out there getting saturated.' He still didn't seem to understand so she made it simpler. 'I like storms.'

Deputy slouched down in front of her blazing fire and his big black eyes flicked between the two of them. Jed's hand and the matchbox still hung out there in space, so Ellie took it from him and placed it gently next to the existing one on the woodpile. 'Thank you, Sheriff. Would you like a coffee? The pot's just boiled.'

Colour soaked up Jed's throat, though it was lessened by the orange glow coming from the stove. Had he forgotten his own woodpile came with matches?

'Sorry. I thought you might be frightened.'

'Of a storm…?' Ellie swung the pot off its bracket and back onto her blazing stove, then set to spooning out instant coffee. 'No.'

'I'd only been home a few minutes when the power cut. I had visions of you trying to get down the stairs in the dark to find candles.'

Further evidence of his chivalry took second place to inexplicable concern that he'd been out there in the cold for hours. 'Trouble?'

He shrugged out of his sheriff's coat and draped it over

the chairback closest to the heat. 'The standard storm-related issues—flooding, downed trees. We've been that long without rain the earth is parched. Causes more run-off than usual.'

The kettle sang as it boiled and Ellie tumbled water into his coffee, then passed it to him. He took it gratefully. 'Thank you.'

She sunk back into her spot on the sofa and he sat himself politely on the same chair as his dripping coat. Overhead, the storm grizzled and grumbled in rolling waves and sounded so much like a petulant child it was hard not to smile.

'You really do love your weather, don't you?' he said.

'I love…' What? The way it was so completely out of her control and therefore liberating? No one could reasonably have expectations of the weather. 'I love the freedom of a storm.'

He sipped his coffee and joined her in listening to the sounds above. 'Can I ask you something?' he finally said. 'How did you know it was going to rain?'

She thought about that for a moment. Shrugged. 'I could feel it.'

'But you know nothing about Texas weather. And it was such a long shot.'

'Intuition?'

He smiled in the flickering firelight. 'You remind me a bit of someone.'

'Who?'

'Clay Calhoun.'

Her heart and stomach swapped positions for a few breaths.

'Jessica's father. That man was so in touch with his land he could look at the sky and tell you where a lightning bolt was going to hit earth.'

Awkwardness surged through her. Clay Calhoun was dead, just a legend now. Getting to know the man at the start of all her emotional chaos was not something she expected when she came to Texas. Yet, there was something intensely personal about discovering a shared…affinity…with the man that might be her father.

Was. She really needed to start digging her way out of denial and into reality. Her mother had virtually confirmed it with her bitter refusal to discuss it. And Jed had just reinforced it with his casual observation.

Maybe her weather thing was a case of nature, not nurture. Her Texan genes making their presence felt.

She cleared her throat. 'Past tense?'

He shifted his legs around so that the heat from the stove could do as good a job drying his trouser bottoms as it was doing on his dog. 'Yeah, Larkville lost Clay in October. Hit everyone real hard, especially his kids.'

Some harder than others.

He turned to look right at her. 'I thought that might be why you were here. Given Jess's recent loss. To bring condolences.'

'I'm...' This would be the perfect time to tell someone. Like confessing to a priest, a stranger. But for all she barely knew him, Jed Jackson didn't feel entirely like a stranger. And so, ironically, it was easier to hedge. 'No. I... Jess is helping me with...something.'

Wow...Eleanor Patterson totally tongue-tied. Rare. And exceedingly lame.

'Well, whatever it is I hope it can wait a few weeks? Jess won't be back until the end of the month, I hear.'

It had waited thirty years; it could wait a couple more weeks. 'It can.'

He stood and turned his back on the fire to give the backs of his calves and boots a chance to dry off. A light steam rose from them. His new position meant he was five-eighths silhouette against the orange glow. Imposing and broad.

But as non-threatening as the storm.

'Have you eaten?' he suddenly asked, his silhouette head tilting down towards her.

Even after all these years she still had a moment of tension when anyone mentioned food. Back when she was sick it was second nature to avoid eating in public. 'No. I was planning on having leftovers.'

Though her idea of leftovers was the other half of the apple she'd had at lunch.

'Want to grab something at Gracie May's?' he asked, casually. 'Best little diner in the county.'

The olive branch was unexpected and not entirely welcome. Was it a good idea to get friendly with the locals? Especially the gorgeous ones? 'But you just got dry. And won't her power be out, too?'

'Right. Good point.' He launched into action, turning for the kitchen. 'I'll fix us something here, then.'

'Here?' The delightful relaxation of her stormy evening fled on an anxious squeak.

He paused his tracks, cocked his head in a great impression of Deputy. 'Unless you want to come next door to my place?'

How did he manage to invest just a few words with so much extra meaning? Did she want to go next door and sit down to a meal with Sheriff Jed Jackson? Surrounded by his cowboy stuff, his Texan trappings? His woodsy smell?

Yes.

'No.' She swallowed. 'Here will be fine. Some guy delivered enough groceries for a month this morning.'

His smile did a good job of rivaling the fire's glow and it echoed deep down inside her. He set about shaving thin slices of ham from the bone and thick slices of bread from the loaf. Then some crumbly cheese, a sliced apple and a wad of something preserved from a jar labelled Sandra's Jellies and Jams.

'Green-tomato jam. Calhouns' finest.'

That distracted Ellie from the sinking of her stomach as he passed a full plate into her lap and sank down onto the other half of the suddenly shrunken sofa. She turned her interest up to him. 'Sandra Calhoun?'

'Jess, technically speaking, but a family recipe.'

Her family's recipe. That never failed to feel weird. For so long her family had been in New York. She picked up her fork and slid some of the tomato jam onto the corner of the bread and then bit into it. If she was only going to get through a fifth of the food on her plate, then she wanted it to be Jess's produce.

Jed was already three enormous bites into his sandwich and he tossed some ham offcuts over to Deputy, who roused himself long enough to gobble them up before flopping back down.

She risked conversation between his mouthfuls. 'The Calhouns have quite a presence.'

'They should. They're Larkville's founding family. Jess's great-great-granddaddy put down roots here in 1856.'

'And they're...well respected?'

The look he threw her over his contented munching was speculative. 'Very much so. Clay's death hit the whole town hard. They're dedicating the Fall Festival to him.'

'Really? The whole thing?'

'The Calhouns practically ran that festival anyway. Was fitting.'

'Who's running it now?' With Sandra and Clay both gone, and all the kids away?

'Jess and Holt will be back soon enough. Nate, too, God willing. Everyone else is pitching in to help.'

She filed that away for future reference. 'What happens at a fall festival?'

He smiled. 'You'd hate it. Livestock everywhere.'

Heat surged up her throat. 'I don't hate cows...'

'I'm just teasing, relax. Candy corn, rides, crafts, hot-dog-eating competitions. Pretty much what happens at fall festivals all over the country.'

She stared at him.

His eyebrows rose. 'Never?'

The heat threatened again. 'I've never left New York.'

'In your entire life?'

She shrugged, though she didn't feel at all relaxed about the disbelief in his voice. 'This is my first time.'

'Summers?'

Her lips tightened. 'Always rehearsing.'

'Family vacations?'

'We didn't take them.' The way he'd frozen with his sandwich halfway to his mouth got her back up. 'And you did?'

'Heck, yes. Every year my gram would throw me and her ducks in her old van and head off somewhere new.'

The ducks distracted her for a moment, but only a moment. 'You lived with your grandmother?'

His eyes immediately dropped to his plate. He busied himself mopping up the last of the jam.

She'd grown up with Matt for a brother. She knew when to wield silence for maximum effect. Jed lasted about eight seconds.

'My parents got pregnant young. Real young. Dad got custody after Mom took off. Gram was his mother. They raised me together.'

Mom took off. There was a lot of story missing in those few words. If only she didn't respect her own privacy so much—it necessarily forced her to respect his. 'But your dad wasn't in the van with you and the ducks every summer?'

'He worked a lot. And then he—' Jed cleared his throat and followed it up with an apple-slice chaser '—he died when I was six.'

Oh. The charming cowboy suddenly took on an unexpected dimension. Losing your parent so young... And here she was whining about having too many parents. 'That must have been tough for you to get over.'

'Gram was a rock. And a country woman herself. She knew how to raise boys.'

'Is she still here in Larkville?'

The eyes found hers again. 'I'm not from Larkville, originally.'

'Really?' He seemed so much part of the furniture here. Of the earth. 'I thought your accent wasn't as pronounced as everyone else's. Where are you from?'

'Gram was from the Lehigh Valley. But my dad was NYPD. He met my mother while he was training.'

New York. Her world—and her hopes at anonymity—shrank.

She moderated her breath just like in a heavy dance routine. 'Manhattan?'

'Queens, mostly. He commuted between shifts back out to the Valley. To us.'

'And he's the reason you became a cop?'

'He's part of it. He, uh, died on duty. That meant there was legacy funding for my schooling. It felt natural to go into law enforcement.'

Died on duty. But something much more immediate pressed down on her. 'You studied in New York?'

His eyes hooded. 'I lived and worked in Manhattan for fifteen years.'

Her voice grew tiny. 'You didn't say. When I told you where I was from.'

'A lot of people come from New York. It's not that remarkable.'

So she just asked him outright what she needed to know. 'Do you know who I am?'

That surprised him. 'Why? Are you famous?'

His cavalier brush while she was stressing out didn't sit well with her. She took the chance to push her plate onto the footstool next to them. 'Be serious.'

He stared at her. Doing the math. Consulting his mental Who's Who of New York. She saw the exact moment that the penny dropped. 'You're a Patterson Patterson?'

She stared back. 'I'm the oldest Patterson.' By six minutes. Or…was. Charlotte was now. Wow. That was going to freak her middle sister out when she discovered it.

He chewed that over as thoroughly as his supper. But his inscrutable expression betrayed nothing. 'Wish I'd known that before I rescued you from the steer. I might have kept on driving.'

Not what she was expecting. Nervous wind billowed out the sides of her sails and was replaced by intrigue. 'Why?'

Tiny lines grew at the corners of his eyes. 'Your father's politics and mine differed.'

Ellie sat up straighter. 'You knew him?'

'Nope. Didn't need to.'

'Meaning?'

'Meaning some of the circles he moved in weren't ones that I had a lot of time for.'

Defense of the man she'd called father for thirty years surged up. Despite everything. 'If you were really from New York you'd know he hasn't moved in any circle for the past two years.'

'I came here three years ago. Why? What happened?'

She wasn't about to discuss her father's Alzheimer's with such a vocal critic. And—really—what were the chances he'd truly cut all ties and not even kept up with what was happening in the city he'd lived in. 'He's been unwell.'

'I'm sorry.'

'Why? You didn't like him.'

'I didn't like his politics. There's a difference.'

'Even if he lived and breathed his politics?' To the exclusion of all else? At least that's how it felt, although his increasing detachment to his two oldest children started to make more sense since she opened Jess's letter.

His eyes grew serious. 'I know what it's like to lose a father. So I'm sorry.'

He did know. But did he know what it was like to lose one three times over? Her father was no longer her father—first in mind, now in fact. And her apparent biological father was dead.

'Look at us having a real conversation,' he joked lightly after the silence stretched out like Deputy in front of the fire. The storm had settled to a dull rumble.

She'd failed to notice it easing. How long had they been talking?

His eyes fell on her plate. 'You going to eat that?'

For everyone else, eating was just a thing you did when you got hungry. Or at parties. For her, eating was something personal. Private. She took a slice of apple and then slid the rest over to him. He started to demolish it.

'What made you leave New York for Larkville?' she asked, nibbling on the sweet fruit.

Instant shutdown.

She watched it happen in the slight changes in his face. But not answering at all would just be too much for his Texan courtesy. 'The politics I told you about,' he hedged.

There was something vaguely uncomfortable about thinking that her family was responsible for anyone uprooting their life. Even by association. She scrabbled around for a new topic. 'What about Deputy?' The dog lifted his horse's head on hearing his name. 'Is he a New Yorker, too?'

Dogs were apparently neutral territory because Jed's face lightened. 'Born and bred.'

'You said you and he had a deal? About how he behaved. What did you mean?'

He shifted more comfortably on the sofa. 'Deputy had some… behavioural issues when I got him. Our agreement was that he got to spend his days with me if he could manage his manners.'

'He's a rescue?'

'He was a canine-unit dropout.'

She looked at the big brute sleeping happily on the floor and chuckled. 'What do you have to do to flunk being a guard dog?'

'He wasn't trained for guard duty. Unit dogs were used for detection—drugs, firearms, explosives, fire, bodies.'

'Locating the dead?'

Jed nodded. 'Others are trained to take supplies into dangerous situations or to recognise the signs of trauma and approach people in need of comfort and therapy.'

Ellie glanced at Deputy—all fur and teddy-bear good looks. 'He'd be good at therapy. Is that what he did?'

Jed shook his head. 'He was a tracker, tracing criminals through the back alleys and sewers,' he said. 'He was good, but he…was injured.' His eyes flicked evasively but then settled on Deputy again. 'Couldn't earn his keep.'

Ellie had seen the police dogs working with their human partners on Manhattan's streets. 'What happens to the ones that can't work?'

He stretched his leg out and gave Deputy a gentle nudge with his boot tip. 'The lucky ones end up with me in a town full of people that spoil him. Hey, boy?'

Deputy's thick tail thumped three times, four, against the timber pile...but the rest of him didn't move. The boot kept up its gentle rub.

So Sheriff Jed had a big, soft heart. Why did that surprise her? 'Well, he's fortunate he met you, then.'

'Depends on how you look at it,' he muttered.

She shot him a sideways look.

Suddenly Jed was on his feet flattening his hand in a signal to Deputy to stay put. 'I should get going. Storm's easing. I'm going to leave him here with you tonight.'

Here? With her? The half-baked dog certainly looked content enough, but...would he be so compliant once his master had gone? 'That's not nec—'

This time Jed's hand signal was for her. It said don't argue. He snagged his dry coat off the chair back. 'You'll feel more secure with him here.'

'In what universe?' The words slipped straight from her subconscious to her tongue.

Jed chuckled. 'You didn't have dogs growing up, I take it?'

'We had a cat. And it was pretty standoffish.' Her mother loved it.

'Think of it as an opportunity to bond, then.'

Bond? With a hundred-plus pounds of wet dog? 'What if he needs to...?' She waved a hand to avoid having to use the words.

'He's already...' Jed imitated her gesture. 'Just let him out quickly before bed. He knows where to go if his bladder's full.'

'What if it's raining?'

'Then he'll get wet. Or hold on until morning. Seriously, Ellie. It will be fine. He'll just lie by the fire and help you ride out the storm.'

'I don't need help. I like storms, remember?'

He wasn't going to take no for an answer. Who knew, maybe the sheriff had a hot date tonight and wanted a dog-free zone.

She looked over at Deputy, who lazily opened one eye and then closed it again.

Okay, so she was a dog sitter. Stranger things had happened...

She followed Jed to the door. He turned and looked down at her.

'Well, thanks for supper, Ellie. I appreciate it.'

She shrugged. 'You made it.'

He wasn't put off. 'You humoured me.'

'I didn't mind the company.' Though she'd not realised she was craving any until she had his. 'It was...nice...talking to you.' And, strangely, that was true.

He stared down at her for an age, a slight frown in his voice. 'We should do it again.'

Or...not. Deep and meaningful discussions were not her forte. 'Maybe we shouldn't push our luck?'

His sigh managed to be amused and sad at the same time. 'Maybe so.' He snaffled his hat off the doorknob. 'Night, Ellie.'

'Good night, Sheriff...' He turned and lifted one eyebrow at her. 'Jed. Good night, Jed.'

And then he was gone. She watched his shadowy form sprint up the path in rain half the strength of earlier. Even knowing he was just next door she felt a strange kind of twinge at his departure. Enough that she stared for a few moments at the vacant spot he'd just been in. But then the cool of the night hit her and she backed inside, closed the door and then turned to look at her house guest.

Deputy was sitting up now, his thick tail wagging, a big doggie smile on his face. Looking like he'd just been waiting for the party pooper to leave.

'Good boy...' she offered, optimistically.

His tail thumped harder.

'Stay.'

The big head cocked. Ellie took two tentative steps towards him. He didn't move. Two more brought her parallel to him in the tiny accommodations and two more after that had her halfway to the kitchenette. Still the dog didn't move.

Maybe this would be okay.

She reached for the kettle and filled it again with water, then turned back to put it on the cast-iron stove.

There was nothing but air where a dog had just been. Her eyes flicked right.

Deputy had made himself at home on the sofa, stretching his big paws out on Jed's beautiful hand-crafted throw and looking, for all the world, like this was something he was very accustomed to doing.

'Off!' she tried.

Nothing.

'Down?' Not even an eye flicker. She curled a hand around his collar and pulled. Hard. 'Come on, you lug…'

Nada. Eventually she gave up and just squeezed herself onto what little dog-free space remained on the sofa.

And there she sat as the tail of the storm settled in for a long night of blustering, the golden glow of the fire lighting her way, her own breath slipping into sync with the deep heavy canine ones beside her.

And as the minutes ticked by she didn't even realise that her hand had stolen out and rested on Deputy's haunches. Or that her fingers curled into the baked warmth of his dark fur.

Squeeze…release. Squeeze…release.

Or that her mind was finally—blissfully—quiet.

CHAPTER FIVE

THE tapping on his door was so quiet Jed was amazed it cut through the three hours of sleep he'd finally managed to grab. Ninety minutes after leaving Ellie's, he'd been called out again to assist with a double vehicular out towards the interstate and then he'd just rolled from one stormy night task to another until he finally noticed the light peeking over the horizon and took himself off the clock.

Never a good look, the county sheriff driving into a post because he was so tired.

Unfortunately, dragging his butt out of bed just a few hours after falling fully dressed into it really wasn't high on his list of things to do on his rostered day off. He yanked the door open. Deputy marched in with a big grin on his chops. The woman behind him wasn't smiling.

'He slept on my bed!'

'What?' It took Jed a full ten seconds to even remember he'd left his dog with Ellie last night. Bad owner.

'Deputy. He helped himself to the other side of my bed. Made himself right at home.'

Deputy? The dog who'd staked out the mat by the fireplace in his house? The dog raised to live in a kennel? The dog that'd been so slow to trust anyone? 'What have you done to him?'

Her fine features tightened. 'I didn't do anything. He climbed up after I'd gone to sleep. I woke up in the middle of the night to his snoring.'

Jed turned. Deputy thumped. 'Opportunist,' he muttered. He turned back to Ellie, rubbing the grit from his eyes. 'Maybe he was scared of the storm. Or maybe the fire burned out.'

Her delicate fingers slid up onto her hips and it only made him more aware of how someone could have curves without seeming curvy.

'Or maybe he's just a terrible, undisciplined dog,' she suggested.

'That seems a bit harsh...'

'He was on my bed.' Those green eyes were trying hard to look annoyed.

'It's a big bed, there's plenty of room for two.' Not that he actually knew that from experience. He'd had it to himself the entire time he lived in the barn. Her coral lips opened and closed again wordlessly and he realised she actually was genuinely scandalised. Time to be serious. 'Did you ask him to get down?'

Whoops. Wrong question. Determination flooded her face.

'He ignored me, Jed. He's uncontrollable. No wonder he flunked out of the canine unit.'

The instinct to defend his old pal was strong. Flunking out of the unit was never Deputy's fault. 'Well, now... That's not true, watch this.'

He took Deputy through his paces, sitting, dropping, staying, presenting a paw. He responded to every command exactly on cue.

A pretty little V formed between her brows. 'He didn't do that for me.'

'I guess he doesn't recognise your authority.'

'What do I need, a badge?'

The outrage on her face was priceless. Maybe princesses from the Upper East Side were used to their name automatically carrying authority? Where he came from—and where Deputy came from—respect was earned. He ran tired fingers through his hair, tried to restore some order there. 'You just need him to accept that you come above him in the pack.'

Her whole body stiffened, and he thought he'd be in for an

earful, but then her face changed. Softened. Slim fingers crept up and clenched over her sternum. 'I'm…I'm part of his pack?'

The unexpected vulnerability shot straight to his chest. 'Sure you are. You shared a den.'

She stared at Deputy, a haunted fragility washing briefly across her face. 'But he thinks he's boss?'

'Not for long.' Jed snagged his coat off the rack and swung it on, before her confusion weakened him any further. 'Come on. I'll show you around Larkville.'

Sleeping in your clothes had some advantages. First, he was fully dressed and much more able to just walk out the door than if she'd caught him in his usual morning attire. And second, being in uniform helped legitimise what they were about to do. Appear in public, together, on an early morning stroll. Not that it would stop certain tongues from wagging.

'We're going for a walk?'

'Exercising a dog is one of the fastest ways to show it where you fit in the pack.'

'I'm going to walk him?' He might as well have said they were going to jump from a hot-air balloon. 'But he's huge.'

Jed pulled the door shut behind them and slid the snout harness over Deputy's eager nose. 'Dogs. Horses. Cattle. They're all the same. Just get their heads pointed where you want them to go and they'll do the rest. Every command you give him will reinforce your dominance.'

Her brow folded. 'I don't want to dominate him.'

'I'm not talking about him cowering at your feet. I'm talking about him trusting you to be his leader. Respecting your choices. Believing in you.' He thrust the lead into her unprepared hands. 'If he pulls, stop. When he stops pulling, go again.'

And so it began…two of the most entertaining hours he could remember having. Ellie was a natural student; she remembered every single instruction he gave her and applied it consistently. In no time Deputy was glancing to her for direction as they moved through the streets of Larkville.

Even Ellie loosened up. And that was saying something. 'How did you learn this?' she asked.

'I had dogs, growing up. But the boys at the canine unit are the real specialists. I learned something new every day.'

The words were out before he even thought about it. Dangerous words.

She gently corrected Deputy when he pulled in the opposite direction and then brought her eyes back to him. 'You worked for the canine unit?'

Sure did. Not that he usually told anyone about it. His only course now was to give her some information, but not enough. Definitely not everything. 'I headed it up. For my last couple of years in the NYPD.'

That stopped her cold and Deputy looked back at her impatiently. She glanced at the stars on his shoulder. So, because he'd had rank in the city he was instantly more credible?

'Changing your opinion of me?'

'I… No. It kind of fits. I should have guessed it would be either the dogs or the mounted squad.'

It fits? Was he that much of a country hick in her eyes? 'Both those units are sophisticated operations.'

'I don't doubt it.' She looked puzzled. 'But I'm wondering why you'd trade working with dogs for working with people. Here.'

She made his old job sound so idyllic. He could hardly tell her that he'd had as little heart for his job as Deputy did at the end there. 'More like trading a desk and filing cabinet for an SUV and a radio.'

'You missed active duty?'

'I missed a lot of things.' The easy days pre-promotion—pre-politics—particularly. The days when his responsibility didn't get people killed. 'I like policing in the county. It's more… personal.'

'Sheriff…' On cue, two older ladies nodded their elegant hairdos at him and failed miserably at disguising the curiosity they sent Ellie's way.

He tipped his hat. 'Miss Louisa… Miss Darcy…'

They walked on. Ellie was still looking at him sideways. She really had that New York knack of tuning out everything around her. 'But just as political, I'm guessing.'

'I don't mind politics if I agree with it.'

She narrowed her eyes. 'Politics is just a game. You just have to know how to play it.'

And just like that the enjoyment evaporated right out of his morning. 'I'm not interested in playing it,' he said flatly.

Her laugh sprinkled out across Larkville's still-quiet streets. 'No one likes it, Jed. You use it.'

He threw her a look. 'Speaking from experience?'

'Right people. Right dinners. Right connections.' She shrugged. 'Money follows.'

His laugh was more of a snort. 'What does a Patterson need more money for?'

She tossed back her head and her eyes glittered. 'Oh, you know… World domination, buying out crippled economies and selling their debt to hostile nations, that sort of thing.'

He wanted to believe that. It fitted very nicely with the picture of her he had in his head. The picture that allowed him to keep her at arm's length. They walked on a few paces.

But he couldn't help himself. He had to know. 'What do you really need it for?'

Right in the corner of his eye he saw her tiny smile. She meant it to be private, but it speared him right between the ribs. He'd just pleased her.

'I fundraise.'

'For?'

Deputy's jangling collar was the only sound for a few moments. 'For research into Alzheimer's disease.'

Ah. 'Your father.'

Again, more silence, then her voice came lower and breathier. 'You'd think with all the money at our disposal we could have bought him a cure, huh?'

The contrast between the very public place they were having this discussion and the incredible pain in her voice hit him low in the gut. He got the sense that it wasn't something she usually spoke of. Just like him and his New York years. He thought about his own father—how a full police escort failed to get him to hospital quick enough, and all their departmental resources later failed to bring the shooter to justice. How he'd had to learn to live with that reality growing up. 'It's not always about money. Or resources.'

That was the irony. Everything else on this planet revolved around resources.

'Well…I'm hoping that my work might make a difference to someone else's father someday.'

Shame curdled in his belly. Her words weren't for show or effect. Suddenly the wicked stepsister of his mind morphed into a gentle, hardworking Cinderella. He'd always considered that those on the lucky side of the privilege rat race had some kind of advantage that people on his side could only dream about. Some magical shield which meant their hands weren't being forced every other day. To make decisions they weren't happy with. To make compromises with the lives of others.

But all the money in the world literally couldn't save Cedric Patterson.

He stopped and slid his hand onto her forearm. 'Don't give up,' he murmured. 'Science changes daily.'

Ellie stared down at the masculine hand on her arm as a way of avoiding the intensity she knew would be in Jed's eyes. It was only a touch, but it stole the oxygen from her cells. She wanted so badly to believe him, believe in him. It had been so long since she'd been able to confide in anyone, and trusting Jed sort of happened by accident.

Jess Calhoun's secret weighed on her like stocks. Would it compromise the universe if she just told one person that her father was not her father? If she tried to talk through the confusing mess of emotions that discovery had left her with? The deeper reasons as to why a stupid dog accepting her into his pack had nearly had her in tears?

She lifted her eyes and opened her mouth to try.

'Jed! Hey. Didn't know you were on duty today.'

A fresh-faced young woman with thick auburn hair met them in the middle of the sidewalk, greeted Jed with a brilliant smile and Deputy with a thorough scratch behind the ears. The dog's eyes practically rolled back in his head and he leaned his full weight into her legs.

Jed's seriousness of a moment before evaporated. 'Sarah...'

Ellie immediately stiffened at the affection in his tone and the way he met the woman's cheek effortlessly for a kiss. She was very friendly with both man and dog....

'Was out on calls all night,' he continued. 'Heading home soon.'

Ellie stared at him. He'd been out all night? And she'd barged in at the crack of dawn. Why didn't he say?

'Oh, poor you.' Her eyes drifted to Ellie. She thrust out her hand. 'Sarah Anderson.'

'Sarah's born and bred in Larkville,' Jed hurried to say, belatedly remembering his manners.

No wonder he was distracted; Sarah was a natural beauty, all willowy and classic even in running pants and sweats. Feminine curves were somewhat new to Ellie and she knew hers didn't sit quite as well on her. She slid her hand into Sarah's. 'Ellie Patterson.'

'You're new in town?'

'Just visiting.' Jed said it before she had a chance to.

'You know you'll have seen everything Larkville has to offer by the time you've finished walking Deputy.'

First-name basis for the dog, too? Ellie looked from Sarah to Jed. Then she put on her best cocktail-party face. 'It's a beautiful town, I love the antique stores.'

'Oh, my gosh, I know! Have you been to Time After Time down on Third? Probably Larkville's best.'

Jed threw his hands in the air. 'If you ladies are going to talk antiques Deputy and I might go find some breakfast...'

'Sorry, Jed.' Sarah laughed, then turned her focus back to

Ellie. 'If you're in town for a bit maybe I can introduce you around, scour the markets with you on Saturday?'

I'd like that. That's what someone polite would say. But until she understood a bit better what Sarah's relationship with Jed was—and until she'd examined why she cared—her personal jury was out. 'Sure, great.'

The brunette turned her keen focus straight back onto Jed. 'I have a favor to ask. I've taken on the volunteer coordination for the Fall Festival and I'm looking for extra hands.' Before Jed could take more than a breath she barrelled on. 'I know you have your hands full in the lead up to the event with permits and stuff but I'm thinking more…nowish…to help with the planning. Darcy and Louisa have withdrawn their services given the unpleasantness over last year's bread bake. I'm caught short.'

'Unpleasantness?' Ellie risked.

'They didn't win,' Sarah answered, in perfect sync with Jed. 'How about it?'

'What would I be signing up for?' he hedged.

'Don't suppose you know what a Gantt chart is?'

Jed's blank stare said it all. 'Something you use to measure fish?'

The laugh shot out of Ellie before she could restrain it. Both sets of eyes turned on her.

'Okay, Manhattan, what's a Gantt chart?' he challenged.

'A project-planning tool. Helps you to schedule your resources. Project your timeline.'

Sarah stared at her like she'd grown enormous, iridescent wings.

Awkwardness cranked up Ellie's spine. 'I used it for fundraising,' she muttered.

'Do you have project-planning experience?' Raw hope blazed in Sarah's eyes.

'I'm only visiting.' Except that wasn't strictly true. She had no fixed return date. And she was going to get bored with nothing to do…

A deep voice pitched in. 'Bet the two of you would get a lot done in two weeks.'

She threw Jed a baleful look.

'Could you?' Sarah only got prettier as excited colour stained her cheeks. 'We'd probably get a month's worth done.'

But Ellie's natural reticence bubbled to the fore. She barely knew Sarah. 'This was supposed to be a holiday…'

'Jed!' Sarah flung her focus back on the suddenly wary-looking sheriff. 'Jed will make up for any time you lose helping Larkville pull its Fall Festival together. He can show you the highlights after work. Introduce you to people.'

'Oh, can I?'

Sarah trundled right over his half-hearted protest. 'And you'll meet people on this project, too.'

That's exactly what she was afraid of. Just because she schmoozed and smiled in the ballrooms of Manhattan didn't mean she enjoyed it. She was kind of happiest on her own.

Jed didn't look all that pleased about it, either. 'Sarah…I think Ellie—'

'Okay, look, my final offer. One week, a few hours a day, and I will personally teach you to line dance. Texan dancing lessons from a real Texan. What do you say?'

Should she tell her that she'd danced for the joint heads of state in her time?

But Sarah's enthusiasm was infectious. And there really weren't enough stores in Larkville to keep her amused for long. And how hard could a fall festival be after some of the top-line soirees she'd pulled off since giving up dance?

'Okay, one week…'

That's as far as she got. Sarah squealed and threw her arms around Ellie's stiff shoulders and then did the same with Jed. He didn't look like he hated it, particularly. But—interestingly—neither did Ellie. And that was quite something for someone uncomfortable with being touched.

'How can I contact you?' Sarah rushed.

'She's at the Alamo.'

Sarah's eyes said *oh, really?* but out loud she just said, 'I'll come for you early Saturday morning. We can strategise after we've stripped the markets bare of antiques.'

'Sounds great.' Every breath she took was one further away from anonymity. First the sheriff and now Sarah.

The awkwardest of silences fell and Sarah's focus darted around them before returning. 'Have you heard from Nate, Jed?'

Even Ellie could read between those innocent words—see through the bright, casual smile—and she'd never met Sarah before. To his credit, Jed answered as if she'd just asked him the time. 'Not since the funeral. No news is good news when it comes to the military.'

'I guess.' A deep shadow ghosted over her dark eyes. 'Well, Deputy's going to pull Ellie's arm off if I don't let you two get going. See you Saturday, Ellie? Take care, Jed.'

They farewelled Sarah and she jogged off, continuing her run.

'Thank you for helping Sarah out.'

Ellie shrugged. 'I'm going to need something to do with my time. Might as well throw a party, right?' She hoped she wasn't as transparent as Sarah had just been. She really wasn't in the mood for celebrations. 'You don't need to give up your time to show me around. I'm happy to help, no strings attached.'

'I don't mind doing my bit. I like Sarah, she's had a rough time these past few years.'

She studied him closer. Liked Sarah or *liked* Sarah? But the thoughtful glance he threw down the street after her had nothing more than compassion in it. Rough times were something she could definitely empathise with. Maybe that's why she'd felt so instantly connected to the bubbly brunette.

'Breakfast?' Jed hinted. The second mention in as many minutes. 'Gracie will let us eat out in her courtyard with Deputy.'

Did all country towns revolve around the social nexus of food? She lifted her chin. 'Sure. I'd love a coffee.'

'I should warn you, Gracie's coffees come with obligatory berry flapjacks midweek.'

Great.

She glanced at Deputy. Maybe she could sneak hers to him. He'd be a willing accomplice for sure.

Jed wasn't kidding about the flapjacks. They didn't order them but a steaming stack came, nonetheless, and no one else around them looked the slightest bit surprised as theirs were delivered.

Ellie stared in dismay at the fragrant pile. 'Are they free?'

Jed laughed. 'Nope. Standing order. Flapjacks on weekdays, full fry-up on the weekends. Gracie believes in promoting her specialties.'

And reaping the profits. Gracie May had a fantastic sales angle going here, and the locals clearly thought it was charming. 'Nice scam,' she muttered.

Jed laughed. 'Totally.'

She selected herself the smallest of the fluffy discs and spooned some fresh, unsweetened berries onto it. Jed heaped his plate high. 'Come on, Ellie. You can't function all day on that.'

He might be amazed how little a body could function on, although—to be fair—it never was proper functioning. 'I'm not exactly going to be burning it off strolling Larkville's streets.'

He watched her as he chewed his first big mouthful. She sliced her pancake into eight identically proportioned strips and then folded the first one carefully onto her fork and then into her mouth. Ignoring his interest the whole time.

'You eat like a New Yorker,' he said as soon as he was able.

He didn't mean that to be an insult. He couldn't know what it really meant to survive in the world of professional dancing. 'When I was dancing I would have probably just had the berries.' If she had anything at all.

'Seriously? On the kind of stresses you must have put your body through?'

'Dancing's a competitive industry. We all did whatever we could to find that balance between strength and leanness.' Smoking. Exercising.

Starving.

Jed nudged the half-ravaged stack towards her. 'Live a little.'

Ten years ago she might have literally recoiled as a plate of food was shoved towards her like that. Sitting calmly in the face of it was extraordinary progress and knowing that bolstered her confidence. Every day she was reminded how far she'd come. And she was proud of it, given she'd done it practically alone. But this was going to keep coming up if she didn't head it off at the pass.

She took a deep breath. 'Food and I have a…complicated relationship.'

That stopped the fork halfway to his mouth. 'Meaning?'

'I've taught myself to look at food purely as fuel for my body. As the total sum of all its nutritional parts.'

He glanced at the pancake pile. Then back at her. 'You don't like food?'

She smiled. 'I like good food, but I don't eat it because it's good. I eat it—just what I need of it—because it's nutritious.'

His eyes narrowed. 'Are you one of those organic, bio-birthed, grown-in-a-vacuum kind of people?'

She laughed and it felt so good. Most people wouldn't speak so casually about this. 'I actually don't mind where it comes from as long as it's good food.'

'Healthy?'

'Bio-available.'

'To your body?'

'Correct.'

She'd never felt less understood. Sigh. But it wasn't from a lack of willingness on his part.

'That is complicated.'

'I know.'

'Does your whole family eat like that?'

'No.'

'So where did it come from? I'm interested.'

Was he? Or was he sitting in judgment? Sincerity bled steadily from his gaze. But talking about her past wasn't easy for her.

She pushed her plate away. 'I had a few problems, when I

was younger. Part of my treatment was to come to terms with the role food plays in our lives.'

The policeman in him instantly grew intrigued. She saw it in the sudden keenness of his expression. But the gentleman won out. He let it go. 'And you came to the conclusion that food is only about nutrition?'

She shrugged. 'That's its primary function, in nature. Cows don't eat straw because it tastes good, they eat it because it's what their bodies need to run on. It's fuel.'

Excellent, a cowboy analogy. Way to condescend, there, Ellie!

But he didn't bite. 'You don't think a steer would appreciate the sweet tips of spring shoots more than old summer grass?'

'They might. But that's just a pleasure thing. They're actually eating it for the energy.'

He stared at her. 'Got something against pleasure?'

The way the word pleasure rolled off his tongue, the way he leaned in slightly as he said it, sent her skin into a prickly overdrive. And it threw her off her usual cautious track. 'It took me ten years to believe that food wasn't my enemy. Just getting to the point of accepting it as fuel is more than I once thought was possible.'

That shut him up.

Heat immediately began building at her collar as she realised what a big thing that was to dump on someone who was just making polite conversation. But he didn't look away. He didn't shy from the awkwardness that poured off her in waves.

She watched him put the puzzle together in his mind. And it looked like it genuinely pained him.

'You have some kind of eating disorder?'

'Had.' She lifted her chin. 'I'm better.'

This is where he'd hit her with twenty questions, grill her for the gruesome details that people loved to know.

Can you ever truly be better after anorexia?

How low did your weight get?

Is it like alcoholism, something you manage forever?

Yes, pretty low, and kind of. She readied herself to utter the stock-standard answers. But Jed just flopped back in his seat and considered her.

'Good for you,' he said, then got stuck back into his pancakes. Ellie blinked. 'That's it?'

He glanced back up, thought hard for a moment and carefully reset his fork on his plate. 'Ellie, I've been expecting people to take me at face value since I arrived in Larkville. It would be hypocritical of me to do anything other than accept you for who you are. Or were.'

Gratitude swelled hard and fast in her ever-tightening chest. Acceptance. Pure acceptance. This is what it looked like.

'Just like that?'

'Just like that.' His eyes dropped back to his flapjacks. 'Although I would like to make you dinner tonight.'

The ridiculous juxtaposition of that statement with what she'd just revealed caused a perverse ripple of humour. 'Why?'

'Because I reckon someone needs to induct you into the pleasures of a well-cooked, well-presented, just-for-the-hell-of-it meal.'

The idea should have made her nervous, but it only made her breathless. 'And you're that someone?'

'Who do you think does all my cooking?'

'Uh, Gracie May, judging by the number of times you've mentioned her.' And by the fact they knew exactly how he took his coffee, and had his own hat hook by the door.

'Fair call. But Gram taught me how to cook. I might surprise you.'

He already did, in so many ways. She took a breath. 'Okay. But make sure it's been grown in a vacuum.'

Silence draped like a silken sheet after they'd finished laughing. Jed called for the check. Ellie used the moments that followed to gather her thoughts and to finish her solitary pancake. Dinner was almost a date. It had been a long time since she'd even been on a date, let alone actually wanted to be there.

She'd done it because it was expected.

Her mother's horrified reaction when she gave up dancing

was very telling. As if she'd just thrown in the most remarkable and appreciable thing about herself. So she'd done her best to find in herself some other marketable value at the ripe old age of twenty-one, but she'd spent so long in her determined battle to dance she really didn't have a lot of other skills. Organising fundraisers was something she was good at but it wasn't going to make her a career. Certainly not a fortune. Not the way a good marriage might. So she'd dated banker after stockbroker after up-and-coming media mogul. Year after year. She'd bluffed her way through an endless series of meals, held her emotional breath at the end of the date lest the good-night kiss become too much more and tactfully extracted herself from the most persistent and slick operators.

And she'd felt nothing. For any of them.

To the point that she wondered if all sexual sensation had withered along with her muscle mass. Was that the lasting damage her doctor had warned her so constantly about?

Yet, here she was going positively breathless at the thought of a man putting on an apron for her. Doing something just for her. Not because he wanted to get into her pants or wanted her name or her money, just because he thought she might enjoy something he had to offer. Something he enjoyed.

They paused at the entrance to Gracie May's alfresco courtyard. 'I'm going to give Deputy a proper run before heading home for some more sleep,' he said. 'You'll be okay to find your own way back?'

She nodded, intrigued and absurdly breathless. 'What time should I come round tonight?'

'I'll pick you up at six.'

'But you're right next door.'

'Ellie…this is step one in "food is more than just kilojoules." If we're going to do this we're going to do it right.'

A ridiculous lightness washed through her. 'At six, then.'

He smiled, and it soaked clean through her. Then he lowered his voice. 'Wear something nice.'

CHAPTER SIX

JED dropped the heat on the simmering rice and turned to survey his little cottage. Not perfect but tidy enough. He wanted lived-in and welcoming, not spotless and cold. Deputy snoring by the fire sure helped with the lived-in part. So did his pre-loved Texan furnishings and the original 1885 fixtures.

He glanced at the antique clock face and frowned at how short a distance the little hand had moved since he last looked. Tension had him as tight as an arthritic old-timer.

What had possessed him this morning to offer to cook Ellie a meal—after what she'd just told him? A lush dinner for two was not exactly the easiest route to arm's length for him and nor would it be the easiest of experiences for her. She'd be under pressure to eat whatever he prepared. She might end up hating it.

And him.

But the words had just tumbled from his lips as she laid her soul bare over pancakes. Maybe it was the sleep deprivation. Maybe it was the tremulous defiance in her expression after she let it slip about her past. Maybe it was his total inability to think of anything else but helping her while she sat across from him.

And then the words were out. He was committed.

Six o'clock crept marginally closer.

The crushing pressure to do something spectacular weighed down on him. He wondered if she had any idea how long it had been since he cooked for someone. Dates had been sparse enough in the past few years—but to have someone inside his home and to prepare a meal for them…

Someone like Ellie…

He felt like a rookie around her. Just a little bit in awe. She wasn't getting any less striking with the passing days. And she was knocking down his misconceptions one by one.

Not quite the princess he'd thought.

Not quite the charmed life he'd imagined.

In fact, he could only imagine how uncharmed her past must have been. He knew enough about eating disorders to guess which one she'd had and to imagine the damage that would do to a young girl's body. And mind.

Not that you'd know it now. She was slim but healthy, toned, curves in enough places, her skin and eyes clear. He only got the briefest of looks at her hair that first morning, dropping off her supplies, but it was natural and golden enough to make him wonder why she punished it by dragging it back all the time. If she'd been sick when she was younger, did she have a clue what a spectacular comeback she'd made? Maybe not, judging by the whole food-is-fuel thing. That was just…

He wanted to say weird but it was obviously what she'd needed to get healthy. So it had worked for her. And he was the last one to judge anyone for doing what they needed to do to get by. But, boy, what she was missing out on…

He gave the rice a quick stir in its stock base.

Ellie Patterson liked to know where her boundaries were. She liked things as well lined up as those flapjack pieces she'd carved so precisely. Her carefully pressed clothes, her librarian's hair, her preference for seclusion. Knowing what he knew now, he could only imagine how tough she must have found the whole situation with the steer.

Yet, she'd been impulsive enough to come to Texas without checking whether Jess Calhoun was going to be home. That meant she was capable of spontaneity. She just needed the right trigger.

What was your trigger, Ellie?

She'd still never said what her business with Jess was. Not that he could ask. The whole nosy-cop thing still stung. She just wasn't used to how they did things in Texas. And why would she be if she'd never left Manhattan?

The more he got to know her, the less like Maggie she became. Similar on the surface, but Maggie was confident from her cells up—overconfident quite often—whereas he had a sneaking suspicion that Ellie's perfect facade masked something quite different.

Quite fragile.

The two hands of the clock finally lined up and cut the clock into perfect hemispheres.

Showtime.

'Stay,' he instructed Deputy, then threw a jacket over his shirt and jeans. Casual enough not to freak her out, dressy enough to show some respect. Two seconds later he was out the door and turning down her laneway. Twelve seconds after that—including some time to make sure his shirt was tucked in—his knuckles announced themselves on her door.

His door. But amazing how fast he'd come to think of it as hers.

Like she'd always lived there. Thank goodness she hadn't. He couldn't imagine managing this attraction he felt for longer than the few weeks still—

'Hey.'

The door opened and filled with designer heels and long, bare legs. His eyes trailed up over a knee-length blue cotton dress, hair disappointingly pulled back hard but this time captured in a braid that curled down onto her bare shoulder and curved towards one breast like an arrow. His heart hammered harder than his first day on duty.

'You'll need a sweater' was all he could manage.

'Really? Just to run next door?'

'Better safe than sorry.' And better for him so he could string more than clichés together over dinner. He shook his head to refocus while she reached for the light cardigan hanging by the door. The stretch showed off more of her dancer's tone.

'Okay. Let's go.'

Either the brisk air was getting to her or this felt as weird for her as it did for him, because there was a breathlessness in her voice that gave her away. And made him think of other ways she might get breathless.

Okay...! Shutting that one down. Was he doomed to behave like a kid around her all night? He sucked in a lungful of evening air and told himself this was just a one-off. It wasn't a date. It wasn't the start of anything.

It couldn't be.

'So... Am I overdressed?' She glanced at his casual jeans and frowned. 'I can change.' She even faltered and half turned back for the house.

He slipped an arm behind her to prevent her retreat. 'You're perfect, Ellie.' And she was. The dress was so simple and so... fresh.

So not New York.

'I got this in Austin.' The woman was a mind reader. 'I drove in earlier. I didn't really bring anything appropriate with me.'

With two bulging suitcases he doubted it, but he liked that she'd gone into a fashion crisis for him. And then as rapidly as the thought came to him he shoved it away.

This wasn't a date. This was a...demonstration.

'Good choice,' he said, and hoped the appreciation didn't sound as gratuitous in her ears as it did in his.

They turned the corner and his hand brushed her back as he guided her in front of him. She flinched at the contact. When he was younger he would have chalked that up to a physical spark, but her hasty steps forward told another story. His touch made her uncomfortable. That killed any fantastical notion that she was breathless about this dinner.

She was just plain nervous.

He paused on his porch and indicated the outdoor sofa. 'I'll just set the risotto to simmer and then we're heading out. Make yourself comfortable for a few minutes.'

Deputy dashed out and went straight to Ellie. Her hand went absently to the thick of his fur. So it wasn't all touch that she was averse to.

Just his.

He found the lid for his pot and dropped the heat down to almost nothing. Gram taught him the best way to slow-cook rice but it needed an hour longer than he'd left himself. Hopefully Ellie didn't mind a late supper. New Yorkers always ate late. It was one of the things that used to bug him about Maggie. He wanted to eat half the furniture on getting home; she wanted to wait until the streets grew more lively.

'Okay, let's go.' He pulled his front door shut behind him.

She stared at him. 'Wasn't tonight about a meal?'

'It was about a meal appreciation. Part of appreciation is anticipation.'

'In other words you're going to make me wait?'

'Not good with delayed gratification?'

She smiled, tightly. 'Are you kidding? Self-denial is what I specialised in.'

'Right. Well, then, I'll ask you to trust me. Would it help if I told you we were heading over to the Double Bar C?'

She stood. 'We're visiting the Calhouns?'

'Just their land. Their foreman, Wes Brogan, is going to meet us at the gate.'

'So we just…roam around on their land? Dressed like this?'

He smiled as he opened the SUV's door for her. 'We won't be roaming. I have a specific destination in mind. But I figured you might be curious to see a bit of the Double Bar C.'

'Yes. I'd love to. Now I understand the sweater.' She climbed in, neatly evading his proffered hand.

Deputy was most put-out to be relegated to the back seat and his harness meant he couldn't even stretch his head forward for a compensatory scratch. But a car trip was a car trip and he was happy enough to stick his head out the back window and snap at the trees whizzing by.

Ellie watched him in her side mirror. 'I can't imagine him in the canine unit.'

He glanced over his shoulder at his old friend. 'The thing with Deputy is that he's a real obliging animal. That made him easy to train and super-responsive in the field. He loved being on task and he had a fantastic nose.' He brought his eyes back to the road ahead of them. 'He was our first choice for tracking. His size was a deterrent for perps, but he was next to useless in close contact. He just didn't have the aggression we needed.'

'Is that why he flunked?'

It had to come up sooner or later. Jed chose his words carefully. 'He never really flunked, it was more of a...retirement situation.'

She smiled. 'Really? He got his 401(k) and gold watch?'

He hissed under his breath. Had he really thought he could only half explain? 'Actually he had some trauma in the field. He never really recovered from it.' True yet not entirely true. The truth was too shameful.

Her smile faded immediately and creases folded her brow. She sat up straighter. 'He was hurt?'

'He got beaten, Ellie. Pretty bad.'

She spun around in her seat and looked back at Deputy, so content and relaxed now. Jed's own mind filled with the images of how they'd found him down by the river.

Her eyes came back to him, wide and dismayed. 'Who would do that?'

'Bad guys don't discriminate. Deputy could have led us to them.'

'What about his...person. Where was he?'

His stomach tightened into a tiny, angry fist. He cleared his throat. 'She... His handler.'

'Where was she?'

Shame burned low and fierce in his gut. 'She was right there with him. But she was...in no position to stop them. When it was over he dragged himself to her side and wouldn't leave until she did.'

In a body bag.

Those clear blue eyes filled with tears. 'Oh, my God...'

Nice date conversation, stupid! He tried to wind it up, as much for his own sake as hers. Those were not days he let himself revisit. 'After that he had trouble with close conflict, which made him a liability in the team. He was retired. But he was miserable doing the PR rounds and there were no openings for therapy dogs. I decided to take him in with me.'

'And he's okay now?'

'About the most action he sees with me is car chases and some casual steer mustering.' Which brought him nicely back on topic. 'Wes was grateful you called the fence breach in the other day. Saved his team a lot of time. He was happy to do this return favor.'

The sadness in her eyes lifted just a bit but he noticed she kept casting her eyes back to Deputy in her mirror. As though his physical trauma was something she could relate to.

'Well, I'm glad those hours on the rooftop were valuable for someone!'

The gates to the Double Bar C were perpetually open and Jed cruised on through and followed the well-maintained road for about a mile, then threw a right and headed on up a much less groomed track.

Up ahead the Calhouns' foreman waited for them near a rusty, wide-open gate. The padlock swung free in his thin fingers.

'Wes.' Jed pulled the SUV up to the gate opening.

'Sheriff.' Wes leaned his forearms on the lowered window and dropped the padlock through it into Jed's hands and smiled. Not his mouth, his eyes. 'Lock up when you're through?'

'Sure will. Wes, this is Ellie Patterson from New York City. Ellie, Wes Brogan, he's been foreman here on the Double Bar C for near as long as either of us has been alive.'

'Right grateful for your help with the stock on Monday, ma'am.' He dipped his broad, battered hat and did a good job of not looking curious at seeing his sheriff not only out of uniform but with a woman. At night. Alone.

Ellie leaned forward. 'You're welcome. I hope they were all okay?'

Jed stifled a snort and waited for Wes's reaction. Brogan was proud of his stock *en masse* but he didn't have a lot of time for the intellectual talents of cattle individually.

'Damned fool livestock were just fine. Was the fence came off second best.'

Ellie sagged back in her seat.

'Why don't you leave Deputy Dawg with me, Sheriff,' Wes offered. 'He can mix it up with some of the hands till you pick him up from the homestead. Then he won't get in your way up at the mine.'

It was crazy to think of a dog as a chaperone but having Deputy along made this whole thing feel less like a date and more like an outing. Leaving him behind threw everything into a new light. But saying no would only raise more speculation in Wes's shrewd hazel eyes. 'He'd enjoy that, thanks, Wes.'

Deputy leapt—literally—at the chance to get out of the car and visit with Wes. He was still running the older man in circles as Jed rumbled the SUV up and over the hill. The side of his face tingled and he knew Ellie was staring at him. He met her speculative gaze.

'Mine?' she queried. 'We're going hunting for gold?'

Of course she didn't miss Wes's slip. 'Part of the Calhoun fortune was made on mineral rights,' he said simply. 'The Double Bar C is dotted with speculative mines going back a century.'

Her brows dropped. 'And you thought a dress and heels would be appropriate attire for exploring an old mine?'

The image made him smile. If there was a woman to pull that off it was Ellie Patterson. He had a feeling she'd tough out any situation with finesse. 'We're not exploring it, exactly.'

'What are we doing…exactly?'

Here we go… Make or break time. He'd come up with this idea in that crazy, anything's possible, just-before-you-fall-asleep moment after he collapsed back into bed this morning. Seemed to him that Ellie lived her life trussed up in expectations and

New York niceties and he wondered what she would do if she
let go of all that, just for a moment.

Let herself just...be.

But this could go only two ways.

He took a breath and just leapt right in. 'How do you feel
about bats?'

CHAPTER SEVEN

'BATS?'

Ellie stared at Jed. He didn't seem to be joking so she dug a little further. 'Baseball or vampire?'

Those gorgeous lips twisted. 'Just regular bats.'

'I…' Was this a trick question? But he looked serious enough. 'I've seen bats before, feeding high over Central Park.' She almost dared not ask. 'Why?'

'I want you to see one of Larkville's most amazing sights.'

'You must have a low opinion of your town if a bunch of bats in an old mine is one of its highlights.'

'That's not a "no."'

'I'm not going to say no or yes until I know exactly what you have in mind.'

He stared at her long and hard. 'Can I ask you to trust me? I don't want to spoil the surprise.'

Any surprise that had bats in it couldn't be all that great. But this was Texas, her genetic home, and he was looking at her with such optimism…

He pulled the SUV up on a ridge top and pulled the handbrake on hard.

'I'm trusting you that this won't be bad, Jed.' She hated that there was a quaver in her voice as she stepped out of the vehicle.

'It's not bad. And I'll be right here with you.'

Her body responded to his low promise in a ripple of shivers.

The sun was half hidden behind the hills and ridges of Hayes

County but Jed left the SUV's headlights on for illumination. They pointed across the void where the earth dropped clean away.

'If we're here for sunset we should have driven faster,' she joked, not entirely comfortable with having no idea what they were doing.

'Trust me,' he murmured, close behind her. 'Just let something happen to you, not because of you.'

Ellie's breath caught. That sounded awfully intimate. And he was standing pretty close. In the heartbeat before she remembered how hard she found physical contact, her body responded to his words with something that almost felt…sensual.

You know…if it had been in anyone but her.

The sun seemed to pick up momentum the further it sank.

'See that opening down there?' He pointed down into the void while they still had any light at all and she squinted her eyes to see what he meant. 'One of the region's biggest colonies of free-tailed bat roosts in there.'

'It's a long way down,' she whispered, still transfixed by his closeness.

'Not a problem. We're not going to them…'

Almost as he said the words she caught a momentary glimpse of a small black shape cutting across the stream of light coming from the SUV. She gasped. 'Was that a bat?'

'Keep watching.'

A second black shape shot across the headlight beam. Then another. Then another. Crisscrossing the shaft of light like big, dark fireflies.

'Those are scouts,' he said, closer again to her ear. But the magic and mystery of the evening had taken hold. She forgot to be sensitive to his proximity.

'What are they scouting for?' she breathed.

'To see if it's safe.'

'Safe for what?'

She heard his smile in the warmth of his words. 'For the colony to hunt.'

And then it happened. A surge of small black shapes formed a wave and rose towards them from below. The raw sound of so many flapping wings made her think of a flood surge. She stumbled back, right into Jed. He held steady.

'You're safe, Ellie,' he said, low into her ear so she could hear him. 'They can navigate around individual blades of grass, they're not going to have any problem missing us. Just let it happen.'

Just let it happen.

How many times had her soul cried back in dance training after her instructors promised her it would happen if she just let it come—the magical, otherworldly sensation of letting the dance completely take over. She watched it happen in her fellow dancers, she watched the joy on their faces, and she wanted it for herself.

But no matter how her soul had bled it had never just happened for her.

Just like the rest of her life.

The bats drew closer, moving as a single body, and the first members flicked past her a little too close for comfort. She flinched away from them and reached behind her to curl Jed's shirt in her anxious fingers.

'You're okay.' His arms crossed down over her shoulders to keep her still. But nothing felt more unnatural than to stand here on the very edge of a precipice while a tsunami of wild creatures enveloped her. Every part of her wanted to rush back to the safety of the vehicle. Surely she could watch it from there?

More bats whizzed past, and then more—the closest managing to miss the two of them by an inch, until she felt like they were being buffeted by a hurricane of tiny wings, whipping close enough to feel the tiny sting of disrupted air against her skin and hair but never actually touching her.

The wave kept coming, thicker and deeper until the air around them seethed loudly with life.

'There's two million of them in there,' Jed half shouted as the windstorm from twice that many wings hit her.

The sheer scale of the life around them sent her senses spinning off into the dark sky. She felt small and insignificant against such a powerful collective mind, but safe and so very present.

Two million creatures knew she was there. Two million creatures were taking care not to hurt her. Two million creatures were relying on her not to hurt them.

Being frightened suddenly felt…kind of pointless. But she wasn't ready to be alone up here.

She slid her arms up between Jed's still crossed over her and then ran her hands along his forearms until they curled neatly within his. His fingers threaded through hers and anchored there so that the two of them formed their own, primitive set of wings.

Ellie carefully unfolded their joined limbs until they were stretched as wide as the bats' must be. Still the tiny black shapes did nothing more than buffet them as they surged past and up into the Texan dusk. She lifted her left arm—and Jed's—and then her right, a flowing exploration, testing the bats' sonar skills. They continued to miss her by the shallowest of breaths.

Incredible lightness filled her body until she felt certain she could take lift on the bats' air. She bent and swayed amidst the flurry of bats and closed her eyes to just feel the magnitude of the power in their numbers. Her hair whipped around her face, coming loose of its braid in the updraft caused by their exodus.

Jed stepped back slightly and dropped her right hand.

Anchored to him by her left, Ellie stepped ever closer to the drop of the ridge—ever closer to the tempest of tiny mammals coming over its lip—and she stretched her body up and out blindly, feeling the music of their flight, the melody in their subtle turns and shifts. Seeing the mass of bats as they each must: through their other senses.

Twisting as the airborne fleet did felt the most natural and right thing in the world. She used Jed's strong hold as a pivot and twisted under his arm in a slow, smooth pirouette as she'd done a thousand times onstage. But it had never felt this right onstage. Or this organic.

This…perfect.

She bent and she straightened and she moved with the flow of the bats—inside the flow—her eyes closed the whole time, predicting their intent in the mass of the flight. Being part of it.

Was this it? Was this what real dancers experienced when they hit that special place where everything just came together? When they let their minds go and just felt? She was eternal. As old as the planet and as young as a baby taking its first breath. Every synapse in her body crackled with life.

The whole time she was tethered to earth by Jed's touch, by the warmth of the intense gaze she could practically feel against her skin.

She danced. Sensual, swaying and shifting, and reaching out on the precipice, letting her body have its way.

Finally, the density of the bats around her lessened, the flurry of their millions-strong zephyr dropped, the sounds of their flight faded. Until only the last few laggers whizzed past.

And the only sound left was Ellie's hard breathing.

Her eyes fluttered open.

She stared out across the empty void of the dark Calhoun gully and felt the exhilaration slowly leach from her body. She missed it now that she'd finally—finally!—had a taste. But, deep down, her heart pulsed with joy that she was capable of feeling it at all. Utter sensual freedom. Infinite possibility.

After a lifetime of believing otherwise.

'Ellie?' Jed was as breathless as she was.

A dark heat surged through her and swamped the last vestiges of golden glow. What had she done? Dancing like that in front of a man who was virtually a stranger. It was like suddenly realising you were naked.

But she was nothing if not resilient. She turned and used the move to twist her fingers out of his. Ready for his laughter.

But he didn't laugh; he stared at her, silent and grave. 'That was—'

'Not what you were expecting, I'm sure.' She forced the levity into her words. Better to laugh first…

'—amazing.' His face didn't change. His focus did not move. 'I was going to say that was amazing.'

She stared at him, searching for signs of condescension. 'I just…' What could she say? How did you explain one of the most moving moments in your life?

'Why are you crying? Are you hurt?'

Unsteady fingers shot to her cheeks. Sure enough, they were wet.

'No.' Not outwardly. 'But that was—' the most free she'd felt in her entire life '—so beautiful. So wild.'

He stepped forward, arms open to comfort her, and she couldn't help the learned response of her body. She flinched.

Jed froze.

His voice, when it came, was thick. 'Is it being touched in general you don't like…or is it just me?'

CHAPTER EIGHT

SHE'D hurt him.

After he'd done this amazing and lovely thing for her. After he'd not judged her at all this morning when she dumped her whole illness on him.

'It's not you.' She shook her head, and golden strands flew all around her. Trembling hands went immediately to the destruction that was her carefully braided hair. Between the side-swipes of four million tiny bat wings and her own twisting and rolling, it was a complete wreck. She fumbled trying to tuck the largest strands back in.

'Why don't you just take it out?'

Her eyes shot to his. As if she hadn't made enough of a fool of herself tonight, getting freaky about her hair would be the final insult.

'No, I'll just…' Her fingers moved more quickly, shoving and tucking, but it wasn't easy, reinstating the prison after the freedom of just moments before.

'Ellie…' Jed's hand slid up onto hers, stilled it. She forced herself not to snatch it away. 'Don't make it all perfect again. Don't undo everything you just experienced.'

She didn't want to. Deep inside she longed to just let it loose, or leave it wild and shambolic like right now. 'What must it look like…?'

'It looks like you just took a ride in the rear of a World War

Two fighter, or galloped hard across all of the Double Bar C.'
His eyes held hers, penetrating. 'It looks good.'

She stared at him, trapped in the intensity of his stare. His
hand slipped off hers and slid down to the small band holding
her braid in place. He closed his fingers over it but didn't pull.

He waited for her.

She took a breath, still locked in his gaze and whispered, 'I
don't wear it out.'

'Why not? It's beautiful. Amazing colour.' He stroked the
hair sticking out from under the band. For a bunch of dead skin
cells they certainly came alive under his touch.

Beautiful? Hardly. 'It was a symptom…of my illness. For so
long it was brittle.' For so long she was too ashamed to let people see it. 'And it fell out in patches.'

'Not now,' he assured her, slowly sliding the band down and
curling it into his fingers as it slid off. 'It's healthy and strong.
Like you are.' He worked the bottom of the braid loose, his fingers gentle but a little bit clumsy. The braid unwound more.

It was his clumsiness that stole her breath. It was his clumsiness that stilled her hands when she burned to disguise her
shame and pull her hair back into a ponytail.

He was as nervous as she was.

For her this was a major step. What was his excuse?

He let gravity do most of the work, but he helped it along by
arranging her long tresses around her shoulders as the braid finally gave way completely.

Ellie stood stiff and ready for some kind of reaction from him.

'Why did you give up dance?'

The unexpected question distracted her from the discordant
sensation of having her hair unbound and free in front of someone.

'What I saw just now…' he continued, 'and the fact you made
yourself sick to be good at it. It makes me wonder why you'd
give it up.'

Tonight had been way too monumental for her to be able to
retreat to her usual private shell. She was unravelled in more

ways than one. She answered as honestly as she could, despite
her very cells crying out for her not to.

'Not eating was never really about dancing,' she confessed,
and then wondered where the heck she went next. Brown eyes
just watched her. 'But professional dancing was a good environment for a sickness like that to go unremarked. Everyone was
hungry in those dressing rooms, everyone was lean, everyone
was exhausted all the time.' She felt it now, just for talking about
it. The cell-deep fatigue they all danced through six days a week.

'It certainly wasn't conducive to me getting better, but I didn't
leave because of it.'

'Then, why?'

Her eyes dropped. Would he understand? Or would she just
sound like the precious princess he thought she was? Only one
way to find out.

'Turns out the Patterson trust was a major benefactor of the
company I danced for. My father donated six figures every year
to it.'

'So he was proud of what you did?'

Her smile even felt token. 'I traced his contribution back in
the company's annual reports. It started the year I was recruited.'
She cleared her throat. 'Just before.'

His eyes said more than any words could have.

The old shame sat heavily on shoulders that had felt so light
just minutes ago.

'He bought you in?'

'When I was feeling particularly glass half-full I'd imagine he
saw how hard I was working and wanted me to feel validated.'

'Did you?'

She thought about that. 'At first. It had been my dream for so
long. But the harder I trained the further behind everyone else
I slipped. The more I saw what they all had that I was missing.'

'What was that?'

'Passion,' she snorted. 'Heart.'

His eyes blazed. 'I don't believe that.'

She tossed her head back. 'Are you a regular at the ballet?'

Colour peeked out above his collar. 'So trust me to know where I sat in the company food chain. I loved the logic and the certainty of choreography but I lacked spirit.' Her breath shuddered in. 'I made a great chorus member, but I was never going to be a principal.'

'You threw it in because you didn't get to be the star?'

Even after just a few days she knew when he was being provocative for effect. He had to recognise by now how little she liked being the center of attention.

She smiled. 'No. But my father bought my spot. And I knew how many real dancers had earned it. Their chance. I decided to let one of them have it.'

Angry colour crept up his neck. 'You gave up your childhood for it. You gave up your health. Don't tell me you hadn't earned it.'

'I didn't want it all that much, it turned out.' She shrugged. 'It was everything I knew growing up, something I could excel at, something I could be technically proficient at. That proficiency probably would have kept me there until my body literally couldn't do it but, in the end, I couldn't face being reminded of my lack of passion every single day.'

'No. Not after what I just saw.'

'Earlier today I might have disagreed with you on that point,' she murmured. 'But with what I felt just now…' She turned and stared down at the old Calhoun mine. Then she brought her eyes back up to his and pressed her fist between her breasts. 'Maybe you're right. Maybe there's passion in here…somewhere…just looking for the right voice.'

Maybe? Jed watched Ellie's blue eyes glitter in the low light thrown by his SUV. Was she serious? Underneath the neatly pressed outfits and perfectly groomed hair, the woman oozed sensuality, but obviously didn't know it. The way she'd danced as the sun set… He'd never seen anything as moving. How someone could be one hundred per cent focused and one hundred per cent absent at the same time. Off…somewhere…otherworldly.

He recognised the feeling, though it had been a long time

between sensations. He'd had it back when he was a kid and learning to horseride with his dad. The first time he'd galloped—petrified but exhilarated—alongside the man that he admired and respected so much. The man who only came home to him from duty on weekends and whose time and attention on those days was the whole world to a boy of six years of age. It was a feeling that had had to sustain him for a very long time after his father died.

Until he eventually forgot how it had felt.

Until years passed between incidences of remembering it.

He almost envied Ellie the experience she'd just had except for the fact that his own body had responded vicariously to her complete immersion. He'd seen her experiencing the thrill for the first time. He'd felt it in the tight grip of her fingers, the way she wanted to fly away from him but didn't at the same time.

It fed a need in him that he'd barely acknowledged. It stirred his blood in a way that probably wasn't helpful out here in the privacy and dark. Under a rising moon. This whole night had gone a totally different direction than he meant. He hadn't prepared himself to feel...drawn.

He cleared his throat. 'I have a confession to make. I brought you out here to show off a bit of Larkville, to help you see that the country has its merits, too. And to get you loosened up a bit so you might enjoy dinner rather than viewing it as something to be endured. But I'm glad that it has affected you so strongly,' he continued. 'And I'm thankful I could experience a little bit of it, through you, too.'

They stared at each other wordlessly for moments. The growing awareness in her gaze intrigued and frightened him at the same time.

'You still up for dinner?' he risked.

For three hard heartbeats he thought she was going to say no. But then she tossed back that hair she was so ashamed of and took a deep breath.

'Depends,' she said, and Jed realised he'd do just about anything at all to keep this connection they'd unexpectedly formed between them alive a little longer even if it was a mistake. It had been too, too long.

Her eyes twinkled. 'Will there be bats?'

No bats.

But something delicious was bubbling away on the stove when they walked back into Jed's cottage half an hour later. They'd had to pry Deputy away from the men lazing around the Calhoun hand quarters—he was in his doggie element—but he was happy enough to be back in front of his own fire now.

So was Ellie.

'Sure gets cold fast at night here,' she said.

'Yep,' Jed agreed. 'As soon as that sun sinks behind the mountains…'

Excellent. Talking about the weather. A new social low. Conversation had been pretty sporadic since returning from the Double Bar C but, for the life of her, Ellie couldn't manage anything more fascinating.

When had she got this nervous? And why?

'Give me ten minutes—I'll just serve up…' Jed cleared his throat. 'Washroom's through there if you want to freshen up.'

She did, but there'd be a mirror in there and if she looked in the mirror there was no way she was walking out with her hair hanging loose around her shoulders. And given how Jed would almost certainly feel if she came back with it perfectly pulled back, Ellie figured it would be best all round not to go in at all.

Plus it felt pretty good having it down. Kind of…risqué.

Her eyes automatically went to Jed, but she dragged them away when she realised what they'd done. Risqué and Sheriff Jed Jackson didn't belong together in the same thought process.

At all.

They went instead to Deputy. Much safer territory. He was such a good-natured dog. She'd thought he was just plain dopey but he couldn't have been to make it into the canine squad, even as a tracker, if he wasn't smart. They had to be pretty focused and resilient. Her heart squeezed… Though apparently every dog had its breaking point.

Just like humans.

Whatever kind of a dog he used to be he approached life much more simply now. She certainly understood that desire.

'Ready?'

Jed pulled up two seats at the timber breakfast bar. Then he added a bottle of wine and two glasses to the two steaming bowls already there.

'We're eating here?' she queried.

'Yup. A meal doesn't have to be fancy to be good.'

She frowned at him. 'I feel like I need to let you know I've had good food before. Despite my—' idiosyncrasies '—rule.'

'Good dining is about so much more than the taste.' He held one of the two tall seats out for her to perch on. Then he held an empty glass up and raised an eyebrow. She nodded—barely—and he splashed two inches of white wine into the glass. She wiggled more comfortably on the seat, starting to enjoy the pageantry of this meal, coming as it did so close on the heels of one of the most exhilarating experiences of her life.

'Texan wine?' she tested.

'Naturally.'

He slid a plate towards her and she took an anxious breath. But he'd been careful; she had a bit of everything on her plate but nowhere near the quantities on his. He wasn't out to overwhelm her. She appreciated that.

She peered closer. 'What is this?'

'Cuisine à la Jackson. Texan ribs, risotto and salad.' He smiled. 'A tribute to my past and my present.'

She could see something Mediterranean in the colour of his skin and eyes, bleached by generations of cold Atlantic winters. That side of his family came endowed with old legend and crazy anecdotes and he shared some of them as Ellie tried the moist risotto and the tangy salad. But when she got to the lone rib on her plate she hesitated.

'Just like Texans do,' he said, anticipating her question. 'With your fingers.'

'I don't think I've eaten with my fingers since I was four,' she joked, lifting the rib to her mouth.

'About time you rediscovered the art.'

Ellie tentatively wrapped her lips around the sticky goodness. Her eyes rounded at the divine taste. 'Ofmigof…!'

Ribs were good. Really good. Rib muscles were constantly being worked out just breathing, so it made sense they'd be lean and tender. That meant that they got a tick in her 'good fuel' box. But in this case they also got a tick each in the boxes marked 'yum' and 'plain fun to eat.'

She nibbled her way along one piece of bone, then licked her fingers individually. Jed reached over for the flat-iron pan the ribs had come out on, his muscles bunching under his shirt. He tonged another one up and lifted an eyebrow.

She only hesitated for a moment. 'What's it cooked in?'

He placed one more rib on her plate and shook his head. 'Old Texan secret.'

'Come on. I'm more Texan than you are—'

Ellie hid the accidental slip-up behind his full laugh. A mistake like that was not like her, she was normally so guarded with her words. She glanced at her wine—only an inch missing. How relaxed had the bats made her? Or was it Jed?

In the end she barely noticed the passing of time, or food over her lips. The conversation roamed all over the place and she was most rapt by the accidental snippets of information about the Calhouns—any one of her sisters or her brothers. Her Texan sisters and brothers, she allowed, thinking of Alex and Charlotte and Matt. Though Matt was as Texan as she was, technically.

Then, barely realising it had happened, she found herself curled up on a sofa just like her own, a cup of steaming hot cocoa in hand. Cocoa. The drink that got no ticks in any of the boxes except the one marked 'sigh.'

'Jed, I have to admit—' and admitting she was wrong took some doing '—this has been a pretty awesome evening.'

'Even the food?'

'Especially the food. I never quite got why people insisted on eating when they got together but...' She looked at him curiously. 'It's kind of nice. Relaxing.'

'That's the cocoa.'

She barely had the energy for more than a low chuckle. 'Right. That must be it.' She shifted more comfortably on the sofa.

'So you didn't hate it?'

She stared at him, recognising genuine anxiety flirting at the back of his careful expression. 'On the contrary. I'm not sure when I've ever been this relaxed and comfortable with someone. Thank you.' She ignored the squeezing sensation deep inside.

'Are you thanking me for dinner? Or for being comfortable to be around?'

She tipped her head onto the thick-stuffed top of the sofa and let it rest there. 'Both?'

Confusion battled it out in his silent gaze. 'For what it's worth, the feeling's mutual. Though I wouldn't have expected that when I first met you out on the road to the Calhouns'.'

She groaned. 'You got me at an especially difficult time. End of a long drive, a bad week.'

'Drowning in steer.'

Ellie laughed. 'And the steer.'

'Why the bad week?'

Could she tell him? She wanted to—a lot—but until she'd spoken to Jess it really wasn't her secret to share. How ironic since she was the secret.

She leaned over and placed the last of her hot cocoa on a side table Jed had dragged over next to the sofa. Then she brought her eyes back to his. 'Back home I'm...expected to uphold a certain standard. A level of output. It's a crazy kind of pace.' Though it's quite handy when you don't think you have much else of a life to lead. 'But add a few emotional upheavals to the mix and it all gets a bit overwhelming.'

Upheavals—suitably broad and non-specific.

'Who expects it? This standard?'

She blinked at him. 'Everyone. I'm Eleanor Patterson.'

'You say that like you're the First Lady, with obligations to the whole country.' He shifted his leg slightly to point the soles of his shoes towards the fire and it brought him a hint closer to her. 'Define "everyone"?'

'My parents. My brother and sisters. The people who count on me to work their events, to attract a crowd, to make them money.'

'What about you?'

She frowned at him. 'What about me?'

'Do you have high expectations of yourself?'

'I do. But not unrealistic, I don't think. I have a good idea of my strengths and weaknesses. It's not all bad.'

Suddenly his gaze grew more intense. 'Throw me a couple of strengths.'

When had he moved that close? 'Okay. Well… People call me driven. Focused. Tireless. They're all good things.'

'Depends how you look at it.' Jed stared steadily at her. 'You don't look tireless to me. You just look tired.'

For absolutely no reason, the compassion in his lined face was like a sock to her guts, robbing her of air. Her chest squeezed in, collecting into a tight, painful ball. She held his eyes.

'I'm exhausted,' she confessed. Exhausted by life. Exhausted by faking it. Exhausted by all the angst and worrying over something she couldn't control in any way.

Like whether or not she was a Calhoun.

He turned his body front on to her and took her hand between his.

It wasn't a come-on. It was humane compassion, pure and simple, but it wasn't something she could let herself do. She pulled her hand free and then, without meaning to speak, words were leaving her lips. It suddenly seemed extra important to her that Jed understand it wasn't him she was afraid of touching.

'I don't like physical contact because I was always so self-conscious about how I must feel to people,' she blurted. 'How frail.'

How skeletal.

He didn't react, but she was starting to expect that from him now. Jed Jackson was a man who was careful to think before he spoke. Plus the deep shadows in his gaze gave him away. 'You don't want to seem fragile?'

'I'm supposed to be strong.'

He slid one hand along the back of the sofa and his eyes were steady on hers. 'You can't be strong all the time. It's okay to ask for help.'

His body language was obvious, his message clear. He was there to lend her strength if she wanted it.

But she had to come to him.

She stared at the big barrel of a chest just a foot away from her, imagined resting there. How had they got there, the two of them? At the place that a virtual stranger could ask her if she wanted to absorb some of his apparently endless strength and the place that she was actually considering doing it.

But there they were and it didn't feel weird, just…foreign. She hadn't had someone touching her in a long time but it had been even longer since she'd been the one to initiate contact. Beyond the necessary courtesy with the necessary people. Beyond her sister's life-sustaining hugs that she only allowed because it was Alex. Beyond the quickly evaded clinch at the conclusion of the endless first and only dates she went on to make her mother happy.

Heart hammering, her eyes slid to the soft denim shirt covering his broad chest. It did look extremely comfortable. And it was so close.

She was as slow to move as trust was to come but, once she started, momentum took over. She reclined into the sofa back, against the length of Jed's arm, her breath suspended the entire time.

He did nothing. No words. No actions. He didn't trap her within the curl of his arm or force some kind of intimacy for which she wasn't ready. He just sat quiet and undemanding and understanding as she grew accustomed to the feel of someone's body against hers.

'There's a reason I took Deputy in with me,' he rumbled from next to her. 'More than just him needing a home.'

His pause wasn't an invitation for her to speak, it was an opportunity for him to gather his thoughts. Something about the slight stiffness in the body pressed so warmly against hers told her that he was rewarding her vulnerability with one of his own.

Making this easier for her by making it harder on himself.

Ellie inched in closer to the crook of his arm. Why she thought such a tiny gesture would bolster him… Yet, it seemed to work.

'Police presence was massively increased in Manhattan after the 9/11 attacks,' he started. 'The NYPD got an influx of new recruits wanting to make a difference, to defend their city. For a while there we had rookies coming out of our ears but, by the time I was promoted to the canine unit, the enthusiasm to serve had waned, yet the required service level stayed high.'

He stared into the fire.

'As captain of the unit it was my job to oversee training and rosters and staff development as well as dealing with budgets and resources and procedures. It was my job to deal with the expectation of management, too. Sometimes those two things didn't fit together at all.'

'Expectations and resources?'

She felt his nod in the slight shift of his torso. 'I made some decisions that I wasn't all that comfortable with.'

Ellie changed the angle of her head so that she was looking up at him. Mostly into that gorgeous jawline. 'Did that include Deputy Dawg?'

The hard line of his jaw flexed. Pronounced creases formed between his brow. 'Deputy's handler…Officer O'Halloran. She and Deputy were inseparable, she was as good a trainer as Deputy was a tracker, but she was no more suited for the front line than he was. I knew that even if she didn't. I knew she was misplaced from before she'd even arrived in the section.'

'But…?'

'But reassigning her would have meant my team was down by one and the others had already carried her for the weeks it takes to train up a new handler and dog pair. And it would have compromised our output at a time we were being hammered for results.'

He paused for so long, Ellie thought maybe he'd changed his mind.

'So I sent her out while we scouted other units for likely replacements. Despite knowing she wasn't ready—that maybe she never would be. I exposed her and Deputy to risk before they were ready.'

Ellie's breath tightened in response to the sudden tension in Jed's body and she remembered his earlier words. 'The waterfront.'

'She died there, Ellie. And Deputy was beaten half to death defending her. And both of those shames were on me. My lack of judgement. My haste.' He swallowed again. 'My weakness in not standing up to the game-playing and the bull dust from higher up the food chain.'

'You were doing your job,' she murmured, though it wasn't a whole lot of consolation.

He threw up his hands angrily. 'My job was to look after my team and my district and make informed, careful decisions. Not to throw a rookie to the wolves.'

His frustrated outburst over, his hands dropped back down and one fell lightly onto her shoulder, but Jed was so lost in his memories he didn't even notice. And, for the same reason, Ellie couldn't bring herself to protest. Plus the small and surprising fact that she didn't entirely mind it.

'Is that why you quit the department?'

'I let that team down as badly as I would have let Deputy down by leaving a working dog to rot in some public-relations role. Me stepping aside made way for someone who deserved the stars on their shoulder.'

'That sounds vaguely familiar,' she murmured, lifting her

eyes to seek out his. He dragged his gaze back from the spot on the far wall he'd been pinned to and lowered it to stare down his cheekbone at her.

His thick lashes fringed a thoughtful expression. 'It's not the same.'

'No, it's not. But it's close. Sounds like we walked away for similar reasons.'

That caused more than a few moments' silence. 'I'm happiest out in the field interacting with people and doing an honest day's work,' he finally said.

'Ditto, as it turns out. Minus the job.' She laughed. 'And the people.'

His smile transformed the shadows in his gaze into contrasting highlights for the sudden lightness there. He nudged her sideways. 'You're not so bad with people once you get warmed up, Ellie Patterson.'

All this time she'd thought pressing into someone like this would be uncomfortable and exposed. But she only felt warm and somehow restored. If Jed was to pay the slightest attention to her body pressed against his, she knew he wouldn't feel stringy muscles and vacant hollows under his fingers. He'd feel flesh and curves and…woman.

Teenage Ellie would never have been able to conceive of a day she'd feel proud of her convex butt and actual bust. But she did right this second.

She felt…desirable.

Brown eyes caught and held hers. Jed's pulse kicked visibly against his skin as his strong, honest heart sped up. Her shallow breathing betrayed the fact that hers matched it exactly.

His gaze dropped to her lips.

'Well.' She cleared her throat. 'Deputy's a lucky Dawg to have ended up with you.' She averted her eyes before he could read too much into her glazed expression.

Jed sat up straight and then used the dying fire as an excuse to break the contact between them. Embarrassed heat surged up her body as he stood and selected a large log piece to add to the embers.

And the moment—so surreal and rare—was well and truly lost.

Ellie stood. 'Thank you for a great evening, Jed.'

'Have I changed your mind about food being more than just nutrition?'

'You've change my mind about a few things, actually.'

Speculation filled his careful gaze. 'Really?'

'But my jury's still out. One good experience doesn't undo the lessons of a lifetime.'

Did he even know she was only partly talking about food now?

He grabbed a spare coat from his stand and helped to drape it around her shoulders. 'That sounds like a carefully disguised opening for a repeat performance.'

Did she want to do this again? Did she want to risk exposing herself to Jed? For Jed? 'You set the bar pretty high tonight. It's going to be hard to beat.'

He paused with his hands on her shoulders and spoke from behind her. 'Is that a challenge?'

She turned and stared up at him and hoped everything she was feeling wasn't broadcast in her eyes. 'Maybe.' Then she turned for the door and opened it herself just to prove she was a modern woman. But secretly she'd loved how he'd so naturally helped her into his coat. How he'd held the car door for her. It gave her an idea of the kind of thoughtful man he'd be in…other ways. Awareness zinged in the air around them as she stepped out into the bracing cold.

Jed followed close behind.

'Walking me back, too, Sheriff?'

'I picked you up, I see you home.'

How many of those New York dates had even bothered to wait while she hailed a cab? Not counting the ultimately disappointed ones who assumed they'd be getting in it behind her.

'Personal rule?'

His voice shrugged. 'Just good manners.'

But as her doorway loomed so, too, did the moment she'd struggled with her whole dating life. The moment she had to hint—or just blurt outright—that they weren't getting inside her wing of the Patterson home. That they weren't getting inside anything else, either. The few that had actually gotten as far as her door weren't there because they were chivalrous; they were there because they were persistent or amazingly thick-skinned. Or presumptuous.

Jed was there because… Well, because she'd been far too busy being aware of his smell and the deep sound of his voice to get busy planning her exit strategy. So here she was just steps away from her door and she had no choice but to wing it.

She turned on the ball of her foot and Jed lurched to a halt to avoid crashing right into her.

So…good night! She opened her mouth to utter the words.

'Don't forget Sarah's coming for you on Saturday.' Jed's pedestrian reminder threw her off her game completely. So did the fact that he was just standing there staring placidly at her. Not making a single move. Implying that she wasn't going to see him again.

'Coat,' he said, when she just stared her confusion up at him.

'Oh…' She shrugged quickly out of his warm jacket.

But the tiniest of smiles played on his face and she wondered if she was being played, too.

'See you on the weekend, maybe,' he said as he folded his jacket over his arm and turned to walk away, casual as you like.

Where were the corny lines? The grasping arms? Ellie reached behind her to open her door, but irritation made her rash. 'You're not going to make sure I get in okay?'

He turned three-quarters back and threw her a glance so simmering it nearly stole her breath. It fairly blazed down the darkened path. 'Do you really think that's a good idea?'

Every molecule of oxygen evacuated through the walls of her cells and escaped into the night. His dark gaze held her, even at this distance.

He wanted in. If she just stood back and opened the door to

her little house, he'd be in there in a flash, sweeping her up as he went. Realising was as shocking as discovering she almost—almost—wanted it to happen. After so many years of wondering whether she'd starved the sensuality right out of her, coming to terms with two arousing experiences in one evening was going to take some processing. And she couldn't do that with company.

No matter how tempting.

But it took her so long to make her lips and tongue form the necessary shape, Jed had turned the corner and was gone by the time she whispered, 'No.'

Instead the word breathed out and tangled with the frost of the cold evening and was gone.

Just as her better sense apparently was.

Heads he'd go for it, tails he'd cool it.

Appropriate, really. Heads meant he was completely out of his mind. Tails meant he should tuck his tail between his legs and run a mile.

The moment he was out of Ellie's view earlier he'd kept walking right on past his front door and taken himself for a quick, restorative sprint around the block. Three blocks, actually. Better than a cold shower any day.

He paused at the bottom of his porch steps, before his heavy footfalls gave him away to his sleeping dog.

His version of heads or tails involved his trusty companion. When he opened the front door, Deputy's head would either be facing the fire or his butt would. There was a fifty-fifty chance of either.

Deputy could decide.

Given he apparently couldn't.

Jed bunched his fists into his pockets and hunched his shoulders against the cold, one foot poised on his bottom step. The third option, of course, was to do nothing. She would be gone in a few weeks. He could tough it out that long. But doing nothing didn't feel all that possible. Ellie had a way of wheedling under his defenses if he wasn't actively patrolling them.

Course, if he dropped them altogether it wouldn't be a problem.

Princess ballerinas from New York City didn't meet the definition of Ms. Right and they had another great thing going for them.

They were transient.

Passing through meant *won't get attached.* Passing through meant he could explore this bourgeoning something without risking the expectation of more. Pinocchio could live like a real boy for a few weeks. Flirt and seduce and romance a woman the old-fashioned way.

Except faster.

Three days ago he would have said he wasn't interested in being some New Yorker's holiday fling, but Ellie Patterson had taken him by surprise. He'd clicked with her. He was definitely attracted to her. And she intrigued the hell out of him. There were much worse ways to spend a few weeks than getting to know someone like that.

A couple of weeks wasn't long enough for either of them to form any kind of permanent attachment. But it was long enough for him to give his romancing skills a healthy workout. It wasn't really about sex, per se, but it most definitely was about the hot, vivid feelings that came with the getting-to-know-you phase. He missed that.

The question mark.

The flirting.

The touch.

The kissing.

The chase.

He really wasn't into casual relationships. He'd tried a one-night stand—necessity and raging hormones being the mother of invention—but he'd been unable to have another, his mind not able to go through with a repeat performance even if his body was willing. Which it wasn't, particularly.

So he took up running instead and he pounded out on the pavement all the frustration he felt from doing the whole Zen-monk thing for so long.

Three years of virtual abstinence.

But there was nothing casual about the way his body responded to Ellie's when she was around. There was nothing casual about the way he'd opened up and told her about New York, though he hadn't come close to connecting all the dots for her. And there was nothing casual about the look she'd thrown him just before they left his house.

The look that was part gratitude, part curiosity, part awareness and part just plain sexy. And a whole lot complicated. The beginning of something he had no business to be encouraging.

Something he'd surrendered a right to ever expect.

And so that was why he was delegating this one to the universe. Or to Deputy, more rightly.

If he walked inside and Deputy was toasting his big shaggy butt, that could only be good news. He'd just run more. Exercise Ellie right out of his system. Go back to having a nice, straightforward, uncomplicated, monastic existence. His body would forgive him—eventually.

Though, if he pushed open that door and Deputy's big black and tan head was hot from radiant heat… His body wouldn't have to forgive him. He could spend the next few weeks together, inducting Ms. Ellie Patterson into the wonders of her own body.

Deputy—or rather the universe—could decide. It couldn't do a worse job of his life than he had.

He took the steps quietly.

Turned the handle. Paused. Gave himself one last chance to change his mind. To reconsider whether Ellie Patterson with her New York independence, her burning need to control things and her disinclination to touch him, might end up being the committing type. Totally the wrong type for him.

His fingers twitched on the doorknob.

Nah.

He pushed into the room and reached for the light switch. Deputy lifted his head, his big, brown half-asleep eyes blinking slowly. Away from the fireplace and towards the door where his master stood.

Jed took a deep breath on a weird kind of fated feeling at the same time as his body went into mourning.

Tails.

Probably just as well. He could do without the entanglement.

CHAPTER NINE

A WHOLE new day without Sheriff Jed Jackson…

Already that felt so weird. But it had to be a good thing, right? Given how badly she craved his company. Anything that felt that good simply couldn't be good for you. Denying the craving was one step closer to mastering it.

Ellie frowned.

Except that's pretty much the path she'd been on when she got so sick. Denying her hunger, denying the needs of her body. Mastering it. A daily show of control in a world where she felt she had very little.

Sarah was still speaking but she barely heard the words. She'd done that a lot in the couple of hours they'd been together. Even more in the three days since the bat date.

So… What was the right thing to do? Indulge the craving or deny it? Neither one seemed ideal. Unless… Maybe it was like an inoculation—allow a tiny bit under your skin so that your body could build up defenses.

A little Jed…but not too much.

'Is what possible?' Sarah said, glancing at her as she pulled her car into Jed's street.

Ellie's head snapped around. 'What?' Had she spoken aloud?

Sarah tipped her pretty face. 'You know. If I hadn't been through much worse in my life I might be developing a complex right about now. I get the feeling you haven't really been with me all morning.'

Head flooded up Ellie's throat. 'Sure I have.' Um… 'You were talking about parking for the festival?'

Sarah smiled. 'I was. Ten minutes ago.' Her eyes grew serious. 'Are you okay, Ellie? We can talk festival another day if you like?'

Self-disgust curdled the tasty afternoon tea they'd just had. 'No, let's do it now. I'm fine. Just distracted. I'm sorry.'

Sarah pulled on her park brake right out front of the Alamo. 'Don't be sorry. I'm the one strong-arming you into this. With your background I figure you could do this with your eyes closed. I just didn't actually expect to see that in play.'

Ellie laughed at the image. It was pretty apt. 'God, I'm sorry. I've been pretty present-absent today.'

'So what's on your mind, Ellie? Maybe I can help?'

'Uh…' No.

'Seriously. I know we've been kind of thrust together today but you've been good enough to listen to me talk—' she grinned '—kind of. This is my opportunity to give back.'

Ellie stared. She didn't do girl talk. Not with strangers. And even if Sarah didn't feel much like a stranger, confidence wasn't something she gave lightly. Yet her amber eyes were so open and so intent…

'Have you…' She stopped and tried again, encoding it. 'What are your views on inoculation?'

Sarah scrunched her face. 'Like immunisation?'

'Right.'

'Humans or livestock?'

Ellie laughed. 'Human.'

Those sharp eyes narrowed. 'Oooh, human singular?'

Damn. 'No, I—'

'Never mind, never mind.' Sarah waved the intrusion away. 'I'll just answer it on face value. I am—' her eyes drifted up and to the right '—pro-inoculation.'

'Why?'

She shrugged. 'Because how can you know how your body is going to react to something you've never had any experience of?'

Ellie stared at her. Speechless.

Somehow, despite the worst analogy in the living world, Sarah had managed to actually answer it in a way that was both meaningful and which resonated for her. Ellie could guess what her body would do around Jed, based on previous experience, but until she actually tested the theory…

'We're not talking about foot-in-mouth disease, are we?' Sarah dropped her voice.

More heat. More awkwardness. But she couldn't help herself and a laugh broke out.

'We're not,' she answered, seriously. 'No.'

Sarah stared, visibly battling with something. 'Is it… Are we talking about Jed?' Her expression was virtually a wince. She clearly didn't want to be wrong. Unless she didn't want to be right? But she was saved from the hideousness of asking as Sarah rattled on. 'Fantastic, if we are. Jed's way too good a catch to be going wanting.'

Ellie glanced at her left hand. 'Aren't you single?'

Sarah flushed. 'Now. Yes. But Jed's not…my type.'

Really? A man like that? Wouldn't he be everyone's—?

Oh.

There was someone else for Sarah. And just like that it all made sense. Her warm affection for Jed in the street. Her high opinion that leaked out in a few things she'd said about him this morning. Her total disinterest in him any other way than platonically.

'He'd have to be some kind of guy… Your type.'

'He sure would,' Sarah said, the tiniest of smiles playing around her lips.

What could she say that wasn't stupidly patronising? Not much. So she just nodded, smiled and said, 'Good luck with that.'

'Thank you. Nice try with the deflection, by the way.'

'Rats, I thought you might fall for that.'

'Afraid not. So, back to Jed.'

Ellie glanced nervously into the street as if he might be conjured by their low whispers. 'No, really, let's not.'

'Back to inoculations, then. What are your feelings on the issue?'

Ellie took a deep breath. 'I might be coming around to your way of thinking. But it's not without risk.'

'The best ones never are.'

So much more risk for her than for most people. So many hurdles to overcome. Was Jed worth it? Ellie frowned.

Sarah adopted her strictly business tone. As if sorting things out between herself and Jed was part of the Fall Festival planning. 'Well, he's a regular at the Association Hall for the monthly mixer. He doesn't really dance but given half the single women there come to see him, I'd say they definitely think he's worth taking a chance on.'

A dance. It had been so long since she'd danced for pleasure—if you didn't count the indiscretions of a few short nights ago. But she didn't want Sarah focusing on Jed any more than she already was.

'Who do the other half go for?'

Sarah smiled. 'Holt Calhoun. Not that he'll be there and not that he goes often, but no one wants to miss the one dance he actually comes to.' She shook her head. 'He sure got his brother's charisma.'

Ellie frowned. 'His brother's…?'

Nate?

Sarah blinked; those wide eyes flared a tiny bit more. It was the first time Ellie had seen her anything less than fully composed. She stuttered, 'His father's—Clay Calhoun.'

Awkward silence fell.

Well… Wasn't that the most Freudian of slips? And wasn't that the most furious of blushes. But given how amazingly gracious Sarah had just been about Jed and the whole bumbling inoculation analogy, she was hardly going to repay it by making the other woman uncomfortable.

'Sounds good,' Ellie lied, clambering out of the car. 'Will you be there?'

Sarah smiled and climbed out after her. 'You betcha.' But

not for Jed and not for Holt Calhoun. So maybe it was for the line dancing? 'It starts at sunset with a side of beef on a spit.'

A sea of brown, grousing cattle filled her mind. Back on her first day in Larkville she'd have happily consigned any one of them to a rotisserie, but with the benefit of distance and a few personal introductions she felt a whole lot more warm and fuzzy towards the poor dopey creatures. 'A whole side?'

Sarah threw her a curious look.

Ellie pulled herself together. 'I think I just smacked headlong into a big-city double standard. I guess I can't complain about someone throwing half a cow on the barbecue when I happily ate Jed's marinated ribs three nights ago.'

Sarah laughed. 'Get used to it, honey. Out this way they call it "bustin' a beast." Enough for half the town and one of Jess Calhoun's fresh-baked biscuits each.'

Right. Yet another reminder about why she was really here. 'Calhouns again. Seems like they're everywhere I turn.'

'The Calhouns founded Larkville and they practically own it still. You can't move without running into one of their businesses or their animals. Or one of them.'

What would she say if she knew she was walking with one?

'By the way…' Sarah murmured, following Ellie down the laneway to her door. 'Ribs? Seems like you're doing just fine with that inoculation, huh?'

'Ellie…'

Amazing how a single male utterance could whisper so many things. Relief. Confusion. Foreboding. And only the last one made a bit of sense given what had passed between them last.

Caution wasn't the reaction she'd hoped for when she lifted her knuckles to his door, but she had a theory to test. And, given she was already so far out of her comfort zone by being here at all, she had nothing to lose by proceeding.

She stood taller in his doorway. 'I came to take you up on your offer to show me Larkville's highlights.'

His eyebrow twitched but he didn't let it go any further. The effort of keeping his expression neutral showed in the sudden line of his mouth. 'Sarah's offer?'

His words could not have been a clearer reminder that it was their friend and not he that had committed him. She figured she was supposed to be feeling some level of shame right now for making him go through with it. Possibly even graciously relenting and scurrying back to her front door.

Screw that. She had a point to prove to herself.

She was still a tiny bit tetchy after checking her email this morning and realising there was still nothing from Jessica. And she was a lot tetchy that Jed hadn't so much as said hello since that steamy moment at her door four nights ago. A lifetime!

'Wrong side of bed this morning, Ellie?' She turned her distraction up to him. 'You're forming your own Grand Canyon between your eyebrows there. Something on your mind?'

You.

'No. I'm fine.' Habit got the better of her. 'Is now a bad time?'

His mind was busy behind his careful eyes. But when it finished flicking indecisively between yes and no, it settled on no. 'Happy to be out on a beautiful Sunday showing off my district. Besides, I owe Sarah. She was really welcoming when I arrived.'

In her head she reached out and shoved him in the chest just to jolt that careful beige mask from his face. Wednesday night he looked like he wanted to eat her whole, now he was only doing this for a friend? 'You know I'd help her anyway.'

That earned her the first hint of the Jed from the top of the Calhoun ridge. His eyes landed on her softly. 'Yeah, I know you would.'

'Okay. What time should I come back?'

He reached inside and grabbed his jacket from its peg and whistled for Deputy. 'Now's as good a time as any.'

Don't do me any favors. She followed him out into the street where his chariot awaited. His lips shifted slightly as he walked alongside her and she wondered—again—if she'd muttered aloud.

They rode in silence and Ellie busied herself looking at the architecture in the streets they passed. It was easy to see where 'old Larkville' began and ended in the switch from earthy colours and stone construction to brighter timbers and cladding on the more modern buildings.

Twin bells clanged as Jed pulled the SUV under a sign that said Gus's Fillin' Station. 'Just need gas,' he said unnecessarily, and then didn't move.

Over to her right a weathered man sauntered towards them. 'Fill her up, Sheriff?'

'Thanks, Gus.'

'Wow,' Ellie said, watching the man go about his business. 'An honest-to-goodness service station. I thought these were legend.'

Jed laughed. 'You really need to get out of New York more.'

For a man well past fifty, Gus certainly had superhero hearing. 'Pfff…New York,' he grunted as he passed back along the vehicle to slop a window-washer in its bucket.

Jed half winced, as though this was an argument he should have predicted.

Ellie leaned out her window just a bit. She'd always believed in calling someone's bluff. 'Something wrong with New York?'

'Don't go there, Ellie…' Jed murmured through the wince. 'I was hoping to show off the good things about Larkville.'

Gus shuffled around the front of the SUV and took his time slopping the windshield with soapy water. 'What's right with it? Noisy. Smelly. Dirty.' Every word accompanied a strong swipe of the rubber blade across Jed's side of the glass.

Ellie smiled. It was hard to take such blatant prejudice to heart. 'When was the last time you were there?' she asked brightly.

Steely eyes peered up from under his battered old stetson. 'Back in eighty-one. Gave someone a ride.'

'Eighteen eighty-one?' she said under her breath, and then, much louder, 'A lot has changed in three decades.'

'Would want to,' Gus muttered.

He crossed to her side of the SUV and sudsed up her side a

little too zealously. But, as he drew long streaks of clean across the soap, his eyes found hers.

His motion faltered. His black pinpoint pupils doubled in size. Some kind of prescience nibbled low in Ellie's gut.

He finished what he was doing, then crossed around to her side again, replaced the gas spout in the bowser and appeared at her window. The smell of old-school tobacco wafted with him. 'How old are you?'

'Gus—' Jed sounded literally pained as he passed a bill via Ellie and into Gus's wrinkled, sun-spotted hand.

'Just a question, Sheriff.'

Ellie hurried to head off the inevitable condescension. 'I'm thirty years old. So, yes, I do remember New York from when I was a child. I know for a fact it's changed.'

But Gus wasn't even thinking about New York City any more. His head tipped. 'You look mighty like her.'

Ellie's gut clamped. The oxygen in her lungs sucked into a void.

'Who?' Jed stepped in smoothly when it was obvious she wasn't going to.

'The woman I gave a ride to the Big Apple.'

Her mother mentioned she'd lived briefly on the Calhoun ranch. Stood to reason she would have been into town. Met Gus, maybe.

Ellie forced what little air she had left in her lungs up and past her voice box. She tried to pick a fight to distract him. 'Are you suggesting all women from New York look the same?'

Gus frowned. 'I'm sayin' that you look just like her.'

'Come on… You remember some woman you gave a ride to thirty years ago, Gus?' Jed tried to be the voice of reason. But he glanced at Ellie, too.

She didn't take her eyes off Gus. Exposure suddenly blazed bright, possible and totally unexpected. 'Hard to forget this one. She wasn't here for long but she had a big impact on the town.'

Desperate to end the conversation before it went any further, Ellie turned to Jed. 'Shouldn't we get going?'

'Keep the change, Gus.' Jed put the car straight into gear.

Gus stood back and Ellie wasted no time in smiling briefly and then raising her tinted window pretty much in his face.

He could add rudeness to New York's list of failings.

'I'm so sorry about that, Ellie.' Jed's apology was immediate; they hadn't even bumped out of the gas station yet. 'He's obviously confused.'

Ellie grunted. 'He seemed pretty sharp. Was the New York thing a dig at you or at me?'

'Not me. No one knows my background and that's how I like it.'

'I can see why.'

He rubbed both his temples with one hand, then refocused on the road. 'Would it help if I said ninety-eight per cent of Larkville isn't like that?'

'Would it be true?'

He chuckled. 'There's a reason stereotypes get started. You just met one.'

She was relaxing more and more every meter she got from Gus's Fillin' Station. 'It's fine, Jed. I shouldn't have taken the bait.'

'He's grown too accustomed to speaking his mind. Not many people stand up to him. Certainly not on first acquaintance.'

'Go me, then.' She glanced at him, looking for signs he was patronising her, but his expression was totally open for the first time today. It was the only reason she risked a personal question. 'So...seriously? No one knows your past?'

Trees whizzed by. 'A trusted two. The rest haven't asked, though I'm sure there's been indiscriminate internet searching.'

She stared at him. 'Yet you told me.'

'I did.' Silence. 'Figured you shouldn't be hanging out there all alone on the revelations front the other night.'

So he did at least remember the other night. 'Well, thank you. You can be assured of my confidence.'

His eyes darkened. 'If that's a very formal way of saying I can trust you, I already know that.'

Would he, if he knew how many secrets she was keeping? Not exactly relevant to national security—lies by omission. As he'd almost found out just now.

She shook the trepidation free. 'So, what's on the agenda today? More bats?'

'I thought you might like to see the aquifer where it bubbles to the surface.'

Chuckling let off a tiny bit of the tension she'd been carrying since opening the door to his textbook indifference. She let it come. 'Another highlight on Larkville's social calendar?'

He shrugged and glanced at her. 'Since when were you all that social?'

'Point.' Besides, he'd be there. And that had taken a dangerously short time to being all she really cared about. She held his eyes longer than was sensible, or safe while he was behind the wheel. At the very last moment, something changed right at the back of them. Something realised. Something…decided. Then he turned back to the road.

'Tell me about your family,' he said after a moment of silent driving. 'Something I couldn't guess.'

The words *Which family?* hovered on the tip of her tongue. He'd never guess that. 'I'm a twin,' she offered optimistically.

His head snapped around. 'There's another woman like you in the world?'

The genuine appreciation in his eyes flattered her stupidly even as he tried to wipe the evidence of it from his expression. 'Boston, actually. And, no, a brother. Matthew.'

'Twins…' He spent a moment getting his head around that. 'You must be close.'

Ellie frowned. 'I… We used to be. When we were younger. But Matt changed right about the same time I quit dancing. Kind of went underground. Lost his joy. I'm closer to my baby sister, Alex.'

She sighed, thinking about how much easier all of this would be with Alex here. Jed glanced sideways at her, drawn by her sorrow.

'I miss her,' she explained.

'She's back in New York?'

Ellie shook her head. 'Australia. But might as well be the moon for how far she seems.'

'That's tough.'

She smiled at his transparent attempts to identify. 'Says the only child.'

He chuckled. 'I can empathise. Gram's too old to travel much now. I miss her.' His lips tightened briefly. 'So there's just the three of you and your folks?'

'Four.' If you didn't count the Calhouns of which there were also four. 'Charlotte's in the middle.'

'And what's she like?'

Ellie glanced at him again. 'Are you really interested or are you just being polite?'

'I never had—' He frowned. 'Families interest me.'

Ellie's heart squeezed. No siblings, no mother, virtually no father. Family dynamics would be a curiosity.

'Charlotte marches to her own beat. Never tethered by convention. We're very different.' And not always that close because of it. But Charlotte and Matt... Charlotte's lightning-streak intelligence fitted perfectly with Matt's dark thundercloud.

'You walked away from dance. You fought your way back to health in secret and alone from what I can gather. You don't think that was sufficiently outside the square?'

She stared at his profile. 'Do two acts even count in a lifetime of conforming?'

'They do if they're significant enough.'

Maybe she and Charlotte had more in common than she'd thought. 'That's high praise from the man who gave the establishment the finger.'

He thought about that as he took the SUV out onto the highway. 'Don't canonise me just yet, Ellie. It took me a long time to be brave enough to leave New York. I might never have if—'

If...?

'Why did you finally do it?'

His gaze shadowed immediately and his eyes unconsciously went to the rear vision mirror. They drove on in silence.

The incident where Deputy got hurt?

Eventually Jed pulled the SUV back off the highway onto a road that had seen better days. A road with a big Authorised Personnel Only sign on it.

'Do you know where you're going?' she asked.

'I'm authorised. And I'm authorising you.'

They fell back to silence. Blessed silence. Something she'd come to really appreciate about Larkville. And about Jed. Here, no one needed you to fill every waking moment with contribution. Saying nothing was okay. Being in your headspace was okay.

'Wow. The rain's really brought her up.'

Jed craned his neck to see the wetland they were approaching. It sparkled and glittered under the midmorning sun and small white and black birds flitted across its surface. 'Texas has been in drought for so long, but Hayes County practically sits on top of a deep aquifer and this is one of only a few places it comes to the surface. This soak's usually more marsh than wetland, though.'

She'd seen evidence of the drought as she'd driven south across the state. Crunchy fields, brown stretches, stock clustered around trucked-in water.

Deputy woke from his back-seat snooze and pressed his nose to the glass. Moments later Jed was hauling his door wide and the dog was out and off, sniffing around the edge of the water.

'It's so pretty,' she breathed.

'Seemed appropriate,' he said. Ellie glanced at him to see if he was making a joke but his eyes weren't on her, they were lost out on the water. As though he didn't even realise he'd spoken.

After a few moments he turned back to her. 'So, two younger sisters and a twin brother. Where does Ellie Patterson fit?'

She took a breath. 'I'm not sure she does.' Or ever did. Accepting that was the key to her eventual recovery. Just as not fitting had been the cause. Only now she had a much better idea of why that was.

'Can I ask you a question?'

He turned.

'Your gram... Have you never thought of bringing her to Larkville?' He glanced at his feet. 'If she's your only family I imagine you're hers, too.'

His sunglasses shifted slightly as his focus moved up to her eyes. 'All her friends are in the Valley. I wouldn't move her unless I had something for her to come to. Grandkids. More family.'

'You don't consider you're enough?'

His shrug looked uncomfortably tight. 'I work all the time. Why would she want to be here?'

'Because she loves you? She could make friends here, too. Maybe hook up with Gus.'

Jed's laugh startled some nearby birds out onto the water. 'Lord, that's an awful image. The damage that the pair of them could do over a few beers...'

He glanced after Deputy to make sure he was behaving himself in this wild place. Ellie stepped closer to the water. Closer to him.

You shouldn't be alone.

That's what she was trying to get at. Trying hard not to say. Because it was ludicrous she would want to. 'Then maybe you should get onto finding a wife and having some kids. Then you can bring her down. Have all your family together. You're not getting any younger.'

Huh. When had she grown so fond of families?

His eyebrows both rose. 'Uh...'

'I'm not... That's not an offer or anything.' Her laugh was critically tight as heat rushed in. Although suddenly it didn't seem quite so ridiculous. But something in his suddenly wary stance told her it was. Very much so.

Old self-doubt rushed back.

The permanent few lines in his brow doubled and his hat tipped forward slightly. 'I try not to mix business with pleasure.'

Curiosity beat embarrassment. 'Meaning?'

'Meaning I prefer not to date where I work.'

'Never?'

He shook his head.

Wow. That took some discipline. But how amazingly liberating. To be able to not date if you didn't want to. 'I wish my mother subscribed to that theory. She's so busy trying to marry me off—'

His face snapped around to hers. 'To who?'

'To anyone,' she laughed. 'The highest bidder. Apparently my true worth lies in my Patterson genes.' Except—it suddenly hit her—Fenella Patterson had to know that her oldest daughter didn't carry one single Patterson gene. Maybe that didn't matter when it came to high finance. 'When I quit dance she decided that my only course left in life was to become someone's trophy wife.'

Jed snorted.

'I know. Crazy, right? Unsurprisingly I haven't been all that successful.' She squeezed the words out through a suddenly tight throat.

The sounds of Deputy snuffling around and ducks quacking broke up the awkward silence.

'Ellie…' A warm hand on her shoulder turned her more fully back to him. She hadn't even realised she'd turned away. 'I meant that I couldn't imagine a woman like you settling for being someone's trophy wife.'

Heat spread up her throat. 'Oh.'

'You assumed I was saying I don't think you're worth trophy status? Or attractive enough?'

She forced her eyes away, out to the sparkling blue water. Maybe there'd be a miracle and the aquifer would surge up and wash her away from this excruciating moment.

'Can you literally not see it?' he murmured.

The open honesty in his voice beckoned. Her heart thumped. She slowly brought her gaze back around. 'I spent a really long time doubting every part of myself, Jed. And I know how I must have looked to people back then. It's hard to forget that.' And to forgive herself for letting it happen.

'Back then.' He stepped closer. Removed his sunglasses so that she could drown in his eyes instead of the aquifer. 'You're not that girl any more.'

'I'm still me inside.'

He stopped a foot away. 'Take it from a man who never knew you before a few days ago, Ellie, and who doesn't hold those past images in his head. You are—' he struggled for the right word and her heart thumped harder at the caution in his voice '—arresting. You might have detoured on your path to beautiful but you're unquestionably here now. Has no one ever said that before?'

The back of her shirt collar was fast becoming a furnace.

'Or did you just not believe them?'

She took a breath. 'They would have said anything.'

'You think they were just trying to get into your bed?'

'My bed. My inheritance. My seat on the board of Daddy's company.'

He stared at her. 'Wow. That's a horrible way to live.'

She shrugged.

He stared. And stepped closer.

'So, what happens when a man who isn't interested in your money or your name tells you you're beautiful? Do you believe him?'

'I don't know.' She swallowed, though there was nothing to swallow. 'Words are easy.'

'What if he shows you?' He closed the final inches between them, paused a heart's breath away. 'Would you believe him then?'

Words couldn't come when you had no air. Ellie stared as Jed blazed sincerity down at her and the moment for protest passed. Then he lowered his head, turned it so that his hat wouldn't get in the way and stretched his neck towards her.

'I'm supposed to be staying away from you,' he breathed against her skin.

Her head swam; making sensible words was suddenly impossible. 'Whose idea was that?'

Sensuous lips stretched back over perfect teeth. 'Deputy's.'

All she had to do was shrink back, like she had a hundred times in New York on curbsides, in doorways, under lampposts, in elevators. The good-night moment of truth. Step away, mutter something flippant and flee into the night. But, as Jed's broad silhouette against the midmorning sun bore down on her, both his hands out to the side as he made good on his promise not to touch her, Ellie couldn't bring herself to evade him.

Euphoric lightness filled her before her chest tightened.

She didn't want to escape. She wanted Jed to kiss her. And she wanted to kiss him back.

'What does he know?' she whispered. 'He's just a dog.'

He continued his slow sink, his body twisting forward so that only one part of them was going to touch, his eyes gripping hers the way his hands were careful not to. A tiny breath escaped his lips and brushed hers a bare millisecond before their mouths met.

His lips were soft and strong at the same time. Dry and deliciously moist.

Heat swirled around the only place they made contact, and Ellie's head swam with his scent. His warm touch grew stronger, pressed harder, fixing her to him as though they were glued. She moved her mouth against his, experimenting, tasting. Exploring. He reciprocated, meeting her stretch halfway.

She made the tiniest sound of surprise low in her throat. Her stretch? But, sure enough, she stood tipped forward on her toes using every bit of her ballerina's balance to make sure their lips didn't separate. Jed's breath coming faster excited hers. His lips opened more, nibbling gently, then smiling into the kiss.

She leaned into his strong body.

Initiating contact was as good as giving him permission. Two large hands slipped up and into her hair where it hung over her shoulders, working their way up to the twin combs that kept it neatly back from her face. He slid them free and let her thick hair fall forward over both of them, and he deepened the kiss, his lips and his teeth parting and his tongue joining the discussion.

Ellie's entire body jerked, breaking away from him. Jed's kiss was so much more than she might have imagined but she'd never had someone kiss her like that—never let them—and her body reacted before her head could.

'I'm sorry—'

He didn't seem the slightest bit put-out. Though his pupils were the size of saucers. 'You didn't like it?'

It wasn't really a question. He seemed very clear on the impact his kiss had on her. His own chest was heaving, too. He just wanted her to deny it.

But old habits died too hard. 'I thought you didn't mix business and pleasure?' she hedged, desperately trying to manage the sudden tumult of emotion.

He blew a controlled stream of air through tight lips, getting himself back under full control. Like she should. 'You're from out of state.'

Guilt surged up fast and intense. Technically, yes. Would he have kissed her at all if he knew she was a Calhoun? 'But I'm your customer at the Alamo.'

'Consider this your eviction notice.'

He was having too much trouble getting his breath back for her to take him at all seriously. A rare sensation flooded her body—a rush at having his obvious and intense interest focused on her, and a tingly kind of awe that she wasn't hating it.

On the contrary.

Power surged through her disguised as confidence. She chuckled. 'That won't be necessary. If you're happy to abandon your principles the first time you get a girl next to a romantic lake—'

'Wetland.'

'—then I'm willing to be your accomplice.'

His eyes grew serious. A silent moment passed. 'Can I touch you again, Ellie?'

It was impossible to know where dread finished and anticipation started in the complicated breathlessness that answered.

She forced herself to inhale. 'Depends. What did you have in mind?'

'I'd just…' He frowned. 'I'd like to hold your hand. And just stand here for a little bit.'

Gratitude very nearly expressed itself as tears. Two firsts on the same day. Her first proper, toe-curling kiss, and the first time anyone had asked her permission about her body.

Ellie took a breath and held out a surprisingly steady hand. Jed curled his palm around it and threaded his fingers through hers and let their combined weight sink it down between them. She turned out to stare at the water. So did Jed.

And they stood there.

Like that.

For maybe ten silent minutes.

Jed's steady heat soaked through into Ellie's tense fingers and, bit by bit, her nerves eased, until she could genuinely say she liked it. It was quiet and mutually supportive and—a tiny smile stole across her face—who knew holding hands could be so sensual.

'Would you like to go to a dance tonight?' The words were out before she even realised she'd thought them.

Jed's chin dropped to his chest and he chuckled. 'I've been standing here working my way up to asking you the exact same thing.'

She tossed her loose hair back. 'Snoozers are losers.' Where was this incredible…lightness coming from? Since when did she flirt so unashamedly?

Since now apparently.

'I get to take you to out.' He smiled. 'That's not losing.'

She smiled up at him and fought her body's instinctive desire to protect itself. Like Jed never meeting someone if he didn't go outside of his county, she'd never find the sort of closeness she craved if she didn't lower her shields from time to time.

Clearly this wasn't going to be forever—Jed had basically

said so—but she'd been waiting her whole life to feel what she was feeling now. She'd just about given up on it. So she wasn't going to take that for granted.

'You do realise it will involve dancing,' he teased.

'Sarah still owes me line-dancing lessons.' And she would die for a chance to dance with a real Texan sheriff.

'Larkville is an amazing place,' she said softly, her eyes looking out over the water. It was almost as if Larkville Ellie and New York Ellie were different women. Cousins. Maybe she would have grown up to be a totally changed person here, with the Calhouns. A woman with a great relationship with her mother, her siblings. A woman who was free to be wild and crazy if she felt like it. A woman who wasn't at war with her body. Then again, if she had, would she have been available when Jed came strolling into town three years ago? Or would she have hooked up with some cowboy and have a dozen kids and a double mortgage by then?

Meeting him and not being able to have him. Impossible to imagine.

Yet she had no trouble at all imagining herself sitting on a porch rocker with Jed's kids at her hip. It was disturbingly vivid. And most unnatural, for her.

'I'm so glad I met you.'

There. It was said. Six short little words but they communicated so much.

She extracted her hand from his under the pretense of finding a stick to throw for Deputy. He exploded into ecstatic life and bounded after it, before bringing it back to her on wet paws. She threw it again. In her periphery she saw the shadow pass over Jed's angular features before he masked it.

Ellie Patterson—Ellie Calhoun—was a work in progress and she had been since she first started to get well. If Jed couldn't deal with baby steps, then he wasn't the man she thought he was.

The man she secretly hoped he really was.

The man that was going to be hard to top when she went back to New York.

Assuming she went back at all.

It all rested on how Jess and her other siblings felt about her arrival. But they contacted her; they invited her down to the memorial festival for Clay Calhoun. They opened the door to her and Matt becoming a part of their family.

But what if that was just a one-off, 'love to see you at the festival but then go on back to New York' kind of thing? What if she'd badly misinterpreted Jess's letter. There was a big difference between 'come visit' and 'come stay.'

She glanced at Jed as he got into the throwing game with Deputy and chewed her lip. Of course, staying and being a Calhoun would kill any chance of something more happening with Sheriff Never-Mix-Business-with-Pleasure. But there wasn't a whole lot she could do about it now. That die was cast the moment she got in her rental car and headed south out of New York.

Actually, it was cast thirty years ago when her mother first did.

Her stomach sank. Mind you, not staying was going to do the same thing. Jed left New York far behind him three years ago.

There was something just a little bit tragic about the haste with which her body accepted that she might have to walk away from Jed. Like it was conditioned to being denied.

There was only one way to fix that.

She glanced at the strong back and shoulders playing tug of war with one-hundred-plus pounds of dog and wondered if she had the courage.

He wasn't promising forever but he could change her life for now. They had two more weeks.

And 'for now' started this evening at the Larkville Cattleman's Association mixer.

It was just like something she might have seen on a movie. Or a Texan postcard. The residents of Larkville tricked up in their newest stetsons, their shiniest boots and their tightest jeans. Little miniature cowboys and Miss Junior Corn Queen wannabes running around between the legs of the bigger, adult versions and the rest perched on hay bales stacked around the old hall. Chatting. Laughing.

Pointing.

She was a bit of a spectacle since she'd arrived with Jed who, it seemed, was generally spectacle enough himself—at least with the women present—but no one looked so surprised that she believed her arrival was totally unheralded.

Clearly the gossip vine had done its job.

On walking in, Jed went straight into public-officer mode, greeting people, asking about their barn conversions and their heavy-equipment licenses and their wayward teenage sons, and Ellie trailed politely alongside smiling and nodding and shaking hands just as she had at so many New York events. She was well accustomed to arrival niceties with strangers and to being the one everyone showed interest in—a Patterson at their party—so the speculation she was fielding from all angles didn't really faze her.

But it bothered Jed.

It took her some time to register the way his spine seemed to ratchet one notch tighter every time someone asked for an introduction or every time they didn't ask but their badly disguised curiosity drifted to her.

Jed's lips tightened as another beaming face made a beeline for them.

She couldn't hide her chuckle. 'I'll get you a drink.'

Whether he wanted one or not, she knew from personal experience that one's fingers couldn't twist with anxiety while they were otherwise occupied negotiating a glass. In his case, maybe holding a beer would allay those tense fists he was making and releasing down by his denim-covered thighs.

The Starlight Room in New York or a Cattlemen's Hall in Texas, people were people no matter what zip code they came from. There was one sure way to end all the speculation… Feed the beast.

She put on her game face and marched straight up to the bar, faking it one hundred per cent.

'What can I get you, darlin'?'

She threw a blinding smile at the man behind the bar and earned herself a slightly dazzled expression in return. 'Hi, I'm Ellie Patterson. Can I have a sparkling water please? And a light beer for the sheriff.'

Within minutes the whole place would know who she was, that she wasn't cowed by the pointing, she wasn't going to get drunk and do something scandalous, and that she was here—officially—with their sheriff. For some reason all those things felt enormously important to get settled straight up.

Especially the last one.

Her eyes went to Jed through the crowd and she could tell by his rigid posture that things weren't improving. Sure enough, two pairs of eyes flicked her way for a heartbeat. Only one pair looked comfortable.

She made herself smile at them and then turned casually back to the barman who was finishing up her order. These people might find out later that she was a Calhoun and so she wanted their first impression of her to be a worthy one. And if Jed was having some kind of change of heart about coming here tonight…

His problem.

'Miss Patterson…' The man slid her two drinks and a few bills. From darlin' to miss in twenty seconds. Mission accomplished. She slid the considerable change straight back to him and earned herself his loyalty as well as his appreciation.

'Ellie!'

Sarah! 'Thank goodness,' she muttered under her breath. Just because she was used to living life under the microscope didn't mean a moment's relief from it wasn't welcome. She leaned in for an air kiss.

'Forget that, Ellie, you're in Texas now.'

Two slim arms were around her, hugging hard, before she even had time to think about what was about to happen. The air left her in a rush. But Sarah looked completely unaffected when she pulled back and launched straight into a run-down of what they'd missed in the half-hour since the dance started and the progress she'd made on planning the Fall Festival. Most of it meant nothing, in fact most of it washed right over her because she was so busy concentrating on how very pleasant that hug had felt and how very little the universe had imploded because of it.

Maybe she was as normal as anyone else now. If she let herself be.

The novelty of that stole her breath.

'I'm so glad you came. I have an agreement to make good on. Line-dancing lessons in exchange for your event-management services.'

Ellie tuned back in fully. 'I was a dancer for ten years, Sarah,' she confessed belatedly, and wished she'd just said it back when it was first suggested. 'Ballet.'

Sarah took the surprise in her stride. 'Ballet? Pfff…you don't know what dancing is, woman! Come on.' She dragged Ellie by the forearm across the room where Jed now stood talking to an elegant woman. 'Excuse us, Mayor Hollis,' Sarah interrupted brightly. 'We need to borrow the sheriff for a bit.'

Jed immediately turned his focus on to Ellie. 'Mayor, this is Eleanor Patterson visiting from New York City. Ellie, Mayor Johanna Hollis.'

Ellie knew how this went. She passed Jed his beer and reached her free hand forward. 'Mayor, I've been enjoying your town very much.'

The mayor knew how it went, too. Her smile was professional but tight enough to suggest she thought she was being patronised by the city slicker. 'Thank you, Eleanor. We're very proud of it.'

That should have been it—niceties exchanged—but Ellie felt a burning need to make sure Johanna Hollis knew she meant it. 'I've been reading up on the architecture in this part of Texas. You have some amazing stone facades still standing. I gather not all towns are as committed to retention as Larkville is?'

A different light blinked to life in Mayor Hollis's eyes. And in Jed's. 'No—' she turned more fully towards Ellie '—you would not believe how hard it is to convince people to maintain our heritage…'

The mayor warmed to her topic and Sarah was momentarily distracted off to one side. Ellie specifically ignored Jed's eyes burning into her in favor of showing the mayor her courtesy.

'Sheriff,' Mayor Hollis finally started when the conversation about Larkville's masonry frontages drew to a comfortable close. She turned a smile on him that was four parts maternal concern and one part admiration. 'I'm so pleased you've found yourself such a lovely and informed lady. I was beginning to despair for you ever settling down.'

Jed disguised his discomfort behind taking a sip of beer. Ellie only noticed because she'd had her share of that awful, neutral expression in the week she'd known him and she'd already learned to read the tight discipline of his muscles.

'Sarah,' he ground past his rigid jaw, ignoring the comment entirely and drawing his friend's focus back to them. 'Did you want something when you came over?'

'Yes! I need you and Ellie. Time for those dancing lessons I promised. I'll see you out there.' She snaffled the mayor's attention on the subject of the Fall Festival and the two of them turned away.

Jed actually glanced around for escape.

Okay…

Ellie placed her half-drunk sparkling water next to Jed's barely touched beer on a sideboard and touched his arm. He pulled it away carefully. But she toughed it out and found his eyes. 'You've never been seen in public with a date, Jed. Did you not expect a level of community interest?'

Or should she be flattered that he'd wanted her here enough not to be swayed by that?

'It's not their interest that concerns me…'

'Then, what?'

Emotion warred behind cautious eyes. 'People think we're together.'

She straightened. 'We are together.'

His frown was immediate. 'We're together, but not...' She lifted her eyebrows as he floundered, but stayed silent. 'You know... Together.'

'Jed—'

'You were practically working up a platform for public office with the mayor just then with all the talk about preserving Larkville's heritage. What message does that send?'

She glared at him. 'It says I have good manners. Not that I'm hunting for real estate.'

Dark conflict ghosted across his eyes. Her mind served up an action replay of every single instance that he'd taken such care to introduce her as just visiting. Tonight. Before tonight. And right behind that was the realisation that the only particularly public thing they'd done was walk a dog and have pancakes. As though by being private he couldn't be held accountable for what else happened between them.

'What are you really worried about, Jed?' She frowned. 'That they might think there's more to our relationship or that I might?'

Frustration hissed out of him. 'Ellie...'

But she knew she was on to something. Every single one of her insecurities triggered, but if she gave in to the fear she'd never let herself feel like this again. So she tossed her hair back and echoed the smile she'd given the barman. Every bit as bright and every bit as fake.

'They're just curious, Jed, they're not queuing up to witness a marriage certificate. Lighten up. Dance. The next time you bring a woman to a mixer—' she took a deep breath at the unfairness of having to say that '—it will barely cause a ripple.'

His eyes lifted long enough for her to spot the doubt resident there. He sighed, but he couldn't keep the tension out of his voice.

'You're right. I'm sorry. Let's dance.'

Line dancing was much harder than it looked from the outside. Even for someone trained in movement. It took Ellie a few minutes to get used to the requirement to anticipate the steps so that they finished on the beat instead of starting on it—more military than musical—but, before long, the repetition and string of steps started to feel pretty natural.

She was pleased that it was a non-contact sport on the whole because touching Jed right now was not high on her wanted list, not while she was still so fresh from his overreaction to the mere thought of being connected with her. Men would have fallen over themselves for that impression back home.

Not that he was most men. If he was she wouldn't be in this position.

'Well, darn,' Sarah said over the music from right next to her. 'You're a natural. Looks like I'll have to find something else to trade you for your time.'

The best part of ballet for her had always been choreography—building complicated dance sequences from established balletic steps. Line dancing was the same in principle. Even dancing in file didn't feel that foreign; she was well used to the ranks of the corps.

Jed moved in perfect sync with everyone else who clearly knew this music a whole lot better than she did. Not flashy but not awkward, either. Just…proficient. And perfectly in time. Exaggerated swagger in his steps, and more hip sway than was healthy for her already-straining lungs.

She glanced at him sideways.

He was watching her move. Both of them trying so hard not to look too interested in the other. She made herself remember that she was mad.

Her cheeks warmed with exertion and her heart thumped steadily. Much more of a workout than she might have imagined. Around them, people whooped and clapped and threw in the occasional 'yee-haw' as they danced, but Ellie's focus kept drifting back to Jed's eyes.

He may be incomprehensible at times but he was still just as attractive and intelligent as the man she'd kissed just hours before. She dropped her lashes and smiled, concentrating on the movement of his feet to stop her losing her place.

And possibly her heart.

They danced like that—ignoring each other and becoming increasingly aware of each other for it—for thirty minutes straight. But it flew past. At last, the band slowed the pace up onstage. Sarah turned to her from her other side as everyone clapped and started moving off.

'I'm going for a drink,' she panted. 'Be right back.'

Ellie's feet went to follow but she was stopped by a warm hand on her forearm. 'Dance, Ellie?'

Jed never dances. Sarah's words echoed in her mind.

Her heart, only just beginning to settle, lurched back into a breathless pattering. There was an apology in his deep brown depths and more than a little regret. It made her breast even tighter.

'We just did.'

He pulled her gently towards him. 'Oh, no, that was fun but…this…is dancing.' He stepped in close and slid one arm slowly around her waist, giving her time to get used to his touch. Around them, others did the same.

'Won't this just draw more attention to us?'

'That horse has bolted.' He smiled, pulling her closer. 'Right about the time you started moving to the music.'

In heels she would have been eye to eye with him. Pity she'd kicked her shoes off once the line dancing hit full speed. As it was, she had to lift her eyes slightly to see into his. She stared at his chin instead, though it was disturbingly close to his full bottom lip. Her breath caught.

'What dance is this?' she asked, as if that made the slightest difference to whether or not she wanted to be back in his arms.

'Texas slow dance.' The way he said it…with that tiny curl in his voice. He made it sound sinful.

Their neighbors shuffled left and right, some glued together like teenagers, some father-daughter pairs with little pink-pumped feet balanced on their fathers' boots, others with a respectful, first-public-dance distance.

Like theirs should have been.

Jed pulled her into him and lifted one of her hands up to his neck. The other he collected in his big palm and threaded his fingers through hers. The arm around her lower back tightened.

'Relax,' he murmured into her hair. Then his feet started moving.

A middle-aged woman who'd stepped up with the band started crooning the lyrics to 'Cry Me a River.' Slow and sensual. Deep and moving. She looked like she tossed hay bales by day. It was amazing the secrets some people had.

Maybe Ellie didn't hold them all herself.

Her muscles loosened in increments as Jed swayed her from side to side, and she did her best to anticipate his moves.

'Let me lead, Ellie.' Soft and low against her ear. 'Let go.'

Letting go meant so much more to her than he knew. He was asking her to undo the habits of a lifetime. The fears and hurts. But if there was a man to be holding her up while she let go, Jed was it.

She let herself be distracted by the feel of his denim thighs brushing against her soft skirt, by all the places she fitted neatly into him. Their bodies constantly rubbing.

'That's a girl.' He grinned. 'You might even start to enjoy it.'

His gentle words teased an answering smile out of her. She let herself lean into him a tiny bit more.

Jed led Ellie around and around in a small arc, taking care not to dance her into anyone else, to protect her from the accidental physical contact he knew would rip her out of the happy place she was slipping into.

Synchronised. Swaying. Lids low. Breath heavy.

In fact, every part of him felt heavy—lethargic yet excited at the same time. Somewhere at the back of his mind he knew he should be worrying about what message this might send her but, right now, his world began and ended with the woman in his arms. He'd sort the rest out later.

'How are you doing?' he murmured.

'Mmm...'

She was practically asleep in his arms. On Ellie, that was a good thing. It meant she trusted him. Enough to drop her guard and let herself relax. Be mortal.

He hadn't planned on creating a dance-floor sensation tonight. He'd planned on keeping his separation of the six-degree variety for both their benefit. Ellie didn't need her emerging awareness trampled all over by a man with no intention of honouring it the way it should be. But somewhere between 'God Bless Texas' and 'Cactus Star' her energy and presence affected him in a way he was still scrabbling to understand. It wasn't just the catlike movement of her long body—although that undoubtedly drew the attention of more than one male in the room—and it certainly wasn't the high-energy, synchronised moves. That only got him thinking of all the other ways the two of them could be synchronised.

It was her focus. Her determination to do the best job she could, even at something as ridiculous as line dancing.

Ellie Patterson had a big, flashing perfectionist gene. And an equal part of him responded to that. He found capability pretty attractive. It was right up there with intelligence and compassion on his list of must-haves. And Ellie had all three in multiples.

All the more reason to stay the heck away from her.

'Ellie?'

Thanks for the dance, Ellie...

There's someone I need to speak to...

If you'll excuse me...

'Mmm?' Her head was nestled in right next to his now, and the warm brush of air from her barely formed response teased the hairs on his neck. Excited them.

'The band's taken a break,' he whispered. It was the best he could manage just then, though he knew he should have been walking away. Fast. Her head lifted enough to turn towards the now-empty stage and then her eyes tracked the band members making their way towards the bar.

'Oh...' She straightened awkwardly and he hated being the trigger for the return of carefully controlled Ellie. A deep something protested with a rush of sensation that tightened his hold.

'Or we could just stay here, dancing.' Drowning.

Her head lifted fully. Her skin flushed. The space between them increased. 'No… I could use a drink.'

He crossed with her back to where their drinks still waited, warmer and flatter now, loath to let her go but so aware of how many curious eyes were trained on them again following their slow dance. He kept a gentle hand at her back to let her know he was there, and to let everyone watching know anyone messing with her was messing with him. Even that felt like a mistake. But it stayed glued there of its own accord.

She paused to slide her heels back on and somehow that act signaled the end of relaxed, free Ellie.

He wasn't ready for that to happen.

'We should get going.' The words were out before he thought about what they meant.

She turned to look at him. 'Already?'

'You want to stay?' The question was so very loaded, she'd have to be blind to miss it. He wanted her out of this crowded fishbowl. To get her alone somewhere that they could talk, get to know each other.

God help him.

She stared at him, weighing up her options. 'No,' she breathed. 'I don't.'

It took fifteen long minutes to edge their way around to the exit, making polite conversation all the way. The departure conversations were more excruciating than the arrival ones because there wasn't a person there who had missed the floor show he'd just put on and he knew he'd set himself up for that. Ellie departed first, ostensibly to use the restroom, but on completion there she turned left instead of right and was gone. He gave it a few more minutes, for appearance's sake, and then followed her out to his truck. Fooling no one, probably, but at least he'd made an effort to protect her privacy.

He knew his own was already lost. But that was a small price to pay for moments more of the heaven he'd felt on that dance floor.

'Hey,' she said as he tumbled into the driver's seat, her eyes vivid in the moonlight. 'Thought you might have got snared again.'

There was only one person he was ensnared by. He turned to her, not prepared to make polite small talk. If he was going to hell he didn't want to waste a moment. 'Ready?'

'Yup.'

Home was a two-minute drive. Deputy was ecstatic that they were home so early and only took a further minute to dash outside and lift his leg against the nearest cypress tree. Jed used the time to throw another log on the dwindling fire.

'I feel like I've missed so much of normal life,' Ellie mused from the shadows. Her arms wrapped around her even though the cottage was warm.

'What do you mean?'

'I didn't go to my first party until I was twenty-two and that was a full-on New York soiree. To represent the family.'

He lowered his long body into the sofa, trying hard not to look as desperate as he felt. Trying hard not to feel it. 'Nothing before that? At all?'

'Not a party. Not a celebration. The occasional end-of-season dance after-party but they tended to be serious kinds of affairs. Lots of sitting around being introspective and deep. Most people had to be up early for rehearsals on the next performance. I was always studying.' She uncrossed her arms. 'So this was my first hoedown.'

He chuckled. 'It wasn't a hoedown. But it was fun. Did you enjoy yourself?'

She studied him across the space and he couldn't have been more aware of how not close she was keeping herself. But at least she smiled. 'I think I did.'

He struggled for easy conversation, to take her mind off the fact they were alone in his house with a bed just a few feet above them. 'Why did you work so hard as a kid? Dancing. Studying.'

Confusion riddled her voice. 'To be good at it. To get good grades.'

'Did you need good grades to be a dancer?'

She frowned. 'Not especially. I guess I wanted…a fallback.'

'In case you didn't make it?'

'My parents had expectations.'

'They expected you to have good grades?'

'They expected me to work hard. I wanted to have good grades.'

'Why?'

Her frustration showed in the flap of her hands. 'Because that was what I did. I was good at things. Why the inquisition?'

He kept his cool, stayed reclined, relaxed. Though what he really wanted to do was drag her out of the shadows into the furnace of the fire. Of his arms. He regretted drawing her attention to the absent band back in the dance hall. They might still be entwined now if he hadn't spoken. 'Just trying to decide who you wanted to prove something to.'

'No one.' It was too immediate. Too practiced. Her eyes flickered. She waited a moment and then whispered, 'Me…maybe. I just wanted to do well.'

'What would have happened if you hadn't?' he asked.

'They would have been disappointed. So would I.'

'They wouldn't have loved you anyway?'

She inched closer to him. To the fire. Eventually she perched carefully on the very end of the sofa. She pressed her hands in her lap. 'Let me paint you a picture. When I was twenty-one, a couple of days after I resigned from the company, I heard my mother talking to my father, bemoaning how I'd shown such promise earlier in my life.'

Jed's stomach squeezed in sympathy. 'Past tense? Ouch.'

'They never would have verbalised it but I felt that expectation my whole life. Mostly coming from my mother. The necessity to prove myself. To earn my place in the family through excellence.'

'You didn't have to earn it, you had a birthright.'

'I was a fraud.' Sorrow saturated her features.

It was his turn to frown.

'I was Eleanor. The capable one. The flawless one.' She looked at him. 'It's what they wanted to see.'

'You're not a fraud, Ellie—'

She turned pained eyes to him. 'I'm not a Patterson.'

He sat up straighter. 'What?'

'My mother was already pregnant when she met my—' She pressed her lips together. 'When she met Cedric Patterson.'

Hurt for her washed through him. There was nothing he could say to that.

'I felt so vindicated the day I found out—that all those feelings I had weren't just neuroses. There was a reason I felt like I didn't belong.' Her bitter laugh betrayed the tears thickening her words. 'Because I didn't.'

He was up in a heartbeat, scooting along the sofa and gathering her into his arms. She came willingly. 'No, Ellie…'

'I was so angry with her, Jed. I'd been through so much, struggled alone for so many years because she made it clear that failure wasn't an option. Just in me and Matt. Nobody else. Not Alex. Not Charlotte.' She shook her head. 'Maybe she thought he'd renounce us the first time we made a mistake.'

'Was your father that kind of man?'

She was silent for a moment. 'She must have feared he was.'

He paused, wondering how much of this scab to scratch off. 'Did he know?'

He felt her nod against his shoulder. 'Always. Two little cuckoos in his nest.'

'Ellie…' He turned her chin up to look her in the eye. It broke his heart to see them full of tears. It made him want to wrap her in his arms and protect her forever.

Forever?

The intensity of that shook him. He pulled back a little. 'He chose you. To raise you and to love you.'

Her shrug was sharp. 'We were a package deal. He wanted my mother.'

Compassion settled in his gut. Who was he to say what motivated Cedric Patterson or didn't, or what kind of a father he'd been to Ellie? What experience did he really have with parents?

Ellie was the one who'd had to live the life, deal with it as best she could.

And it had nearly ruined her.

'I guess I understand, then, why you feel such an intense need to control things.'

'I don't.' But it was so patently ridiculous even her own protest was half-hearted.

'Then why aren't we naked in front of that fire right now?' He needed to shock some life into those suddenly dead eyes. It worked, two green-tinged blue diamonds flicked up to him. Heat flooded her cheeks. But she'd been nothing but honest with him since they'd met.

'That's not about…control…exactly.'

Sure it was. 'Then what's it about?'

She smiled, a poignant sort of half effort. 'I'm not sure you appreciate how rare it is for me to feel this way.'

He narrowed his eyes, a stone forming in his gut. 'What way?'

'Attracted. Comfortable.' She took a deep breath and twisted upright against him. She locked gazes with his, though there was fear behind the bold words. 'Desirable.'

Chemistry whooshed around them but it tripped and tumbled over heavy boulders of reality. Ellie wasn't like other women. She didn't operate on the same plane as everyone else. She had no real experience with men, from what he could gather, yet here he was offering her a good time but not a long time.

Jerk.

Yet beneath all the chivalry, a really primal part of him tipped his head back and howled that she trusted him with her soul and her body. Could he really walk away from that?

Regardless of whether or not he was worthy of it.

He shut that part of him down and refused to look closer. 'Ellie… You know what you're saying? Is this something you really want to do?'

She met his eyes. 'I'm thirty years old, Jed. Old enough to make my own decisions. I'm ready.'

He knew he was. He'd been ready from the moment he met her out on the road to the Calhoun ranch.

He settled her more comfortably against him and cupped both sides of her face, staring into her eyes intently. They sparkled with provocativeness and defiance. So much so he almost bought it. But her own words echoed in his head in the half a heartbeat before he let his lips touch hers.

'Fraud,' he breathed against her lips. 'You're terrified.' She was nowhere near okay with this.

'A little.' Her eyes smiled where her lips couldn't. 'But I feel safe being terrified with you.'

Unfamiliar emotion crowded in, wanting to awaken her and protect her at the same time. He knuckled a loose thread of hair away from her face. 'I don't want to hurt you, Ellie.'

And he would. Because that's what he did. He couldn't be trusted with hearts.

She lifted her face. A dozen thoughts flickered across her expression and he wasn't quick enough to grasp any of them. 'I don't want to be like this forever.'

'Like what?'

She stared at him, long and silent. Then finally she whispered, 'Broken.'

Compassion flooded up from that place down deep he wouldn't look, washing away any hope of him doing the rational, sensible, smart thing. Part of him rebelled against that, stormed at him that healing her was not his job, that it was not conducive to the kind of short and sharp relationship he wanted. But the primal part shoved past those concerns and spoke directly to his soul.

Ellie needed him. Ellie wanted him.

And he wanted her.

He wasn't a fool. He knew tonight wouldn't be the night that he really got to know her. And he didn't want it to be. With Ellie he wanted to take it slow.

They mightn't have long but they could make it count.

The raging, warning part of him slammed itself against the

casing of the box he kept it in way down deep. He ignored it. There were a dozen reasons this was a bad idea but, for the life of him, he couldn't think of one strong enough to stop the motion of his body as he swung his legs off the sofa and pulled her upright with him.

For some reason—despite everything that happened in New York with Maggie and despite the kind of man he was—he'd been gifted this beautiful woman and her courageous soul.

He wasn't going to throw the opportunity away.

Ellie saw the decision in Jed's gaze the moment he made it and the reality of what she was about to do hit her in a flurry of sharp nerves. She swallowed hard. 'How do we...start?'

His fingers against her jaw eased some of the flurries. 'What about where we left off?' he breathed.

Already she was half hypnotised by the new intensity in his heated gaze. The hunger. 'The dance or the lake?'

'The best parts of both.' He took three steps towards the fire. Then he pulled her into his arms for another slow dance.

She tipped her face up. 'We have no music.' It was a pathetic attempt to head off the inevitable, even if she wanted it. And she really, really did.

His eyes softened. 'Let go, Ellie. We'll dance to the rhythm of the fire.'

And so they did, shuffling left and right in the cozy space between the stove and the sofa. Jed trailed his fingers up and removed her combs, freeing a tumble of hair. She let herself enjoy the sensuality and anticipate his next touch.

'Okay?'

Her heart pounded against her ribs. She nodded.

On they danced, Ellie sliding her arms around his waist and curling her nervous hands into his shirt. His fingers travelled up and down her spine, stroking her once again into the comfortable place she'd been back at the dance.

It didn't take long.

Warm breath teased her jaw, her neck, as his lips dragged back and forth across her blazing skin. She leaned into his caress and slid one hand up under his hair, then—finally—turned her face towards his.

Their blind lips sought each other out.

And then they were kissing. Soft, sweet. Hot, hungry. Slow, lazy. Every part of her body throbbed with a mix of uncertainty and yearning. Sensory overload. Jed's strong arms kept her safe and created a place where she could explore and discover without fear. Desire washed through her starved cells, fast and tumbling.

He breathed her air and fed her in return. She felt the hammer of his heart against her own chest and knew it wasn't uncertainty, like hers. It was passion.

Jed wanted her. And he cared enough to take it slow.

He cared.

Guilt shoved its way up and into her consciousness just as he slid his hand around to her ribs so that his thumb sat just below her breast. Her skin tingled then burned where his skin branded hers. She tried to focus on the new sensations he brought.

Then his thumb brushed across the tip of one breast.

'Wait…' Ellie tore her lips from his. 'Just wait…'

His breathing was as strained as hers. 'Too fast?'

'I need to—' she stepped back and pressed her fingers to her sternum '—I need a moment.'

'It's okay, Ellie. Take your time.'

Distress tumbled through her. He was being so kind. 'No. Not that. There's something I need to… Before we go any further.'

She had to tell him. She should have already told him. A dozen times.

He collected her frantic hands and brought them together, in his. 'Take it easy, Ellie.'

'I need to be honest with you, Jed. I owe you that.'

It was such a risk. She knew how he felt about—

'Honest about what?'

She stared at him, wide-eyed. Her feet tipped on the very edge of no return. 'Ask me who my father is.'

He blew out a strained breath. 'Unless you're about to tell me that we're actually related, I really can't see how—'

'Ask me, Jed!'

Her bark shut him up. He stared at her, his mind whirring visibly amidst the confusion in his eyes. He took a deep breath. 'Who is your real father, Ellie?'

She stared at him, sorrow leaking from every pore. Wondering if she was throwing away any chance of ever feeling normal again. Wondering if she was throwing away her only chance at happiness.

But knowing she must.

She took a breath. And told him.

CHAPTER TEN

DEPUTY slamming full into him couldn't have done a better job at knocking the air clean out of Jed's body. He stood, frozen, and stared at her.

'You're a Calhoun?'

'It's why I'm here in Larkville,' she whispered.

Visiting Jess. He'd not let himself quiz her further on that once he got to know her. It was none of his business then. But now…

'You're a Calhoun.'

He stepped back, a deep, sick realisation growing in his gut. She was here to meet them. He knew the Calhouns; there was no way they wouldn't ask her to stay, to bring her into their care. He regulated his breathing to manage the roar building up inside him.

She'd say yes; why wouldn't she? He'd never met a woman crying out more strongly for somewhere to belong.

She'd say yes and she'd never go back to New York.

'I wanted you to know, before we—' Ellie swallowed '—went any further.'

Further? His body screamed. He'd gone quite far enough. Yet nowhere near where he wanted to be. He lifted his eyes and stared at her. 'I thought you were only here for a few weeks.'

Her face pinched. 'I know.'

'But you waited until now to tell me?'

'I didn't know if…this morning was a one-off, an accident…'

'You think my tongue just fell into your mouth?'

She winced at his crude snipe. 'I'm sorry that you're shocked but it wasn't my secret to tell.'

'So why tell it now?'

'Because we were about to…'

'What?' Do something irretrievable?

'Go further,' she whispered.

He searched around for something to hang his anger on rather than hating himself for being stupid enough to let this happen. He knew how hard she was searching for something more meaningful in her life. Yet he'd let himself want her anyway. To need her. And that scared the hell out of him. 'You could have told me this morning. At the dance. Any time before this.'

On some level he knew he should be grateful she spoke up now and not even later. But he just wasn't capable of more than a raging kind of grief. Ellie was a Calhoun. That meant she wasn't just passing through; she was about as forever as it came.

Her colour drained more. 'Yes. I should have.'

His snort damned her. 'You think?'

It was her wince and Deputy's quick slink away around behind the sofa that told him his voice was too loud. His anger was really disproportionate to what she was supposed to be to him—a casual thing—but it was burbling up from deep inside him just like the soak did from the aquifer.

Confusion only made him madder. 'That's it, then. We're done.'

The pale shock left Ellie's skin, pushed aside by her own angry flush. 'Why? Why does it make any difference to us now? Either way I'm out of your life in a week.'

'You're part of my town's biggest and most influential family. You couldn't be more off-limits to me.' He clung to that like a lifeline. It was better than risking exposing the truth.

'Why? Just because of your rule…?'

Her pain burned him harder the more he tried to ignore his body's response to it. She had no idea what she was stumbling towards. 'My values, Ellie.'

She frowned, half confusion, half distress. 'I thought…'

He threw his hands up, frustration eating at the body that just moments ago was humming with sudden and long-absent life. 'What? That you were different? Special?'

Her gasp was like a reverse gunshot.

She did—he could see it in the hurt awakening in her eyes. She thought he might make an exception for her. For them. She didn't understand that it was bigger than whether or not he wanted to make an exception.

Deputy peered out from behind the sofa at the sudden silence, the whites of his eyes betraying his anxiety.

'You know how big a deal this was for me, Jed,' she whispered. 'To get myself to this point.'

Shame gnawed hard and low. But so did the raging frustration of who she was. And what that meant. And the fact she'd effectively lied to him. He flung open the door to the stove and stabbed at the crumbling coals.

But this wasn't really about her keeping secrets. This was about grief. His grief that Ellie was now so thoroughly and permanently out of the question. There was no way he was risking her in any way. And since he couldn't be trusted…

His body screamed at the denial and his soul echoed it softly.

That betrayal of his own heart outraged him even more.

He didn't want to look into her eyes and see the growing emotion there, her growing connection. The dream of the cartload of kids they'd have tumbling over a greying Deputy or Ellie grown round and healthy with new life inside her. Even if secretly— desperately—he did.

He'd been down this road before and it didn't lead anywhere good. A woman wanting more. A man wanting less.

He needed her to walk away. Fast. And she wasn't going to do that unassisted.

He mentally brought out a revolver.

'Why did you tell me now?' he gritted, loading an emotional bullet into the barrel.

'Because it was the right thing to do,' she whispered.

'It was the safe thing to do.' He loaded another for good measure. 'That way you wouldn't have to step outside of your comfort zone at all. When things got heavy.'

'Jed—'

Her chest rose and fell faster and he forced himself to forget how the curve of that flesh had felt under his fingers just moments ago. Soft and innocent. Vulnerable.

He'd betrayed someone else's vulnerability once...

Her eyes glittered dangerously. 'Why are you being like this? After everything I told you, did you seriously imagine that my past wouldn't still raise its head? It's going to take some time—'

'We never had time, Ellie.' He spun the barrel and snapped it into place. 'That's what you didn't understand.'

'I know. But it's a start.'

'The start of what?'

Confusion bled from her beautiful eyes.

His voice dropped. His pulse throbbed in the lips that were about to hurt her so badly. 'What we were about to start would mean more to you than any other woman I know.'

Her nod was barely perceptible.

'That's not something you'd do lightly. Yet you were willing to do it, with me, for just a few short days?'

'I... Yes.'

'Because you hoped for more?'

'No. You've been very clear.'

Liar. He could see the hope even now, shining brave and bright. And terrible. She wanted more. 'Then, why?'

Her entire body stiffened. 'Because I thought that it might just be the only chance I ever have. To feel like this. I wasn't going to give that up.'

Her only chance. Forever? The responsibility of that pressed its force outward from the dark place inside. He didn't do forever.

He lifted the emotional gun and fought to keep his hands steady.

'Right man, the right conditions,' she went on. 'I can't imagine that happening again. Not for me.'

Anxiety twisted up live inside him. 'What conditions?' What was she expecting?

Ellie's arms crossed her body. 'Trust. Patience. Commitment.'

Panic tore its way out of that box deep down inside. Somewhere distant—far, far away from its angry tirade—he knew that she didn't deserve this. But he couldn't stop it.

He lined her up in his sights. 'I haven't offered you a commitment.'

'I know. You've been painfully clear.' Her voice thickened. 'Why is that?'

She was going to fight back. Intense pride warred with disbelief, but he pushed it away. 'Commitment doesn't come on tap, Ellie. I have to feel it.'

Her face blanched and those slim arms tightened around her torso, steeling herself for the blow. 'You don't feel anything?'

'I feel something.' He wouldn't lie to her but he wouldn't string her along, either. He was no one's Prince Charming. It didn't matter how much he felt. Nothing good could come of her wanting him. 'But it was never going to be happy ever after.'

She withered before his eyes and breathed, 'Is that so inconceivable?'

And there it was.

The disappointed awakening. Hope dashed. Fear realised. Heart broken.

All the things he was best at. Self-loathing burned in his gut. 'I know myself, Ellie. I'm not the committing type.'

'Ten days ago I wouldn't have said I was the kissing type. Yet here we are.'

Did she need it spelled out? He disengaged the safety on the gun she had no idea she was facing. 'I don't do commitment, Ellie.'

'You've committed to Deputy. To Larkville,' she argued, holding her own. 'So you're clearly capable of it. Is it just women?'

Ready...

'Don't do this, Ellie.'

'Why not? My flaws are so clearly up for discussion, why can't yours be?' She tossed her hair back.

Aim...

'Look, we gave it a shot, it didn't work out. It happens.'

She clenched her jaw and locked eyes with him. 'I imagine it happens to you a lot.'

His finger trembled on the trigger. 'What's that supposed to mean?'

Deputy dropped his snout flat to the floor and cast anxious eyes at them both, whining, as Ellie gave as good as she got.

'It means that limiting yourself to meeting women outside of the county when you have no intention of going out of it is a convenient way to ensure that no relationship is ever going to work out, don't you think?'

She was fighting for her life and—God help him—he was starting to fold. He urgently fortified his resolve. The more she fought him the more he was going to hurt her.

'You have a problem committing to women,' she cried. 'Just admit it and let's deal with it.'

He closed his eyes. 'Why does it have to be a problem? Why can't it just be because I don't want you?'

...Fire.

Her sharp intake of air was the only clue that he'd struck her way, way down deep. Where she was the most raw and exposed.

A prideful woman would have walked out. A bitter woman would have railed at him. A vengeful woman would have struck back. But Ellie just lifted her chin, to hide the devastation at the back of her defiant eyes.

'Is that true?'

Self-disgust burned and he spun away tossing the useless gun far away. 'We've shared a few kisses, Ellie. And now you're asking me for a commitment. That's not normal.'

Silence stretched out.

And out.

Deputy crawled closer to them on his belly.

Not normal.

Ellie had to make herself breathe. Jed probably had no idea how much more that last accusation hurt than any of the other things he'd said since this beautiful evening started to go so very, very wrong. All she ever wanted was to function like everyone else. To love and be loved just like everyone else.

Was that really so much to ask?

But she wasn't like everyone else. She was all back to front. She needed the trust and respect and surety of a man before she could even do the simple things that usually fostered trust and respect and assurances.

Like hand-holding.

Kissing.

Touching.

No wonder it had taken her thirty years to even find one. What were the chances of ever finding another?

Jed prowled around his tiny living room, his expression so crowded it was unreadable. 'Believe me, I'm just saving us both a lot of time. The novelty of your physical response to me would have worn off sooner or later.' He crossed his arms across his chest and clenched his jaw until it was pale. 'You're a good person, Ellie, but I'm not interested in a relationship with you. And I don't think you'd be interested in anything less with me. What else is there to say?'

She stepped forward. 'Jed...'

He barked his frustration. 'Ellie, I don't know how to be clearer. My life is complicated enough without having to make allowances for a high-maintenance princess with body issues.'

She froze.

Having her life—her illness—so summarily dismissed burned much more than it should have. She'd guarded herself her whole life against the judgment of others. And her own. But, sometime in the past two weeks, she'd lowered those shields. Opened herself up to hurt.

And this is what hurt felt like. Amplified a thousand per cent by love.

She stumbled against the arm of the sofa on the realisation.

Love.

Oh, God, was that what Jed could see in her eyes? Had she let it show? Somewhere between rescuing her from raging cattle, helping her fly with the bats and dancing with her as if they were making love she'd fallen head over heels for Sheriff Jerry Jackson. The woman who thought she wasn't capable of feeling it.

Of all the moments to realise she was wrong, discovering it just as he was rejecting her was the cruellest blow of all.

Her whole body ached.

Love.

That was a mistake she'd be careful not to make again. Not if this was how it felt.

'I need to go.' The words came out as a croak. She turned and stumbled for the doorway. Deputy cringed and ducked as she passed him, then he circled around her, his shoulders low and tail tucked between his legs.

Exactly how she felt.

'Ellie—'

She yanked the door open.

'Ellie, wait…'

Not compassion. Not from him. Not now. She couldn't bare it. She turned back—heartsore—and said the only thing she knew would hurt him.

'That's Ms. Calhoun to you, Sheriff.'

It hit its mark with shocking accuracy and every bit of colour drained from his tanned face. She was too numb to feel any triumph.

She turned and lurched down the pathway to her own little haven, leaving the door gaping behind her as wide as her chest cavity.

Drinking was almost pointless.

It didn't even feel good. Like the calluses that formed on his weapon fingers during training, or the ones that formed on his thumb in his pen-pushing years, the liquor he'd hit so hard after losing Maggie only formed a hard, impenetrable casing over his stomach and his heart that meant he never got drunk...

He only ever got numb.

He resettled his cheek on the old leather cushion.

Numb was good enough.

He lay on his front on the sofa, head turned to the side, eyes lost in the orange glow of the dying fire he couldn't be bothered stoking.

Thinking.

Trying not to.

It had been hours since Ellie had stormed out of his house and he'd raged across the room and slammed the front door shut behind her. What followed was three hours of pent-up grief and denial. Latent stuff left over from New York that he'd never fully expressed. It had to be. He'd not let his emotions get that firm a hold on him...ever. The whole lot liberally lubricated with the bourbon he kept for when his gram visited.

He'd stopped short of breaking stuff but only just. He had too much respect for his inherited furnishings and the many lifetimes they'd endured before his. Much harder lifetimes than his, too—war and drought and hardship and loss.

Real, unimaginable, barely survivable loss.

So he'd slammed and cursed and raged around instead, lecturing himself at half volume and doing a damned fine impersonation of his training sergeant until his legs got sore from being upright.

And then he'd fallen into this exact position and not moved for the next hour. The luminosity of the fire held him transfixed. It glowed exactly the way Ellie's eyes had as she'd stared up at him, offering herself.

Back when she was still in his arms.

He'd done the right thing. If he said it enough he might even start to believe it. He wasn't about to repeat the mistakes of his past and stay with someone out of a sense of duty, because they needed him. That wouldn't do anyone any favors, especially someone as damaged as Ellie.

He got a flash of the extra damage he'd done tonight—patently reflected in her traumatised expression—and clenched his fists. Better a short, sharp pain now than longer and much worse later.

Before he really hurt her.

Then right behind that he got a flash of the same expression on the face of Maggie's sister. She'd taken it on herself to clutch his hand by way of support, surrounded by all his girlfriend's family and friends in their funereal black, as he heard over and over how happy Maggie had been with him and how in love they'd been.

He'd stopped in at a liquor store on his way home.

Limiting yourself to meeting women outside of the county when you have no intention of going out of it is a convenient way to ensure that no relationship is ever going to work out, don't you think?

He did think. He'd been very cautious all this time to justify it that way. But Ellie had torn that careful excuse wide open and called it for the BS it was.

He'd been so close to telling her what had really happened in New York. What kind of a man he really was. But something had stopped him. Maybe he thought Ellie would understand.

And he didn't deserve understanding.

And he sure as hell didn't deserve her acceptance.

So he'd pushed her away with everything he had, and he'd done as thorough a job as he did with everything. You don't keep people at a distance for years without developing some powerful strategies. Never committing, never letting yourself feel.

You've committed to Deputy, to Larkville.

His vow to his dog was more about atonement than anything else. As long as Deputy was alive and well—as long as he'd salvaged something worthwhile from that train wreck of a situation in New York—then he didn't have to look too closely at his own demons.

His eyes rolled sideways to Deputy's mat expecting to see

the big lug stretched out in his usual position. But the mat was vacant.

Jed lifted his head. Squinted into the corners of the room.

Silence.

He pushed to his feet. 'Deputy?' He swung the bathroom door open, then took the steps up to the loft by twos.

'Deputy?' Loud enough to be heard by a sleeping dog but not so loud that he'd wake Ellie next door.

Nothing—from this cottage or the old barn.

Raw panic seethed through him and he had a sudden vision of slamming his front door closed. What if Deputy had gone out for a nature break and he'd locked him out? He sprinted back down the stairs and flung the door wide, emerging coatless into the chilly, empty street.

He gave the whistle command that Deputy had been trained to respond to—a dog never forgot that primary signal, no matter what—and then held his breath for the *galumph* of approaching feet.

Still nothing.

Nausea washed through him and his mind served him up a fast-action replay of his fight with Ellie as it must have looked from a fragile dog's perspective. The moment where he slammed that front door closed. The noise he was making for the hours that followed. If Deputy had come home, it would have scared him off again.

Ellie…

His body called straight out for her. Ellie would help him. She would hold him together as he lost it. She'd keep him grounded as his past fears threatened to rise up and swallow him. Because she had more strength than she realised and maybe he didn't have as much as he liked people to believe.

If ever there was a woman to understand weakness, wouldn't it be a woman who'd battled her own dragon and survived? A woman who knew the many aspects of fear by their first names? If ever there was a woman who could help him, wouldn't it be Ellie Patterson, with her insight and compassion and courage?

But that spoke of so much more than just wanting her.

That was needing her.

And he didn't do need. Needing was not something you could come back from.

He gave it a moment more, then dashed back inside and reached for his coat and police-issue flashlight. Hadn't Deputy been let down by humans enough times? And now he'd consumed too much liquor to even get behind the wheel and find him fast. Self-reproach oozed through the surges of adrenaline.

Dogs. Hearts. Souls.

He was so right not to trust himself with anything fragile. But still he burned to find Ellie and beg her help. Not just for Deputy's sake, but for his own. Failing someone that needed him again would send him back to that place he'd been three years ago. To a much worse place than he'd let himself go because—all this time—he'd been holding on to his one, furry reminder of New York like a talisman.

As long as he could love that stupid dog, then he could love. He caught himself on her doorstep just as his knuckle rapped once on the timber. He pressed his hand flat on the wood to stop it knocking again. Rousing Ellie to help him was not something he should be doing.

It was three in the morning.

He'd just evicted her from his life.

He curled his fingers into the flaking paintwork. And he couldn't bear to see her face when she realised what little care he took of things that he loved.

He pushed away from her door, turned back up the laneway and switched on his flashlight, then jogged out into the cold night.

CHAPTER ELEVEN

'LEAVING SO SOON?'

Ellie dragged her tired eyes back from the place on the horizon she'd let them drift and turned her head to the man wiping his wrinkled hands on an oily cloth. She'd vowed only yesterday never to bring her car to Gus's Fillin' Station, yet here she was. Fillin' up.

But she just wanted gas. She so wasn't in the right emotional place for another stoush with someone. Last night had spoiled her for courage for…pretty much ever. And she had as little energy and drive for a fight as she had at the height of her sickness.

She'd lain awake for hours after storming out of Jed's place. She'd lain awake and listened to him through the paper-thin drywall between his cottage and hers—pacing, slamming, cursing. The intermittent yet all too frequent *clank-clank* of glass on glass.

She'd lain awake, crying silently in the darkness for his pain as much as her own, and trying desperately to divine the truth from every footfall, every slam, every muttered phrase that she couldn't quite make out.

Barely breathing past the hope that the next noise she heard would be pounding on her front door to make all the pain go away.

Dying by degrees every time it wasn't.

And then beating herself up for having dared to dream.

Only when Jed had raged himself into an exhausted silence

had she let herself follow, tumbling into the only place pain had never followed her.

Oblivion.

Even then she'd dreamed of one short, tortured rap on her door.

'I have to get back to New York,' she lied, dragging her gritty focus back to Gus. Although technically not a lie. She couldn't stay here to wait for Jess. So home was pretty much the only place she could go.

The path of least resistance. Letting down Sarah was easier than staying in Larkville and seeing Jed every single day. Running out on Jess was easier. Going home to face the mother she'd so cruelly stormed out on—the mother who'd lied to her daughter her whole life—was definitely easier.

And that was saying something.

Everything was going to be better than staying in Larkville with a man who didn't want her. Or worse, didn't want to want her.

'Got yer business seen to?'

'No.' Not that her business was any of his.

He nodded, and watched her surreptitiously from the corner of his vision. Finally, he bent down to her, placing both hands on the edge of her lowered window. Her heart clenched.

Here it comes.

'Reckon I owe y'all an apology.' Her eyebrows lifted as he hurried on. 'An' I don't do that very often or very easy so let me just get it out.'

Something in Gus's awkwardness spoke to her. Maybe it was the soul of one misfit calling to another.

'You took me by surprise yesterday, sitting there all calm and unexpected. You reminded me of someone else and it put me out of sorts.'

Ellie smiled inwardly at how much this apology sounded like him blaming her.

'Anyways, my reaction didn't really belong to you, so I'm sorry if my actions caused offence.'

She smiled, though it wasn't without effort. The last thing she felt like being today was civil, but she'd changed since getting to Larkville; opting out of dealing with the world was no longer an option.

'Thank you, Gus. I'm sorry I let it get to me.'

That should have been that, but just as he was about to step away, he rounded back, looking a decade younger. Yet older at the same time. 'Your mother. Was she ever in Larkville?'

She could play innocent, she could lie, she could do any number of things that would send Gus back into his office scratching his head and wondering until the day he died. Or she could treat him better than she'd so recently been treated and put him out of his misery. Because, she wasn't sure why, but she knew unquestionably that this man was miserable way down deep inside.

She nodded. 'Fenella Groves, back then.' Or Calhoun, really.

He kept his feet but for one moment she feared he wouldn't. His knuckles whitened on her lowered window. 'I thought so. You look so like her. Sound just like her.'

'You knew her?'

'Yes. For the short time she was here. A lovely woman. How…' He slid his hat off to reveal thinning grey hair. 'How is she?'

He feared she was dead, it was all there in the way he clutched his hat respectfully to his chest in readiness for the worst.

'She's fine. Healthy, happy, busy with my father's business.'

His eyes lit up. 'A New York businesswoman. I should have guessed.'

Drive away, Ellie. But something wouldn't let her. The chance to salvage something valuable from this trip loomed large. 'How did you know her?'

'Through Clay Calhoun. We was friends and he and Fenella was—' his eyes shaded '—friends.'

He's guessed. Not guessed that her mother was pregnant when he drove her seventeen hundred miles to Manhattan, necessarily, but that Ellie was here because of Clay. She should have figured; it was too big a coincidence in a country this size. She met his speculation head-on. 'I came to meet Clay's children.'

'They're all away.'

'So I gathered. I'll come back another time.' But as soon as the words were out she realised she might not be able to. Even for the Fall Festival. Jed would still be here.

Silence fell. Dirty boots shifted on the tarmac surface. Ellie glanced at the clock on her dash. 'I should get going.'

Gus stepped back. 'Right. Sure. Y'all drive carefully.'

But old pain was resurrecting in his eyes. Something was hurting him. And Ellie didn't want to be responsible for more pain in under twenty-four hours. She blew out a breath. 'Unless... Do you sell coffee?'

'Better than Gracie May's,' he bragged, relief live in his voice.

She sighed, glanced in her mirror at the empty road that led back towards the Alamo and then pushed open her driver's door. Minutes later she was seated at the cramped little counter inside the store filled with car polishes, air fresheners, snacks and magazines, cupping a coffee she didn't really want between her hands.

But at least it went some way to warming the hollow, cold place that was her heart.

'How well did you know my mother?'

Gus frowned. 'Well enough. The three of us spent some time together. She was the talk of the town being squired around everywhere with two such good-looking young men.' He chuckled at his own wit.

Her mother...firmly in the center of the spotlight? 'I'll bet.'

'Don't you go sassin' the woman that gave you life,' he scolded and, astonishingly, Ellie felt some shame. 'Weren't her fault she was cut from such different cloth to everyone else. Everything she did was interestin' to folks around here. Won't be no different with you.'

'Except I won't be staying long enough to make an impression.'

'Heard y'all made an impression last night at the dance.'

Her heart sank. 'If by "impression" you mean "spectacle," then, yes, I probably did.'

They'd danced close enough and slow enough to ignite a dozen rumors.

Gus busied himself cleaning his counter. 'Weren't no surprise to me when I heard. Y'all looked right cozy when I last saw you. I told him so when he came through this morning, too—'

She hated the way her heart lurched at that news. 'Jed was here?'

'Not for long. Searched round the back, lookin' for that mutt of his.'

Ellie sat up straighter, her chest tight. 'Deputy?'

'Not the first time he's slipped his collar. Won't be the last. He's probably getting himself a second breakfast with Misses Darcy and Louisa.'

Probably. It wasn't her right to worry about Deputy or Jed any more. Not that it ever had been, apparently. She forced her mind onward.

'So you drove Mother home to New York?'

He snorted. 'Not what she most preferred, but only choice she had.'

Ellie paused midsip. 'She didn't want to go back?'

'She didn't want to admit defeat to her folks. She'd burned a fair number of bridges coming here at all. Marryin' without their approval.'

So she returned with her tail between her legs. Just like me. And a belly full of babies, thankfully not like her. How much more awful must it have been, discovering that? Her mother must have had strength she'd never seen.

Or just never looked for.

'Do you know why she went back?' Ellie studied him, watching closely for a reaction.

She got none. He just shrugged wiry shoulders. 'She wouldn't stay in the same town as Clay and have to face him every day.'

Every day. Just like Jed.

'And he never went after her?'

'Clay was a proud man. Proud of his heritage and his business. It never sat right with him that he'd picked a woman who couldn't settle here in the country. Whom he couldn't make happy. Whom he couldn't give children to.'

Ellie nearly gasped. 'She told you that?'

'Not on your life. She'd have never spoken about him like that, even to me. But he told me. After she'd left. About how desperate she was for offspring and how none ever came.'

'He got over her quick enough. From what I hear Holt Calhoun is my age.' She surprised herself by feeling actual, genuine umbrage on her mother's behalf.

She knew how she'd feel if she heard Jed took up with someone from last night's dance the moment she was out of the picture. That he was kissing someone else in front of his fire just days after she'd stumbled down his steps.

Gus wiped down his spotless counter one more time. 'Weren't no shortage of women eager to have her place. Turns out any fertility issues didn't lie with Clay. He got himself the heir he'd been wanting so bad after just one night with Sandra. Once that was done, there was no question he'd marry her as soon as the divorce papers came through.'

So he couldn't reconcile with her mother even if he'd wanted to. But that didn't explain why he never acknowledged her and Matt. Why wouldn't he at least seek them out? 'He got the family he always wanted.'

'Yup.'

'And my mother got hers. Just not together, I guess.'

'Love don't hardly ever strike two people equally, Ellie.'

Her mind went straight to Jed.

Was it really that simple? Had she let all the new and overwhelming feelings she'd had since coming here skew what she felt for Jed? Had she misread the level of his interest? What experience did she have to call on? Sudden heat joined her aching heart.

Just how much of a fool had she made of herself?

'Well, thanks for the coffee, Gus.' Despondent, Ellie pushed up and away from the counter and turned for the door. The bell above it tolled. 'I'll tell Mother you asked after her?'

His head shot up, his eyes grew bright and keen. He looked like asking after her was just the first of a hundred things he wanted to say to her mother.

'That would be a kindness. Thank you.' Gus cleared his throat again. 'So when do you leave Larkville?'

'Right now. That tank you just filled will get me halfway home.'

His brow folded. 'Now?'

'Got a long drive.'

'Before seein' Jess?'

'She's on her honeymoon.' He even told her that; did he have a touch of her father's Alzheimer's?

'Sure, but she's back this morning. Her best friend, Molly, mentioned it yesterday.'

Ellie's heart leapt in her tight chest. 'Today?'

'A week early. Something to do with her boy getting home-sick. Would be a shame if you missed her.'

Imagine if she hadn't come to Gus's station to top up her rental. She would have left Larkville and probably passed Jess Calhoun on the way out of town. 'Yes, it would. Thank you, Gus, I really appreciate that.' She threw him a gentle look. 'It really was a pleasure meeting you.'

And in his understated Texas way he agreed. 'Mutual.'

Then she was out the door, back in her car and lead-footing it in the direction of the Double Bar C.

She almost, almost didn't miss it. The dark shape that lurched out of the bushes on the side of the highway feeder and darted across the front of her rental. First cows, now wolves. How many wildlife incidents was she destined to have in Larkville?

Maybe the cows had been a sign. Maybe she was supposed to turn back there and then that day? Maybe she'd just been too slow on the uptake and everything that happened afterwards with Jed was the price she paid for staying.

Except—despite the awful end—it was hard to regret meeting him. To know that such a man existed, that such new parts of her existed… They had to be worth everything that followed. No matter how awful.

She kept her foot steady on the brake as the dark shape dashed out of her periphery. Behind it, like a consciousness shadow, came recognition.

'Deputy?' She craned her neck back to see into the bushes on the other side of the road where he'd headed. 'Deputy Dawg!' she called out the open window.

Maybe it was the formal use of his full name, maybe it was because she was a voice he vaguely knew, or maybe it was just because they'd had that one special night crammed into her bed together, but after a moment of breathless silence his big horse head poked back through the bushes and wild eyes stared at her as she climbed out of her car. She looked both ways for traffic and then crouched.

'Come on, boy!'

He didn't hesitate. He rushed straight towards her, his tail slinking between his legs as he approached, his ears flattening. The first things she noticed were the terror in his eyes, the wet of his thick coat and the muddiness of his paws. The next thing she noticed was the pace of his heart.

He shoved his wet body against her and lifted a sopping paw against her crouched hip.

'What are you doing out here?' she queried, wrapping her hands around his shoulders and snagging his collar. His body was roasting, and drool hung off his usually dry chops in strings. His gums were pale in the split second she saw them, and a series of anxious whines issued from the back of his throat.

Deputy was stressed. Really stressed.

Had he been hit? Injured?

She glanced left and right again to make sure they were still traffic-free. A semi could come along any moment and find a car, a woman and a dog taking up their lane.

'Come on.' She opened the back of the car and gestured for

him to jump in. He did so with an unseemly amount of haste and then sat, trembling top to toe, crowded in amongst her suitcases.

'Where's your dad, boy?' His big head cocked at the sound of her measured voice and he seemed to relax just a hint. 'Oh, you like me talking to you, huh?'

Deputy blinked, refocused, came back to the same plane as she was on.

Yeah, he did.

So she started a gentle monologue as she slipped the rental into gear and pulled forward on the highway. 'I don't have your dad's cell number or I'd call him.' More head cocks in her rear vision mirror. 'I can't call 911, boy. Even for you.'

She thought fast as he *humphed* back against her luggage, relaxing further. 'But we're so close to the Calhoun place. Why don't we go there? They'll have his number. And we'll ask Wes to take a look at you, hey? You like Wes, he's a good guy, and you like the Double Bar C, I know....'

On and on she rambled, as Deputy zeroed in on every tone and nuance of her voice and inched back down the stress Richter scale. She told him about meeting Gus Everett and about Jess's letter and how her mother had loved Clay Calhoun enough to betray her family's wishes and marry him. Enough to uproot her city life and move out here.

'Must have taken some courage, huh?'

Deputy tossed his head up and smacked his lips clean of the prodigious amount of drool. It was almost an agreement.

Courage. Though it was hard to know whether it took more courage to stay or to go.

'But then she left...' How bad had things become between the newlyweds that she was willing to bail so soon on their marriage?

Ellie knew, firsthand, how deficient she felt just for having her aversion to touch. The hundred different ways the world had of reminding you that you didn't measure up. How much worse must it have been for her mother to believe she was infertile when the man she loved wanted an heir so very much?

At least she had Jed in her corner helping her, not judging.

Had being the operative word.

A sudden realisation shimmied through her. Whether or not Jed had withdrawn his interest in her, he could never withdraw the difference he'd made to her soul. And to her body. She could never—would never—go back now that she'd tapped into that passion inside of her.

Jed gave her that.

Yet here she was running away rather than staying and toughing it out. But didn't it take two to work things through? And could she even face him knowing how awfully she'd misread his interest?

'I've messed things up, boy.' She groaned and Deputy cocked one brown eyebrow. 'I said things I shouldn't have. I hoped for things I shouldn't have.'

He just blinked at her.

She turned at the Calhouns' access road that she'd first met the cows on. 'He's a good man, your dad. Got his share of issues but nobody's perfect.'

By the time she pulled under the big entry statement to the Double Bar C she'd offloaded her entire childhood onto the poor old dog, who'd dropped to his elbows some time back and now his eyes were drifting shut. But they shot open as she pulled her car up to the Calhoun homestead.

That big tail began to thump.

Ellie's own tension eased. Maybe he was going to be okay, after all.

Up ahead a handful of people were unloading luggage from a fancy truck. Ellie recognised Wes Brogan immediately, and the ranch hand she'd spoken to on her first visit to the Double Bar C. Next to them, a tall, dark-haired man with killer bone structure looked up from the back of the vehicle.

Ellie pushed her door open.

Up on the homestead porch the door swung open and a young boy dashed out, skipping down the steps and running over to the man whose eyes were fixed so firmly on her arrival. Behind the boy, a blonde, willowy woman stepped out of the house.

Ellie's breath caught.

Jess.

Suddenly she became critically aware of her appearance. Barely groomed from her desperate exit this morning and patches of damp and mud and dog slobber where Deputy had leaned on her and pawed her. Ordinarily she'd have been mortified that this was going to be Jessica Calhoun's first impression. But Deputy's needs came first. There was no time for preciousness. And besides, something essential in her had changed since arriving in Larkville.

She turned and pulled open the back door of the car and the whole car lurched as Deputy leapt out. Wes Brogan's eyes flared wide. The boy dashed forward, squealing. The tall man snatched him up before he could get far.

'The sheriff's been tearing the county up looking for you,' Wes said in a loud voice, coming towards her.

Ellie's breath caught, low in her throat. 'Me?'

Wes laughed and his eyes dropped to her side. 'Deputy Dawg.'

The breathlessness hardened into a lump and embarrassed heat soaked up her neck. She forced speech past it. 'He's… I'm not sure what's happened to him. I found him on the highway. He was in a bad way.'

Wes instantly sobered and barked over his shoulder for the younger hand. 'Cooper! Grab Misty's kit and clear us a space in the tack room.' Then he lifted his eyes back to hers and said quietly, 'I'll check him over, Ms. Patterson.'

'Ellie, please…' Ugh. All so hideously awkward. And none of it really mattered anyway. She'd be gone in a few minutes.

Some fuss and bustle and all three men and one very tired, miserable dog disappeared for some much needed care. The surprise must have still shown on her face after they all trooped off because a soft, polite voice spoke right behind her,

'Deputy's part of the family around here.'

Ellie's back muscles bunched. She took two deep breaths

before turning around…and her eyes met a pair so similar, yet different, to her own. There was absolutely no question of their owner's identity.

'Jess.'

Jessica Calhoun's pretty face folded in a frown. Ellie could see her trying to place this newcomer who'd arrived with their sheriff's dog. But just as she thought to introduce herself, Jess's eyes widened and her lips fell open on a gasp. 'Are you…?'

'Eleanor Patterson.'

'Oh, my Lord—' Long slim fingers went to her chest and her eyes welled up dangerously. 'Oh…'

'I'm sorry to take you by surprise,' Ellie rushed.

'No! Molly told me someone was looking for me in town. I had no idea…'

The two of them stood awkwardly, their respective hands dangling uselessly at their sides. Ellie said the first thing that came to her. It was the least poised and professional she'd ever been but also the most honest. Another thing she'd learned to be.

'I don't know what to do.'

Jess's nervous laugh bubbled up. 'Me, neither. Can I, um… A hug?'

Old whispers instinctively chorused in her head and she grasped for a legitimate excuse. 'I'm filthy—'

Jess laughed properly this time. 'You're on a working ranch. Everyone's dirty here.' She stepped forward, undeterred.

Ellie knew this moment counted more than any other she'd ever have with her half-sister. She tamped down the whispers, held her breath and stepped into Jess Calhoun's open embrace.

Warm, soft, strong arms closed around her, and Ellie felt her body flinch on a rush of emotion.

Good emotion.

Jess hugged just like Alex. The discovery brought tears to her eyes.

The hug went on just a bit too long but neither one wanted to be the one to end it. Eventually Ellie pulled away but kept her hands on her half-sister's arms. 'This is so…'

'Odd?'

She laughed, sniffing back tears. 'But good!' she added lest Jess think she wasn't cherishing every moment. 'There are four of you.'

Oh, no, she was rambling.

But Jess knew she was talking about Calhoun offspring. She smiled. 'I know. And two of you. Twins!'

They stared again.

'I'm sorry I came without checking,' Ellie said.

Jess shook her head. 'Don't be. It was quite a bombshell I dropped on you. I'm sorry I wasn't here.' She pressed her fingertips to her coral lips and shook her head. 'I can't believe I have a big sister.'

Ellie laughed. 'And a big brother.' Matt may not be here but he deserved to be counted into this moment.

'Holt's going to freak out…not being the oldest any more.' Her laugh then was pure delight, yet Ellie could tell it came from a solid and dedicated affection. Her eyes went to the little boy who peered around his mother's legs.

'And…do I have a nephew?' Ellie breathed.

'Oh! Brady Cal—' She caught herself. 'Sorry, still getting used to that… Brady Jameson, I'd like you to meet your aunt Eleanor.'

Ellie reeled back. 'My goodness that makes me sound a hundred years old.' Then she bent down and shook a very serious Brady's hand. 'Call me Ellie.'

'You sure don't look a hundred,' he said, pumping her hand formally.

Everyone laughed then and the silence no longer felt awkward. 'So…the letter…'

'Do you want to see it?' Jess was quick to offer.

'No, not right now. I don't need a letter to know the truth. I can see so much of Matt in you. And maybe a bit of me.'

'I thought the same thing. The rest of you must be your mother?'

'I look a fair bit like her, yes.' Much to poor Gus's distress.

'She was very beautiful, then.'

This time, accepting the compliment—believing it—wasn't quite as hard as it once would have been. Maybe Jed had helped her grow accustomed to that, too. Or…just grow.

'She's quite a legend in our household. This mystery first wife we could never ask about.'

Ellie grimaced. 'She's pretty ordinary in real life.' Except that wasn't true any more. Fenella had walked away from a man she loved, pregnant with his children, and built herself and them a whole new life. That took amazing courage. So did maintaining her stiff New York veneer when Ellie had blurted the fact of Clay's passing to her so carelessly. She wondered how she would have reacted if someone threw news of Jed's death at her so carelessly.

She owed her mother a really long conversation. And several apologies. Starting there.

'I think I have a photo in my phone if you'd like to see it.'

Jess answer was immediate. 'Oh, I would.'

'I'd love to see a picture of your father if you have one?'

One beat. Two. 'Our father, Ellie.'

The niggling hurt of disloyalty to the man who'd raised her sharpened its teeth. Honesty compelled her. 'That's going to take a while to sink in.'

Jess's eyes darkened with compassion. 'I'm sure.'

'He never…' She paused, wondering how heartbroken Jess still was about her father's death twelve weeks ago. 'He never told you about us?'

Jess stared at her. 'Ellie… He never knew. He never got the letter.'

Everything whooshed around her feet. 'Not at all?'

Oh, her poor, poor mother. That was going to break her heart.

The crunch of vehicle tires on gravel drew their eyes around behind them. Her gut squeezed harder than a fist as she turned.

Speaking of broken hearts…

'Sheriff!' Brady called, and dashed over to the now-stationery SUV.

Jed's empty eyes hit Ellie's almost immediately but that careful nothing had always been his particular talent. He slid them to Jess's instead. 'I wasn't far away when I got Johnny's call. Where is he?'

Jess waved him in the direction of the tack room. Brady followed him.

It wasn't reasonable to be surprised—or disappointed—by his intense focus on the dog he felt so responsible for. But his barely cursory glance still hurt. She forced her attention back onto her half-sister.

'Sheriff Jackson,' Jess explained. 'Deputy is his dog.'

'I know.'

'Oh, you already met him?'

'I was staying in his barn conversion. He's shown me around town a bit.' Her heart squeezed. *I fell in love with him.*

Jess looked bemused. 'I'm surprised he didn't say hello.'

So it wasn't just her who saw nothing but a passing glance in that moment. 'Just anxious for Deputy, I'm sure.'

'Are you okay, Ellie? You've gone quite pale.'

She forced her lungs to inhale. 'Yes. This has been quite a morning, that's all.'

'Sheriff Jackson doesn't need our help, buddy.'

Jess turned to the striking man emerging from the tack room with a protesting boy in his arms. He was easily more handsome than Jed, but Ellie felt nothing but aesthetic appreciation for his beautiful angles and stunning complexion. He was fire to Jed's earth.

And earth appealed to her so much more.

'Ellie, this is my husband, Johnny Jameson. Hon, this is Eleanor Patterson.'

The way she only put the tiniest of inflections on the surname told Ellie she'd been the topic of quite a few conversations.

Light grey eyes widened and Johnny extended a hand. 'Ms. Patterson, it's a real pleasure to meet you.'

She took it without hesitation. 'Congratulations on your marriage.'

The newlyweds looked at each other with such focus then;

the passion and love between them stole Ellie's breath and hurt her already bruised heart.

That's what she wanted. Someone to look at her like that.

'Thank you,' Johnny said, all courtesy.

'How's Deputy?' she asked when what she really wanted to know was how Jed was. Did he hurt like she did? Did he feel anything at all? Or had he already exorcised all trace of her from his system.

'He's good now that the sheriff's here. Apparently he's been missing since last night.'

'Last night? But he—' She snapped her mouth shut. She could hardly admit that Deputy was right there when she was kissing Jed. Although then she had a flash of the dog cringing as they argued and of her bolting from the house and leaving the door wide open. Guilt swamped into the empty place inside her.

'Oh. Poor boy.'

'He'll be okay. He's had a rough run in life and he's easily spooked these days.'

He doesn't deal with conflict well, Jed had once told her. Like two members of his pack tearing each other to emotional pieces.

Behind them, all three men and one infinitely more relaxed dog emerged from the stables.

'Is he okay?' she asked Wes, specifically, determined not to give off any unhappy waves while Deputy was around. Jed's eyes finally fell on her but he didn't speak.

Her chest ached.

'Right as rain,' Wes said. 'Or he will be when he gets home. Cooper gave him a quick once-over with a brush for the mud on his fur. Sorry about your suitcases, Miss Patterson.'

Jed's head snapped up, then around to the still-open rear door of her car. Exhibits A and B were on plain view complete with muddy paw smears. Finally his brown eyes came back to her and this time he couldn't hide what burned there.

Betrayal.

'You were leaving?' Jess gasped. 'Imagine if we'd missed each other!'

You were leaving? Jed's dark eyes accused.

She faced Jess. 'Lucky Gus told me you were back. I was on my way over here when I found Deputy.'

Finally Jed found speech. 'Why didn't you let me know?' he asked, low and deep. 'That you'd found him.'

Why are you leaving? It was all there right between what he was actually saying.

'You're welcome,' Ellie said, pointedly, her eyes fixed on him. 'The Double Bar C was closer. I thought Deputy might need some first aid.'

They stared at each other, a crackle of pain reaching from her to him. Jess's eyes flicked between them and then to her husband, wide with concern. For a heartbeat Ellie truly thought that maybe she'd dissolve into tears here in front of her new family and the Calhoun hands. And Jed. She willed her body not to.

And some miracle—or maybe years of dominating it—meant it listened.

Jess broke the silence. 'Ellie, why don't you stay for brunch, if this is the only chance we'll have to talk? We can swap those photos. You, too, of course, Jed.'

'Thank you, Jess, but I should get Deputy home. Get him settled back in. Maybe another time?'

Would it be that easy? He'd just leave and that would be that? Ellie's breath grew shallow.

Not easy. Not at all.

'Sure, Sheriff,' Jess said. 'I'm glad everything's worked out okay.'

If you didn't count a broken heart and some hurtful truths.

'Yep.' He curled his fingers into Deputy's coat as she had so many times. 'Something like this sure makes you think about what's important.'

His eyes flicked to her again as he said that, but then he turned, gave them all a Texas wave and signaled for Deputy to follow him to his vehicle. Ellie watched him go, wondering if that long-legged lope and those square shoulders would be branded in her mind forever.

She stared, unblinking, to make sure they would be.

As they turned for the house, Wes Brogan muttered, 'He's a good man, that sheriff. Most people would have shot that dog.'

Johnny grunted. 'Jed's not the sort of man to give up that easily when there's a bit of hope.'

Those words anchored Ellie's feet to the ground. Her whole body lurched to a stop and the air in her lungs made a word all of its own volition. Was she giving up too easily? Was there truly not even a sliver of hope for her and Jed?

'Wait—'

He was going to disappear from her life not knowing if she didn't do something.

Brown eyes and grey looked back at her. 'Ellie?' Jess said.

Um… 'I'm just going to need a couple of minutes. Can I meet you inside?'

Jess's head cocked in a great impression of Deputy, but her eyes flicked for a heartbeat over to where Jed walked away. 'Sure, just let yourself in the front door and follow your nose through to the kitchen.'

'Thanks.'

She hadn't sounded that breathless in years. Since she'd come rushing out of her first-ever dance class busting to show her parents what she'd learned. Wow, those sure were innocent days. Who might she have become if she'd taken up tennis instead of ballet?

A burned-out tennis player instead of a burned-out dancer probably. She couldn't go on blaming her childhood for everything. Those years were long behind her. What she did now was what counted.

Right now.

She pivoted on one foot and then sprinted off after Jed, refusing to call out to him. Hoping to preserve some modicum of dignity. He was loading Deputy into his vehicle when she caught up.

'Jed,' she puffed.

He stiffened, but finished securing Deputy into his harness

before turning. He nodded like he was passing her in the street. 'Ms. Calhoun.'

The words coming back at her the way she'd flung them at him were exactly the insult he intended.

Her tension coiled so far up inside it threatened to strangle her. 'Can I speak to you?'

'You are.'

Now that she had his full attention she didn't know where to begin. 'I talked to Gus today.'

Not what he was expecting. One eyebrow lifted under the brim of his hat.

'He knew my mother. How she came here, why she left. How hard that was for her.'

Despite what had happened between them, Jed was still a decent man. If he felt any impatience at her bumbling beginning his country manners didn't let it show. 'You didn't know?'

'I knew that she left, not why. She couldn't tell me.'

He frowned. 'Bad?'

'She believed she couldn't give Clay an heir. They ended their marriage over it. And she left feeling inadequate. He let her leave feeling about as inadequate as a woman possibly can.'

Jed suddenly realised which way the wind was blowing and he straightened two inches. But his eyes didn't go back to their careful neutrality. Maybe there were some things he couldn't hide.

'These past two weeks have been life-changing for me, Jed. You may never understand the difference knowing you has made for me.'

'Ellie—'

'Don't worry, I'm not going to make a scene or put pressure on you. I just wanted to thank you.'

'Thank me?' He frowned. 'Why?'

She looked down at her strappy sandals, covered in Calhoun dirt. 'Everything in my life started spinning wildly a month ago. My father is not my father. I'm not a Patterson. My Fifth Avenue mother was married to someone else and lived on a ranch. My sisters aren't my full sisters…' She wrapped her arms around her front. 'I arrived here feeling…disconnected to everything and wondering where I belonged.'

She took a breath. 'And then I met you. And you were like… a rock. Predictable and sure.'

Offense flirted on the edge of his silence.

'But at the same time you were a surge I had to go with or get buffeted. Like the bats in the gully. Every moment with you challenged me and made me really look at myself. At the person I've let myself become.'

His gaze dropped to his steel-capped boots.

'I've developed so many strategies in life to keep from having to face the reality of who I've grown into, they've become excuses.' Every word was harder to get out, every breath tight. 'Dance was an excuse for not eating. But not eating was about controlling my body, controlling something in my environment where I felt otherwise invisible.' She twisted the fingers of both hands together. 'Studying or rehearsing all the time, that was an excuse, too. My distancing myself from relationships was about hiding my disorder from people who might notice it.'

She took a shaky breath. 'Not touching anyone was about disguising my internal deficiencies. Blaming it on something external was just an excuse.'

His eyes closed briefly. 'Ellie, you don't have to do this—'

'I do. I do, Jed, because I'm lucky. I won't be leaving Larkville like my mother did, believing I'm inadequate. You showed me what I have inside me and I will always be grateful for that. Whether or not you wanted me, ultimately, I know you wanted me at least for a moment.'

She took a breath and he pressed his lips together, almost as if to stop himself speaking.

'But more importantly,' she said, 'I wanted you. I know now that I'm capable of that. So…that's it really. Just…thank you.'

He nodded, his eyes intense.

She turned back for the house.

'You were right when you said I told you about being a

Calhoun to stop us getting physical,' she said, spinning back around just as he pulled the door to his SUV open. Stalling, and they both knew it. Her eyes fixed on his. 'But it wasn't because I didn't want you touching me.' Her voice cracked. 'I can't imagine being touched by anyone else. I can't imagine wanting to touch anyone else.'

Jed's lips pressed tighter together.

'But I will. And if I don't, well…so be it. But I want to explain because I don't want to drive out of town leaving you feeling inadequate, either.'

His laugh was so very cowboy and so very awkward it warmed her heart. He no longer had a prayer of hiding the pain in his gaze.

She took a really deep breath. 'I've never…' How was she even having this conversation? 'My whole adult life I thought I couldn't…'

She closed her eyes and remembered the bats. Remembered how that felt. Then she opened them and remembered how he felt. 'I was petrified of how you were making me feel. Totally out of control. My body reacting in complete contravention of my will. I've never felt that before.'

Jed the good man wasn't far away. 'That's the best part, Ellie.'

'Look at what I did to myself to maintain control growing up. You think I did that by choice? It's not a conscious thing. It's something I'm going to have to work on.' She curled her nails into her palms to stop herself reaching out. 'I get that we're not going to happen. I'm still leaving today. I just want to leave with us both understanding what happened between us. How it went so very wrong. Because up until then I thought things were going pretty right.'

The distant keening of cattle filled the silence.

'You're still leaving?'

She turned back and stared at him, no energy or heart for more.

'What about Jess? You came to get to know her.'

She summoned some words. 'I came to find out who I was.

Mission accomplished.' At least she knew, now, who she wanted to be. 'I'll stay in touch with Jess by email.'

'And Sarah, the Fall Festival—you're just going to dump her?'

It sounded so much uglier when phrased like that. Defensiveness washed through her and tangled with the exhaustion. 'I can help her from New York. Come back in October for the big event.'

Maybe.

He stepped closer. 'Visit once a year? Is that what you want?'

She took a sharp breath and met his eyes. 'That's what I can manage. You've helped set me on a new path but I'm not a masochist. I won't find it easy coming back in the future.' She swallowed. 'Maybe finding you with someone else.'

His eyes echoed her pain. 'You think I'm going to do that?'

Her breath caught, but she fought hard not to make assumptions about what that meant. She'd done more than enough of that since arriving. 'According to Sarah you're Larkville's Most Wanted. I think you'll have no choice.'

'What if I don't want to be wanted by one of them?'

Her heart shrivelled. 'You'll figure it out,' she said instead, the best she could offer. She turned to walk away again.

'I'm not a good man, Ellie.'

The raw pain in his voice brought her back. 'Says who?'

'Says me.' He stared at her, and something indefinable shifted. Right at the back, in the space between blinks. 'Not wanting to get involved with someone where I live was not just about avoiding relationships. It's because I had a relationship with someone I worked with once and it didn't end well.'

Oh.

Had she somehow imagined that he'd been as loveless as she all this time? Or had she just not let herself ask?

'A woman in my unit. Maggie. We were together for five years.'

Her heart twisted. Five years? That didn't spell commitment issues. So maybe it truly was just her?

He'd tried to tell her.

'Why did you break up?' She didn't want to know, and yet she had to.

'We didn't break up,' he gritted. 'She died.'

Shock and empathy responded to the pain bleeding off him. All this time she'd been battling a ghost that she didn't know existed.

'We'd been together in another division, careful to keep things on the down low. Most people didn't know we were a couple. Maggie followed me over to the canine unit when I was promoted.'

The idea of Jed—her Jed—loving someone else. Spending time with someone else... Five years. It felt impossible.

'My superiors would have transferred one of us out of the unit if they'd twigged. So I worked hard to treat her like everyone else.' His eyes flicked away. 'Too hard.'

Her silence was a question in itself.

'She begged me to let her go out before she was ready. Not to make a big deal about it in front of the team. She wanted to be equal.' He turned half away from Ellie. 'Thing was if I'd truly been treating her equally I would have grounded her and let her deal with the fallout.'

'She went out?'

'And she died. And Deputy got beaten.'

Ellie gasped. 'Maggie was Deputy's handler?'

He looked across the seat of his car at the dog that'd looked up when he heard his name. His head nodded, brisk and small.

'I'm so sorry.' The urge to touch won out. She slid her hand onto his arm. 'You loved her.'

The bleakness in the eyes he turned up to her took her aback. 'That's just it. I didn't love her.'

Maybe someone had to live with it to recognise it in others, but Ellie suddenly wondered how she'd never seen it in him before.

Blazing, damning shame.

'Oh, Jed...'

'Five years, Ellie, and I kept her at arm's length the whole time. So much so she had to chase me from department to department to stop me slipping away.' He swallowed past the pain. 'I dishonored her the whole time. Deep inside. Overcompensating for the love I just didn't feel.'

'Why did you stay together?'

'Because she adored me, because she'd put our relationship ahead of her own career so many times. Because she was willing to take whatever I could give her.'

Ellie felt sudden and cell-deep empathy for the woman who had tried so hard to win Jed's love. Who'd died trying.

The pain in his eyes told her exactly how deeply he felt that, too.

'Being together was the perfect excuse not to be with anyone else. Work was the perfect excuse to keep things superficial. To manage Maggie's expectations.'

Excuses. Didn't that sound familiar?

He turned to her, self-loathing blazing in his eyes. 'That's the kind of man I am, Ellie. That's why I know I can't commit no matter what I feel for you. You deserve someone who's capable of loving you with everything in them.'

Deputy's heavy sigh punctuated the silence. Was he afraid they were going to start fighting again? Ellie fought hard to keep her body language relaxed. 'You're not that man,' she whispered.

He turned to her suddenly and pain glowed real and raw in his plea. 'Then who am I?'

She shook her head. 'A man who's been really hurt in his past. A man who protects himself from loss before it can happen.' She took a breath. 'You're the male version of me.'

Jed stared at her, pain giving way to confusion.

'Do you think your Maggie would blame you for what happened to her?'

His answer was a frown.

'Do you think she would blame you for not loving her more than you could?'

'I blame me.'

'I don't,' she breathed. 'Not for her.' She bent lower to stay connected to eyes that suddenly dropped to stare at the dirt. 'And not for me.'

And it was true. She could no more blame Jed for not loving her the way she needed than she could blame Deputy for falling to pieces at the sound of raised voices.

But she could love him.

And she would.

And she wouldn't hide it.

She curled her hand around his arm, touching him. Letting every feeling and emotion and hope run through her body and into his. Letting her know she accepted him.

He shrugged her hand free and she slid it back on, refusing to let him back away again.

'I can't love you, Ellie.' His volume betrayed his pain. 'Not the way you want.'

Her heart hitched. *Can't*. Not *don't*.

'Why?'

'Look what I did to the last person who loved me.'

'She would forgive you, Jed.'

He shook his head, not hearing. Not wanting to. 'You can't know that.'

'I can know it, because I know you. And because I love you like she did. And I know that I would forgive you if I had the chance.'

He stared at her, eyes roiling with a mix of pain and confusion.

'Give her the chance,' Ellie pleaded, and slipped her fingers in between his. 'Forgive yourself so that she can, too.'

He stared at her, the options tumbling visibly in his gaze, and then—exactly like the houselights used to come on after she'd been lost in the depths of a performance—the shadows leached out of his eyes and he almost blinked in the sudden brightness of hope.

And in that exact moment, Deputy chose to nudge his wet, cool nose into the place their hands entwined. He'd moved more

silently than a dog his size should ever have been able to and he
blazed his wide, dark, loving eyes straight up into Jed's.

It was Maggie's forgiveness.

And his own.

And it broke the last of Jed's strength.

Ellie slid her arms around him and let him bury his face in
her neck. His hold tightened hard around her, hard enough to
last them forever. Ellie didn't care how many of the Calhouns
might be watching out of the window. She was through with
worrying about appearances.

'Stay.' The word croaked against her neck, but Jed's tight
arms reinforced it. And the four tiny letters carried a universe
worth of meaning. 'I don't want you to leave.'

She pulled back a little. 'I can't stay.' Not without being certain.

He cleared his throat and lifted damp eyes. 'Remember the
bats? The way I stood behind you on that cliff top and kept you
safe while you danced? How scared you were?'

Her chest threatened to cave in. Those memories would be
the ones replaying on her deathbed in a half-century. She pushed
the words through her tight throat. 'Of course.'

He paused and there was confusion in the dark depths of
his eyes. But it was greatly outweighed by something new.
Something she'd not seen there in all the time she knew him.

'I'd be willing to do that again, to help you heal.'

She scrunched her forehead. 'With the bats?'

Intensity blazed down on to her. 'With me. And with you.'
His fingers rose to trace her jaw. 'Slowly. Until you're ready to
feel yourself fly again.'

His meaning finally dawned on her and her lungs cramped.
'Are charity cases part of your job description?'

He smiled down on her, and didn't let her hide behind sarcasm. 'I want you to stay, Ellie. With me.'

She refused to let herself hope. Old habits died way too hard.
'Just like that?'

He stroked the hair from her face. 'No, not just like that. Feeling like this absolutely terrifies me.'

She could see the uncertainty live and real in his eyes. But it wasn't alone. Something else flanked it, keeping it at bay. It shifted and flirted at the edges of his gaze, ducking and weaving just out of view so that she couldn't quite place where she'd seen it before.

'Feeling like what?'

The golden threads between her eyes and his were enough to let a little piece of his soul cross over. 'Like my world will end if I let you drive away today.'

Her breath faltered and her chest tightened as he took her hand, pressed his fingers to hers and returned her own words from last night to her. 'But I wouldn't feel safe being terrified with anyone else, Ellie.'

Every old instinct she had urged her not to allow this hope. But something newer overruled that. The same something she saw fighting the fear in his eyes. And in a moment of intense clarity she suddenly knew where she'd seen it before.

Just now—in the look passing between Johnny and Jess.

In the look she must be blazing up at him now.

Love.

Jed would keep her safe while she learned to accept every part of herself. She'd do the same until he could recognise the feelings he harbored. Understand them. She absolutely would.

He lowered his mouth until it was just a breath from hers and his hat blocked out the sun. 'It's been so fast, Ellie, it's hard to trust. But if this isn't love, then God help us after another week together.'

It was love, for both of them. Inconceivable and miraculous. She knew that way down deep in the oldest part of her soul, the part that held all her truths. And she so badly wanted to be in the room the moment it finally dawned on him.

'I want to stay,' she whispered against his mouth. 'I want to feel like that again.'

He touched his lips lightly to hers and her soul sang. He

nibbled the corner of her mouth and then turned it into a fully fledged kiss. A searing kiss. They were breathless when they pulled apart.

That rich, golden glow now consumed his eyes. There was no fear.

'The bats, Ellie? That feeling? I give you my word, that was only the beginning.'

CHAPTER TWELVE

THE bats were only the beginning. It took a scandalously short number of weeks for them to discover, tucked up in her comfortable loft bed, they could reach a place Ellie never imagined actually existed. A safe place. A place where the feel of their two bodies moving in sync was the most poetic and seductive kind of dance ever.

Jed was patient and gentle and forceful and strong in just the right amounts and he let her fly when she needed to and shelter when she had to.

When she wasn't with him, she hung out with Jess or Sarah, and she'd started teaching ballet to the local schoolchildren and, thanks to a bizarre request from the eighty-year-old Misses Darcy and Louisa, to Larkville's senior ladies. Now she taught three times a week.

And it meant she was dancing again.

She still loved her solitude, but alone had so quickly come to mean just her and Jed and Deputy. The word had failed to apply to Ellie by herself because she just didn't feel alone any more even when she was.

Jed kissed his way from her thumb, up her inner arm to the crook of her elbow, and then murmured against her strong pulse there. 'I have something to ask you.'

She matched his gravity. 'Okay.'

'Gram's coming down next week.' She pushed up onto her

elbows. 'I wanted the two most important women in my life to meet.'

She stared at him. For Jed, that was quite a pronouncement.

'I'd like that.' But then something occurred to her. 'Where will she stay?'

'Right here in the barn.'

'Then where will I stay?'

His face grew serious. 'I thought that you could move in with me.'

Ellie's lungs refused to inflate. 'Just while she's here, you mean?'

He took her hand in his and absently played with her fingers. It was the least casual casual thing he'd ever done.

What was happening here?

'Sure. Or we could keep the barn for her visits. Or if one of your family visits.'

She sat bolt upright and the covers dropped to her waist, leaving her naked and exposed. That no longer troubled her. In fact, she positively adored the way his face and body changed in response to hers.

'Just so I'm clear...' She swallowed past the lump which grew low in her throat. 'You want me to meet your gram and you want me next door with you? For good?'

His eyes sobered. 'I do. And so do you.' He leaned in and traced her collarbone with his lips. 'It's in the special laugh you reserve just for me and the fact you let my dog sleep on your feet in front of the television...'

'He's very warm—' Ellie started, her natural instinct to protect herself creeping through.

He smiled against her lips. 'It's in the way that you touch me and that way you let me touch you. You love me.'

'That's hardly a newsflash.'

His kiss grew more ardent before he tore himself away. 'It's funny...'

Lack of oxygen dulled her capacity to keep up with his mental tangents. 'What is?'

'You hated this body for being weak, but I love it for being so strong. Strong enough to get you through.' His eyes darkened and lifted to hers. 'To get you to me.'

She cleared her suddenly crowded throat. 'You…love it?'

The wonder in his face didn't change. 'Every part of it.' His eyes locked on hers. 'Every part of you.'

Ellie's heart raced her mind. He looked so casual lying there talking about the weather one moment and the next—

Joy contributed to the gentle spin of the room but caution still ruled. Because he still hadn't said those all-important three words. Not exactly. And she knew him to be a man of his word.

When he said it, he'd mean it.

'I'd sort of hoped to do this somewhere more memorable,' he frowned.

More memorable than in his arms after a morning of beautiful intimacy? Did such a place exist?

He took her hands. Both of them.

Her breath froze.

'You've been so strong, Ellie. And so patient while I worked my complicated way around to this.'

She still hadn't breathed.

'Everything before you felt slightly off kilter but I just didn't know why. Everything since that day with the cows has felt… right. Colours got brighter. The air got fresher.'

Words to die for but she hoped it wouldn't be literal, from oxygen deficiency.

'I love you, Eleanor Patterson-Calhoun.'

Elation, gratitude and adoration tingled under her skin and she worked hard not to throw herself straight into his arms. The moment she had the words, she realised that she'd known them all along. 'Would you have said that if your grandmother wasn't coming to stay?'

'You think I'm declaring love to free up a bed for a tenant?'

She smiled and nudged his shoulder. 'I think you'd say anything to get me to move in with you out of wedlock.'

'Who said anything about out of wedlock?' His eyes devoured

her metaphorically and then his lips repeated it literally. When he finally released her he said, 'How would you feel about a fall wedding?'

The earth stopped revolving. 'You're proposing?' Such short words but so very hard to get out.

He took both her hands. 'Ellie... Believing I was worthy of your love was the tough part, marrying you is a no-brainer. If you'll say yes.'

Yes. Oh, two hundred times, yes! She was so ready to love and be loved for all the world to see. 'We'll need a long engagement.'

He flinched, just slightly. 'So you can be sure?'

'I am already sure,' she said, holding his eyes with hers. 'But if we upstage Clay's memorial Sarah will skin us both alive.'

They laughed until the smiles turned to kisses.

'And one thing...' she said, emerging for breath. 'That's Eleanor Patterson-Calhoun-Jackson to you, Sheriff.'

A fire burst to life deep in his eyes and he pulled her back onto the bed before twisting over the top of her.

'Jed,' she laughed from under his weight, 'your gram's going to be sleeping here...'

His powerful arms shoved his hard, naked body out into the cool morning air, leaving her with ringside seats to the breathtaking view.

'That does it. I'm packing your things,' he said. 'You're moving in right now.'

Dearest Alex,
I'm sorry I've been so lax in writing. Though I know you'll forgive me when you understand why.

I'm really not sure what part of this letter will stun you most. That I'm engaged to a spectacular man whom I love and trust beyond either of our wildest dreams, or the other news I have yet to share.

But first the man... I know you'll only skip down to that part anyway.

And out it all came.

Jed. Deputy. Larkville.

Her entire second family and the Fall Festival. The amazing personal leaps she'd made since arriving and how, for the first time, she felt whole. Whole! Not like she'd rattle if she shook her head hard enough. The hard truth she was going to have to tell Matt and her concern that such bad news would be better coming from Alex, or Charlotte.

The ink flowed over the linen weave parchment, her handwriting still as practised and careful as ever.

Love's a funny thing, Alex, the more you have, the more it seems you can fit in.

So, no matter how many secret siblings I turn out to have, you remain—and always will—the sister of my heart.

Please come, if you can, in October.

I cannot wait for you to meet Jed.

xx

Ellie

'Hon, Holt's only back for a few hours. Given you're the guest of honour do you think we should get going?'

He was so handsome, and so impatient. And so beautifully, wonderfully hers. She pressed a seldom-used number in her contacts and held up two fingers to Jed, apologetically.

'Sorry,' she mouthed.

He smiled and shook his head.

A man answered and she brought the phone quickly back to her ear.

'Hi. Matt…?' She kept her eyes on Jed. He looked so proud. And so in love. And so very, very certain.

Pretty much everything she felt.

'Matt, it's Ellie…'

* * * * *